ALMOST DEAD

The bullet hit their right front tire. The car shuddered. Then over the bank they went, experiencing horrible jolts as the car pitched and yawed as if riding a sea of concrete waves.

Instinctively, Maria planted her feet firmly to the floor so that the car's violent shuddering rippled through her body. Flung forward and back despite the bracing posture, her body felt bisected as the seat belt bit into her chest. One crash was like an explosion as they were knocked around, the car plunging forward. Then there was a jolt that felt like it ripped out her ribs. Then silence.

Maria hung from her seat belt and knew they were on their nose. Dust swirled in the partly crushed car, blinding and choking her. Dan's hand on hers pulled her, but she was held in place by her seat belt. Stinging eyes sent tears down her face. Her body felt heavy and began to ache, just now awakening to the bruising.

Above her head was a large tree trunk or branch. Glancing down she saw a breathtaking abyss whose bottom was a ribbon of deep blue—the river.

"Oh, my God," she whispered. They hung in space at least two hundred feet above the river rocks. Somewhere above a gunman could be watching.

They waited in the coolness of the wind, their minds searching for a way to free them from the anticipation of being about to fall and yet not falling. Two or three minutes seemed like ten. The leaves were life green, the sky a hopeful blue, the ants on the luxuriant bark looked busy, unaffected. The chill—was it death or was it a morning's invigoration? In just moments she would know.

She looked at Dan. "If I fall, tell my father I loved him. My mother knows."

"You should tell him yourself." He smiled grimly. "The timber industry won't be that lucky."

"How can you be almost dead and still joking?" she asked.

"Same way you can be almost dead and arguing about it."

BOOK YOUR PLACE ON OUR WEBSITE AND MAKE THE READING CONNECTION!

We've created a customized website just for our very special readers, where you can get the inside scoop on everything that's going on with Zebra, Pinnacle and Kensington books.

When you come online, you'll have the exciting opportunity to:

- View covers of upcoming books
- Read sample chapters
- Learn about our future publishing schedule (listed by publication month *and author*)
- Find out when your favorite authors will be visiting a city near you
- Search for and order backlist books from our online catalog
- Check out author bios and background information
- Send e-mail to your favorite authors
- Meet the Kensington staff online
- Join us in weekly chats with authors, readers and other guests
- Get writing guidelines
- AND MUCH MORE!

**Visit our website at
http://www.kensingtonbooks.com**

AT THE EDGE

David Dun

PINNACLE BOOKS
Kensington Publishing Corp.
http://www.kensingtonbooks.com

PINNACLE BOOKS are published by

Kensington Publishing Corp.
850 Third Avenue
New York, NY 10022

All Kensington Titles, Imprints, and Distributed Lines are
available at special quantity discounts for bulk purchases
for sales promotions, premiums, fund-raising, and educa-
tional or institutional use. Special book excerpts or customized printings can also be created to fit specific needs. For
details, write or phone the office of the Kensington special
sales manager: Kensington Publishing Corp., 850 Third Avenue, New York, NY 10022, attn: Special Sales Department,
Phone: 1-800-221-2647.

Pinnacle and the P logo Reg. U.S. Pat. & TM Off.

First Printing: April 2002
10 9 8 7 6 5 4 3 2 1

Printed in the United States of America

ACKNOWLEDGMENTS

Professional acknowledgments: To Ed Stackler, my friend, editor, and inspiration meister; to Anthony Gardner, my agent, for being a great advocate and a terrific advisor; to all the creative people at Kensington Books, Laurie Parkin for making it all happen, and Ann LaFarge for her editing and thoughtful editorial assistance throughout the process; to Ruth Johnson for her extensive research efforts; to Dan Tomascheski and Ed Murphy, Registered Professional Foresters, for sharing their wealth of knowledge about forests; to author Jennifer Furio for her insight into criminal minds and for editorial comments; to Eric Wilinsky, who taught me the basics of fiction writing; to Justin Kirsch for great moral support and computer wizardry; and to Sara Kalmon-Bauer for the Web site (www.daviddun.com).

Personal acknowledgments: To all of my friends, family, and coworkers from whom I have received a large measure of encouragement and inspiration—some who helped with a few words, some who devoted themselves to many hours, even days, of thought and helpful editorial commentary, not all of whom are listed here. I thank you all for your generosity, support, and hard work. I will undertake the risk of naming a few of these fine folks (in alphabetical order): To Cherie Arkley, on matters of what is fashionable and what is not; to Bob and Carolyn Dietz—Bob on plot points and wine, Carolyn for her sense of what is funny and making me want to try a little humor; to Mark and Marisa Emmerson for editorial comments, especially about children and Nate; to Russ Hanly for action scene comments and character points; to Nancy Hatfield for her comments from the kinder, gentler side of life; to David Martinek for his thoughtful comments about plot and my various characters; to Missy McArthur for her editorial attention to those all-important details; to Bill Warne, a source of encouragement and thoughtful commentary on plot and characters; to Donna Zenor for all of her insights into plot points and characters (particularly Dan); and to my wife Laura, who still manages to love me.

Prologue

Kenji Yamada had never seen anything so magnificent as Catherine Swanson's thighs. He sat beside her in the back of his Rolls-Royce Seraph with the twelve-cylinder motor at idle and the CD player whispering Sinatra love songs.

Her scent filled his nostrils with a heavy-sweet floral fragrance that included a hint of musk. A black linen sheath dress with a high collar left her shoulders bare, the flawless perfection of her skin like emperor's silk.

Her eyes made him feel wanted and close, while her fingers caressed the back of his head, stirring long-forgotten memories. Years ago at prep school, the most beautiful girl in his class lived in an ivy-covered brick house and wore designer tennis shoes from a store in New York. He had taken her in the rain under a maple tree. Shoulders like that.

Over Catherine's left breast she wore a diamond pin emblazoned with the letter C. Her fine chestnut hair was damp velvet in the moonlight.

For the joy of knowing her, of touching her, Kenji was risking both his marriage and his professional perch atop the Amada Corporation. This was not the worst of his sins—it was just the most personal. Still he felt no hesitation, not the slightest pause, as he contemplated his headlong fall into the unknown.

He nuzzled her neck while his attention focused on the thigh and black garter that seemed to be sliding free of the dark linen fabric. He ran his fingers over Catherine's arms, the muscle, and shape, how they flowed down to slender long fingers.

Tentatively he kissed Catherine's mouth. When he felt her tongue in reply, she turned in the seat and he kissed more confidently. Just visible on her inner thigh, at the edge of her panties, was a tattoo—a tiny rose with the initials TS on either side of the stem. Above the old-fashioned silk stockings, her legs were baby smooth.

His experienced fingers felt for the zipper on the back of her dress and, for the first time, he hesitated.

The wife of Senator Tom Swanson, the most coveted but untouchable wife he had ever met, an established, conservative woman with an impeccable reputation, would not be committing adultery in the backseat of Kenji Yamada's car. Notwithstanding that he was a successful businessman, polished, sophisticated, a powerful-looking fellow with exotically handsome eyes. He was also notoriously married.

She looked at him, the moonlight spreading across lips that now formed a challenging smile. Stifling his doubts, goaded by the smile, he pulled the zipper down to her waist.

"Kiss me" was all Catherine said as he lowered the gown.

He had never hungered for a woman as he did for Catherine Swanson. It was love, but love of power; it was the dream, nurtured since boyhood, of forbidden fruit; it was raw animal attraction; it was his circumstantial celibacy,

now five days old; it was his age; and it was that life might
be escaping him without him having grabbed enough of it.

He thought he detected something in her glancing eyes—
he knew it wasn't desire.

And then his world changed forever. The door flew open,
a blinding strobe lit the night air.

"You son of a bitch," Catherine shouted at the photographer.

Kenji said nothing, grabbing for his loafers, trying to
figure out how he could climb across Catherine to the man
popping the pictures. Realizing such a move was impossible,
he reached instead for the door handle on his side of the
car. Catherine tried to cover her brassiere, then get the dress
down somewhere near her knees, but it was too late. More
efficient-sounding clicks and whirs and flashes. The camera
was getting it all.

As Kenji ran around the car, his fear, the humiliation, the
shattering of his sense of personal control, vanished, and
he became the pragmatic old Kenji who had climbed the
corporate ladder with a measure of ruthless ambition equaled
by few.

The photographer was disappearing into the night. Kenji
circled to the front passenger's side and in the glove box
found his 9mm Smith & Wesson semiautomatic pistol, which
his security chief had given him and until tonight he had
shot only at an indoor range.

The disaster of being caught and not in control had brought
about a deadly calm. He got in, slid behind the wheel, and
shot the Rolls down the road, its lights illuminating the
photographer who ran toward a van still a hundred yards
distant. Kenji was a few car-lengths behind and bearing
down fast when the man left the road for the forest.

Kenji stopped the car and got out. Even in the shadows
of the full moon, he could see the layer of dust that covered

the huckleberry, the salal, and higher up the redwood boughs. He could hear only the sound of the man moving through the brush and the purr of the car's motor. As a precaution against something he hadn't yet defined, he shut off the engine and took the key.

"Stay here," he told Catherine. Then he shouted at the forest: "All I want is the film. Then you can go."

Silence.

"I'll give you money," he yelled. "We can talk."

Nothing.

Picking a redwood tree by the side of the road, he aimed to its center and peeled off three shots in rapid succession.

He heard crashing and plunged into the forest after the retreating sounds. It felt like he was wading through heavy water. Vines tore at his silk Armani socks. The thin soles of his handmade calfskin shoes were slick and his feet moved crazily. Densely packed boughs obscured his surroundings. Even the full moon couldn't find its way through the green mass that was a redwood forest. Oddly, he thought of ticks and Lyme disease, of poison oak, of falling in a hole. Still, he moved forward, following the sound, until the quiet compelled him to stop.

His breaths came heavy, pushed by the nagging realization that he could not lose this race.

"You don't want to stumble around in the dark woods with a wild man shooting at you," Kenji yelled.

No response.

"I would pay you ten thousand dollars."

He heard a single sharp crack as though the man had shifted his weight. He listened intently to brushy sounds overlaid with a noise like falling venetian blinds. He staggered foward at a near run.

When the photographer moved, Kenji moved, but his gut told him that he was lagging farther behind.

"All right, twenty thousand cash."

There was an urgency about this situation unlike any other in his forty-one years. The equation was simple. His Harvard-educated Japanese wife would not stand for philandering of any kind. If she left him for adultery, then his position as head of Amada, a subsidiary of her father's sprawling financial empire, would go with her. And under anybody's laws he could be disinherited. Kenji Yamada would become the paper tiger, sentenced to a living death.

Of late, his wife had become wily. She had caught him once. A hot day, a cool drink, a soft leather couch, the brown of it matching the skin of his personal secretary, a woman impressed with his power, his position, and his good looks.

Without artifice his wife would never have discovered his secret, but she had resources and she used them. It was a simple matter to plant a bug in his office. She had heard every groan, each exclamation of success, Kenji's bragging about doing two women in the same day—everything. He had been given both warning and ultimatum: one last chance. That chance was about to be spent by a two-bit photographer running through a darkened forest. He had to find this man hiding in the woods; he had to get the film.

Kenji made his desk-softened body go faster, risking injury. The photographer was getting tired, the pauses longer, the scurrying less frenzied. The chase would not go on much longer; at some point the man would disappear.

The forest seemed sparser. Looking up at an angle through the trees, Kenji saw stars. It signaled a large opening. Maybe a clear-cut, maybe a power line, or perhaps a log-haul road. A place this fellow might run. Without waiting for more brushy footfalls, Kenji estimated the direction and crashed wildly, not caring if he punished his body. Head down, arms out in front of him, he managed to miss the tree trunks.

There were no more sounds of the man running, but he

guessed the reason. He burst out of the brush into the clear-ing. Stars were bright in the watching sky, the moon a fountain of light silhouetting a figure sprinting in its glow. A power line and a maintenance road stretched to the crest of a small hill, where the man's feet flew over the smooth surface of the dirt road. It took only a few strides before Kenji knew he couldn't keep up. This man was a lithe, long-muscled runner.

Fear swept through him. He saw his wife's disgusted, hurt face. He raised the gun. You couldn't shoot a man for taking a picture. But your whole life, everything you value—your honor, your vanishing fortune . . . The finger squeezed in the middle of the debate. Eight times it squeezed. It was an unlucky shot, almost an accident, he would later conclude. Hitting a running man with a pistol at fifty yards is really not possible with precision. He knew the instant he pulled the trigger that he had a hit. His knowledge of the hit, he decided, came from a spiritual union with the hunted, rather than the sickening thud that was the bullet hitting flesh. Startling to think that you would actually hear the strike, hear the thump of expanding lead boring through bone and meat.

For a moment Kenji considered the odds that the body could be hidden, the evidence destroyed. He and his security man, Hans Groiter, would be back first thing in the morning to dispose of the body. For money Hans could do something like this. Already he and Hans were so deep into the dirty deeds of life that he didn't fear Hans or his reaction, although this accidental shooting was rather more dramatic than any-thing they had done previously.

It was a sick moon with stars strewn across the sky like diamond teardrops. There were already crickets and frogs, the scurrying of the newborn in the brush, and other sounds of dawn in springtime. Kenji wondered why a night like this could not be left to love.

He covered the fifty yards to the body, taking in the moon, the stars, his life, the law, the jail cell, the publicity, the whole panoply of what-ifs that encompassed both capture and escape. He played it through his mind first one way, then the other, careful to give equal time to the possibility of failure. It was bad luck to assume a win.

The photographer lay flat on his back in the middle of the road, his sport coat looking tattered. To Kenji's horror, the body still moved; there were strange breathy sounds gurgling through frothy blood that looked black in the moonlight. Oddly, or maybe it wasn't odd for bohemian photographers, the man wore denim jeans and a white T-shirt sporting a heavy bloodstain that in a well-lit photo would have made a dramatic statement.

The clip of his pistol was empty. Kenji waited a moment and realized the wheezing and choking could go on quite some time. Obviously, it was a lung shot that missed the heart. He had made a mistake, and he knew that to escape his mistake he needed to control his mind. Justice lay in his own consciousness, not in the sovereign state. Kenji would make his own justice. He walked away until the choking was a whisper.

This man's death dragged on. Walking back, Kenji decided that he was strong enough to partake in this man's death.

"Help." The man was trying to talk. Looking down to find the camera, Kenji couldn't escape the sight of the seizing body, head thrown back, mouth gaping. "Help me."

For whatever reason, he felt nothing. He yanked the camera over the man's head, cursing as the photographer tried to push out the word "help" through cups of blood.

"You die hard." Kenji opened the camera and pulled out

the film, then grabbed the man by his feet and pulled him out of the road and into a thicket of stickers that tore at his clothing and his flesh. He noted the distance between the giant electrical towers, about halfway between. The blood would make the body easy to find.

Kenji remembered this power line, knew it eventually intersected the logging road about a half mile from where his Rolls sat with Catherine, who by this time would be shivering. He elected to walk back through the woods, letting the trees thrash him, recalling that white people had whipped themselves to receive some strange absolution from their wrongdoing. Already he wondered whether tomorrow or the next day he might feel something. Perhaps when he lifted his little boy over his head or touched his wife in the night, he would feel the weight of his guilt.

He reached the car and walked to the back door on Catherine's side, took off his coat and brushed himself off. For a few moments he had allowed himself the luxury of infatuation. It would never happen again. But this time there was no question that he would yet have Catherine physically.

"What was all the shooting? Thank God you're all right. I mean, my God, no one should get shot over pictures." She was terrified, rambling. "The photographer is all right. Please, dear God, tell me he's all right."

Kenji paused. And then he lied. "He's fine. I was so pissed that I made him dance. He danced and I shot. I stripped out the film. It's OK."

Kenji walked around the burgundy car, noticing the gleam of the moon in the satin finish. He got in the back on the other side and motioned Catherine to him. The strain showed on Catherine's face.

"Guess you took care of him," she said a little too brightly.

"Shall we resume?"

"You've got to be kidding—after that?"

"But you were so ... ," he started, casually reaching for her purse.

"What are you doing?"

It took only a second to find the small transmitter.

"How crude."

She looked pale, the skin on her face even tighter. He dropped the 9mm in her lap. She shook, but at first he said nothing.

"Talk."

"Please don't hurt me." Her lip was quivering.

"You've got the gun, not me."

She held her hands up as if the gun were a loathsome creature.

"My husband has very little, just his government pension from the Senate. We have huge debts, legal fees. Your assistant wanted to test you. He wanted evidence if you failed the test. He promised we'd get a little part of Amada. He said there might be some discovery that would make Amada very valuable. The details ... I'm unclear."

"All you had to do for the money was seduce me?"

"There were other things. . . . Political favors."

"Ah, that would be after he took over for me." Kenji chuckled but felt only hatred. "What do you know of this ... discovery?"

"All Satoru would tell us is it could involve a lot of money. There was a guaranteed minimum of fifty thousand cash no matter what happened. Otherwise, I never would have done it."

"I assume the pictures were to be given to my wife and father-in-law as an excuse to throw me out."

"Only if you took me up on my offer."

For a fleeting moment he wondered whether this was all

Satoru's idea or if his father-in-law had a hand in it—probably the former. Satoru was ambitious.

Putting his arm around her, he put his face an inch from hers, holding her tight. Chanel again filled his nostrils. He didn't worry about his sweaty smell or unkempt hair.

"Here's what you'll do. You will tell Satoru that I wouldn't touch you. We were never here. After the restaurant I took you home. I will give you and your husband the stock you were promised in a revocable trust. It will be revoked automatically upon my death. Only I can take the stock back during my life. You will get your millions if I decide so. So save some of your income from the trust and wish me a long life. But you will never deny me your body—ever. Agreed?"

A pause.

"OK," she said, looking out the window at nothing but the darkness.

"OK," he repeated. "Our deal starts now."

1

It was spring, and Dan Young's front-yard dogwood was showing the tips of its taupe blossoms. Normally, Dan didn't give domestic shrubs or trees or gardens a second thought, but Tess's favorite tree had been their dogwood, planted on their first anniversary, and that made every dogwood important.

Here, not two feet from his nose, someone else's early-blooming dogwood grew outside the window of the small antique shop. This downtown store had a timeless feel to it—reminding him that there were those certain moments that could make a person's destiny. Dan wondered if this might be one of those moments, for he carried $500,000 in cash in his leather briefcase. It was an extraordinary sum and he was delivering it to a rather unusual person.

Amid the store's velvety brown hues of old wood, the smells of scented polish and beeswax, shoppers talked in lower tones and seldom let their cigarette ash hit the floor.

The place exuded personality. When he had stepped inside to kill some time, Dan instantly knew that the proprietor's hand was connected to his heart instead of his wallet. In this small town by the sea, where the locals made lumber, caught fish, worked for the government, or catered to the tourists, and consequently had modest budgets, such a store could have been more profitably filled with cheap furniture sold on easy terms.

A freestanding armoire from Gascony, France, shone with quiet grandeur. According to the placard, it had been hand made in the mid-1800s. Beside the armoire hung the object of his attention—a photograph seemingly yellowed with age. It intrigued him. He'd been around the perimeter of the place twice—the consequence of being early—and this was his third time back to the narrow space in front of the photo.

The photo had been taken in black and white, probably with a large-lensed box camera manufactured around the turn of the last century. He had a passing interest in photography and knew the look created by large, slow cameras using photo plates. Or maybe it was the clothing of the subjects that made him think the camera was from another era. A giant redwood tree served as the backdrop for the composition. In front of the tree stood a woman, a man, a dog, and a young woman. Dan somehow knew the dog belonged to the man. It was doubtful that the woman even liked the dog, although he could surmise from the look of things that she liked the man.

But it was the younger woman who piqued Dan's interest. She wore a skirt appropriate to the day, drawn in tight at the waist, ballooned out, then falling straight down from the hips to the top of her sharp-toed black boots, not unlike the boots he had seen on female clients at his law office—in winter, never summer.

Her face had a lean angularity, the nose strong but not

too prominent, and the cheekbones high. If only he could see the detail of the eyes that looked at him, that tugged at the darkest recesses of his mind. He knew that those eyes held a child's innocence, that they owned the sun, that under the sepia tone of the photograph her eyes were golden, surrounded by blue.

The first time he looked at the photo, it had taken him a moment to recognize her. He had watched her from across the courthouse hallway a couple of weeks ago. Last summer, he'd sat a foot away from her in a pickup. It was now apparent that Maria Fischer's reason for choosing to meet at Muldoon's Pub, next door to the antique shop in Old Town Palmer, was that she had some connection to this place.

He checked his watch: 9:55 A.M. He took a new grip on the briefcase. Even though the handle was slick with sweat, its contents growing heavy, he didn't want to put it down. He stroked his lip, where up until this morning there had been a mustache. He was unable to escape the odd feeling that someone might be watching him. Yet the many mirrors revealed no one.

"Can I help you?"

The salesclerk wore a raw silk blouse and black pants that looked modern Italian, and she wasn't quite what Dan expected.

"I've been looking at this photo. It's made to look antique."

She smiled broadly. "Right. It's a good fake. It was taken last year."

"I suspected."

"Actually, it's my cousin with her mom and dad. A friend of hers took it with a plain old Nikon 35mm."

"The dog belongs to Dad," he said.

"How did you know?"

"Your cousin is a lawyer?"

"You know her?"

"The earth woman."

"And you are?"

"Oh, I'm just a colleague, and I'm late. Nice meeting you, though." He tossed the words over his shoulder as he strode out.

Context. Everything was context. You would barely recognize your own mother if you knew, just *knew*, you were looking at a photo that was one hundred years old.

Dan wondered what Maria Fischer would do when she recognized him. He had only had one face-to-face conversation with her and it was about a year ago. He had waded into a demonstration at an Otran mill and had headed for the speaker's platform with a request that the crowd disperse or face the police. Things had gotten a little rowdy in the crowd; she had jumped off the pickup bed that served as a platform and then pulled him into the cab. It was an old red Ford with dents and rust, and with blankets tacked on the upholstery. There they had a shouting match before they made a deal that she would get the demonstrators away from the mill gates in a half hour.

Now he was giving her money. He and his clients had to trust her to keep it quiet—although they had gone over that part very carefully. Everything about the drop was covered by the attorney-client privilege and it was inviolate. Even a judge could not order disclosure of the facts concerning the handoff. He had worked that out carefully and they had reduced it all to writing. Technically at the moment of the drop, she and her clients were clients of his and the opposite was true. Accordingly, for this very limited purpose on this one occasion, the courier and the donor were clients of hers, even though Maria personally had no notion of either the courier's or the donor's identity.

Since Maria didn't know Dan well and he was without his mustache, he wondered if in the dark corner of a tavern he could, for a few minutes, disguise his identity. Even if only for a short while, he wanted to talk to Maria Fischer without her hating him. And it was the sort of humor he couldn't quite resist.

Dan Young was a member of an old-school law firm that worked for private industry, mostly a group of lumber companies owned by one Jeb Otran. Unlike the other attorneys in his firm, Dan was anything but traditional. He had distinguished himself early on, not only because he was daring and shrewd, but because under the country-boy exterior was a man who prepared like a bean counter and spoke with the eloquence of a prophet. He wore cowboy boots, usually without the barnyard mud.

Dan had grown up on a ranch in eastern Oregon near the Deschutes River, outside of Maupin on Deep Creek (pronounced "crick"), in the baking-summer tan-sand hills and winter-bleak snowdrifted valleys. He had learned to string fences, doctor cows, and take in the hay; on Friday nights he'd drink beer and dance with Tess until 10 o'clock; then they'd adjourn to the Young family home and he'd fall asleep on his mother's old tan couch with his head in Tess's lap, her fingers combing his blond hair or tracing the faint white lines that ran across his palms and the backs of his wrists—scars from years of handling barbed wire.

His mother, Gertrude, and father, Lucas, had worked the land all their lives, seldom driving their 1972 Dodge pickup farther than Maupin or the Dalles except when they went to the cattle auctions in Portland. Although neither had a college education, they were well-read, never having owned a TV and not being much on socializing. Winters were long, dark, and cold. Lucas had inherited the family ranch when his brothers and sisters had moved off to the cities. He had hoped the same legacy for his eldest boy, Dan.

Even after Dan graduated from Harvard Law School, Lucas still wanted him to take over the ranch, even conspired with Tess's dad to expand it. There was talk of merging the Young ranch with a portion of the Johnson ranch, making the "JY" a sprawling place with 500 acres irrigated, maybe 20,000 acres total, beginning 2 miles farther down Deep Creek.

Gertrude Young knew what her husband wanted to deny, that Dan was uncommonly gifted and that he wanted to roam and travel places with people who could not be found in the backlands of Oregon. Tess was just like Dan in that regard, and as Gertrude saw it, Dan and Tess would be together forever in some place far away from Deep Creek, barns, mesas, canyons, and livestock.

As Gertrude predicted, Dan and Tess ended up exchanging snow-coffined Maupin for damp-souled Palmer. But Tess always said, once a cowboy, always a cowboy, and to this day Dan occasionally roped a calf, although he'd long since gone cold on the bronc and bull riding.

When he had a chance and an invite, he still went to roundups and brandings for a local northern California rancher or two, but never to Oregon, never back to the high desert. Once he had left, he was done there for good except for family gatherings and holidays. Tess and he had made a life for themselves on the northern California coast in a medium-sized city by Oregon standards, and there Dan had made a name. He had even considered running for state senate when the party pushed him. In fact, some said that if Tess hadn't died, he'd probably be wearing his cowboy boots in Sacramento on his way to Washington, D.C.

If he never went into politics, he was destined to one day

lead his firm or another one like it. He was always popular with the court clerks because he never took himself or his successes too seriously. The judges liked him fine when he wasn't pushing the line on the rules of evidence or procedure.

Dan still usually won at arm wrestling, never played golf, and drank his scotch neat if he wasn't having beer. Seldom if ever did he miss a 49ers game, and he never failed to analyze new players and game plans. Although he bet only in office and tavern pools, his track record at picking winners and spreads was nothing short of phenomenal.

But Dan had struggled to maintain his winning approach to life after the loss of Tess. Previously he had been possessed of exceptional good humor; now he tended to brood while he drank his beer. He always had a sharp wit, but lately he used it as a sword rather than a foil. Light furrows of melancholy and little forehead lines cut by the anxiety of perpetual sadness gave his face a rugged brand of character that added years.

His life consisted of small things: parent-teacher conferences, sleep-overs for his son, Nate, and his friends, helping out his sister, Katie, taking out the garbage, washing the cars, picking up groceries for Pepacita, roping a few calves, and tending his law practice. Every Saturday morning when he was in town, he went to a fried-eggs-and-coffee place overlooking the ocean and sat alone at the very table where he and Tess had dined.

Sometimes he would remember Tess the wrong way— her lifeless body wrapped around the steering wheel of her car, reduced to a grotesque arrangement of flesh and bone. He would remember her just the way he had found her, still warm, just after a drunken driver had put the steering column through her chest in a head-on collision. The red lights flashing, pouring onto the rain-slick, shiny black street; the rank, bracing smell of petroleum; the blubbering, slurred

"I'm sorries" of the other driver; and the hurt, cold and deep, and seemingly endless—all of it had clung to him.

At first his friends said he had bounced back quickly— up early every morning, concentrating on his cases like never before. He had become quieter at work—a little more garrulous socially. But eventually the forced cheerfulness at dinners with friends became nearly real. People stopped giving him books about grieving and depression. Now he had a smile for most every occasion, a joke or two like usual, and he no longer had to pretend at every party.

Dan had stopped seeing the counselor almost before he started. The counselor claimed that a man's life could become like an iced-over pond. A thin veneer on the surface that looked solid, but a man could drown if he fell through. "Well," Dan explained, putting on his coat after the last counseling session, "if I fall through, I'll swim on over to see you."

It was a year after Tess's death that his father died, but Dan didn't feel like he had much more "stuffin' " to be knocked out of him, so he sucked it up and continued on.

Muldoon's Pub stood five blocks from the downtown university campus, such as it was. As Dan had expected, there was only a light Saturday-morning crowd, most of it near the TV at the end opposite the fireplace. He found a booth far from the other patrons, in a dark and quiet corner of the room.

He blew out the candle on the table, deepening the shadows. Without his cowboy boots he felt naked, but he had deliberately shed his little trademarks for the meeting. Remarkably, he had come without his hat.

He asked for water and corn tortillas with salsa, no real drink, pledging to keep this meeting short and keep it sober.

This rather brash cash-delivery plan was amusing, but it had to work and it had to be completed in absolute secrecy. Although he and Maria had never actually done battle in the courtroom, their jousting confined to pre-court skirmishes, he was rapidly becoming her nemesis. Still, context would work for him here just as it had momentarily fooled him with the photo. Maybe they'd have a talk before she came unglued.

And then—five minutes early—Maria Fischer entered the pub ramrod straight, her stride measured and steady, searching for a tall gentleman dressed in a herringbone sport coat.

This was not at all like the Maria Fischer he knew. Perfectly coiffed, she wore gold earrings and necklace flat against her smooth, bronzed skin, complementing the smart-looking silk blouse and tan business suit that she wore with all the panache of the French model who first took it down the runway. Her dark hair, with the sheen of its reddish highlights, made the most of the brighter light at the center of the room. Even a casual observer would have recognized her immediately as someone on her way to something important. But for a careful watcher, there was something more. It was vulnerability, a quality that, for Dan, had remained completely hidden in his observations of her at the courthouse and their encounter at the demonstration.

He'd heard stories about her. That she'd studied law with a correspondence school while living somewhere around Fairbanks, Alaska, in a one-room cabin. That in winter there was no way to access her cabin except by cross-country ski, snowshoe, or snowmobile. That she had come out of Alaska to save the forests and for that reason alone she had become an attorney.

People all agreed, friend and foe alike, that the woman's power came from her absolute guilelessness. She could be accused of being a zealot, of being overly passionate and too serious about everything, but no one doubted her absolute sincerity. Since in Dan's mind she was often sincerely wrong, that made her a particularly dangerous adversary.

She paused, searching, and Dan waved, sticking his hand out of the dark corner, keeping his face back. Natural, unpretentious warmth lit up her face. For just a second he felt an odd pang of guilt.

"I enjoyed your lecture so much." She spoke their prearranged code sentence with perfect ease.

"That's flattering coming from an attorney with your considerable speaking talents." He mouthed the correct response. In accordance with their understanding, he didn't rise from his chair.

Dan searched her face, looking for any sign that she might recognize him in the gloom or remember the timbre of his voice. Looking into her unsuspecting eyes, he understood in a new way the extent to which, in another life, under different circumstances, his soul could have become mortgaged to the look of her. The soft light masked both the autumn gold at her pupils' edges and the light blue of her outer irises. She was waiting for him to speak next.

"Well"—he tried a chuckle—"here's what you came for." He shoved the briefcase with his foot.

"I just want to say how much we appreciate what you're doing." She paused as if such expressions did not come easy to her.

"All for the cause," he replied as she took a seat. "Will you have something to drink before I walk you to the bank?"

"Iced tea would be good."

The waitress came through the murk to their dark corner. Dan ordered two iced teas, then changed his mind, called her back, and ordered a beer as well. What the hell, he might as well enjoy himself.

"I would love to tell you about our work, if you have a minute."

He responded by nodding, knowing that it would be safer to take her and the money to the bank.

"My work is the wilderness. . . ."

Thinking Dan a city man, Maria gave him a verbal slide-show, enriched by Dan's own memories of exploring the mountains with his grandfather: an August moon, heavy and round like an ancient, knowing face, looking down on silhouetted peaks shouldered by jagged, granite ledges spilling down into the shadows above a river. There were rocky crags, crystalline waterfalls, and miles of white-water rapids, enormous gorges carved by the river, rock walls covered with mosses, lichen, and ferns.

Dan studied Maria as she spoke, not hearing every word.

The waitress came by, and Maria paused until she left.

"Are you part of the movement?" she asked without warning.

"Oh, I'm not much a part of anything."

"You don't have to tell me, if you don't want to." The sincerity in her eyes felt like a weight on his chest.

"I'm a nameless courier, in a darkened tavern, secretly passing cash in a briefcase."

"I wonder, could I ask you to sit forward a little? I just can't see you back in that corner."

He couldn't help but smile as he leaned forward.

"Well, I'll be . . . Dan Young. You shaved your mustache."

"Tell me something I don't know." He chuckled.

"Oh and what could I possibly say to you, short of you giving me lots of money, which you are. I can't believe this. I'm speechless."

"Doesn't sound that way to me," he said.

"Now I feel completely stupid dressing up this way. Why are you doing this?"

"I'm only a lawyer, just like you. They didn't ask me what I thought."

"Why'd they send *you?*"

"Nice smile?"

"This isn't a joke, is it?"

"The briefcase is full."

"So what do you want?"

"To give you the money, get a little info."

"Info? This"—she gestured at the briefcase—"is to help us get the Highlands Forest designated as a park. Lobbyists and court battles cost a fortune. Patty McCafferty and I and a lot of others are determined to save it."

"Well, I know that." Dan had watched Patty McCafferty speak in a voice that transformed her words into religion for the faithful. Maria Fischer's voice was a lesser instrument of that same fervor—a more interesting voice.

"So how do you feel about helping our cause?"

She waited for his response. He took the last gulp of his beer and contemplated the iced tea.

"You want my views on another forest preserve?"

"Well, maybe not."

"Let's talk about it sometime when we don't have to go to the bank."

"I know I'm not supposed to ask. But why all the secrecy? Why doesn't whoever it is just write a check for such a huge amount and take credit? Not to mention the risk of loss. Isn't it just crazy to carry around cash?"

"I guess I don't know, really."

The waitress asked if they'd like something more to drink.

"You?" he asked Maria.

"Thanks, no."

"I don't care for anything, thank you. Just the check."

"It *is* an individual donor, right?"

"You don't give up easily."

"Well, maybe you guys regularly sneak around with cash paying people, but we don't."

"I could take it back. Tell them you don't want it."

"Yeah, right."

"Tell me," he said. "What drives *you* to save an old-growth forest?"

"It's still there. It's part of where we came from and what ties us to our past."

"No. I don't mean that. What created this fire in your belly?"

"That's a bigger subject than a beer and a bowl of chips. Listen, I know we said we'd both go to the bank, but I can handle it from here. The bank is just down the street."

"You think that's a good idea?"

"Nobody knows what's in here. It's just a briefcase. And I don't really want to be seen with you."

"Ouch."

"It's nothing personal."

He gave her the I-don't-believe-you look with a little smile. "So would you meet me again in a dark corner?"

"You get us another half million and we'll talk about it."

Of course before she knew the courier was Dan Young, she had had many reasons to impress the man; she was talking to a big donor, after all, or at least the donor's representative, and the coalition desperately needed the money. But when she first saw him, there was more. She had felt him looking at her; he had seemed attuned to every detail of what she was saying—then again, maybe it wasn't what she was saying.

Aside from the fact that she hated his politics, Dan Young had always seemed to possess some quality that she found attractive. He was wide-shouldered and had the quiet confidence of someone who knew exactly what he was about. But he didn't quite swagger, although like all cowboy types he tortured animals, ate meat, did what his kind usually did. She wasn't quite sure what made him interesting.

Once at a county fair, before Dan's wife had died, Maria had been working a booth devoted to registering Democrat voters. She'd taken a break, gotten some hot tea, and moved to the back of the booth where she watched the people passing by. Not thirty feet away, Dan Young had been standing around with an odd mix of professionals and a few cowboys, but he looked more like the cowboys even if his jeans were a little new, his heavy blue work shirt laundered and starched.

Because he was Otran's lawyer and represented industry, she had been curious about him. But it struck her that unlike the other men in the group he had no roll of flab above the oversize belt buckle. Remarkable for a guy who had to sit in a chair hours on end. He was tall, she guessed 6'5" in boots, maybe 6'4" in his bare feet. Blond, obviously blue-eyed, he tended to half-smile under his bushy mustache and concentrate on whoever was talking, periodically shifting his weight from one foot to the other while he listened.

He had big hands and used them when he spoke. There was an earnestness about him that made people listen although he seemed to stay silent more than speak.

There was a dimple in his chin, and he had eyebrows that looked like they got regularly trimmed, and over the right brow was a faded scar. As she watched, the group of men had become more animated, one of them obviously trying to tease Dan.

Dan smiled at the fellow poking him in the shoulder,

adjusted his hat, and walked away over to the far side of the arena where the bull riders were coming out of the chute.

"Hey, man, we were only kidding. Those big fuckers will kill you. Come on back here," one of the men called out.

In a few minutes Dan Young was riding a bull. Everybody had heard about Dan—he had grown up riding everything on four legs—but when he jumped off the bull, a woman and a boy came running toward the arena. By the way the woman approached Dan, Maria could tell it was family. He tried to put his arm around her, but she shrugged it off and squared off to him, holding the boy on her hip. It was obviously his wife, and Maria was guessing that she hadn't been consulted about the day's adventure.

Maria had watched as the woman cut loose a verbal barrage. But when she was in his face, he sobered. Without hearing a word, she suspected that the woman was reminding him that he had a son, a family, and responsibilities. A trip to the hospital was not what their little family needed. The look on his face, the honest appraisal of what he was being told, gave Maria some information.

Reluctantly she had admitted there was some good in this timber-industry mouthpiece. Maybe it wasn't much, but something. Then she had seen him at the demonstration, where they had argued. But as ugly as their verbal sparring became, spurred on by her bloodred anger and his I-fear-nothing determination, she still secretly liked him at the end. It was something she didn't understand about herself and didn't want to understand.

Getting involved further with him, even in casual conversation, would not be practical, she knew. *Practical.* According to her father, she wasn't at all practical, and she was still trying to figure out exactly what that meant.

Living in an Alaskan cabin wasn't practical, but it was good, it was uncluttered, it was simple, and it enabled her

to form visions of herself and her life. She lived free of the
noise of civilization. The hardness of the place, the relentless
cold, the backbreaking work, the isolation, the energy that
she had to expend on preparing a simple meal, all had
enabled her to see things that couldn't be seen on a hillside
mansion in southern California. The impractical sometimes
bore fruit. She wasn't sure that she ever wanted to be practical.

For a good part of her life, she had been considered
attractive. Perhaps before her teens people thought of her
as an ungainly and skinny tomboy with braces. Later, she
became beautiful, but still it was a beauty that was off the
beaten path and depended to some extent on her smile and
an inner something that beamed out of her countenance.
Some said she was vivacious, others that she was a natural
inspiration.

Maria's mouth was a little large, her lips full, and after
the braces her teeth were sensational. If anything was ordinary about her, it was her brunette hair and a hairline that
was not perfectly clean when she pulled it up atop her head.
But she never did that, except on Saturday while she read.

There was her scar. She called it Amy's scar, in honor
of the little girl she had been rescuing when injured. A full
six inches long, it was an inch wide, right across an otherwise
perfect belly. Everybody had something—well, almost
everybody. If you were lucky, it was only flat feet. But
Maria wore her scar with gratitude. She was thankful that
she had been there to collect it. Two-piece bathing suits
were out and she was a tad shy about the scar when it came
to men.

Maria craved new ideas and new ways of thinking. She
was like a walking investment bank for creative thought.
Stubbornness was the other side of that equation, and she
had not yet learned to tolerate ideas that challenged her

fundamental beliefs. In truth, she had only a handful of fundamental beliefs: She should practice yoga; she should save old-growth forests; her mother was inherently wise and good, and to whatever extent she might fail, it was probably due to her father; she should be doing unto others what she would have them do unto her except when she lost her temper; anything worth doing was worth doing passionately; children were sacred trusts. And she believed fervently in love, but wasn't sure she'd ever find it.

Certainly, the man before her was puzzling and had aroused a heated curiosity about two basic issues: Did he want to save the planet—more specifically the trees? And did he look as good naked as he did clothed?

As he watched the waitress return with their check, there seemed a sadness about him. It was a peculiar contrast to the square-jawed maleness that he exuded.

He caught her noticing him. "You wanna have coffee sometime?"

"No," she said. "Not exactly. I mean maybe if we weren't so, well, opposite. We're just about as opposite as two people can be."

He nodded and she could see the sincerity in his eyes. She pondered that one. Something about this man reminded her of her father—the way he used to lavish attention upon her before their great falling-out and her migration, as she called it, to Alaska. Old feelings stirred inside as she reminded herself: This isn't my father. And it isn't my boyfriend.

As the crowning complication to her life, Maria was still her father's daughter and hadn't yet decided how she would finally deal with business and materialism. Nor had she decided how to deal with her predictable, maybe even boring boyfriend.

"Hey," Dan said. "I gotta go. But I did enjoy your company." He nodded at the door as she reached for the briefcase. "Maybe you should go first."

Dan followed her out of the pub, concerned about her decision to go alone to the bank, even though it was only a couple of blocks. The easy way she had with him, her passion for everything, the trees, life, her work—it was attractive. Watching her move briskly down the sidewalk, he found himself wishing there were a way to prolong their contact. But reason prevailed, and he walked to the right and she to the left, he fighting the impulse to follow. It was a slow morning, the shops just preparing for the onslaught of afternoon foot-traffic—traffic that might not come on this noticeably quiet Saturday.

Maybe because he was uneasy about the money, or because he had more to say, or because of that damnable intrigue, he turned to watch her one last time. As he did so, a figure in a long brown leather coat and cowboy hat came at her rapidly from behind.

He didn't actually reason out that it was too warm for a long coat; it was more that everything about the situation appeared wrong.

Then it hit him.

The briefcase.

"Wait," he shouted. And ran.

2

Maria jumped as if stabbed. He imagined her eyes widening with the realization of the coming assault. From under the leather trench coat a policeman's side-handled baton appeared. Her attacker, his face hidden under the brim of his hat and a nylon stocking, swung the weapon. Maria was quick, though, and she deflected the baton with the briefcase. The assailant moved in. A swift jab of the baton caught Maria hard in the ribs. As she staggered, the assailant snatched the case and ran.

Dan sprinted, reckless from adrenaline, but he was too late. A black Chevy with a shine on the chrome came to a squealing stop, the assailant leaped through the open rear door. Inside, the thief's head turned, partially revealing through the nylon stocking the finer details of his profile— the nose and a slender face and jaw. In that moment, as Dan's fingers missed the closing door by inches, he realized that the assailant was a woman.

Tires squealed, and the Chevy raced away.

Dan took Maria's arm, looking her over to make sure she was all right.

A couple stood befuddled across the street, a shopkeeper shook a small carpet in front of his store.

"Follow her," Dan screamed. "Where?"

Somehow she understood that he was asking about her car. She pointed even as he moved toward the Ford Taurus.

"Keys," he said, watching the black sedan turn the corner.

He opened the passenger side and slid across to the driver's seat. "Stay here."

"I'm coming." She slid in as he hit the accelerator.

The car's momentum slammed the door. He squealed around the corner. No black sedan. Maria fastened her seat belt as he accelerated through a red light.

"Take it easy," she shouted.

"Not while they've got the money."

They were on Fifth, the main street through town, going north.

"There." Maria pointed at the black car's tail end, which was disappearing around another corner far ahead. The car had turned off onto an old two-lane highway that eventually headed into the mountains. Dan swerved into the oncoming lane, passing a young woman whose mouth went wide in shock.

"Let's call the cops. For once they could do some good."

"We can't do that," he said. They went around a curve; the rear tires broke loose and started to slide.

"Will you be careful!" she screamed as the car fishtailed from an overcorrection. "Why can't we call the cops?"

Before he answered, she saw some kids crossing the road, and he slammed on the brakes, then swerved into the parking lane, barely missing them.

"Stop this right now," Maria shouted. "We can't kill people because we want the money."

"We aren't killing anybody," he said through clenched teeth. "And we can't call the police because this is not supposed to be public."

The car lurched around another curve, almost leaving the road. His foot remained on the accelerator. Here the road was fairly straight, slightly diminishing her tension. Strip malls and an odd assortment of fast-food places flashed by. Doris and Jerry's steakhouse and a liquor store all fronted against subdivisions.

It appeared they were gaining. The muscle in his jaw bulged, but he looked otherwise unfazed. Except for the speed they could have been on a Saturday outing.

"I insist we call the cops," she said.

"Remember we made a deal. This is all attorney-client privilege."

"That was before someone stole the money, for God's sake."

They flew by a small school and entered the first grove of trees, then dropped to flatland pastures. Towns ended abruptly in these sparsely settled regions. Maria knew this road well. Along this area the coast rivers and streams had deposited silt for millennia, making a narrow band of grassy bogs. Behind this lush green ribbon were towering foothills, redwood country that butted up against the mixed conifer forests of the coastal range of northern California. The two-lane road on which they drove meandered along the coastal lowlands at the toe of the hills. Mountain roads spurred off it. One in particular led to a maze of graveled ranch and logging roads that cut deeply into the mountains to the east. This was the route to the backside of the Highlands Forest.

They passed a pickup as though it were standing still. Its blaring horn was lost in the wind.

"Slow down—" Then the car rounded a gentle turn, hit some loose gravel, and began a slide. She saw the white guardrail approaching. "Jesus." She stiffened her legs and tensed every muscle, anticipating the crash. By some quirk of spinning tires and centrifugal force, the car came completely around, missing the white steel railing by inches. "You're gonna kill us," she said as the car straightened out after the 360.

"Who gave you this money?" she asked as they fishtailed past a slow-moving van. She didn't really expect an answer. "The thief knew exactly what he was doing." Realizing that she was half-yelling, she told herself to talk calmly. Maybe it would help slow him down. "That guy knows you're back here."

"That was no guy. And if they were thinking about us, they wouldn't be doing this. They'd be weaving around town."

"Not necessarily—there are cops back there. In the mountains there are no police. Maybe they want us to follow."

She studied him, wondering if he'd thought of that. His hands were clenched around the wheel, his expression all grim determination.

"You lost the mustache so I wouldn't recognize you?"

"At least for a few minutes."

"What exactly is going on here?"

"I was giving you money for a worthy cause. Somebody stole it. That's it."

Now they were maintaining an even distance of a few hundred yards behind the black sedan and traveling at about eighty miles per hour.

"You're not being straight with me. Tell me who you work for and what they really want. Then maybe I can figure this out."

"I can't, all right?"

"Fine," she said.

But of course it wasn't fine.

Ahead, the black car had disappeared from sight. For a few moments neither said anything as Dan increased their speed around the tree-lined curves, squealing the tires and keeping her knuckles white.

"They're up there. As soon as we get around this bend, we should see them." She was hoping that would slow him down.

As they rounded the hill, she saw the black sedan take a smoking-tire right up into the mountains. The road followed the Wintoon River Canyon to thousands of square miles of rugged wilderness owned primarily by the government, some by ranchers, some by timber companies, and some by the Hoopa, Yurok, and Tilok tribes.

They drove in near silence up the canyon, the country getting steeper as they went. They passed the first major ridges near the coast and a gorge where hundreds of feet below them there was a series of waterfalls.

"I figure the best way to identify these people is to see where they're going," he said. "Fortunately, you started with almost a full tank."

"It's a rental car. My Cherokee's in the shop."

"There are no gas stations until you get to Johnson City. On these back roads that's over one hundred twenty miles."

"Maybe they live up there."

He didn't reply or say what he thought, but he was obviously planning something.

"So what do we do if we follow them to a house?"

"I stay and watch the place while you tell the clients where the money is."

Ahead she saw the dark sedan pull to the shoulder. They had entered an isolated stretch of road high on the mountainside. The last mailbox was about two miles behind them.

Dan slowed to normal highway speed. They both peered forward. Barely two cars wide, the asphalt was old and intermittently striped down the center. Narrow gravel shoulders dropped off steeply into a stand of young-growth redwood maybe twenty feet high.

"Oh God," he breathed. "They're—"

Maria saw two figures crouched near the back of the sedan when an explosive sound startled her. The bullet hit their right front tire. The car shuddered; another thundering report rang out. The car veered, and Dan's mouth remained unwavering in a determined line, his elbows locked. The outside tire hit the gravel shoulder; rocks shot into the wheel well, creating a clamorous racket. Then over the bank they went, horrible jolts as the car pitched and yawed as if riding a sea of concrete waves.

Instinctively, Maria planted her feet firmly to the floor so that the car's violent shuddering rippled through her body. Flung forward and back despite the bracing posture, her body felt bisected as the seat belt bit into her chest. Small trees disappeared under the front end, but others rose to replace them. Then everything rolled to the right, and she was hurled against the door. One crash was like an explosion as they were knocked around; the car was plunging forward; then a crash was followed by a jolt that felt like it ripped out her ribs. Then silence.

Maria hung from her seat belt and knew they were on their nose. Dust swirled in the partly crushed car, blinding and choking her. Dan's hand on hers pulled her, but she was held in place by her seat belt. Stinging eyes sent tears down her face. Her body felt heavy and began to ache, just now awakening to the bruising.

Above her head was a large tree trunk or branch. Glancing down, she saw a breathtaking abyss whose bottom was a ribbon of deep blue—the river.

"Oh my God," she whispered. They hung in space at least 200 feet above the river rocks.

An oak branch had speared the windshield and come out the back end as though a giant rapier had run the car through.

The spread of torn and buckled roof from which they hung stretched like a spring, giving bounce to the car as it dangled in the wind.

"Don't move," he said in a low voice, as if even a small noise might break the ribbon of sheet metal. An eerie mountain wind blew through the twisted openings in the car and made a sound like sighing. The tree was rooted in a tiny shelf on a nearly vertical cliff. The main trunk grew out away from the cliff for a distance of twenty feet or so before curving up to rise nearly parallel to the steep rock face. If the car had slid another three feet down the branch, the front end would have hit the main trunk.

"Maybe we can go out the side window over the roof and into the tree," he said.

Maria noticed her knee shaking through her tattered nylons and quickly took inventory of her body. Everything was painful, but nothing excruciating.

"We're gonna get out of this," he said.

Wham! A bullet from a high-powered rifle slammed into the car. There was a creak as the metal stretched.

"God, no," she heard herself saying.

She froze. She looked at his face and found him appraising her.

"I'm OK," she muttered.

Another bang shuddered the car. Neither said anything, waiting, feeling the agony of their own mortality.

Looking down at the gray rocks and green river below, with the twisted metal groaning, Maria imagined the long free fall superimposed over the sound of her pounding heart.

"Please let them stop shooting," she prayed.

"We gotta get out of here. Any second this thing could bust free of the tree."

But they waited, in the coolness of the wind, their minds

searching for a way to free them from the anticipation of being about to fall and yet not falling. Two or three minutes seemed like ten. The leaves were life green; the sky was a hopeful blue; the ants on the luxuriant bark looked busy, unaffected. The chill—was it death or was it a morning's invigoration? In just moments she would know.

"Come on," he said, snaking his right arm around her small waist even as she felt his fingers fumbling for the latch on her seat belt.

"Wait, be careful, I'm liable to fall right out of here." Immediately in front of her, there was a gaping hole through what used to be the front windshield and beyond that, the abyss. Somehow his right arm wasn't enough. By putting out both arms and both feet against the jagged metal, she secured herself.

"OK," she said.

At that moment a third bullet slammed the underside of the car, just missing Maria and punching a hole in the roof.

For all of five minutes they waited in near silence. His arm remained around her and her right hand had found its way to his, down at her waist where he still gripped her. There were no more shots.

"Ok, I'm going to release your belt."

The belt came away and she rolled toward him. On his side the opening was smaller and she realized the roof in front of the driver's seat was sunk in, whereas on the passenger side it was torn open by the branch.

Shattered glass was everywhere.

"Wait, let me," she said when she saw him about to crawl out the driver's-side window. "I'm a climber. I can do this." Despite her dread of further shooting, she crawled over the top of him and stuck her head outside. The front of the car was hanging free about two feet above the L-shaped main trunk of the tree. There was nothing to grab. The branch that had punctured the front windshield and exited the rear window was large and smooth and moss-covered like the main trunk. It was without any hand- or toehold for a sufficient distance, so it would be difficult to climb. Ripples went down the side of the fender, some angular enough that they might make a foothold.

"Maybe we can climb down the side of the car to the trunk of the tree and then try and scale the cliff. It's either that or wait and hope somebody finds us."

"We aren't waiting," he said.

"I've hung off cliffs. It's pleasant. This isn't." She wondered how he would react to the high climbing.

"Let's go."

"They may start shooting again," she said.

"They may. The wind may blow a little harder and the car may plunge."

She nodded her assent. Holding out her hand to him, she shook his and looked in his eye.

"If I fall, tell my father I loved him. My mother knows."

"You aren't gonna die today. You should tell him yourself." He smiled. "Industry won't be that lucky."

She began pulling herself through the window.

"How can you be almost dead and still joking?" she asked, trying to get a firm toehold on a small branch held tight against the crushed fender. It was a long stretch as she tried to hold herself with her hands.

"Same way you can be almost dead and arguing about it. Here," he said, holding out his hands. "I won't let go."

They locked their hands on each other's forearms. She could feel his fingers biting into her flesh. With her body fully extended, and Dan hanging out the window, her feet were within inches of the tree trunk; yet she wouldn't hit it square. Even a small slip could have her sliding off the tree and into space.

"Let go, I'll drop," she said.

"You're sure?"

"Do it."

He let go and she dropped, tried to balance by squatting. Both feet slid off the tree and she grabbed.

She groaned when her chest hit the tree trunk. She lay barely draped across it, most of her body hanging in space, digging her fingers into the wood, while she struggled to stay alive. Her feet hung down one side of the log while her arms reached over the top to the other side. Her chin sat on the log's crest.

"Hang on," he said.

"I'll make it," she groaned. But she couldn't think. Her mind was full with spinning, falling fear. Any second her fingers would give way. Slowly she raised her foot until she found a rough gouge in the bark where her toe could get a purchase. She pushed but was able to move her belly up the tree trunk only a fraction of an inch. Again she tried and moved a little farther.

"Hold on, I'm gonna jump," Dan said. He was crawling out the window. A man his size in a free fall would come right off the log, she was certain.

"No! You'll fall."

"I'm coming."

In the split second before he let go, she realized he had kicked off his shoes.

Dropping much farther than she had, he felt his bare feet hit the wood with a loud slap. The pain was a mind-sharpener.

He teetered crazily, arms gyrating. In a squat he hovered over Maria and dropped his hands to the moss-slick bark. His seat-stiffened joints could barely tolerate the maneuver.

Remembering days of football and workouts, of agility and stamina, he tried to get his body to follow his memories. Still draped over a horizontal section of the trunk, Maria moved herself up farther now and was about to push again. He grabbed her armpits and pulled, moving her belly six inches higher up on the log.

"Hold," he said. He did it again and she was able to spring up.

They moved down the trunk to a small shale ledge just big enough for them to stand together. "Well, you potentially saved my life," she said, her eyes searching his. "But you could have killed yourself. And I was making it." She paused. "Anyway, thanks."

"No thanks until we get up there," he said, nodding at the cliff.

Each of Dan's back pockets held a shoe that he now removed to slip on his feet. She began climbing, clinging like a spider, Dan staying just below her. They were using roots and stems from sparse vegetation and gouges in the face of the rock to support their body weight.

"It's dangerous for you just below me."

"Nah. I'll catch you," he said. He thought about stopping to rest but she wasn't, so he forced himself to keep moving.

After another ten minutes of hard climbing, several near-slips, and two short rests, they finally made it to the forest and eventually the road. There was no sign of the thieves or their car. They backtracked at a crisp jog until they came to a gravel driveway.

"There's a house down here, I think," Dan said, noticing her regular breaths. He wasn't used to women who could keep up with him. "I'll find a car and try to track them again. You go back to town."

"Oh no. That was *our* money," she said, jogging right after him. "If you go, I go."

3

They had come to a farmhouse. White, with peeling paint that revealed weather-grayed siding, the single-story house looked as if it were slowly dissolving. Moss-clad gutters appeared useless, and brush and tall grasses had taken over the area around the building. A Ford half-ton pickup truck was parked in a carport to the side. In front of the house was a tired Buick with a visible rust spot near the back window.

The presence of two vehicles looked promising. Dan stopped and blocked her way, as if to settle this matter before moving on.

A million words went through his mind, but he knew none of them would do any good. Changing his mind, he turned to walk to the farmhouse.

"Wait a minute," she said, grabbing his shoulder and yanking him around. "Just stand right here and don't move. You are being crazy and you're making me crazy. If you end up a bullet-ridden, Republican corpse, I have to think about that the rest of my life. And I refuse to spend the rest of my days thinking about a dead Republican."

Looking down at all 120 pounds of her, at her chest heaving with determination, he started to smile, then stifled it. "What can I do for you?"

"Some discussion. Nobody gives us briefcases full of money, and not five hundred thousand at a time. I mean, that in itself is unbelievable. But now we have a robbery by someone who obviously knew what was happening."

"Seems that way."

"So did someone on your end tell somebody, or someone on my end?"

"How many people on your side knew about this money drop?"

"As far as I know, just me and Patty McCafferty. How many on your side?"

"With the exception of the donors, I was the only one who knew it was today and the manner of the delivery."

"So according to what we know, this couldn't have happened except by pure chance."

"Saturday-morning purse-snatchers with a getaway car? I don't believe it was chance."

"I'm with you," she said. "What are you going to do if you catch them?"

"I don't know yet," he said. "For starters, I want to know where they're going."

"They'll be long gone."

"The longer we stand here discussing it—"

"Well, we need transportation no matter what. Once we get a car, we can talk about where to go."

He rapped on the door of the house. A middle-aged woman with obviously dyed flaming-red hair answered the door. A cigarette dangled from a mouth rich in red lipstick.

"What can I do for you?" She seemed intent on their filthy, semi-dressy clothes.

"Need to rent your truck."

"It's not for rent."

"We just crashed our car. We're in a hurry. How about two hundred fifty dollars?"

"How do I know you'll bring it back?"

"I was a Boy Scout." The woman didn't seem amused. "I'll show you picture ID, and give you my home address and phone number."

"We need to use your phone," Maria said.

"What for?" Dan asked.

"Because we're going to call our people and tell them what happened."

"Now hold on—" he began.

"While you two argue, I'll get the keys," the woman interrupted. "You get your checkbook ready."

"This is not negotiable," Maria said.

"Shit—"

"Are you afraid your boss—what's his name, Hutchin?— will stop this insanity?"

"I didn't know that it was any of your damn business what I tell my firm and what I don't."

"I don't want to force the issue. I need a little cooperation here."

"What do you mean force the issue?"

"I could go to the press, go to the police. The money was ours."

"You're a real piece of work," he said.

She just glared at him.

"I hid a radio transmitter in the briefcase. There's a radio signal. I need to follow it, so now you know."

Maria looked stunned.

"I don't have to depend on ESP."

"That's not the point. You put that ... device in the briefcase without telling me?"

"It's called an ADF. It's used to track a target, like a wild animal. But aren't you glad it was in there?"

He pulled the automatic direction finder (ADF) receiver out of his coat pocket, trying to reassure her.

"But this is a really small receiver. We have to be close."

She sighed. "So you were keeping this secret, hoping to get rid of me. You're still holding out on me. If you don't call, I'm going to the cops with the whole story. It's that simple."

"I'll call Hutchin," Dan said, resigned but irritated.

"You can use the phone if you want to." The woman pointed to an oak stand where the hallway opened up into a living area.

Dan told Hutchin a much abbreviated and safer-sounding version of the story, then waited.

"Don't you think you should come back and regroup?" Hutchin said.

"I've got Maria Fischer with me," he told Hutchin. "She's no cowboy. We won't confront anybody, but I've got to do this while there's still a chance of a signal. Once they discover the transmitter, our odds go way down."

Hutchin reluctantly agreed they could drive around public roads and try for a signal, but nothing more. With maddening precision, he spelled out the terms of their understanding while Dan waited for the moment he could hang up.

"Now what do you intend to do?" Maria said when he returned.

"Just what I've been doing."

She nodded and turned to the woman. "Do you have any boots that I could buy? You can put them on the car tab."

The woman waved her new cigarette as if it were part of the thinking process, then nodded. "You can have my husband's old ones. Fifty dollars."

"Fifty dollars?" Dan interjected.

"Don't argue. What size?"

"Eleven."

"Great. And two pairs of thick socks."

"Twenty dollars."

Dan shook his head.

"Relax. You can afford it."

The woman brought the boots and socks, took the hefty

check, and smiled between drags. Before Dan spoke, he ushered Maria out of the house and away from the woman who seemed grateful to close the door on them.

"I'm going to look for a black sedan whose owner lives in these mountains. I'm going to find a Chevy with the letters SRH on the license. I'm ninety percent convinced it was a woman who attacked us, and she knew how to use that billy club. Maybe she's got a police background. She or her accomplice has to be from around here or they wouldn't have headed into the mountains. City people don't do that. Don't know the roads."

They hustled to the truck and jumped in. Dan cranked the engine and it took a few turns before the throaty sounds of the un-muffled exhaust vibrated the floorboards. "Of all the people to get stuck with—to be donating to the coalition ... or representing somebody who would. Why you? I just don't get it," Maria complained.

"I don't like it any better than you do. Why didn't you call *your* office?"

"Don't want to worry people."

"You know that if McCafferty hears about this, she'll have you on the next plane home to Sacramento."

"I suppose."

"And you wanted me to call Hutchin, hoping he'd tell me not to go after the money."

"Someone should know where we are and what we're doing."

"Don't you think we'd both be happier if I did this by myself?"

"Not a chance," she said as he roared back up the mountain road.

* * *

Corey Schneider thought it interesting that her silent partners wanted their half of the money immediately. There was some risk to them in an immediate transfer. Traveling toward the meeting spot, she had fumed at the presence of the man. Nothing had been said about some big macho fucker sticking around after the delivery. Another few seconds and that guy would have been all over her. Even with her baton, he would have been tough. So she'd have used the gun. And wouldn't that have been a mess. According to her sources, it was to have been a simple money drop to Maria Fischer and not a long, cozy rendezvous.

Another puzzle was that Corey's unknown accomplices set up a meeting site on a back road where they could be spotted should someone follow. These people who called her in the night were far too cautious and sophisticated for amateurish plans. She glanced down at the map to make sure Denny was on the right road. Although she knew these mountains well and had traveled most of the ranching roads, the location for the drop was remote, and she could only recall having traveled through that area once before.

"I can't believe you did that. We could have lost them." Denny had looked tense and completely distracted since the shooting. "I'm not going down for this."

"Relax."

Denny was a cheap grunt. He was spineless, and she knew she would need to do something about it. And soon. Other than having the hots for her and his willingness to "help," he was unsuited for everything they did.

She pulled down the mirror over the visor. Even without makeup, which she almost never wore anymore, she looked good. She had clear skin, a small and slightly narrow-lipped mouth, but great cheekbones and good symmetry. Not that it meant anything to her. She flipped the mirror closed as if disgusted that she'd even looked.

"What's this?" Denny said.

A chopper had swooped low over the car and dropped something in a small parachute.

"Chopper's unmarked. Must be somebody who doesn't want to be recognized," she said. They were on a ridge covered mostly by grassland and oaks. "Pull over."

When they were opposite the spot where the chute had fallen, the chopper hovered in the distance. Attached to the chute was a small plastic cylinder, and inside a rolled-up map. On the map an *X* marked the place where she was to meet the mysterious voices on the phone.

Beside the *X* it simply read "no." At another spot very near their current location was a second *X* marked "yes." Now it all made sense. They were almost twenty miles from the originally designated point. They knew her route, could follow with the chopper, see everything for miles around, including someone following. They had picked a different location so that she could not plan a trap. They were in complete control.

"We're going just up the ridge and stopping. I suspect that helicopter will come to us."

"What's *in* that briefcase? Drugs?"

"Nothing illegal."

"I don't think I'm getting paid enough for this."

"We'll fix that. But for the moment just shut up and do your job."

When they had moved up the ridge, the helicopter approached.

"Stay here," she told Denny, and went to the car trunk. She set the briefcase inside and rapidly began counting out ten packets of $10,000 dollars each. The money was all in $100 bills. It took her only a couple of minutes. She paid no attention to the leather pocket in the lid of the briefcase nor the bulge at its center. In a rush she closed the lid the instant she put her portion in a nylon bag in the trunk.

A man dressed in black and wearing a ski mask stepped from the copter. Since he made no move to approach her, she ran to him, wanting at this point to make the transfer and get out of the area. As she approached, she saw an automatic weapon with a silencer clutched in the man's hand. She handed him the briefcase, and with a quick nod he jumped in the chopper. Immediately it pulled up steeply and was gone over the hill, leaving nothing but the mountain quiet.

It was midafternoon and Dan hadn't found anything. They were parked on an old log-landing dark with stirred earth and woody debris, green with naturally sprouting redwood and Douglas fir. The fir loved the bare mineral soil and the sunlight in the man-made clearing. Above them, perhaps 1,000 feet, the hilltop loomed lush with spring grasses and dark with black oak. Below them the hillside fell away in a sea of young redwoods and mixed conifers interspersed with black oak, tan oak, and madrona.

The mountainside redwoods below them, about three years old, had sprung from stumps left from recent logging. Now mere babies, they eventually would obscure everything around them. Stretching below them in a giant bowl grew an old-growth redwood forest—the Highlands.

Dan's receiver had five channels and spindly fold-out antennae. The channel selected had been correct for the animal collar in the briefcase when he experimented with it. There was no reason to try the other channels, but he did so anyway. With the first click on another channel, the receiver gave a very faint beep. The needle barely registered. He switched it back to the briefcase channel.

At that moment they heard the whine of a jet helicopter, then saw it flying low over the trees. The receiver picked up a stronger signal apparently emanating from the copter; then after perhaps thirty seconds, and as the copter was still coming closer, the signal died.

"Damn," he said aloud. "I'm sure I got a signal from that helicopter, but as it got closer, it disappeared."

"It looked to me like it might be coming down," Maria said. "But where would it land over there?"

"It's hard to believe they *could* land. Maybe the signal was coming from something else."

Dan switched back to the other channel and once again got a faint signal.

"There," she said.

"It's not even the right channel," he said. "You stay here. I'll go down and check things out."

"Wait a minute. I heard your call with Hutchin. If you got a signal, that was it. You were supposed to call him."

"Do you see a phone booth? Besides, this probably isn't the signal. I told you I changed channels."

"That helicopter was the right channel?"

"Yeah, but it could be long gone."

"I think we should let Hutchin know what's happening."

Privately, Dan *had* thought the helicopter was landing. "We can't do that from here."

"Then we'll drive back."

"You drive. I'm going down that hill."

White particles of dust and pollen hung in the rays of the sun. Heavy forest scents of musty humus and the sweeter odor of jasmine permeated the air. There was a barely visible animal trail leading into the woods.

"I'm going with you" Maria said.

"No way. You'd slow me down. Stay right here in the car."

"It's a free country. I can walk where I want. As far as slowing you down . . ." She looked him up and down. "That's ridiculous."

"All right." He paused to search for words. "But don't complain and don't ask me to turn around every five minutes."

"You're a boor." Her expression said "asshole." Tension stretched the air as she stood with her hands on her hips. After a time of silence she let out a deep breath. "We're overdoing it here. Let me be the first to apologize. I'm . . . well . . . sorry for being so . . . whatever."

"Stubborn. You're sorry for being so irrationally stubborn. And for tagging along."

He grinned and she allowed a small smile.

"If I were a man, would I be 'tagging along'? I said I would be the *first* to apologize."

"And you did it very well, very well indeed. With a little coaching."

She shook her head. "You are really something else."

"Try to overlook it."

"If we're going to go chasing into these woods, wouldn't it make sense if I knew what you know?"

"Yeah, well, I've got this little problem known as attorney-client privilege."

Strangely, though, he found himself wishing he could tell her exactly what had happened, and why.

4

At the turn of the last century, the wealthiest man in Nolo County was William Carson. Across the street from his mansion, he built a bank to contain his fortune. A hundred years later, William Carson's bank had become the Hutchin Office Building, home to the law firm that employed Dan Young. The front entry of the two-story building was flanked by whitewashed wooden pillars; a balustrade surrounded the lip of the flat roof. Inside, the building looked like a Victorian library. Beautifully restored paneling, crown molding, plinth blocks, ornate cast-iron doors, and heavy wooden window-frames completed the traditional look. With walls made of heavy stone blocks, the building had a cathedrallike sense of integrity and permanence.

On that evening a week ago, Dan had arrived at the office a full fifty minutes early, wondering what could be so incredibly important that Jeb Otran would summon him and Hutchin to a 10:00 P.M. meeting. Not that Dan was about to complain. The intrigue alone was worth it.

Jeb Otran owned more than anyone else Dan was ever likely to meet: a million acres of timberland, a dozen saw-mills, woodworking facilities, huge electrical power plants, fleets of trucks, banks, and mortgage companies. Nobody really knew what it was all worth. But there was more to Otran than his money. Otran was a regular Horatio Alger—from humble beginnings he'd created a financial empire, pulling himself up by his bootstraps the whole way.

William Hutchin arrived almost immediately. Hutchin was a broad man, wide in the shoulders, girth, the face, and in the span of his hands. His six-foot figure, which was topped with a wild mop of silver-gray hair, combined with his booming voice to give him an imposing manner known to everyone in town. He had been with Otran for much of his ride to the top; his firm had been representing Otran for nearly thirty years. Dan had gradually established a strong personal bond with Otran as Hutchin slowed down his personal activity, involved now only in the more weighty matters. Dan handled all the cases and had the day-to-day contact.

After acknowledging one another, Dan and Hutchin walked into the foyer. Moments later, Otran's gray sedan pulled to the curb and Otran, a sinewy, square-jawed man, joined them.

"Evening, gentlemen," Otran said. "Strange time for a meeting, but it's a strange topic."

Hutchin led them directly to the library, a windowless room whose walls were covered by row upon row of thick law tomes. They sat around a large, polished rosewood conference table, well-lit beneath overhead brass lamps covered with green frosted-glass shades.

Hutchin, much to Dan's surprise, said nothing. Instead, he looked at Otran expectantly. Finally Otran cleared his throat and spoke slowly, thoughtfully, as though there was more to say than could easily be said, making it all the more important that he find just the right words.

"Even though it's the middle of the night, and hush-hush, this is not Watergate. Nothing illegal. But it's about as peculiar as Watergate." He looked at Dan. "I guess we might as well plunge right in. I need someone to deliver a bunch of money to the enviros. A hell of a lot of money."

Dan tried not to look shocked.

"It's not as bad as it sounds." Otran smiled. "It's to fund a campaign to convince the government to purchase the Highlands. It's supposed to lead to a government land purchase. The government won't buy it unless there's imminent peril to the trees and a big uproar. Needless to say, the enviros don't want cutting. They'll create the uproar if we plan to cut." Otran paused. "Are you with me so far?"

"But what does Metco say?" Dan referred to an owner of about one half of the acreage of the Highlands Forest.

"Oh, they've got to be cagey. Officially they plan to cut the trees. Hell, they're processing harvest plans right now. But they're sick to death of the bad publicity. They want to sell their whole four thousand acres to the government, declare the world safe, and go on growing and cutting their trees. In fact, Metco would like to sell to me. As for us, we can't log the land we own next to the Highlands. I get calls from Senator Cansfield weekly, begging me not to log anywhere near the Highlands. Says it should be a buffer for the murrelet bird. Metco would have to go right through us to log the Highlands. The senator begs me not to let them, but I've told her they've got an easement."

"So that's the reason we're giving money to the enviros?"

"Well, then there's Amada. The Japanese at first were dead set against giving any money to the enviros and really didn't seem at all anxious to sell. But when Metco got determined to go ahead and fund the enviros' campaign Amada turned on a dime with no explanation and wanted to be the biggest contributor. That I can't figure. Now they're actually the driving force to give money to the enviros. A full half of the money is theirs and the rest is divided up between ten different timberland owners. But they'd rather we deliver it. The Japanese are very discreet."

"Why would they care what happens to the Highlands?"

"It's three thousand acres of prime old-growth redwood,

really the other half of the Highlands Forest. Maybe they worry about their own logging. If you can't grow and cut trees, the land is worthless. It's remote, steep, and they claim they'd like to sell it to the government. I said we ought to hire our own lobbyists, but they say the government never does anything we want. It's better coming from the enviros, and they'll help pay the bill. I hate it. But all the timber owners try to cooperate on this enviro stuff, so I said I'd take care of it. Don't know how much these guys want to give in the end. Plenty the first time, though. Five hundred thousand.''

Dan's jaw dropped.

''Are you with me so far?''

Dan nodded. A few minutes ago the world had been simpler. It was the Wildflower Coalitions of the world against industry. Industry was usually right, and he knew which side he was on.

''A long time ago, I became acquainted with Patty McCafferty. She was out to save the world back then—just like now. Wasn't practical then, either. But Patty McCafferty is a woman that will set you to thinking. She used to talk up a storm. Talked about having some poetry in your life.'' Otran chuckled and shook his head. ''You got any poetry in your life?''

''When I meet Poetry, I'll let you know.'' That got Dan a smile from Otran.

''I hope you find her,'' Otran said, just a tinge more serious. ''Anyway, Patty's hell on this forest and will do just about anything to save it. She wants the government to buy it. And for the moment, that makes us buddies. We just want the whole thing to go away so we can all go back to logging without all the publicity. And damn regulations. People get so excited because these trees are so big and so old. It's like a spotlight on us. Really, I don't think there's any way to appease these nuts. They're never happy. But some of the political types will lay off for a while if they can declare victory. Politicians love to feel like they solved a problem.''

This lash-up between McCafferty and industry sounded to Dan like the alliance from hell.

''Now I suppose you don't have to be told that it would be politically embarrassing for us to make a large public donation to Patty McCafferty. Especially me.''

Dan and Hutchin laughed out loud. Barroom remarks, sly winks at the pub, blaring horns on the street, screamed epithets, the finger—all these and more would await the timberman who gave solace to the enviros, much less cold, hard cash. The grassroots timber support would never appreciate the subtlety of the politics. They were still producing bumper stickers like: EARTH FIRST. WE'LL LOG THE REST OF THE PLANETS LATER.

''We want to give some money to her attorneys, but I can't have the money traceable to me or the rest of 'em in any way,'' Otran said. ''And the Japanese, who are putting up half of it . . .'' Otran rolled his eyes. ''They'd do that hara-kiri thing if it became public. This is all attorney-client privilege, right?''

Dan nodded.

''Absolutely.'' Hutchin's big voice filled the room.

''Let me get this straight,'' Dan said. ''You want to give a half million in cash to the same people who participate in demonstrations outside your mills?''

''Yes. Do you think that's a problem?''

''If it gets out, people may think it's bribery—''

''It won't get out,'' Hutchin cut in. ''And it's not against the law to make anonymous donations. I know how you must feel, but sometimes in this life, the whores lie down with the saints.''

Dan thought for a moment. "So it's a no-strings-attached gift to the enviros."

"Yep," Otran said. "And it's mostly Japanese money."

"But how do we know they'll use it like we intend?"

"Let's not worry about that," said Hutchin. "That's Jeb's worry. Our job's to get the money delivered and to do it carefully. Very carefully." He paused before continuing. "You'll be dealing with Maria Fischer. I'm sure you two will become buddies the way things are going."

"You're okay with this?" Otran asked.

"It's worth a good stiff drink," replied Dan. "But no, I have no problem with it. Indigestion maybe, but no problem."

"When you decide how you're going to deliver this, call me. Only Amada cares how we do it, so I'll have to call them."

Dan left wondering who were the saints and who the whores in this little scenario.

5

The hill was steep through the second-growth trees, but it leveled out after four hundred yards or so when they came to the edge of the old growth. The trees stood like inscrutable old men guarding their prehistoric past, the larger specimens some ten feet in diameter. They formed the upper story of the forest. Below them were smaller redwood trees, stunted under the canopy. In places there was a second layer of shorter trees. These were hemlock—graceful evergreens with drooping tops, not as large as the redwood giants but adapted by nature for growing in the shade. Underneath them were the broad-leaves, tan oak, black oak, and where it was wet enough, alder. These wide-leaf species reached out for every ray of sun that might slip past the upper layers.

"If industry is giving us money, they must have something to gain by it." It was the first thing she'd said since they began their descent. Dan had to admire her persistence.

"I guess."

"Well, do you know?"

"Look, if I could spill my guts"—he gave her an appreciative look, he hoped without any disrespect—"you'd be the logical choice."

"You know you're sexist."

He stopped. "Where I come from, I was paying you a compliment—not making a pass."

They looked at each other.

"Do you have any serious complaints about my compliments?" he asked.

Without answering, she walked on.

They were in the old growth now. A thick layer of clover grew like green carpet over the forest floor. There was little sign of wildlife under these massive trees although Dan supposed their noisy passage through the fern and wild rhododendron would scare into hiding whatever was present. They walked where they could, taking the path of least resistance until they came to something odd: NO TRESPASSING signs nailed to the trees at forty-foot intervals.

"I wonder if this is Metco or Amada land," he said.

"No way to even guess without a compass and a map. Even then I doubt we'd figure it out."

"Don't you guys go on spy missions to guesstimate who owns what?"

"Those 'spy missions,' as you call them, are overrated," she said. "We look from the air more than the ground."

They walked quickly as they talked, weaving in and out of head-high ferns, clawing their way through brush, all the time marveling at the trees, whose massive trunks seemed to belong in a land of giants.

"What's this?" Dan was eyeing a fallen tree with a NO TRESPASSING sign nailed at its center.

"Somebody has cut off the limbs."

"Which makes it impossible to climb over . . ." They began walking alongside it, thinking they would go around. Quickly they came to another NO TRESPASSING sign. "These guys are serious," he said.

After a good one hundred feet they came to a second tree, lying parallel with the first, so that as the first began to taper to six or seven feet in diameter, a second thick log began.

"This is outrageous," she said. "This was done deliberately. How did somebody get a permit to cut these trees?"

"They don't need a permit if they're not selling them or making lumber of them."

"You're right," she said. "It's one of the many flaws in the system."

"It's a token gesture to private property rights."

After a similar distance they came to yet another fallen tree.

"It's like someone was building a barrier," she said. "Help me look for a thick branch we can bring over."

She began looking for a piece of wood; Dan followed her.

"Every second that goes by, I become more convinced that maybe that chopper did land out here in the woods," he said.

"So you think somehow—"

"I don't know what to think. If you'd told me that this

would be out here, I'd have thought you were nuts," he said.

"Let's climb over this and find out what's going on."

"I've heard you're quite the Alaskan wilderness woman."

"Yeah? Where did you hear that?"

"In the courthouse hallway, where the news is on time every time."

"Same place I heard you've been a very unhappy man ever since your wife died."

"You heard I drink too much."

"That too. Here's a log, let's go."

She helped him lift a gnarled, eight-foot limb as thick as a man's thigh.

They carried it to where the nearest barrier log narrowed to its smallest diameter and leaned it up against it.

"You climb, and I'll push."

"I think I can manage," she said.

Maria was still in her business suit and climbing in the long skirt would be difficult. As if reading his mind, she hoisted the skirt up her thighs, revealing the knit portion of her panty hose. To hold the skirt in place, she refastened her belt. Her thighs were hard and well-shaped.

He made it a point to study the barricade, trying to estimate its age. Foliage growing around the log indicated that it must have been on the ground for some months, or even longer.

She began climbing up the branch, using smaller branches as handholds. In a minute she was atop the log. Dan followed easily, though he had physically lost something since Tess's death and his own sporadic exercise schedule. To enable Maria to scale the second log, Dan interlaced his fingers so she could step in his hands. Putting her palms atop the log, she hoisted herself up in one smooth motion. It was impressive.

"You adroitly avoided my question about Alaska by bringing up my somewhat checkered reputation."

"I didn't think you'd notice. It's ten feet to the ground and they've stacked about a billion branches like the worst windfall you've ever seen. Let's concentrate on getting through here."

Dan reached up and grabbed a big knot where a branch had broken off. His foot slipped and he struggled just slightly to climb the second log. When he got to his knees, he saw the situation was bleak. Branches were piled perhaps eight feet high, some large, some small, but nothing that they could walk on for any great distance. Sinking into the loosely piled branches could result in an injury or at the very least a quagmire that would be nearly impossible to get through. Beyond the piled branches the forest was once again thick with head-high ferns.

"I have an idea," Maria said as she began walking down the log toward a small grove of hemlock growing at the barrier. "We can jump to the first of those trees, climb a little higher, then get in the next tree by pulling its branches close enough to jump to its trunk. Do that a couple of times and we should be beyond the man-made windfall."

"A couple of squirrels," he said. "Only one of those squirrels weighs about two hundred twenty-five pounds."

She went first, literally leaping into the six-inch diameter tree and moving nimbly through the thick branches to the relative security of the trunk.

"We did this when I was a kid," he said. "It was more fun back then."

A branch snapped and she moved a few inches down to the next, swung around the tree, and climbed to a point where the tree was very flexible. Using her weight, she leaned the small hemlock into the next one over, grabbed its branches, and easily stepped across the chasm.

He pondered the gulf to the first tree and the flimsy branches that he would be grabbing.

Either he jumped or she went on without him. He reached out, grabbed a branch, and tried pulling the tree to him, but at this height it was too stout to move. He took a deep breath and jumped, grabbing the branches. With his weight, the branches did nothing to slow his fall toward the tree, then were slicked off by his feet for a good three feet down the tree. Reverberations ran up the trunk as he slammed into it. His body quivered with the pain of the trunk hitting his testicles, but not a sound escaped his lips.

"Are you all right?"

"Maybe a little more soprano than I used to be," he said in a forced but natural voice.

"Might help with cowboy-brain syndrome," she said.

Ignoring the pain, he climbed high and grabbed the branches of the second tree pulling it toward him. This time the trunk was much closer and he easily took hold of it.

In only a few minutes they were beyond the windfall and on the ground. Again walking in undisturbed old-growth forest was easy, although they occasionally had to detour around a fallen tree. But unlike the ones in the barrier, these had toppled naturally in a haphazard fashion over many years' time. The resins in the redwood preserved even those that had fallen hundreds of years before.

Dan nodded at the receiver. "We still have a signal, but on the wrong channel."

After a few hundred feet of meandering into the forest, Dan looked up to see something astounding: In the middle of this wild place, as if they had grown there, stood back-to-back chain-link fences running parallel and about twenty feet apart with razor wire atop both. Between the two fences the brush had been cleared and had yet to start to grow again. The place was apparently brand-new or well maintained.

"How did they do this out here?" Maria asked.

"There isn't a road except the one we came in on."

"They did put in a so-called wildlife road allegedly for research purposes," she said. "Maybe we're near that. Let's follow the fence."

They had gone no more than fifty feet when a barking dog moved quickly toward them.

"Oh shit," Dan said, hearing a second dog only a little farther off. "Man's best friend."

The first dog, a black-and-tan German shepherd with bared canines, came around a redwood tree in the area between the fences. He wore a large leather collar with a thickened section of black plastic.

"No doubt about what he'd like to do," Maria said.

The needle on Dan's receiver followed the dog's movements.

"The signal is coming from the collar," Dan said. "Looks similar to the transmitter that was in the briefcase. But it's not the same."

Dan approached the fence, igniting a frenzy: The dog lunged at the fence, growling and barking.

"Let's get back," she said. "The racket's liable to bring somebody."

"OK, OK, just a second. Jeez, that's what I get for changing the channel."

"Come on." She was dragging him back.

Dan followed her with some reluctance, noting that the guard dogs quieted as soon as they disappeared into the woods. "They're trained to be quiet unless they spot an intruder. My dog would bark for an hour."

"Let's just stay away from the fence."

"What if we climb a tree and try to see what's inside the enclosure?"

"Most of the trees have no branches for the first fifty or a hundred feet up," Maria replied.

"We'll find some little ones like the hemlock we climbed through."

What they found after a fairly extensive search was a big madrona with a fork near the ground. Its dense leaves formed a green barrier obstructing their line of sight, making it necessary to peer through what holes they could find.

It grew nearly one hundred feet from the fence with sufficient intervening brush and trees, so they were invisible to the dogs. From the perpetual whining it was obvious the dogs were aware of their presence and had kept pace with them as they made their way through the forest. When they reached the higher branches, they could see nothing but the tops of the chain-link fences meeting at a ninety-degree angle, indicating they were at a corner.

From nowhere there was a whirring sound. A black-and-brown bat flew overhead; they both followed it with their eyes. Just as it was disappearing from sight, headed toward the compound, there was a gun blast. The creature crumpled. Staring at each other in disbelief, they realized that the shooter was within fifty yards.

"What the hell?" Dan whispered. "Do bats come out in the daytime?"

"Rarely," Maria whispered back. "Unless they're mad with rabies. Maybe we need to get more in the middle of the fence to see beyond it."

"I think we better head out."

"How can you say that?"

"We're not going to find the money out here. If it's in there, we can't get to it. We could look for the helicopter better from the air."

"They're shooting bats, for God's sake! Now that we're here, aren't you the least bit curious?"

"I'm here for the money. For bats I've got *National Geographic*."

She put her hand to his ear and spoke through it. "You're impossible. Just when we find something—you want to go back. Look at this, it's totally bizarre."

"Somebody has a shotgun. That's not so unusual."

"A little heat and you melt," she whispered.

"All right. Climb a little higher up into those skinny branches off to the right," Dan whispered.

He watched her as she placed her scuffed black leather shoes tentatively on branches no bigger than his thumb. Now a good ten feet above him, she stretched her neck, attempting a better view of something.

"Oh my God." She sucked in her breath.

"What is it?"

She stretched even farther. Dan heard a strange thump, then watched helplessly as Maria fell. Dropping, she hit a heavier branch near Dan with a sickening thud. He grabbed for her, catching an arm. Still, she was slipping. With his free hand he groped for better purchase on the branch, while with his other he hung on to her, allowing himself to fall rather than to lose her. As they went down, he grabbed branches and they raked his free hand with white-hot pain. Repeatedly he slowed their fall. There was the sound of breaking tree limbs, a horrible pain shot through his ribs, and then the ground rushed up at them.

6

"I still can't believe you did that. I could have ditched them."

"I told you to drive around the city," Corey said. "If you'd done what I asked, this never would have happened."

She shed her trench coat and walked into the family room as Denny closed the garage door a little too hard.

"This place'll be crawling with cops. We don't have a helicopter like your buddies. I'm not going down for this. You did the shooting, not me. They could be dead for all we know."

"Relax," she said. "Go watch your TV."

He cursed as he climbed the stairs to his room. Corey sat back in the easy chair, staring at the ceiling's beautiful polished box beams: gleaming, satin smooth. With its red-brick fireplace, leather furniture, and plaid carpeting, the room had an earthy, masculine feel. On the walls hung wooden Indian masks, grotesque screaming objects, ghouls from some bad dream, the tools of terror of a medicine man.

A bullwhip sat coiled in the glass display box built into the coffee table. It had been her father's and now it belonged to his demon, her name for the memory of him that lingered on, tormenting her, a phantom so elusive she had grown weary of the chase.

She craved a joint but knew she shouldn't. It would dull what was to come. Instead, she lay back and let the image of Maximillian Schneider invade her mind.

* * *

It began in her bedroom, tucked inside a palatial Georgian mansion, on her Queen Victoria canopy bed. It started with a laugh, Corey's long, rolling laugh—her dead mother's laugh. Her timing couldn't have been worse. Her father, drunk as usual, had been pacing by her room, back and forth—pausing only to stand silently outside, then to resume his pacing.

He stormed into her room, white-faced with rage, as if she'd been laughing at him. He yanked her from the bed and pummeled her like a butcher pounding meat. With each punch, her insides felt as if they were coming up her throat. Then he began tearing off her nightclothes.

"Get up," he growled when she lay naked, immobilized with pain, panting and moaning on the cold, tiled floor.

Ten minutes later, she was on her belly; her lips had been painted a sloppy, horrific red by his shaky hand. Her arms, tied with white silk scarves to the bedposts, ached. The strap bit into her bare flesh, searing, penetrating, the white-hot leather whistling at her again and again.

This was much worse than anything he'd ever done to her before. Without warning, he stopped. She turned, looking over her shoulder. He was gulping air, sweat pouring down in little rivulets over the white fat-puffed skin. He hefted the strap for another swing. She vomited, causing his hesitation—and probably her own salvation. With all her strength she pulled at the scarves. The right-hand bedpost snapped off. She hurled it to the side, hitting his soft body.

He made a sound that was pure rage. She rolled to the far side of the bed, trailing the scarf from her right hand, her left still tied. Her fingers worked at the knot as she watched him fingering a huge red welt on his neck.

"Stay put." His voice sounded choked, hoarse.

She ignored him, her fingers working fast. In seconds she was free. She ran around the bed, snatching up her robe. He moved to cut her off but slipped, unsteady on his feet. One hand touched the floor. It was enough of a fall that she was able to slip by him. For once the booze was her ally. Spooked, she ran. Her father lunged into the coffee table with his knees. He rose, bellowing his rage.

She sprinted down the stairs to the massive front door, twisted the dead bolt open, flew off the porch, and dashed into the night.

The world was a blur. Ahead the forest opened its arms to her, ready to take her to its bosom. If she could make it to one of the small breaks in the mountainous green wall fencing the lawn, she could make it to her hiding place—disappearing like a gopher down its hole. He had never set foot in her safe harbor.

In seconds she had found her haven. Engulfed in the heady scents of jasmine, earth, and mint, she stilled her breathing to listen. Outside the cave, the sounds of crickets, frogs, and owls reassured her that she was not alone. The forest, she thought. Mother Earth. My protector. She just carries on, taking care of all her living creatures and growing things. Pure and beautiful, never painful: Mother, indeed.

In the morning she awoke in her bed. She had sneaked back inside, once certain her father had sobered. Strange engine sounds came from the backyard. The window rattled in tune to the throaty bark of a chain saw. She ran downstairs and out into the sunshine.

"Get out of my sight," *her father commanded when she begged him to stop the bulldozers and saws. He had found his ultimate revenge: Before her eyes, he was destroying her forest. As she watched, the machines ripped and tore, dragging and cutting until her only refuge was no more.*

She needed to kill him—a man for a forest—but he never

gave her a chance; he killed her forest, and then he killed her plans for sweet revenge. Later that day, right after tying her spread-eagled between the bedposts, directly following the most gruesome acts she'd ever endured, he called Uncle Jack into the room. Uncle Jack, the one she loved, the only one in the family who had ever shown her kindness, was staring at her with mortified eyes. Then her father shot him dead. Slowly Maximillian turned the gun on himself, shoving it deep down his throat before pulling the trigger.

After that day, anguish never left her. But it was not yet the howling, crushing pain that kills people from the inside, making them shrivel up and literally die, or stare silent, vacant stares out the window for years on end.

That kind of anguish she had known only when, weeks later, she overheard Aunt Jessica tell a friend that Maximillian Schneider had not been her father. Her real father was her beloved uncle Jack Schneider; Corey had been the product of an affair between her mother and Jack. And in an instant, she saw Jack's many kindnesses for what they had been: hollow acts of repentance for his guilt. His concern now felt no better than mockery: far too little and far too late.

It was then, in the grip of soul-crushing pain, that Corey first considered her calling. At first she only felt it, but didn't understand it. In something of a confused state, after the death of both men, and fighting with her aunts and the trustees, she joined the marines and then the military police. Stationed as an officer in administration at a military prison, she found a legally sanctioned outlet for her anger and relief from her aunts. On her twenty-fifth birthday her trust was dissolved; her aunts were no longer in control of her money. She resigned her commission and moved to California.

She had the money to step full measure into her real mission, to define it as a duty, for with the wealth of both

*men, enough to last her several lifetimes and then some,
she could do whatever she chose.*

Corey rose and called up the stairs for Denny. It was a
few minutes before he came down and sat in the family
room.

"You don't like those masks, do you?" She sat on the
leather couch opposite him.

Denny didn't answer for a moment. "No."

"Why not?"

Denny just shrugged. "Don't know if I need a reason.
Just don't like the look."

"You know, in merry old England they used to flog
people. Flay them alive, actually, little metal hooks on a
whip tearing off their skin in strips until they didn't have
much left. To keep them alive as long as possible, they'd
hang them upside down so their heart and vitals would get
the last of the blood. How'd you like to do that, to get
revenge on your biggest enemy?"

"I don't have any enemies that big."

"You're indifferent, right?"

Corey imagined exactly how she would do this. He was
making it easy. She was rolling it around like a ball on a
table, weighing it.

"Did you know that statistically, serial killers are almost
never women?" she asked. "When the cops look for one,
they always start with a man. Always. That's because women
are watchers, mostly. What would you do to your worst
enemy? Somebody that really hurt you."

"I'd shit in his Porsche and shove it over a cliff."

"With him in it?"

"Mm, no."

"Think you could get excited about taking a shower with me?"

"Together?" asked Denny with undisguised amazement.

Corey stood and was already peeling off her clothes in the middle of the family room. "We'll celebrate doing the job. Then we can turn on the cop channel and see if they reported anything."

Denny was smiling now.

"We'll do it until you can't do it anymore, and then we'll wait and do it again," she said.

Fleeting glimpses of her body were all Corey had given him until now. She was amused at the way his eyes darted to her breasts. He made no move to get undressed, out of touch with everything except what he saw.

When she was naked, she stood before him, one hand on her hip.

"Are you just going to look?"

Corey lathered her hands slowly and deliberately with a giant bar of yellow soap. "Stand under the shower. It'll relax you." It was a large stall tiled in blue and turquoise to the ceiling, with two showerheads, but only one of them turned on. Her friends, some pot growers with taste, said the decor was very "boy."

He stood with his back to the nozzle, the hot water cascading over his shoulders, loosening the tightly drawn muscles at the base of his neck.

She began to soap his chest and belly, teasing him. "Should I soap the rest of you?"

Denny's eyes rolled back in his head. Men were such

funny creatures, Corey thought, their minds so easily distracted.

"Turn around," she told him.

Breathlessly he followed her orders. She pushed herself close against his back. Reaching around him with her left hand, she began to do things she knew would utterly transport him.

"Close your eyes," she whispered. "Relax."

Within seconds, sure that he was now lost in sensation, she reached her right hand high to a tiled ledge and a small lacquered box. There, from inside the black-and-red box, she quickly withdrew a small .22 automatic. As she placed the barrel at the base of his skull, time slowed down to let her observe every detail of the scene. There was her hand wrapped around the mother-of-pearl pistol grip. There was the red dot showing the safety off. And his wet brown hair in need of a trim.

"A little present from Mother," she whispered in his ear.

As Corey dragged his body from the bathroom, dread hung like black sheets at the edges of her mind. Then her certainty returned: She had rid the world of a weakling who didn't believe in her cause; Denny would have broken the first time they squeezed him, would have copped a plea to save himself. And she would've gone to jail, or worse.

Denny's absence wouldn't be noticed for months—and perhaps not at all. She had checked his background as carefully as she had planned his demise. A drifter with no family outside a sister who hadn't seen him in years, he had no close friends and only a few acquaintances in the entire county. He had called himself a cowboy—she supposed because he had a hat. She buried him in the woods behind the house, grateful that no one who mattered had ever seen them together.

After it was over, after she had covered the corpse in the

hard clay hole by the charred stump, after she had mopped up the blood and scrubbed herself clean, she sat on the shower floor, exhausted, once again letting the warm water pour over her, letting the blackness fill her head.

The sound of the ringing phone barely penetrated the soothing shower sounds.

"How did it go?" There was a nervous edge to the deep accented voice. She was certain the man was German. It wasn't the usual time for his call.

"Not good. Some stud the size of a mountain gave her the money. He was ready for a fight. They followed us partway up the hill."

"What happened?"

"I blew them off the road with a .300 Weatherby Magnum, that's what happened. Right front tire. They went over the bank."

"Are they dead?"

"Probably. Nothing on the police bands."

"Why did you put a transmitter in the briefcase?"

Her breath caught in her throat. "What are you talking about?"

"You put a transmitter in the briefcase?"

"The hell I did."

"We took care of it," he said. "That's all that matters. What about Denny? What's he know?"

"Nothing. Besides he up and left. Headed for Florida."

"Are you sure?"

"I said he left for Florida." She didn't trust the German voice—especially after today. "Why is industry paying McCafferty? I mean what exactly does she do for them?"

"If you figure it out, let us know. Maybe she just gives in to their demands if what they pay her is right enough."

"I doubt if it's that boring," she said. "Did you know the courier would be built like a brick shithouse?"

"Had no idea."

"You wanted me to get away with the money?"

"Came for our share, didn't we?"

"Why'd they build a big Cyclone fence around that complex of theirs in the Highlands?" She thought she heard a deep sigh. "It's Amada, isn't it?"

"Don't know anything about it. What do you think?" She was sure the voice was tighter. Or was it her imagination?

"Why did you hesitate? What do you know about this?"

"That's not the nature of our arrangement." The voice came back icy. "So if you value our relationship, all the tips, the money, perhaps you would be wise to tell us about this fence."

She needed time to think and wished she hadn't brought it up.

"I know that men come and go. Mostly at night. I know that they have a big permanent staff and I know they spend most of their time inside, not outside. Something glows, iridescent, in the night. I can see it like a halo through the trees."

"Interesting. What else?"

"Guys come in the night. They put on protective suits and unload stuff into the buildings. They work in the dark, never with a light. There's an old mine shaft nearby. They go into that as well. Around the shaft they also built a fence and they're working there during the day."

"What do you think they're doing?"

"At first I thought they might be making Taxol from the bark of the yew tree—like they tell the government. You know, latest cancer drug. I got some government documents under the Freedom of Information Act. They're distilling Taxol, but I don't think that's all they're doing."

"And how do you see all this if it's dark?"

"Government surplus infrared night-vision goggles."

"You see the glowing with these goggles?"

"No, that's with the naked eye, looking down from up in a tree."

"So how did you find out in the first place? You creep around with goggles, or what?"

She was feeling nervous. This guy seemed a little too interested in the mechanics. But she'd gone this far.

"I was watching the Highlands. They were building a so-called research road, which was actually a logging road. Before the fences were done, I told you they were doing work around the mine shaft during the day."

"What sort of work?"

"Just carrying stuff in and out. Guys with clipboards standing around." She waited for some comment. Some hint that the man on the line knew something. "And they've had a couple pipes going into the mine. Now, what do *you* know?"

"I told you, that's not the nature of the relationship."

There was a click and the line went dead.

7

Dan never lost consciousness, but his memories remained hazy. He had the presence of mind to toss the receiver into the brush after he hit the ground and to feign unconsciousness when he heard the voices. The men said nothing of interest, only grunted and complained that Dan was heavy.

At some point he felt a needle prick his arm and remembered nothing more. Blackness for only God knew how long.

He came to with a bright light in his eyes, its intensity magnified by a throbbing headache. He tried to sit up.

"Hey, hey, take it easy there," a deep male voice said. A hand on his shoulder kept him lying flat.

The voice belonged to a gray-haired, white-coated man who looked all business. The age lines in his face were faint but discernible, teeth not quite even. He was carefully dressed in a starched white coat over a pressed blue shirt and his demeanor said "doctor." Two other men, big guys in blue jeans and muscle-filled T-shirts, stood back, saying nothing.

"How many fingers?"

He held up his hands. "Where's Maria?"

"Right here," she groaned. He looked to his left and saw her lying on a folding cot. Glancing around the room, he could see white cupboards with masking tape on the doors with various labels, like FLASKS, BEAKERS, DEWARS, and a lot of names for materials or equipment that he didn't understand. He was also on a narrow, folding cot, narrower than a twin bed, perhaps four feet away from Maria. Everything was white. For some reason he couldn't quite articulate, it appeared they were in a modular building in a room about twenty by thirty.

"She appears to be fine other than a lot of bruises," the man said. "Now, how many fingers?"

"Seven."

"What year is it?"

"2002."

"Who's the president?"

"Dick Cheney."

"Sense of humor's intact."

"What was the last thing you remember?"

"Climbing a tree."

"Why were you trespassing?"

"Where am I?"

"You're in the facility you were spying on."

"What facility?"

"That's private."

"That's baloney," Maria said.

"I can assure you we have legitimate reasons for keeping it confidential. We're protecting the forest."

"How are you protecting the forest?" Maria asked. "And where are my clothes?"

"Being cleaned. What's left of them. I'm afraid they were badly torn in your fall out of the tree."

Dan realized now that he was completely nude under a wooly blanket. Judging from the bra straps on her shoulders, he surmised Maria still wore her underwear.

"I didn't just fall out of the tree. Something hit me in the chest."

"Really, I can't imagine what. Are you sure you are remembering things correctly? You were sort of knocked silly."

"I'm positive."

"Strange. At any rate we'll return your clothes just as soon as they are clean. Then the police will come and get you."

"The police?"

"We're making a citizen's arrest. You were clearly trespassing."

"Oh, come on," she said. "We weren't hurting anything."

"That really isn't the point, is it? We're entitled to privacy for our work. The nature of our project requires that we keep it completely confidential for the good of this ecosystem."

"You're on Metco or Amada land or both. Since when are they concerned about trees? They're in the business of cutting them down and making lumber."

"They're also in the business of growing them back. But I'm not going to bicker. Nothing improper is going on here. Quite the contrary."

"Well then, you shouldn't mind telling us what you're doing."

"Why were you carrying a radio receiver? What drove you deep into a private forest past barriers and numerous NO TRESPASSING signs?"

Maria glanced at Dan. He took a deep breath. "Look, is this going to be a trade? Our secrets for yours? Or is this a one-way street?"

"You were on our land. You were breaking the law. It's already a one-way street. You made it that way. So what were you doing here?"

"OK. We were picking mushrooms and this is a bad dream."

"A friend of Dan's is a biologist for Otran Enterprises," Maria interjected. "It's another timber company."

"We know who they are."

"Well, they're doing a study on land over the mountain there. We must've gotten a wrong radio signal, yours instead of theirs. Of course when we came out into this forest and found the barriers and all the signs, we couldn't imagine what anybody would be doing here."

"So you just kept coming even though you knew you were breaking the law."

"More or less, although we didn't consider that we were doing anything terribly wrong," Maria continued. "Like I said, he's an attorney for Otran Enterprises and was concerned that maybe you had something going on in your forest you didn't know about. Maybe a pot-growing operation or something. I mean, you do work for Amada or Metco. True?"

"And you are?" He ignored her question.

"She's my girlfriend," Dan said. "And she's an attorney as well."

"Also for Otran Enterprises?"

"She does a different kind of work—"

"Yes," Maria interrupted, and cut a look at Dan. "And I'd like my clothes immediately."

"We'll check on it. Your last name is Fischer?"

"Yes."

"And you are Dan Young?"

"You've been checking our wallets." Dan eyed their billfolds lying on a nearby table.

"Had to. We didn't know if you'd regain consciousness. We'll bring you your clothes when they're washed and dried. Please don't leave this room. The door will be locked and we ask that you not try to climb out the windows. The dogs will be right outside." The man started to leave, then turned back as if he'd forgotten something important. "And we're going to leave the lady with her blanket, but once we're outside, we'll ask you to pass yours around the door—we really don't want you leaving."

After they had left the room, one of the muscled arms snaked around the door, the hand beckoning.

"I'm keeping the blanket," Dan said as he rose.

The arm flung the door open, and the two big men walked purposefully over to Dan.

"Pass your blanket or we'll take it," one of the burly bodyguards ordered.

"Maybe you should give it to him," Maria said.

Looking at the dark-haired man, Dan guessed his weight at about 230 pounds. Of the two muscle guys, he appeared the leader. The second, who now stood beside him, was at least as big and a lot meaner-looking. With boots Dan gave himself a fair shot at taking them both. Without, he would probably lose. Giving in didn't occur to him. Making sure his eyes never wavered and his shoulder never dropped to betray his intention, he kicked straight at the lead man's testicles.

The man reacted too late. Doubling over, he groaned, and after a good breath, screamed. With his blanket wrapped around him, Dan moved in quickly with a very square upper-cut to the face. The guy went down deadweight. Now the odds were considerably improved. Instinctively he knew the legal situation might be manipulated if he did it right.

The remaining man assumed a fighting stance.

"Wait." The commanding voice of the white-haired man rang out. "Leave him alone." Then addressing Dan, he warned: "But I'm telling you, if either one of you tries to escape, we will use the force necessary to stop you."

"We aren't going anywhere," Dan said. "We're waiting for the police. In fact, we welcome the police."

Groaning, the man on the ground rolled over, staggering to his feet. With their disappointment clearly showing, the two men withdrew with their boss—the injured man still hunched over.

"That wasn't very bright," Maria said. She smiled a little. "So now that you've done your Tarzan act, what's next?"

"We look around," he whispered, pointing at the door. He had wrapped the blanket around himself as one would wrap a towel, but left a considerable amount of fabric on the floor. She turned away, wrapping her own blanket high on her body, tucked just under her arms.

"You take the drawers; I'll take the cabinets," she said.

"There's nothing interesting in here or they wouldn't have left us alone. It's a storage area for research equipment and supplies."

"So what, then?"

"So we're going through there."

Dan pointed at a vent grate.

"You'll never fit." Her tone betrayed a hopelessness.

"I can try. You'd clearly make it."

"Oh yeah. Right."

Dan began rummaging through the cupboards and drawers. "We need a screwdriver." He found nothing resembling the necessary tool. He did find a spackling knife of the sort Sheetrockers use and immediately stood on his bed, loosening the screws. It was remarkably easy.

With the grating removed, he considered how he would get up into the duct. By putting a chair on the bed, he was able to stick his head in the metal passageway. The metal appeared thin and it was supported by little more than flimsy brackets and the Sheetrock. Even if he could fit, he would fall through the ceiling.

"You might have better luck over here," Maria said.

She had opened a big walk-in closet and had pulled aside a rack of brand-new lab coats. Behind the coats was a wall with an old pass-through door, probably used to access papers or supplies.

"Unless you like falling through the ceiling."

He got down quickly. It looked much more promising.

Taking the putty knife, they pried the drab green door. The flimsy metal bent.

"I'm sure this is a modular unit just set here. The pass-through was probably for another place and another time. I think it's painted shut. We need something stronger to pry with," he said.

Maria began rummaging in the drawers. Dan did the same. He found a first-aid kit with a pair of heavy scissors inside.

"These might do," he said, thrusting them under the sliding door. At first it moved a half inch, enabling him to get his fingers underneath. He needed leverage, so he jumped up on the sill in front of the pass-through, losing his blanket in the process. Maria retained a solemn expression, keeping her eyes fixed on her fingers that were now also thrust under the stubborn door.

They both lifted, straining as hard as they could. Instantly it gave way, sliding up into the wall. He noticed her biting her cheeks and staring straight ahead as if struggling not to smile. Dropping to the floor, he picked up the blanket.

"If you'll allow me," he said, hefting himself over the lip and through the wall. Inside was more storage and one solitary door in the middle of the wall, a sturdy door set on heavy hinges similar to those found on a bank vault. At eye level there was a small window made of very heavy plate glass that allowed visual inspection of the room.

To open the door, one would grab a large metal handle and pull it down. At the moment it was held in place by a heavy combination lock.

"What's in there, I wonder?"

Maria was intent on the door as well. "Let's look."

But neither moved for a moment while they took in their surroundings. Stark white walls with pastel green cabinets brought to mind a medical clinic. The floor was speckled green vinyl, probably laid over a wooden subfloor, up to an area about a foot from the door of the special room, where the floor turned to concrete slab. Stacked to either side of the door were boxes of vermiculite, a growing medium for plants. Down the hall on the opposite side was a more normal-looking door. At either end of the hall were doors that appeared to be interior to the complex, one of which looked composite and economy driven, the other heavy wood with multiple panels.

They approached the double-plated window, looking inside. It was a room about twenty by fifteen. There were two desks, numerous cabinets, and a microfiche reader. In a far corner of the room hung a television camera behind a heavy wire-mesh grid.

"What do you make of that?" Dan said.

"It's a secured document room. The sort of place you'd keep highly confidential information."

"What do you suppose is through that door?" Dan said, nodding to the right to the end of the hall and the economy door.

"I don't know, but I doubt we're meant to find out," she said. He began walking. "Young, let's discuss this." She moved in front of him with one hand on his chest.

"You talk and I'll listen," he said as he reached around her for the knob and began slowly turning it.

"All balls, no brain," she muttered as she stepped from between him and the door.

He peeked through the crack at 3,000 square feet of modern laboratory, packed with all sorts of equipment that looked electrical and chemical. There were at least a dozen people in casual attire, concentrating on their work. In the middle of the lab were two huge vats with a lot of tubing running around them and apparently in them. He guessed they were under pressure.

"What do you see?" she asked.

"Take a look."

She stepped around him and put her eye to the crack.

"What are they doing?"

"Something they obviously don't want us to know about. What if we just walk out there in our blankets and introduce ourselves—maybe they're not all bad guys," he said.

"Dumb idea. We'd never leave with anything."

He put a hand gently on her head, moving her down the crack so that he could hunch over the top of her and get a better view. After a minute or two a couple of technicians began walking toward the door.

"Close the door, they're coming."

"In here," he said, opening a storage-room door. It was a room perhaps twenty feet long and fifteen feet wide, lined floor to ceiling with large shelves stacked with ordinary-looking supplies. Mostly it appeared to be paper products. On the floor in front of a large bottom shelf was a row of five-gallon cans of industrial cleaner. Behind the small aluminum drums the shelf appeared empty.

"Come on," Maria said, moving a couple of cans and crawling onto the shelf.

"Are you crazy?"

"Hurry, damn it."

Dan crawled in backward, only to discover that there wasn't enough room.

"I'll get on top," Maria said, sliding over him. He stayed prone underneath Maria, who lay facedown on his back.

With considerable effort he pulled the cans in front of the shelf.

"If they were coming, they'd already be here," Dan said.

Then a woman's voice.

"I think the file folders are in the big locker."

"You can look, but I think they took them all out of there and I think we've run out. We go through those damn things like bugs on a chicken farm." Male voice.

The door opened.

"Somebody keeps leaving the lights on."

Dan held his breath. Fortunately, Maria was a small person. Neither of them made a sound. He could see the woman's legs in navy blue slacks. She wore cheap white tennis shoes that squeaked over the floor as she rummaged through the shelves. She was working her way back and would surely see them if she began moving cans or looked just over the tops. It was inconceivable that she would miss them. Glancing back, he noticed Maria's petite white thigh on top of his meatier, even paler version, the blankets scrunched to the side. He liked her taste in panties—bikini style but not thong. It surprised him; he would have had her pegged for more matronly briefs. Unfortunately, nothing else in this place was the flesh white of their untanned thighs or the ivory white of Maria's underwear.

One shelf back the lady was searching too thoroughly. They were going to be found.

The door opened.

"If you're looking for file folders, we moved them over to the file room."

"Well, why didn't somebody say something?"

"Hell if I know."

The door slammed; the lights went out.

"That was close." Maria let out a deep breath.

First Dan moved two cans; then he let her slither out, unable to ignore the smooth warmth of her skin sliding on his. More concerned for Maria's safety than he cared to admit, he slowly opened the door, finding an empty hallway once again.

At the opposite end of the corridor stood the heavy wooden door, dark in color, that looked more executive than the rest. Instinctively they were drawn to it. They both hurried, imagining that at any moment the door from the laboratory might open once again. When he tried the door, he expected it would be locked. It opened.

A soft light in the corner partially illuminated the office. Inside, it had been decorated much more lavishly than the other rooms they had seen. There was a window with vertical mahogany blinds, a cherry television cabinet, custom bookcases to match, a large rosewood desk, a beige carpet overlaid with real or imitation Persian. There was a large folding-door, freestanding closet that when opened revealed various items of clothing on hangers, a lot of snack foods, rain gear, golf clubs, two rifles, and a sawed-off shotgun.

"Damn, look at that," Dan said.

Maria flipped up the corner of the rug.

"It's real. Handmade. Let's see what we can find." She went to another door that led into a small bathroom complete with a shower.

Dan tried the filing cabinet behind the desk. It was locked.

They both rummaged through the drawers of the desk but found no key.

"Most morons put the key in the desk," he said.

She went to the other filing cabinets and began looking through them.

"We better do this fast," he said.

"I'm hurrying."

"Oh, look what I found." She held up a flat gray box.

"What is it?"

"Box full of keys, all labeled and each key attached to the bottom with Velcro. And one says fireproof cabinet."

"Bingo."

Quickly they opened it and started rooting through files full of paperwork. Many pages of equations were unintelligible. They found computer printouts with chemical names and numerous spreadsheets that contained numbers and chemical symbols.

"Look," she said, holding a stack of photos. They were pictures of dead-looking bats.

"What's that mean?" he whispered.

"What's any of it mean? Those equations look formidable," she said. "A lot of very fine print. Whoever wrote them must be a math or chemistry person."

"Why do chemistry people take bat photos?" he said.

"Or write stuff about bat neurons," she said, holding up

an equation with an explanation related to brain activity and consciousness. "We better get the hell to the other side of that wall before they find out we know about this."

"I'd like to know what it is that we know," Dan said. "Let's take one bat photo and these pages of chemical equations."

"I wish we knew what we were doing," she said, sliding the drawer closed. Dan was still rifling through another. "You wanna die in here? Come on." She opened the door a crack. "Shhh!" She closed the door quietly. "In here, quick."

"What? Why?" he whispered as she shoved him in the bathroom.

"We have been crapped on by the gods, that's why," she said, opening the shower. They both stepped in and quietly closed the frosted-glass door. "The white-haired guy is at the other end of the hallway talking to the thugs. Listen."

The outer office door opened and closed, then silence for a moment.

"Let me talk to Hans." There was a pause. "Hmm. Hmm. They're in one of the supply rooms." After a time he cleared his throat. "I've already called the cops. They're trespassing." A long silence. "You do that and they could never leave here, Hans. No way. And even if we did, we don't know for sure whether anybody knows they're here.

"I know all about the division of labor." More silence. "Well, you can damn well do as you please next time. But the cops will be here in half an hour." Sounds of the chair rolling on plastic and a deep sigh punctuated the silence.

"I don't *want* to know. That's your deal. Your department . . ." There was a solid smack on wood, then the sound of liquid pouring and the clink of a crystal decanter. "Yeah? Well, fuck you too, Hans." He slammed the phone.

After a few minutes the office door closed again.

"Let's go," Maria said.

"I don't need any encouragement."

The hallway was empty. They rushed through the office door and down the hall to the pass-through, their bare feet whispering over the linoleum.

"Let's get back in there," she said, prying it open.

While she was crawling through, he went to the cupboards in the hallway but was only finding more meaningless computer printouts. He wished they had found something he could understand, something in plain English.

"Will you come on?" she pleaded.

With one photo and five pages in Maria's purse, they lay on the cots and tried to look as calm and bored as possible.

8

The eighteen-foot mahogany table was inlaid with redwood burl and cherry, exquisitely made with feet capped in heavy brass and with fine carvings down the legs. There was a distinctly Asian flavor to the design in keeping with the preferences of the man who sat at its head. The Amada regional headquarters, about fifteen minutes outside of Palmer and forty-five minutes from the redwood-forest research compound, was second only to the San Francisco offices in grandeur and opulence.

Kenji Yamada had married Micha Asaka Yamada, the third daughter of Yoshinari Asaka, one of the ten wealthiest men in Japan. The Asaka family's corporate holding company, Kuru, was heavily invested in the wood-fiber industry, manufacturers of fine paper, pencils, wooden blinds, wooden windows, medium-density fiberboard, and a host of other derivative products.

Kenji had been relegated to the U.S. subsidiary, Amada, which was not a Japanese name but sounded so to the Western ear and was very pronounceable to the Western tongue. Among Amada's chief assets was one million acres of timberland in the United States and Canada. About 250,000 of those acres were located on the north coast of California not far from the Oregon border. Since it was substantially north of San Francisco, not many even knew that this wild area existed.

Kenji devoted every waking moment to furthering Amada's business. At age forty-nine he worried that life was passing him by, and that if he didn't have some outstanding success in the near future his father-in-law would die not realizing that his third son-in-law brought him the most honor. Today he stood on the brink of greatness, thwarted only by some legal technicalities and a stubborn mystery that seemed to defy resolution.

Kenji sat in an ornate chair differing from the others both in the detail of its carvings and its mass. His face remained impassive as he listened to the other three men. Only occasionally did he let his fingers run lightly over his close-cropped jet-black hair—an expression of his annoyance at what he was being told. To his right sat Hans Groiter, his chief of security, a Caucasian man whose skin was deeply freckled and nearly hairless. To Groiter's left sat his bespectacled lawyer.

"I am disappointed Herschel would bring them into the compound without consulting us," Kenji said.

"Well, now they're about to leave," Groiter said. "We'll never know what they know or what they suspect unless we do something, and fast."

"You have this Dan Young's address?"

"If I get your drift, we can start planting bugs tonight."

Kenji merely nodded, dismissing him. The ride from the Amada office to Palmer was short. With luck Groiter would get his work done before Dan Young arrived home.

"Why are the damned bats going crazy?" Kenji asked Kim Lee. "In this country that kind of thing could attract more curious biologists."

"We know they are an undiscovered subspecies," his attorney answered. "And I think we're getting them all killed off."

"Oh yes, and to find that out, we had to kill a goddamned snoopy biologist who asked too many questions?"

"It was a heart attack."

Kenji didn't bother replying. It had been stupid to bring in a man they couldn't control. The second week on the job the man had wanted to bring in an army of his brethren. Another one of Herschel's mistakes.

"So when do we know something?"

"About the bats? About our problem in the mine?"

"How about the railroad?" Kenji asked, shifting his attention to a topic only slightly less vexing.

"They won't sell."

"Why not? For good money they should."

"If we go to them and hint at big money, what do you suppose they will think?" Kim Lee tried, and failed, not to sound condescending to his boss.

"They'll think we have found something of value. So how much should we offer?"

"Ten dollars per acre."

"And why should they take that?" Kenji asked.

"It's a place to start negotiating, but I don't hold out much hope. The railroad always keeps the mineral rights."

"Why we didn't buy everything when we bought this land is a mystery to me."

The exasperation showed on Kim Lee's face, but he remained silent.

"I know I don't have to remind you of the money that each of you will make if this project is a success."

Following a helicopter ride to the police station, Dan and Maria had arranged for the recovery of the ruined rental car and for the borrowed truck to be returned to their "benefactor." Then they were ticketed for a trespassing infraction and sent home. After a taxi ride back to the pub, they retrieved Dan's car and drove through Palmer past darkened houses made quiet for the night.

For the hundredth time Maria wondered aloud what secret the men at the compound could be guarding so carefully.

"No clue," Dan said, "but Hans, whoever he is, wanted some creative persuasion, and our buddy was pointing out they'd have to kill us if that happened."

"Maybe we should have told the cops."

"No. We've got nothing. Nothing that couldn't be explained away. This way we can talk to our clients, get clearance, find some experts, maybe make something of the bats or the equations. Then, if appropriate, convince the cops to go out with a search warrant without warning."

"I don't disagree."

They pulled up in the driveway of the Palmer Inn. Although Maria had not planned to stay the night, she had long since missed her flight and had now decided to attend an early-morning telephone conference with Patty McCafferty and Jeb Otran—a discussion she wanted to hear.

"Look," Dan said, "why don't you come to my house? You have no luggage. You don't even have a toothbrush. I have a guest bedroom. Pepacita, my housekeeper, is there. You wouldn't be the lone female."

"Hey, that's a leap across a giant gulf. In the morning you'd wake up and realize this is Maria the enviro under your roof—the enemy. Isn't that what you guys call us?"

"We call you worse than that. But this is an emergency."

He watched her brow furrow.

"You're going to feel strange walking into the lobby like that. What will you do in the morning?"

"Oh, and you've got a whole size-eight wardrobe?"

"I do."

"You—you didn't get rid of your wife's clothes?"

"No. Not all of them. Not yet. She was a generous and good person. She would have given you the clothes if she were alive, so why not when she's gone?"

"You've got clothes I could wear to a seven A.M. meeting?"

"Absolutely. Size eight. Tess weighed one hundred twenty-five pounds. She was five foot eight inches tall. Pepacita is a great cook. There'll be dinner whenever we get there."

"What if we get the clothes and I come back here."

"You can decide when you get to my place."

"I *am* famished."

"Good. We'll at least get you dinner and a wardrobe."

"You know, any day now we could be in court on opposite sides of a timber-harvest plan, clawing at each other until our fingernails are hanging from bloody stumps."

"What happened to the old saying: 'Let us strive mightily but eat and drink as friends.' "

"This is real life. This counts. If you cut down a grove of redwoods a thousand years old—well, they're gone forever."

He straightened his hat and looked at her as if he had an answer.

"You wanna say something dumb, like they'll grow back."

He laughed. "Let's go to my house before we start an all-night fight."

Hans Groiter liked dried pumpkin seeds. He liked the little ritual of cracking the salted shells between his teeth and sucking out the meat. The trick was that after removing the heart he ate the shell as well.

As he drilled through the subfloor of Dan Young's house, he ground a shell to a pulp between his teeth. Peering around the edge of the venetian blind, he had watched a heavy Mexican woman puttering in the family room. Figuring carefully the location of the large couch, he had entered the crawl space under the house and used a hand drill to create a ⅛-inch pilot hole. Although his spike mike had wood-boring threads, he wanted to make it easy and silent.

He worked by the light of a battery-powered lantern, keeping it turned away from the entrance to the crawl space and hoping that some stray beam of light would not penetrate the darkness outside the residence and give him away. With the predrilled hole he easily screwed the mike through the floor with his right hand while his left arm mindlessly brushed aside cobwebs. Around him the pillar and post foundation supported a crawl space that varied between twenty-four and thirty-six inches over uneven ground. Protruding through the plywood floor were the nails that held the subfloor to the plywood. If he wasn't careful, they would bloody his knuckles.

By the time the mike was screwed through the plywood, the medium-density fiber (MDF) subflooring, and the carpet, he had a strong feeling that he better get the hell out before he was caught. He worked with a fierce sense of urgency. If they did come, his men would trigger a quiet beep on his walkie-talkie and alert him to listen. So far, the silence had been reassuring. Once the mike was in place, he inserted a tri-pronged plug to a wireless transmitter.

As quickly and as quietly as possible, he retreated to the small, hinged door in the side of the house, exited the crawl space, and walked the one block to a waiting van.

In the forest behind the house, buried in an azalea, stood a large, sensitive microphone aimed at the family-room window. Sound waves from inside that hit the window could be picked up by Groiter's hidden paraphernalia and broadcast to the van. Any kitchen or family-room conversation that could not be detected by the spike mike under the couch could probably be heard through this giant ear. Also, Groiter's best surveillance man, a guy too expensive to be anything but an independent contractor, had done a phone tap at the pole, also using a transmitter with a feed to the van.

All they needed now was for Dan Young to come home and talk to someone.

In the van, Groiter pulled out a Clive Cussler novel and poured a pile of pumpkin seeds onto a paper towel. "Now we wait," he told the surveillance man.

In retirement Groiter imagined that he would sit on a South Seas beach with a mound of pumpkin seeds, a stack of thrillers, and some dark glasses that would make it easier to watch the girls go by. A bachelor, he had never felt the need to become attached to anyone or anything with the possible exception of his retirement account that he nursed with a mother's love and a father's devotion.

Over the years he had managed to develop a marvelous detachment where people were concerned. He did not laugh when they laughed, cry when they cried, nor did he ever mentally put himself in the place of another. For that reason he could, if required, strangle toddlers. But he maintained a scientific point of view. If there was no remorse, there was also no joy in wet work, and he employed as little violence as he deemed possible in order to ensure a satisfactory retirement.

He had served Kenji well, managing largely through creativity to avoid killing people even in the most difficult circumstances. His value lay in his availability to do whatever was needed, like a bizarre kind of insurance policy. And since he had absolutely no one to tell, his exploits went utterly unheralded.

Most of his killing had been done in liberated Iron Curtain countries where the Mafia got in the way of some business arrangements of the Petchenkoffs, an old-money European family. He had at least achieved a stalemate after knocking off four highly placed figures in organized crime. To get to the bosses, he had to kill at least a dozen underlings, two with a ten-inch awl, one with a knife, all up close and personal. The Petchenkoffs were allowed a graceful exit at a reasonable price, neither side wanting anything more to do with the other.

He met Kenji while working for the Petchenkoffs. Actually, the Asakas were more or less sideline participants, and Kenji had an inkling of Groiter's exploits. When Kenji hired him and imported him to the United States, things became much more refined. He hadn't killed a soul working for Kenji, although he'd helped Kenji clean up the mess with Catherine Swanson and the photographer.

Perhaps Hans's greatest asset was figuring people, their fear, their greed, their envy, and their lust. If somebody had a mind for mischief, Hans had a mind that could find a way between that miscreant and whatever thing of Kenji's they wanted.

At the moment he was having a bit of a struggle understanding exactly what Maria Fischer and Dan Young might want. The morons at the lab had handled the lawyers' intrusion in typically ridiculous fashion by bringing them inside the compound and locking them in a room without so much as a guard. Amazing that a brilliant scientist could be so mindless when it came to security and so fragile when it came to enforcing it.

Yoshinari Asaka III maintained a five-story, traditional Japanese castle on the outskirts of Kanazawa in the province of Hokuriku near the Sea of Japan. It was his preferred residence, though he had several. On this day he sat in his covered garden, by the koi pond, next to a burbling stream running beneath a small footbridge. Growing near the water at his feet was a calla lily bearing a deep purple, trumpet-shaped bloom. It was a gift from his daughter Micha in America, and he treasured it. He also treasured her: the texture of her voice, her scent, her smile, and her determined squint. These things gave him great pleasure.

But for the moment his thoughts included himself, his company, and all his family. When he was a young man, sixteen hours represented a normal day spent advancing the family wealth. Now he did a better job, and it consumed six hours on a busy day. There were days when he took only a single call. So astute was his handpicked management that the Asaka business conglomerate could be guided down the right path with tiny consistent taps from a small stick. If administered precisely, these taps moved the corporate giant to ever greater success. Yoshinari was a master, his tapping so subtle that it often went undetected to all but the most discerning ear.

As in all affairs in every culture, error was possible. In

the Asaka businesses, departures from the path crept in most easily when the master tapper could not see where to apply the stick. And there was now a blurry fog over the business activities of the Amada subsidiary and Kenji Yamada, its chief executive, his son-in-law. It was a matter of possessing accurate information—a commodity in short supply at Amada. So he had sent a liaison, one Oki Satoru, whom he needed to call now.

A voice answered with a groggy-sounding greeting.

"I hope I did not awaken you."

"I fell asleep watching the TV. Sign of getting older."

"Ah, yes," Yoshinari said. "Are you making any progress?"

"I'm afraid Kenji is not happy to see me. I can learn only what Kenji wants me to learn, which is nothing. I am frankly worried that he tries too hard to keep secrets, especially about the forest compound. One wonders what he is worried about. He claims that if word of their Taxol research gets out, the woods will be full of hunters for the yew trees."

"What does that have to do with you and your need to know?"

"It is an excuse without a reason. I believe he has some other project in progress."

"And why do you think that?"

"He has hired chemical engineers at the research center."

"Is there a reason he doesn't share this with us?"

"I don't know. I'm trying to figure it out. But there is a matter I should speak with you about."

"Yes." Yoshinari did not like Satoru's strained tone. He wondered what Kenji had done that even the ambitious Satoru didn't approve of.

"Your daughter has suspected Kenji of seeing other women. She actually told me this, sir. And I took action, sir. Over here the state senators have a knife at the throats of the timber producers. I thought a political connection could advance the interests of the Asaka family. So I promised a well-placed woman money to get next to Kenji. Like a geisha.''

Asaka forced himself to show restraint. *Like a geisha, indeed.* "Go on."

"It didn't work out well. The woman communicated with Micha on the phone, made small talk. Said how much she appreciated Kenji giving her a ride home. That part, of course, was good. But after the call the woman was found dead in a photographer's van, apparently sexually assaulted by the photographer. I had hired the photographer. And he has disappeared. The police think he's running from the law.''

"Tell me why you hired this woman?"

"It's a long story. As I said, her husband is a state senator with prospects. In the long run he could give us political favors. It's common in America like everywhere else. Especially California.''

"It is against the law."

"The woman could pry information out of your son-in-law. That's not against the law. And Micha would have the answer to her question. If she knew he was tempted, she could confine his ways.''

"You thought all this up by yourself?"

"I did."

"And why did you hire the photographer?"

"For evidence."

"You neglected to mention this scheme to me."

"I didn't want to burden you with it."

"Who do you think killed the woman?"

"I don't know. Perhaps the photographer. Perhaps Kenji.''

"I want you to cease all this. I sent you to gather information, not to trap my son-in-law. He is capable enough of serious errors without you creating them for him.''

''I understand.''

''I want a full report of everything to do with this woman and this photographer. Put it in a computer file with a twenty-digit password. E-mail the encrypted file. Courier the password on a single piece of paper directly to me and show it to no one. I will show the report only to our attorneys. If I didn't need someone over there on an immediate basis, I would recall you. Do you understand?''

''Yes.'' It was the reply of a beaten man.

Yoshinari made few errors, but sending Satoru had been one of them. He instantly saw Satoru's foolish game—a transparent attempt to have Kenji removed so that he could be advanced. But Yoshinari also knew that his daughter might not disapprove of a plan designed to test her husband's fidelity.

As for Kenji's secret project, perhaps Kenji saw honor in surprise and in solitary accomplishment. It was the American way, not the Japanese way. For the Japanese, making many work as one was the highest honor, and the honor went to all.

As he wondered how hard he should search for Kenji's tapping spot, Yoshinari realized he had already made a decision. He knew people from all walks of life. He knew political leaders, he knew business leaders, and he had access to those who served them. But even with his great wealth, it was favors owed him by the emperor's family that would get him what his money could not buy. The emperor had access to the most trusted men of the shadows. These men could blend into a crowd, slip into a bank vault, disappear in the night, kill with a single blow. They were as wise as serpents and much more dangerous. They fought only to protect those who hired them or to save an innocent life.

But when they fought, they fought to win and they fought well.

Yoshinari not only needed such a man, but he required one. One who was schooled in the ways of the Americans and who spoke English.

Using all the political capital he had accumulated in a lifetime of fortune-making, he had his man within forty-eight hours. A day after that, the man Shohei was off to the United States. Although *"shohei"* meant "giant," his height was normal, his body highly conditioned and wiry. Someone needed to determine what mischief Kenji might yet have in mind.

9

Dan Young's house was a large, comfortable rambler surrounded on the back and sides by towering redwoods that made it seem miniature in comparison. Located on a large piece of property at the end of a wooded road, the four-bedroom dwelling appeared secluded from neighboring homes.

As they made their way up the front walk, Maria studied the illuminated shrubbery. Weeds had sprung up among the rock roses and the rhododendrons. One of the azaleas was dead and another appeared on its last legs. There was a splendid dogwood in the middle of the front yard. It had probably been Tess who took care of the gardening, she surmised.

The back door opened into the family room and the

kitchen. They walked in and Dan tossed his hat like a Frisbee. It sailed about five feet onto a prong of a large coatrack.

She glanced at him. "Impressive."

Dan nodded at a large dark-haired woman. "I discovered her," Dan said with his arms flung wide in Pepacita's direction. "The all-purpose live-in mother."

The big woman turned from whatever she was cooking. "I get more *buenos* than most wives." Her lively dark brown eyes appraised Maria with obvious curiosity.

Maria smiled and shook Pepacita's hand.

"You and Dan look like you fell on hard times?" Pepacita asked.

Maria smoothed her tattered and stained clothing.

"I must look awful."

"I told her we would pull some of Tess's clothes out of the closet," Dan said.

"Ah, *comprendo*. I will see what I can find."

"We're dying of hunger. How about something to gnaw on while we wait for dinner?"

Pepacita nodded and whisked out some smoked salmon; then as fast as any chef, she sliced a couple of hothouse-ripened tomatoes and garnished them with crumbled Feta cheese. Dan disappeared for a couple of minutes and reappeared in jeans.

Each taking a plate, they moved to the couch, where Dan sat at one end and Maria the other. After a few genuine compliments about the house, Maria turned earnest.

"So what do we do with these documents?"

"For the moment keep it in your purse," Dan said. "We'll figure out where to put it after dinner."

"I need to use your phone. I've got to call my mom and my boyfriend. Late as it is, they'll think I died."

"Right there," Dan said, pointing to the phone in the family room.

Her mother was easy. In that special tone that said "I'm really tied up," Maria told her mother that she would call her in the morning.

"Hey, you," she said to Ross, glancing at Dan out of the corner of her eye. Thankfully, he rose to leave but not without a little knowing smile tugging at the corners of his mouth. She recalled liking his mustache. She knew she looked uncomfortable and tried not to. *Can't pull it off.*

Dan disappeared down the hall.

"I got hung up. It was a real adventure."

"What do you mean?"

"Don't sound so worried. I'm sorry I didn't call. I'm just fine. I was out in the woods and I ended up in an industry laboratory and it's a very long story. I can't tell you now. It would take too long. I'll call you first thing tomorrow."

"You're at the Palmer Inn?"

"No, I'm staying with some friends."

"Do I know them?"

"It's a lady named Pepacita, and a fellow named Dan Young."

"Why do I know that name?"

"Sometimes he handles environmental cases. Ross, I know this is really going to sound strange to you, but you have to trust me here. He's the lawyer for Otran Enterprises."

"*That* Dan Young? Why the hell would you—"

"Calm down. It's one night. There are a lot of people here and there is a good reason."

"Does this Dan Young know what I don't get to know?"

"Don't say it like that. It's attorney-client privilege for him too."

"Oh great, some industry asshole . . ."

"Wait, wait, I can see this is going to be a thing. I will get permission from Patty to tell you ninety percent of this.

Hey, I don't even know all of it. Dan Young's not telling me what I'd like to know.''

"When can we talk?"

"Tomorrow. I promise." She hung up.

Not so mysteriously, Dan reappeared.

"Do you always eavesdrop?"

"Only when vital national-security interests are at stake."
His eyes were bright, but he betrayed only a hint of a smile.

"I'm not laughing."

"Well then, I guess I won't, either. Hey, Pepacita, how are we doing on the clothes?"

"I will show Maria to the clothing and the shower. Nate's in his room. Supposedly in bed, but probably reading under the covers with a flashlight."

"Excuse me, I'm going to check on my son," said Dan.
"Surely."

The kitchen was redolent with the aroma of home cooking, of spices simmering slowly on long, lazy afternoons—garlic, cloves, onions: a potpourri of smells. Pans of all sizes hung on a wrought-iron frame suspended above the island stove. Racks laden with a wide assortment of spices perched in long rows behind the cooktop. A chopping block of oak alongside the stove in the kitchen's center bore years' worth of stains.

Maria could also make out a faint musty odor among the kitchen smells—understandable, since the house sat like a mushroom in the shade of the monster trees. Her eyes swept the family room's casual, wood-walled interior, spying a lariat and a green sweater on an antique hardwood rack. The sweater had patches on each elbow. It was old, well-maintained, and comfortable looking. That about summed this place up. For one brief moment she fantasized about what it might be like to live here—with Dan.

This end of the house, with its tongue-and-groove pine-board walls and angled low ceilings, had the feel of a cottage. The adjoining family room was chock-full to bursting with books, photos, and memorabilia—every square inch of shelf and wall space was utilized. The bookcases were meticulously constructed, with an eye toward matching the walls—obviously built for someone who treasured their contents. She went exploring. Her eye skimmed over the collection, fascinated by its breadth and depth: Thoreau, Melville, Kipling, as well as a host of modern writers. Given the dust patterns, it looked like he kept the classics but didn't read them much. Maybe they were Tess's.

And there was lots more: the dog-eared pages of a Rutherford novel, *The Forest;* nearby a spy thriller; the fat copy of a Thomas Jefferson biography facedown on the desk—frankly, a surprise; a book of Ansel Adams photographs; three original oil landscapes on the wall by a painter whose signature was indiscernible, along with figure drawings and lithographs by other artists; the CD titles in the neat stack of plastic cases, mostly rock, Bob Dylan, a little opera, more light opera, and a smattering of country-western; the magazines on the coffee table: *Time, Newsweek, U.S. News & World Report, People,* a publication by the Audubon Society; an antique Queen Anne table that might be a skillful reproduction; a spreadsheet of professional football teams and their game scores atop it; and the chair where he sat and drank beer, judging from all the caps in the nearby wastebasket. Front and center on the little table where he parked his beer was a 9"x12" photo of Tess.

The man was apparently a 49ers fan. She hadn't been to a game in years but she still watched them on television. When she did, she thought about her father, and if she'd had a couple glasses of Chenin Blanc, she cried. For a split second she smiled at how much she used to like football—

how she analyzed plays with her father. There was loneliness in the memory, so she shrugged it off.

Maria found the personal stuff: the photos, family shots, Nate Young in every imaginable activity, smiling, laughing, a father engaged with his son. But many included a beautiful brown-eyed woman.

From the coffee table, beside another picture of Tess, she picked up a book of Shakespeare's sonnets. Inside the cover, there was an inscription:

> *To Tess: With the love in my heart taxing my mind for expression, please accept these words of another as a tribute to my devotion.*

For some reason the words shocked her. The cowboy expressed his feelings. And judging from the reading material, he was not all belt buckles and boots. In fact, the real Dan Young came in a very odd and misleading package.

Below Dan's inscription in the Shakespeare was Tess's reply:

> *My dearest: Your words are more to me than a lifetime of spring mornings, because they have only you as their source. I accept this book of verse only as a supplement.*

She considered the closet full of clothes—hadn't it been at least two years since the accident? Thoughts of the beautiful brown-eyed Tess, a stranger in most ways, familiar in a few, ignited in Maria a real sense of the pain Dan kept hidden under his deadpan humor, his relaxed shit-kicker affect. She guessed that Dan had not yet made the transition to life without Tess.

Dan had left his camera on the coffee table. It was a late

model Nikon and she knew how to use it. Again a sixth sense told her she should not have the documents in only one location. She pulled both the photo and the documents from her purse and placed them on the coffee table. Picking up the camera, she turned it on, then turned on the flash and used the auto focus and electronic light meter with flash function to take a series of quick pictures. She'd tell Dan when he came back.

After putting the pictures once again securely in her purse, she went back to the photo albums. Not certain what she was looking for, she kept flipping pictures until she found Dan in bathing trunks, carrying a younger Nate on his back. A heavy-muscled hunk, Dan was very well proportioned, broad-shouldered, with a near washboard stomach and muscle tone everywhere. Not quite that trim now, but almost.

"What are you looking at?"

Maria closed the album and turned around, not sure what to say. Next to Dan stood a pajama-clad boy who looked about nine.

"Well, *you're* a handsome guy, Nate," she said. She saw Dan's bone structure etched in the boy's lean face. "I'm afraid I was spying—looking at pictures of you and your father."

"And my mother?"

"Yes. And your mother. She's beautiful."

"Nate, this is Ms. Fischer. Ms. Fischer, this is my very inquisitive son."

Nathaniel's freckled cheeks broke into a smile. "Hi," he offered.

Attentive brown eyes looked up at her from under a reddish-brown mop of hair that sported a slightly unruly cowlick. She noticed Dan subtly attempting to smooth it.

"Ms. Fischer will be staying with us tonight."

"Well, we haven't discussed—" She thought better of

bothering with an argument. If she felt the need, she would simply ask for a ride. The man was a force.

The phone rang. Pepacita glanced knowingly at Dan. "She doesn't call this late," Dan said.

"Of course she does," Pepacita replied, picking up. "He's right here," she said warmly—with none of the bite of a moment before.

"Well, what grade are you in, Nate?" Maria asked, curious about the call but not wanting the boy to feel left out.

"Can I tell you in a minute?" Nate said. "My dad's really getting good at this."

"It's OK, sis. It's no trouble," Dan was saying. "Now look at the light for me." A pause. "OK and it's red, right?" A pause. "So stay right there in your bedroom. Nobody can get in that house if the light is red." A longer pause.

"I understand. It's a windy night. Have you got the cassette in?" A pause.

"Turn it on." A pause. "Now, you know I can be there in four minutes on my motorcycle. Four minutes!" A pause. "At eighty miles an hour I can." A pause. "I'm just kidding, sis." A pause. "OK, I'm sorry for exaggerating. Six minutes tops.

"Are you doing the tape now? Let's hear the breathing. Come on." A pause.

"I'm calling you back in thirty minutes to see how you're doing." A pause. "OK." A pause. "No, it's no problem. I'm up anyway." Dan hung up and looked at Maria.

"It's my sister, Katie. She has panic attacks. Having kind of a bad week."

"Every week's a bad week," Nate said.

Dan smiled and ruffled the boy's hair.

"It's the middle of the night, *muchacha y muchachos*," Pepacita said. Maria could feel that Pepacita wanted her to stay.

"You're right. Nate, my man, what say I go tell you the story about the time I scared off a grizzly bear?"

"Really?" Nate said. Maria supposed it was a story that never got old for Nate.

Dan chuckled. "Really."

"Ms. Fischer could take a shower and change clothes and then we'll have a midnight dinner."

"That sounds great," Maria said.

The shower was luxurious. A large head poured water down into a spacious Jacuzzi tub set within an ornate three-walled tile enclosure. It had a striking floral shower curtain with rose and blue. In seconds she felt drowsy and lost track of time as the water relaxed her. Leaning forward, she let the liquid heat roll down the back of her neck. Then for some reason she came to with a start and looked to the side. She was almost certain she had seen the bathroom door closing. But it was locked. Perhaps it was Pepacita. *Couldn't have been Dan.* But she thought she saw a hand. And it didn't seem like it was Pepacita's. After trying to reconstruct the fleeting memory, she realized that she was so tired she could be imagining things.

Although she sensed he would not spy on her, and tried to convince herself it couldn't have been Dan, it still unnerved her. Then she decided he might have forgotten something. He was such an independent type maybe he would do something uncouth like grab something out of the bathroom on impulse. Then she thought about it and remembered him putting his arm around her when the car was dangling. She remembered the firm security of it. If he did open the door, he meant her no harm and no disrespect. If it actually happened and it was him, he had a reason. But what would justify that?

Too tired to make an issue of it, or to figure it out, she went back to her reverie, content that if anyone was present they were gone now. When she was out and dried, Pepacita passed her everything she needed, including a pair of jeans and a blouse that fit perfectly. Even the bra was her size. She made her way from the bathroom back to the kitchen, where she saw Pepacita setting the chicken piccata on plates and neatly arranging the vegetables.

"I'll be right back." Once again Pepacita disappeared down the hallway.

Nate came wandering in. Maria walked to the table for one more bite of smoked salmon, when there was a noise at the back door. In an instant the house became pitch black. Then came a crash so forceful she thought it an explosion; black turned to bright whiteness, a giant sheet of flame burned into her face, leaving sparkles of light dancing in front of her eyes. As she fell to the floor, it felt as though someone had violently clapped their hands over her ears. Her body hit the oak flooring and rolled. There was no pain. She tried to remember where Nate was.

"Call an ambulance." She heard a faraway voice, and as soon as she heard it, her head exploded in a throbbing ache. "Call an ambulance."

She shook herself, struggling to regain her senses, trying to see something other than sparklers. She remembered standing in the family room. Now she was lying flat on the floor. Sounds seemed to travel down a long tunnel. Trying to touch the fingers of her right hand to those of her left, she felt—if she could make the contact—as though she would be able to put together her memory of standing in the room and the current certainty that she was now on the floor. Nothing connected.

She heard herself say aloud: "Where's Nate?"

"He's right here. He was farther back. He's shook up, but I think he'll be OK. That's more than I can say for the bastards who did this."

She saw a strange oblong head looking down at her. It was very fuzzy and indistinct and there were still myriad points of light in front of her eyes.

"My head hurts."

"I know." Dan's hand smoothed her brow. Clasping his hand in hers felt good.

His face began to come into focus. Then Nate's. Dan had his arm around him and was holding him to his chest. Nate was looking a little bewildered, but then his dad gently shook him and he smiled.

"Those guys must have thought it was the Fourth of July, Nate."

"What blew up?" Nate said.

"On TV they call them stun grenades. And I'd say Ms. Fischer here was certainly stunned."

"My chest hurts—my purse."

"It's on the floor over there."

"Is the photo there? The papers?"

"Could you hand it to me?" Dan said to a frantic Pepacita, who was studying Nate.

"Are they there?" Maria asked anxiously.

"I'm scared," Nate said. She could see Dan still holding him close.

Dan shuffled through the purse with his free hand. "Gone," he said. "They wanted them so bad they came right in after them."

Finally Maria managed, with Dan's help, to sit up.

"This is a home, for God's sake," Dan said.

"Well, they didn't get what they wanted."

"What?" Dan said.

"I'll tell you later," she said. "I can see both your faces now. What a relief."

"Tell me now."

"OK, OK. I took pictures of the pages with your camera."

"Brilliant. The ambulance will be here in a minute."

"Call it off unless Nate needs it. I'm not really hurt, just disoriented."

"You sure?"

"I'm sure."

"Nate, how are you doin'?"

"Fine, Dad," the boy said, obviously trying to be brave.

"We're going to the emergency room. If nothing is wrong, then they'll release you," Dan said.

"What if the police start asking questions?"

"You may be right about that." He paused. "I suppose we could take you in the car. We shouldn't say anything to the authorities if we can help it until we talk to the clients."

"All they did was steal back what we took from them."

"This was different and you know it."

"Our theft's different from theirs?"

"We aren't like them." Dan hugged Nate to his side. "Not a bit."

Pepacita canceled the ambulance. Dan, Maria, Pepacita, and Nate drove to the emergency room with the camera in hand, and by the time they arrived, Maria claimed she felt "almost normal." Nate, although frightened, was not physically injured. Not wanting to argue any more, Dan acceded and they pulled away from the emergency-room door.

"Let's pack some stuff and go to the Palmer Inn. The door is broken; furniture has burn marks; one window is broken," Dan said as they drove.

"You know there's that logging conference in town," Maria said. "There won't be a decent room left. And it's three o'clock in the morning."

When they got back to the house, Pepacita looked dubious and sighed. Dan studied Nate.

"I'm OK," Nate said.

"Let's all sleep in the living room, like camping," Maria

said. Dan paused as if it was a bit of a stretch. "It's at the other end of the house. They didn't come in there."

"Yeah," Nate said. "We could even put up the tent."

Dan smiled at Pepacita and took her aside. They talked, but Maria couldn't hear.

Then Dan came back to Maria. "We were just saying, maybe if we closed off this part of the house and all got in the tent, it would seem different enough for Nate."

"I'm not scared anymore, Dad."

"Uh-huh," Dan said. "OK, we'll try the tent. But, Nate, if you can't sleep, we're going to the Palmer Inn." Dan turned to Maria. "My wife had a heavy flannel nightgown she used to wear with stretch pants. What it lacks in looks, I was told it makes up for in comfort."

"That sounds great," Maria said. It took her about two minutes in the bathroom to change.

They moved the couches and chairs in the living room back to the walls, then put the tent in the middle of the room, tying off the lines to the furniture. It was a good-sized cabin-style tent. Dan and Maria blew up four air mattresses.

"I'm too old and fat for this," Pepacita announced after surveying the situation. "I think I'll sleep in bed."

"OK," Dan said.

"Don't let the bedbugs bite," Nate said.

After the three of them were in their already-too-hot sleeping bags, the lights were out, and Maria was almost asleep, she was slightly startled to feel Dan's hand cupped over her ear.

"This is unusual."

"Not as unusual as what's going on out there in the woods," she whispered back.

"What did you see when you were in the tree?"

"I'm worried Nate will hear you," Maria said. "I imagine he's pretty keyed up."

"He's out like a light."

"Let's talk in the morning."

"I'm curious."

"Well, it seems like I saw a big green something snaking through the forest."

"A what?"

"I just remember green and round and, like, translucent. Like a giant garden hose winding through the trees."

"You're not going to tell me it looked alive, are you?"

"I don't know what I saw, except it was green. It seemed a block or two long."

"They're probably hiding the Loch Ness monster."

She yawned and turned over.

"Hey, did you hear that?" Nate said in a suddenly alert voice.

"It's the wind in the trees. They creak," Dan said.

"Pretty scary night tonight," Nate said.

"Yeah."

"Are you gonna go out on dates with Ms. Fischer?"

"No, I'm not."

There was silence for a while.

"I won't rub it in," she whispered.

"Thanks," Dan said.

10

"I hate to lose five hundred thousand." Jeb Otran sat with one arm braced straight against the library table. They were in the conference room at the Hutchin firm with Patty McCafferty on the speaker phone. "As for the compound in the woods, that's really the business of those who own it—unless they have our money. I just wonder if what you saw was on Amada or Metco."

"We couldn't tell, although I believe it was at least *near* Amada land, because we were in the upper end of the forest," Maria said. She sat with Dan on one side of the table, Jeb and Hutchin on the other.

"If you tell the police about this locked room and this threatening conversation or whatever it was, I would suppose you'll have to tell them about the money," Jeb said.

"Oh, this is great," Patty McCafferty groaned over the speaker box.

"We could ask the sheriff not to publicize it. After all, there's no particular reason they should. We don't have to officially report the theft."

"So we just ignore the fact that we were assaulted and robbed with a deadly weapon? That we were shot at? That someone tried to kill us?"

"Maria, you're right. It's tough to remain silent," Patty said. "And perhaps even dangerous. On the other hand, at the moment it seems you're safe. We also need to worry about what they're really doing out there. If they *are* doing something illegal, it could be dangerous."

"If they broke in and stole the photos, they damn well know you've figured out they're up to something weird," said Hutchin. "They'll have some explanation for all that stuff if the police go out there."

"Of course," Jeb said, and looked at Dan, "they may have come and taken those pictures for purely business reasons. You may have engaged in an act of industrial espionage without realizing it."

"You mean we stole their property," Maria said.

"One wonders if we're dealing in both cases with the

same people. And that is perhaps the best reason for reporting it. The violence, I mean," Otran said. "What's going on in the woods may be somebody's legitimate business. It's private property. But, of course, breaking into your house, if it was them, makes it illegitimate."

"But, Jeb, you've got to be concerned about what's going on out there . . . ," Patty began.

"Curious is a better word. Like I said, it's private property."

"For the forty years we've known each other, you've been obsessed with a person's right to screw up the world on his own land."

"Relax," Otran said, "I didn't say we wouldn't find out. I was about to say I didn't want our lawyer or, for that matter, your lawyer out breaking the law anymore—subject to the proviso that we need to get the money back legally."

"Well, it seems to me—"

"Patty, if you'll just let me finish . . ."

Dan stared at Maria, who was also trying to conceal her shock. This strange conversation indicated a level of familiarity between Jeb Otran and Patty McCafferty that they never would have guessed at.

Now that Otran was telling them to cease and desist in their investigation of the compound in the woods—except as it might pertain to getting the money—Dan decided he would say nothing in front of the others about the photographs in his camera. Still, for personal reasons, Dan felt compelled to tell Otran privately after the meeting. Maria appeared to be staying quiet on the issue as well.

"We are still left with the theft of the money and the shooting. I think it should be reported," Jeb said.

"And I do too," Patty agreed.

"I can claim attorney-client privilege as to the source of the money," Dan said. "I don't think I have to disclose it.

Just that it was taken, that we gave chase, that we were shot at in our car.''

"What about the break-in at your home?"

"I wouldn't bring it up. After all, we took something from them and we don't know what it means," Maria said.

"Leave it out," Dan said.

"That's it, then," Hutchin agreed. "We won't do a thing, Jeb, except for Dan and Maria telling their story about the theft of the money, the chase, and getting shot off the road."

"I'll make a call to Amada and Metco," Jeb said.

"Once again, I'm sorry about this delivery and the way it turned out," Hutchin said.

"I can't imagine how anybody found out about the brief-case," Dan said.

"Well, I can't, either," Jeb said. "We'll be talking. And, Patty, try not to sue me this month, will you?"

"I haven't sued you in a year, and that was only because you got your back up and wouldn't listen to reason."

"You mean I wouldn't bow to your threats."

"Have a nice day, Jeb."

"You too."

Jeb rose and Hutchin followed, leaving Maria and Dan alone in the library.

"We neglected to mention the photos," she said.

"Uh-huh. I noticed."

"What do you think we should do?"

"Well, I have my own score to settle with these people. They invaded my home. That's personal. Now if you're in this thing, I think we should take the photos to a university and find out what some of the science means. Even if it's just routine chemistry, we might discover what sort of routine chemistry they're into."

"Maybe we should each take a few days off to figure this out. I'm checking into the Palmer Inn," Maria said.

"So formal."

"What's that mean?"

"It means for casual comfort, good home-cooked meals, you should stay at my place."

"You're sweet. But I think we need some separation between good and industry here."

"Listen, men and women have lived in the same house and fought for millennia."

Not surprisingly, she had no response for that.

Dan and Maria waited at the Wintoon County Sheriff's Office for Sheriff Robert McNiel to receive their complaint personally.

A big man with a round pleasant face, a large, droopy mustache, khaki trousers and western riding boots, the sheriff looked the part.

"I understand you want to report a theft."

"I do," Maria said. "Five hundred thousand in cash."

"What were you doing with that kind of money?"

"Accepting it for my clients."

"OK, let's start from the beginning. Aren't you the lawyer for the environmental movement?"

"One of them."

"You don't mind if we tape-record your statement."

"Not at all."

"Give me your full legal name." And so the sheriff began a litany of questions until finally Maria had told the entire story of the theft, commencing with her exit from the tavern. In lawyerly fashion she provided all the details except those she and Dan had agreed not to disclose.

When she finished, the sheriff began asking her follow-up questions. "So you were at the Amada compound because you thought you were chasing the money because of the electronic signal and the helicopter over the trees.''

"That's right."

"And somebody is giving the environmental movement five hundred thousand in cash?" The sheriff looked pointedly at Dan.

"I didn't say that. I didn't say who was to receive the money. You asked me if I was a lawyer for the environmental movement, and I said I was," Maria replied. "It was a legal transfer of money, but we are bound by the attorney-client privilege not to disclose the parties to the transfer."

"A crime was committed here. So we need to know the facts—''

"Sheriff, I think you'll find that in most of the precedent-setting attorney-client–privilege cases a crime had been committed," Dan cut in. "Respectfully, you don't need to know any more."

"I see, we're going to get this attorney-client–privilege mumbo jumbo all the way through this."

"There is a little of that," Maria said.

"Are you suggesting that Amada took the money?" the sheriff asked.

"We just don't know," Dan said. "But somebody took the money and tried to kill us when we followed."

"We could look into this a lot better if we knew more facts. Like the facts surrounding the money."

"We can't disclose more."

"You know it's pretty damn strange you two even being together in the same room."

"Well, that's just an anomaly that will take some getting used to."

"For all of us," Maria added.

"Will you keep us updated on your progress?" Dan asked.

"Yes, we will."

When they rose to leave, the sheriff added, "As much as it pisses me off, I understand about the attorney-client privilege. What I don't understand is why your clients are more interested in their secrets than in bringing armed robbers to justice."

"Maybe there isn't a whole lot more to tell, and knowing it wouldn't help you that much," Dan suggested.

"It's our job to be the judge of that."

When they left the building Dan noticed a dark-haired man, probably in his early thirties, with a slicked-back ponytail. He was slender but strong-looking except in the face, which although symmetrical and handsome seemed passive—as evidenced by a lack of character lines. Neither smiles nor frowns had molded his visage. Approaching Maria, he pointedly ignored Dan. When the man went to kiss her, Dan noticed a slight awkwardness between them and she offered him a cheek.

"Dan, I'd like you to meet Ross," Maria said.

"It's a pleasure," Dan said, trying to smile.

"I'll take you back to the hotel." Ross cut off all other conversation.

Maria hesitated.

"Don't worry about the clothes," Dan said. "You can bring them on your next visit."

"I'll mail them." Maria took Ross's arm.

As Dan watched them leave, the argument that seemed just beneath the surface was obviously taking place between them.

Corey's home had two workrooms, one off the garage, the other off her bedroom. Certain jobs were undertaken only in the room by the garage. When feasible, she liked to work in the room off her bedroom because it was conducive to middle-of-the-night naps during intense and lengthy projects.

On this occasion she was working in the more rugged of the two work spaces, the one by the garage. A functional set of double sinks was on one wall. To either side of the sinks stood a hardwood bench that continued around to the back wall. In the middle of the room was a simple but strong granite-topped worktable on which sat her telephone and, at the moment, her propped feet. The walls were adorned with wilderness photos that featured rock outcroppings and old-growth redwood. A single window afforded a view of the forest behind her house.

"We could make it worth your while if you could recover the film," the caller said.

"How in the hell could I do that if they've dropped it off at a photo shop?" Corey twirled the phone cord around her finger and stared at the terrarium on the table in front of her. She listened to the now-familiar but unknown voice that never deviated from the calm, persuasive tones that had become all at once so irritating and attractive.

"You've always been resourceful in the past."

"I'm good at monkey-wrenching. My first theft didn't go so well. Stealing is a different trade."

Inside the terrarium a white laboratory mouse moved in some straw. The terrarium had been fitted with a flat plastic lid that she put briefly in place and then removed. With the lid, the glass enclosure was nearly airtight.

"This would be worth a lot of money to us."

"So what's on this film?"

"We don't know. But we're worried there might be a picture of the car."

"They were in her rental car. He didn't carry any camera that I saw."

Next to her chair was a five-gallon steel container with

a top that had a four-way-locking mechanism. Four grab hooks fit under the lip of the can and each was attached to a snap-over metal finger that could be lifted and pushed to the center of the top of the can to hold the lid tight. When all four of the snaps were locked down, the lid was airtight and secure. On the outside of the can was a white paper label that went the full height of the can. It said SODIUM CYANIDE with skull and crossbones and the words TOXIC and POISON written around the top and bottom of the can.

"Better to be safe than sorry. We noticed that first thing this morning Dan Young went off to a photo place and delivered some film. We don't think it was a coincidence."

"So you don't even know for sure that they took a picture of anything to do with the theft of their money. We might have pictures of some Little League game."

"True. But we can't take that chance."

"How much if I get you the negatives and the photos?"

"Twenty thousand."

On the corner of her table sat a bottle of sulfuric acid. She picked it up, removed the lid, and half-filled a tiny metal cup a little larger than a thimble.

"My, my, you are lustin' after those pictures. And why me? Why all that money?"

"We've got nobody else."

Next she undid each of the four snaps on the five-gallon drum and donned rubber gloves.

"Cut the crap. If I get caught, you can deny you know me, and I've got a built-in motive. I'm the crazy-ass enviro who already stole their money. The cops would think I was worried they had pictures of me or the car or my sidekick."

"We don't think you'll get caught."

"What if I don't believe you're telling me everything?"

"There's still the twenty thousand. Believe that."

"How do I know you'll pay?"

"You know we value the relationship."

The five-gallon can was lined with heavy plastic and inside it was a white powder. Using a small scooper that would hold about a quarter teaspoon, she scooped up the powder.

"I'll think about it."

"Just get us the film. We don't care what's on it. You'll get the twenty grand."

"Call me back in three hours."

Corey hung up, knowing they were holding out on her. But stealing those pictures *would* give her the chance to find out what was on them. That alone might make it worth it. She had to find out who owned the calm, somewhat detached voice on the phone. Maybe something in the pictures would give her a clue. They sure wanted them badly enough.

She set the scoop of powder on her desk and carefully closed the canister and shoved it in the corner. In a few minutes she would take it back to the outbuilding where she stored it. She was saving it for something big, but at the moment she wanted to reassure herself of its potency.

On the table was a small metal ball. It was comprised of two half spheres the bottom of which was solid and the top of which was filled with little holes. It was used to make tea.

She opened the window of her workroom and placed a large fan in it, turned it on, and created an air current flowing to the out-of-doors. Next she put food pellets in a feeder at one end of the terrarium. Immediately the mouse began eating. Placing the white powder in the solid portion of the ball, she set it at the end of the terrarium opposite the feeder. After opening the ball, she placed a small cupped piece of plastic over the white powder, then placed several drops of sulfuric acid on the plastic. Quickly she placed the plastic lid on the terrarium and stepped back to the doorway of the workroom. It took only seconds for the acid to eat through the plastic and hit the white powder.

Gases, like smoke from a Marlboro, drifted into the terrarium. Within seconds the mouse was stone dead. She stepped out, closed the door to the room, and stuffed a towel under the door. She would wait twenty-four hours for the room to clear of any residual gases.

She had gotten the stuff two years earlier at a metal-plating plant where one of her cousins worked. Although she had not been exactly certain what she was looking at when she first saw the five-gallon canisters, she had a fairly good idea. A few minutes' research at the library told her that by mixing the stuff with ordinary sulfuric acid she could create hydrogen cyanide.

Entering her den, she stopped to study a drawing on the wall. It was a set of plans to the courthouse given to her by a disgruntled, former maintenance man. He had been fired from his job because he had been working on the roof with some tar and caused an unfortunate accident. It seemed that there was a rectangular-shaped cavern in the roof about ten feet deep. On the wall of this chamber, there were louvers that allowed air to enter a mechanical room inside the building. It was the air intake for one of the air conditioners and heating units and it fed the courtrooms on the west side of the building.

Working down in this ventilator well, he was spreading hot tar and didn't think to close off the air intakes. People in the courtroom began instantly choking on the stink. One angry judge demanded somebody's job. Corey had sympathized with the man and said she would consider hiring him a lawyer if he would get drawings that depicted what had taken place. She never got the lawyer hired but did keep the drawings.

Corey looked out the window of her den. Through a

break in the overcast, a shaft of sunlight beamed through the shadows. Looking down at her glass-topped desk, she saw that both the sun and the clouds were reflected there, in an interplay of gray and gold. She sat and closed her eyes.

The sea, the sun, the dolphins, appear, but this time the sound of waves crashing on rocks in a steady, rolling rhythm. She sits in her forest, alongside the rocks. Soon the rhythm becomes insistent, taking over her body. And she becomes the rhythm, relaxing, reveling in it. Like sex. Leaving her forest, she swims. Her hands pulling against the glass-smooth surface, the rhythmic sound of her breath, the bracing smell of salt in the air, the silken sensation of the water's passage under her outstretched arms.

When she woke, she felt suddenly angry, as though she had been in a fight. Sitting back in the oak chair, the straightness of it feeling good against her twisted back, she focused her anger and sorted out her plan. Photographs. The pharmacy on Fourteenth in Palmer would receive a visit.

Getting the film was almost effortless. No one really expected someone to break into the film section of the pharmacy. It was only the narcotics they kept locked up in a safe inside a heavy metal cage. A simple electrical fire that she had ignited in just under five minutes would further confuse the issue. She realized she was getting good at this stuff and mostly because she was calm and just thought her way through it.

On her way home she decided to stop at the courthouse. The irony did not escape her. Much of the epic struggle between mainline environmental groups and the timber industry over the redwoods took place at the county courthouse in Palmer. Often these court battles were attended by twenty or so environmental activists and one industry lawyer.

On occasion, however, the troops for both sides turned out in mass. It was this eventuality that Corey had in mind.

She entered the building by the front door and headed for a narrow staircase next to the main elevators. Running up the concrete stairs for five flights felt like exercise in a mausoleum. The stairwell was encased in rectangular concrete and painted light cocoa in a column that rose to the fifth floor.

On the fifth floor were various, smaller county offices, like the office of the public guardian, and a small section of the county assessors group. There the main stairwell ended at the door to the fifth-floor main hallway. Doubling back from that door, there was a narrow hallway leading to another door. This door had a small 8" x 8" window and opened onto more stairs that went up to the roof.

The stairway to the roof was not a fire exit and was kept locked at all times, but the window in the door could be easily broken with a heavy metal object. There was no alarm.

When she opened the door to the fifth-floor hallway, she observed only one man in the hall, dressed in a suit, looking lost and with a leather satchel under his arm. Entering the main fifth-floor hall, she walked north and then westerly to the equipment rooms that bordered the west wall. Everything appeared as the roofer had described. But she wasn't taking any chances.

Returning to the door to the roof, she slammed the small window with a flying kick. It was well-placed and easily broke out the window. She reached through and opened the door, then went up on the roof. It took only seconds to find the sunken rectangular hole that was the air intake for the west-side courtrooms.

Her confidence was building. She would take a chance that nothing major had changed in the three years since her informant had worked here.

On her way back through the door to the roof, she encountered a man in overalls carrying a tool box.

"Were you up on the roof?" he asked.

"Just for a smoke. I'm sorry, the window was broken out and I just went on up." She favored him with a rare smile. "I hope I didn't do anything wrong."

11

These emergency meetings in the outback of northern California were becoming altogether too frequent. Only Herschel White lived in this godforsaken corner of California all year round, the land of fog, drizzle, and redwoods. Kenji's inner circle sat around the conference table while he led the meeting.

"We think we're close to making the stuff virtually inert," said Herschel.

"What does virtually mean? Will it be a hazardous material?"

"Piss is a hazardous material, but it's easy to dispose of."

"Don't give me gibberish. This substance makes bats crazy and will kill people."

"True enough."

"So give me a straight answer. Can we make the effluent safe enough to satisfy the government when we go public with this process?"

"With all due respect, that's partly a political question. If they find out what happened out here, it could be real tough. Maybe impossible. There'll be public outrage." Herschel gave an inappropriate chuckle. "Probably a major motion picture."

"But if they don't find out. And if we find a way to make it harmless—"

"Then you and the company will be heroes. Environmentally and otherwise."

"You're sure your person got all the pictures?" Kenji looked into the calm blue eyes of Hans Groiter.

"She got the pictures at the photo shop."

"So what are you saying?"

"We'll have to listen. See if they have a duplicate set. I doubt it. But it's possible."

"How long till they discover the eavesdropping?"

"No way to know. They haven't talked about the possibility yet."

"Take the mike out of the bushes," Kenji said. "It's too easy to find."

"We've done that. We have the phone bug and the spike mike under the couch."

Kenji nodded, and turned to Herschel White. "When am I going to have a solution? When can I announce the process?"

"We're going as fast as we can. We can't tell the brightest guys about the spill or the problems with the effluent. It's touchy. It's—"

Kenji held up his hand as if weary of the explanations.

Herschel continued anyway. "I think within two months we should have it."

"We may not have that long with this pair of lawyers all stirred up."

"If they still have copies of those pictures they have some tangential evidence of our discovery and indirectly of our little problem," the lawyer said. "And proof of what we're really doing if they're smart enough to figure it out."

"They aren't going to unravel anything," Groiter said. "It's an obscure leap from what they've got to understanding our situation. And besides, they probably don't have any pictures anyway."

"A little thread, if nurtured and pulled, can make a fatal hole in a pair of trousers," Kenji said. "These people, these lawyers, can be determined and therefore deadly. Life can turn into a typhoon when we depart from the ways of tranquillity. These two need to learn that."

They all understood Kenji Yamada.

Slowly Kenji poured himself the steaming hot sake. It had only required a second five-minute telephone call to the vice president of the railroad for Kim Lee to decide that the railroad would not sell its remaining rights in the property. Worse, Kim wanted to tell Kenji's father-in-law the whole story, including the part about the chemical spill and the bats. Only brute intimidation had kept him quiet to date. When it came down to it, Kim would save his own hide and sacrifice Kenji.

This was the chance of ten lifetimes and Kim had given up without coming up with even one creative plan. Success could advance the Asaka holdings beyond anything that any of them had ever dreamed about. By comparison, the computer giants of America would be midgets.

Kenji wondered about himself—how far he would go to attain his goal. He was a realist, dealing honestly at least with himself. So far, he had stolen and taken two lives. Kim Lee was now nothing but a liability. Kenji had watched the nervous tremor as Kim had wiped his brow. He could feel the man's weakness. Kenji felt as if he were being suffocated by the ineptitude of those around him. And all on the brink of greatness.

In the larger context of the Kuru holding company, Kenji's was a relatively minor post. On a fiscal basis Amada accounted for less than 8 percent of the family's net worth. Still, with the jolting discoveries of the past two years, it seemed possible at last that on his father-in-law's death Kenji might very well take over the parent company. If his ideas proved successful.

As the magnitude of the discovery became apparent, his ambition also grew. Slipping into violence would have seemed unthinkable even five years ago. Ambition had slowly seduced him and now had him in a stranglehold.

If he had not fallen under the spell of Catherine Swanson, his life would have been simpler. Fortunately, Groiter executed a perfect setup with the photographer. A few of the photographer's hairs and some of his semen was all it took. Groiter had been very clever about extracting the man's semen. And about removing from Catherine all traces of Kenji.

Now that he had killed twice, taking a third life (or fourth and fifth) to protect his plan didn't really matter. Getting rid of Kim had side benefits. It was important that someone in the Amada fold suffer violence at the hands of extremists. That would tend to eliminate Amada as a suspect.

Dealing with the fear was the hardest part. All great leaders had to overcome it or it ate them alive. Fear of the derision and ridicule of others was the worst. But he had already learned to live without them. Learned that he didn't need to be in the "in group." For just a moment with Catherine Swanson, he had forgotten that lesson. Once he remembered it, he had her anyway. And when he had her, it was without the anxiety—it was the way a man should have a woman.

He had felt like a man, not some street scum who had landed in the palace between her thighs.

He stabbed a preprogrammed dialing button. Groiter answered immediately.

"I've been listening to tapes. They still have a set of pictures."

Kenji's breath hissed like steam from a ruptured boiler.

"Anything else?"

"They've gone to the library. Found articles on the disappearance of Catherine Swanson."

"Why would they do that?"

"Well, it happened just a month ago, and violence is rare around here, so they're looking for any connection to the person who took their money. Dan Young's got a bulletin board at home, and he's plastering it with stuff just like a good little detective. They're making a list of everybody who lives in the mountains. It's a pretty good profile. I think it's only a matter of time before they add Schneider to their list."

"We should never have let them in. Never. Make sure you let me know the minute they are on to something that matters."

"I'll let you know a minute before."

"I called about another issue."

"Oh?"

"I will be deeply moved by the death of our associate Kim Lee at the hands of extremist elements."

There was a long silence, and then an exhale of breath from Groiter. "Are you sure?"

"He's been talking to Satoru about things that could profoundly affect your retirement."

"Corey is crazy, but it'll take some doing to get her to pull this off."

"I didn't say that Schneider actually had to pull the trigger.'' But something told Kenji that Groiter would protect himself and the best way to do that was to find someone else with an obvious motive. ''I'm confident you'll think of something. I think it's time you got another bonus.''

There was a steady rhythm like a drumbeat that echoed through his body, deep breaths that sounded like muted snorts, the leather, and the sweat smell. His body floated over the horse, its gallop impeccably regular as he raised the six-foot wooden bow. The target stood to his right at ninety degrees.

The contest took place on a three-foot-wide dirt track about one hundred yards long with three targets equidistant along the run. As the arrow slid from his fingers, he saw the exact spot on the bull's-eye where the arrow would strike. And it did.

The sport was called Yabusame and was conceived by a ninth-century warlord whose family name was Ogasawara. Yoshinari's horse was a big bay girded with the armor of the samurai, as was Yoshinari's own body. Twenty years previous he had been the Yabusame grand national champion of all Japan. As a senior he had held that title in the over-sixty class, five times running. Only a few of the younger men could best him, and only due to their superior physical endurance. They could retain the absolute stillness of mind and body required for perfection over many attempts. Today the crowd bowed and displayed appropriate awe, making him smile inwardly at his vanities.

Finished for the day, he rode back to his stables. As often as possible he held tournaments at his castle, for those were the only contests that he attended. He wanted to sit by the koi-pond bridge and sip his wife's tea. It seemed that he always returned there when troubled about his son-in-law.

Since Kenji regularly excluded Satoru from meetings and activities that would give him the opportunity to report back, it was necessary for Satoru to rely upon subterfuge, a practice most noxious to Yoshinari. And it had evolved into nonsense.

Shohei had made a report more complete than Satoru's on the bizarre seduction plot. According to Shohei, and consistent with the obvious, Satoru's real motive was to depose Kenji, to take over, and to use Catherine Swanson's political influence with her husband to benefit Amada.

Purportedly, the woman had presented Kenji with an opportunity to be unfaithful. There was little doubt in Yoshinari's mind that if one paved the path to an extraordinary woman's bed with incense and warmed earth, Kenji would oblige his nose the fragrance and his feet the warmth. It was no mystery that Kenji loved his manhood at least as much as his nose and feet.

Shohei was certain that Kenji had taken the bait and most probably killed Catherine Swanson. According to Shohei, Micha knew of Satoru's attempt but believed Kenji had not succumbed to temptation. Meanwhile, Kenji's optimism regarding his secret project never flagged, and in this one thing Satoru believed Kenji was sincere.

Yoshinari found Shohei on his cell phone.

"I want to know more about the Highlands Laboratory," Yoshinari began. "I think you should go in unannounced. Kenji still mustn't know that you exist. As it is, he resents Satoru."

"I will break in?"

"Only to the extent you can do so without detection. I do not know what you are looking for, except to say I want to know about anything that doesn't appear to be Taxol research."

"Of course, I am not a chemist."

"I know. Do the best you can." Yoshinari disconnected.

Kenji kept Satoru from the laboratory at all costs, allowing him to visit the facility only twice. On both those occasions it had seemed evident to Satoru that they were experiencing temporary workforce reductions, as if everyone but a skeleton crew had gone on holiday in honor of his visit. Although they were supposed to be studying Taxol with pharmaceutical chemists, they were hiring molecular industrial chemists. Furthermore, Satoru was convinced that there were areas of the compound that he was never shown.

Yoshinari waited an appropriate number of hours before calling Shohei again.

"How are you progressing? I have great concern."

"I am building my database."

Yoshinari nodded, smiling. Modern spies must use modern ways. "I am most interested in your technique."

"I am downloading the names of all the people involved and their phone numbers. I am also downloading all phone records of every Amada executive, including Groiter and Kenji. As far as those that they call environmental extremists, it is harder. I am downloading car licenses and grouping names of people together that I know keep common company. I am also gathering all available information about the two lawyers."

"I want you to hire two of the best investigators you can find. Discreet men."

"Yes."

"They are to do nothing but assist you in building your database. Hire men with friends. Men who know the police."

"Yes. They call that being 'connected.' It will be done."

Shohei found the forest intriguing. He had learned some of his art in the Okudake Mountains of Yakushima. There he had learned to become a ghostly whisper in the forest.

By painting himself with ash and pine scent even the animals did not know of his passing. Here the trees were much larger than back home and the undergrowth different. Many of the plants he did not recognize. But the humus scent and the cool quiet were the same.

Quickly he found the fence and avoided the dogs because they neither heard nor smelled him. His nimble body was able to elude everything but the razor wire atop the fence. Cutting the razor wire might set off an alarm.

Tunneling under the fence would not be a problem but for the dogs who might hear the activity. Cutting the chain link with bolt cutters seemed the best option, though it would leave a permanent record of his passing. It took only a couple of minutes. He had cut the first links of the second fence when he heard a low growl. Whirling, he saw two Doberman pinschers coming at him like bullets.

He squared himself toward the dogs, his fingers slipping his tanto from a pocket. He let his mind focus. The dogs' eyes were points of deadly determination. Seeing him calm, ready, they missed a stride measuring him and the distance for their leap. Shohei sensed their uncertainty and let his power grow. He threw the dagger.

He felt the first dog lose its will as the razor-sharp metal buried itself in his chest. He turned and baited the second dog with an outstretched arm. As the dog's body came at him, he dropped to the ground and kicked upward under the animal's throat. There was a loud snap and the dog went down—dead.

Such a nuisance. He was not to be discovered. With some effort he pulled the tanto from the first animal's chest, crawled under the fence, and moved off through the bushes. He had gone about fifty yards when he stopped to listen, to ensure that no one followed. There was something moving in the brush. From the pattern of its movement, he could tell it was a man. Painstakingly he followed. They were moving slowly back toward the compound fence but at a location some distance away.

He followed for six hours. Two of those were spent watching a woman in a tree while she studied the compound. She had found a place of good elevation and a big climbable madrona. It provided a view of a small clearing. When she left, he followed her to a truck that he later learned was registered to a Corey Schneider. That was the word he got from his connected men. In hours they had her address and unlisted phone number. She lived in the mountains.

When he put her phone number into the database, it immediately cross-referenced Hans Groiter's phone records. One short call from Hans Groiter's private line. Why did Groiter initiate a call to a woman who spied on Amada, who lived in the mountains, and who was a fringe-radical environmentalist? Why even once? Shohei viewed the telltale call as a slip—part of a pattern of communication normally undertaken from a phone booth or somewhere else untraceable. In a moment of impatience, perhaps, the call had been made from the office. Such mistakes were the undoing of great mysteries.

Shohei decided he would follow her some more.

12

Dan had just gotten off the phone with the sister of the photographer wanted in the investigation of the rape and murder of Catherine Swanson. It seemed that the photographer had been writing a novel and had it on a laptop. Supposedly, he had fled without his computer, hence without his manuscript. According to his sister, that was unthinkable. It was one of many reasons for her certainty that he was dead and not a fugitive. But she had told it all to the police.

He dialed his own sister.

"Hey, you gonna come over and take Nate and Jonathan to the park? They really wanna fish. But they need an adult."

"I feel tired, so tired."

"Maybe a little apprehensive about going out?"

"A little."

"Take your pills?"

"I just hate taking pills."

"Uh-huh. But remember what the doctor said. To keep the old hard drive on the right track, we need the medicine. Then we can reprogram that brain of yours."

"I know. I know. I'll take my meds and come get the kids."

"Katie, you know it means so much to Nate and to me."

"Of course it means something to you. You're a workaholic, and I'm an enabler. Nate's a fisher-holic. How's Maria doing?"

"I guess fine. She doesn't always tell me."

"I think your boy is falling for her about as fast as his daddy."

"Oh, come on. There is nothing between us. I'm not ready for that and you know it."

"You should be, Dan. You should be. She died two years ago. She wouldn't want this. I'm sane enough to know that even if you don't. Why don't you ask Maria on a date?"

"You think she'd go?"

"Do pigs grunt on Sunday?"

"Well, it's not that easy."

"Is your tongue stuck to the roof of your mouth? What's hard about it?"

"It's like I said, I'm not ready. And we're adversaries."

"Yeah, it's a regular civil war. Sleeping in the same tent must be tough."

Dan found Nate and got him excited about fishing, then played catch until Jonathan showed up. Dan returned to his study and barely felt Katie's good-bye peck on the cheek.

Beside Dan hung every news article about the murder of Catherine Swanson. Since it was bizarre, violent, and had happened on Amada land, he'd thought it was worth investigating.

In front of him a giant bulletin board hid behind pictures and notes. Down the side of one bulletin board, every fact they knew or suspected about the person who took the money: female about 5'10"; lived in the mountains between Palmer and Interstate 5; probably single; lived alone; some police or military training; wore broken-in western riding boots; had connections either to industry or to the environmental movement; drove a black Chevy sedan with a license that included the letters SHR; used a .300-caliber rifle, according to police ballistics; had a partner; was physically fit.

On a second bulletin board was everything they knew about the Amada compound. Dan had his secretary, Lynette, gathering information every moment she wasn't working on a critical legal project.

He had a huge stack of aerial photos and had begun trying to account for each house through the mountains in a swath 50 miles wide and over 120 miles long. Even though he started with the ones nearest the point of last contact, it was nearly impossible. There was Johnson City and other tiny towns along the rivers and hundreds of ranches. But he had a feeling in his gut that the person they were chasing through those mountains lived in them—somewhere.

He had just hung up from the photo shop and was getting ready to settle into his morning cup of coffee before calling Maria Fischer in her Sacramento office. It was his fifth try to the photo shop to make absolutely certain they had found no trace of his pictures in the rubble.

In his hand was a list of persons owning a residence within twenty miles of the point he and Maria had been blasted off the road.

His pen ran down the list, making checks by the names: Corey Schneider, Mary Jenkins Smith, Betty Franklin, Jennifer Mills. Most of the entries had two names, a husband and wife. Some listed only a man. Only a few bore the names of single women. These were the next four of those entries, and they were all names about which he had no information. He would check them.

After a couple of good sips of coffee, he got Maria on the line.

"They still claim the pictures were destroyed in the fire," Dan said. "At least they have a sense of humor."

"I thought it was a one-hour photo place and you were going to wait."

"Nate had his soccer game. Look, I need you to find a female enviro who lives between here and I-5 and who is *really* nuts."

"Why do you think we were attacked by an 'enviro'?"

"Just humor me."

"All right, I'll ask around. You gonna check on crazy loggers' wives?"

"Absolutely."

"I have a confession to make," she said.

Dan sat forward in the chair. "What?"

"I think maybe you opened the bathroom door when I was showering. It's bugging the hell out of me."

"Well then, I have a confession to make as well," Dan said. "I have another camera in my bedroom, and while you were showering, I also took a picture of the bat photo and the documents. They're still in the camera."

"How the hell did you know when you opened the door that I would be in the shower?"

"Small window high in the shower. The top of your head is visible as a shadow from outside."

"You're unbelievable. You picked that little lock and opened the door?"

"Ah." He let out a long breath. "I'm just happy that you're being so good-natured about this."

"We know that Kim Lee, an industry man, is now in control of the environmental movement. He's the one who's passing the money. Stealing five hundred thousand won't stop it. Kim has already hushed it up. He controls the press, you know," the German caller said. "And he's got plenty more money to co-opt your people."

"Why are you telling me this?"

"For the good of the cause."

"How do I know I can believe you?"

"Was I right about the money? Was I right about who would deliver it?"

Corey could feel the manipulation, and yet everything he said rang true.

"Why would killing Kim Lee make any difference? Someone will replace him."

"Fear. They would know someone knows their dirty secrets."

She was still unconvinced. She liked to do things her own

way in her own time. The voice on the line was pushing
her and she didn't like it.

"I'm not trying to tell you what to do. You seem to
manage fine in that department. Just think it over. Oh, and
turn on your TV. The local news, channel three. It starts in
three minutes."

The line went dead. Hanging up on her was a form of
control. One of these days she would make him regret it.

Sweat poured down the young man's chest in little rivulets
and beaded on his face like rain on a wax-slick car. Corey
gently squeezed his testicles, sensing that any moment he
would come despite her attempt to hold him on the edge.
Sitting in a slump against the headboard, his back supported
by pillows, he obviously struggled to find release, to overcome her maddening rhythm that was just fast enough to
keep him excited but not brisk enough to end his torment.

She had been waiting for this for a while, starting even
before she brought home Denny, watching this Mike guy
every day as he painted her house and did the landscaping.
But every time Mike had touched her, she had shrugged and
turned away, teasing him, waiting until she was ready. And
then today she had looked at him while he painted the wood
trim on the patio and said, "We can have sex if you want
to." And now here she was astride him, one foot on the
floor, her knee on the bed, her eyes closed, concentrating
on the very moment she had pulled the trigger in the shower.
Killing Denny still excited her. Her orgasm was long and
slow, unfolding like a distant peal of thunder.

When she finished, Mike reached for her, trying to pull
her to his chest, but she slid quickly from his grasp, picking
up a towel and wiping herself. Then she turned to pull on
her shorts. She had stripped only minimally—just enough

to accomplish her purpose—and when her shorts were on, she was dressed and ready to go.

"You're not particularly cuddly for a woman who just made love." Mike watched her from the bed.

"It was good sex," she replied, otherwise ignoring him.

"You could be a little more friendly about it, that's all. Do you hate all men?"

"I need to work."

He shook his head incredulously. "When can I see you again?"

"When my shades aren't pulled, I suppose you'll see me through the window."

"That's not what I mean."

"But that's what I mean."

After he had dressed in silence, she watched his curly brown head disappear down the stairs. At least he had the fortitude not to whine like Denny. She wouldn't kill this one.

She opened a locked door off her bedroom, accessing another large room. It contained nothing but numerous shelves, a rack from which hung a wide assortment of tools, and a single large table.

On the table was a twenty-four-inch length of six-inch diameter pipe, crammed with nails and TNT. Next to the pipe was a battery, and the innards of a clock lay beside a pile of clocks. Even an untrained observer would have been able to tell that she was building a bomb.

As the time drew near, the adrenaline rush began. A feeling of power surged through her veins. The time of the blast, its lethal force, the manner of its placement— everything was hers to decide. The only problem with the arrangement was that she wasn't certain that Kim Lee's car would still be in the parking lot after dark. On Monday nights his habit was to leave late, between 9:00 and 9:30.

According to a local human-interest article, many Amada executives and supervisors ordered pizza and watched Monday-night football together. On two Thursdays in a row, Kim Lee's car had been in the lot.

Once again the voice on the phone had instructed her to turn on the news. And there was Kim Lee explaining that violence against timber companies only strengthened their resolve. Damaged logging equipment could and would be replaced and more effective safeguards were being implemented. Then Maria Fischer was interviewed, claiming that people who committed violent acts against others could not be considered environmentalists. She and Lee were two different faces of the same liar.

Something about the arrogant confidence of Kim Lee as he read the words had infuriated her. Perhaps because they had been preceded by the prodding voice on the phone telling her that the only way to get the attention of the masses was to move directly against the spokesman for Amada. It would draw the world's attention to the plight of the redwoods unlike anything else. Then the facade of the industrialists' power would crumble, their vulnerability exposed.

The likelihood of press coverage was good. She was certain the media would ask—and answer—the question of why anyone would want to blow up Mr. Kim Lee's car with him inside it. She had included the nails in the pipe bomb for a heightened sense of drama. Nails could have no purpose other than shredding the body. The concussion from the TNT would be enough to kill.

Taking up the six-inch pipe, she felt its heft, much as a hunter might take stock of his rifle. Running her fingers along its rough gray surface, she noted the little pits left by the galvanizing process, then studied the flawless threads she had turned herself in her work shed. There was a clink when she placed the end piece on top, and a quiet sound like glass sliding on metal when she screwed the heavy cap slowly into place, noting with satisfaction that the threads were smooth and unmarred.

"Come on, lover boy," Corey said to herself as she caressed the large bomb.

She walked through the master bedroom, past the hand-carved hope chest, made in China for a wealthy socialite in the 1920s; she passed the sideboard and the paintings in the wide hallway, several of which were worth thousands. Occasionally she supposed her little painter friend imagined that he might steal some of these things when his work was completed. But then he would think about her rock-hard core, the trappings of her military training, the strange, scary looks she gave him sometimes, and decide it just wasn't worth it. She knew that he was afraid.

Back in the bedroom, she placed the bomb in a nylon travel bag. Pipe and timer were packed in a rectangular wood box, about twice the size of a shoe box—because of its weight the muscle rippled on her arm when she handled it. Suddenly she felt an even bigger rush. That box was real. She was actually going to hurt somebody who mattered.

There were three entrances to the Amada office complex that were passable by vehicle. She took none of these. Instead, she entered via a park and wooded area of several hundred acres nestled between a huge rock and gravel quarry on one side and the office buildings on the other. After parking a large Ryder rent-a-truck several miles away, she had opened its rear doors and rolled out a white Ford Mustang, about as plain vanilla as there was—except for the bored-out engine and the custom suspension. She sped through the dusk to the park, where she left the souped-up car. Using a dim red light, she proceeded down a trail through the forest for about a quarter mile, arriving at the edge of a large parking lot.

It was well lit. Metal stanchions rose at least forty feet into the air, before splitting into a T-shaped top. There were very few cars remaining, no more than ten in the area that she could see. A very black 1998 Buick with a gray interior and specialty license plate (KIM LEE AM) was parked within thirty feet of the tree line. Probably he had come to work later than most and therefore had to park in this far corner.

She thought it odd that a big shot like Lee didn't have an assigned space near the front door. When she first observed his customized license plate at a demonstration, she had felt a great sense of superiority. Her adversaries were dumb shits.

Like a lot of company cars, it sported a small black telephone antenna in the back windshield. She could put the bomb under the car, but it wouldn't be absolutely guaranteed to penetrate the floorboards and kill him. On the other hand, she wasn't sure the bomb would fit under the seat. The stock-model Buick she had experimented with had just enough clearance under the seat to hide the bomb.

Staying low, she made her way to the vehicle, crouched down, and removed her field pack. She took out the two rodlike tools—the kind used by emergency vehicles to aid motorists who have locked their keys in their car. Although she had practiced at home, she didn't have a lot of experience and she had never tried a Buick. She inserted the two rods and attempted to grab the lock bar.

As she worked, she began to think about the voice on the phone. Whoever it was had prodded her to do this. While killing Kim Lee was something she might have thought about doing herself, it unnerved her that she had this unknown accomplice. Suddenly she felt like the puppet instead of the puppeteer. Though no one had told her to kill him, the thought had somehow slithered over the phone line even if not embodied in a word.

Did Kim Lee know that this unknown someone wanted him dead? Would he know why? What was the real reason for the money? Would he know anything about it? Slowly a new idea began to emerge. Maybe she shouldn't kill Kim Lee right away. Maybe she should take him home and toy with him.

Corey Schneider had always been careful to follow her own meticulous plans. Being spontaneous was dangerous, given her vocation. But somehow she couldn't shake the feeling that she was being manipulated for reasons she didn't understand. And she wanted to understand.

The door lock to the Buick clicked open as she pulled gently upward on the internal latching mechanism. She paused and tried to fathom how she might kidnap this man without any preparation. She had a roll of heavy duct tape to hold the bomb under the seat. It would certainly bind him sufficiently. The truck would be very useful. She could hide the Mustang and Mr. Lee as well. Without further equivocation she determined she would do it. Quickly she put the bomb back in her pack and retreated to the forest.

The forest edge was so quiet that a ringing in her ears made the silence uncomfortable. Winter brought with it cold dank air, along with a moisture-laden forest that seldom enjoyed the sun's warmth even on its uppermost parts. A pocket of black shadow created by the light of the halogen bulbs of the parking lot seemed to deepen the bone-chilling cold. Occasionally she heard the rushing air from a passing car in the distance. The access road to the office complex was a quarter mile or more from the two-lane highway that served it. Most workers had gone home two hours ago. Only the management football fans remained.

She could feel her heart beat as a slight pulse in her

stiffening neck. Her mind sorted through her rapidly forming plan. Considering that she might even build a cage in the basement for her resident corporate asshole, she contemplated whom she might hire to construct it and how she could explain it to him.

A beam from a spotlight mounted on a security vehicle swept across the trees on the far side of the lot. Cruising around the edge of the parking area, the patrol would be one more impediment to a kidnap. If the security people were around when Lee exited the building, she would be forced to abandon her plan.

For this new scheme to work, Lee had to disappear. When she was through with him, his body could be discovered in a manner that would maximize publicity for the cause.

She considered what she might do with the bomb. It would make a great gift for Dan Young or that the bitch Maria Fischer. Since Young and Fischer were becoming such buddies, maybe it would suffice for both of them.

As the patrol car swept past, she noticed a figure coming down the lit glassed-in stairs in an outside wall of the Amada office complex. It looked like Lee. He was alone; apparently he was leaving early. The patrol car was moving away now.

Waiting was an ordeal. Every second brought a hope that no one else would come, that the patrol car would not double back. One person seeing nothing more than two shadows in the night could spark an inquiry that would lead them to her.

The chair was a 200-year-old solid wooden affair from Spain. A nobleman had been tortured to death in it. She had been kind enough to tell Kim Lee that. There was a creaky friction between ancient dowels and their sockets every time he moved vigorously. Held together with some sort of premodern glue and wooden pegs, it was massive and still stout. Slightly frayed fabric, probably the fourth or fifth recovering, played under Kim's fingers. Some other heavy thinker had also squeezed his fingers on the rich material. Kim did it just to remind himself that he was alive, to allow his mind to sense something in the blackness even if it was only tired fabric against his fingertips.

His chest and back were bathed in sweat; sometimes his hands gripped the chair so tight the last knuckle of each finger ached with the strain. He tried to think—about the chair, the room, the details of each. It worked for a few minutes at a time, but then the terror would return.

He didn't want the fear to grip him so fully that he quit feeling, quit thinking. It was amazing really that his mind could be suffocated, his emotions clamped in a vise, with just a simple description of what she intended to do to him. It was incredible luck the way she managed to discern his deepest fears. Of course he was afraid of dying. He wanted to live. He wanted to live so bad it hurt inside, so bad that the sum of his life had become this moment and his sole mission to survive. But beyond the fear of death, there was a much greater fear—the fear of her kind of death.

When his chest hurt and his sides ached, when he had run out of tears, he made himself think about his wife and young child. Perhaps at this moment he actually felt closer to his wife. Only twenty-five, she had frizzy black hair that touched the tip of his nose when she sat in his lap and giggled—just curled up like a ball, scrunching her toes under her bottom, her big white teeth grinning out from her skinny lips. That's what he called her sometimes to tease—"skinny lips." Then she would rub her nose against his and make little snarling yaps like a mad Chihuahua. And he'd run his hands up her shapely dark arms, and the love would be pouring over him and out of him, and that was the best thing in life.

Then there were his dreams of their baby girl growing up. Now she gurgled and smiled, barely able to walk, knowing her parents only as the source of all comfort and sustenance.

But one day she would know them as people: their favorite books, what they did on Sunday afternoon, which relatives were invited often, Dad's favorite sake, and Mom's favorite perfume. Kim wanted to be there so that she could know him. He wanted to watch her roll her eyes and smile at his jokes. But he had forgotten these things and had started thinking that being a rich and successful corporate lawyer was the best thing in life. Now here he was locked in a black closet, sitting in an antique, history-making chair, waiting for a madwoman to come and do something he tried desperately not to think about.

He had a sense that whoever had taken him was cold to the core, completely unreachable. Now he thought of the watchmen who had lost their ears, and recalled the terror in their eyes. Now he understood.

Then he heard someone climbing stairs—he'd figured out about the stairs, because of the stair-climbing footfall, marked by a feather-light stride on the wood, and the sound of a barely discernible slide on the ball of the foot. Whenever she brought him food or water, or led him to the toilet around the corner from his dark little room, he heard these things.

Just missing Kim's knees, the door creaked open to the inside and there stood his enemy.

"If you'll just let me out of here, I'll do anything."

"Tell me why the timber industry wanted to give five hundred thousand to the environmental movement."

"Most in the industry want the government to buy the Highlands Forest to stop all the protests."

"Who wanted me to steal the money, and why?"

He hesitated. Sweat broke out on his forehead. Kenji Yamada had grown dangerous. Perhaps his boss was as dangerous as his tormentor.

"You really aren't willing to take the steps necessary to escape the fate I've promised you."

In the dull light, before he noticed what she was doing, she took out heavy shears and snipped off the end of his little finger. The torture she had promised was so elaborate and what she had just done so simple, that it was a surprise. It was a moment before he began to scream. For a time he couldn't think; he could only yell. Then suddenly he was sopping wet and terribly cold. She had dumped a bucket of ice water over him.

"I'll tell you! I'll tell you everything. Just don't hurt me anymore. It's a new process. Incredible. But the bats, they're—" He gasped. A heavy weight pressed on his chest and pain shot up into his throat. He tried to take a breath. What could she be doing to him? What could he tell her? The room spun around and then there was nothing.

Lying on his belly on the massage table, Kenji began to relax. The young woman's hands were working on his buttocks and along with a slight erection came a general feeling of well-being. Because it was sexual it was the only part of the massage that compellingly did the job of distraction so that relaxation was possible.

When she got to his lower thighs, his mind departed to the cares of Amada, and his muscles took on a resilience that made deep relaxation impossible.

He picked up the phone, heard his masseuse sigh her discontent, but knew that she would say nothing about his placing a call. She normally tried not to irritate him when he was in these moods. What no one knew was that these moods of late had Dan Young's name written on them.

"How is it going?"

"I was going to call you in an hour," Groiter said. "I'm afraid it's not going so well. Turns out they did have another set of photos. Young sent them to Fischer in Sacramento and she's had them developed. Apparently she's given them to Patty McCafferty who has forwarded them to some university."

The erection was long gone. "Can't you get control of this? They're crawling up our ass."

"We are carefully going through and figuring out what papers were taken. There is a very good chance they didn't get the right stuff."

"I'm supposed to wait around and see if they can eat my heart out? What else are they doing?"

"Young is talking to relatives of the photographer. They say it's impossible that he would have raped the woman and run off."

"Shit. Is there anything we can do?"

"Not really. But this is the same stuff the police were told."

"Is there any way Young could have seen the money drop?"

"No. He saw the copter coming back to the compound after we got the money. He may have made a connection."

"How?"

There was a brief pause in Groiter's quick responses.

"We found a transmitter in the briefcase—"

"Did you say transmitter?"

"We destroyed it on the way back to the compound."

"You didn't tell me this. You didn't tell me."

"Didn't think it was important. He thinks he got a signal before we destroyed it. That's all. It's a hunch."

"A hunch? He's investigating because of it."

"So far, he has nothing. I think it's dangerous to jump to conclusions."

"I want you on this. I want you all over this."

"What did she do to Kim Lee? He's dead, right?"

"She was supposed to bomb the car. But it's in the parking lot and he's vanished into thin air."

"What do you mean supposed to?"

"You know. We've got surveillance. We were pretty sure that's how she was going to do it. But I didn't come right out and discuss the method. It doesn't work that way. She's gotta believe she's working for Mother Earth. We're just sort of fatherly advisers in the cause."

"I don't care about the shrink stuff. I just want to know."

"I'll get the details, but it may take a little time."

"Well, get them. And get control. Push back."

13

The iridescent green of the alarm showed 3:00 A.M., and the sound of the bathroom fan reminded Dan that he had gone to sleep listening to its comforting hum. He got out of bed, went to the bathroom, then to the kitchen, where he got a beer on his way to the den. There was by now an even greater clutter of maps, news clippings, and lists. The bulletin boards were full of scribbles. But nobody, not he, Maria, nor the sheriff, was making any real progress.

Although it was another long shot he had learned that Corey Schneider was indeed a single woman, thirty-six years of age. Interestingly, she was an environmental activist, although in these parts that wasn't unusual. Maria knew who she was and commented that she was a loner, an extremist, and weird. Two years ago she and Maria had gotten into a screaming match over invading a congressman's field office and chaining themselves to furniture, but Maria was certain it wasn't this woman who had robbed them. Robbery and political statements were two different matters.

Dan had been lobbying for Maria to have someone call this woman, perhaps the fund-raiser person at Wildflower who knew Schneider as someone who was wealthy, occasionally gave money, and often wanted information. He was determined to discover whether Schneider had an explanation for her whereabouts on the day of the robbery.

The other clue that he had done nothing about was the helicopter. In northern California timber companies, public utilities, or the government usually owned the jet helicopters. Amada had one, but he had never seen it. Perhaps a look would give him a clue as to whether the copter that emitted the radio signal belonged to Amada. One easy way to see the chopper was to fly over the compound. But there was a much more compelling reason to do that, and that was in preparation for another trip inside. Something was going on behind that fence. Somehow it all related to the missing money, the break-in at his house, and the guys who almost killed them on the road.

Dan wanted to do the flyover next Sunday morning at daybreak. He had a growing certainty that the all-white unmarked helicopter had emitted a radio signal precisely because it contained the missing money. It also followed that if it had been landing it would have come down on the pad near the compound.

If it was the same aircraft, it would further link the compound and Amada with the missing $500,000. That information plus what he might discover on a second trip inside would perhaps help convince Jeb Otran and Hutchin that Amada and their compound were not as benign as they claimed. And it would get him one step closer to the men who had invaded his home. His fingers tapped nervously on his knee. There was no way that he could not tell Maria, especially since she was back in town. Obviously, she would want to come along for the flight. That was a complicating factor because a contract logger by the name of Anderson was harvesting Otran's land immediately adjoining the Highlands. So far, it seemed that his preparations were undiscovered by the enviros. By commencing on a weekend, Anderson hoped to get a jump on any court order the enviros might obtain. If the enviros had known about this cutting in the old growth immediately adjoining the Highlands, they would have sought a court order before the weekend—they still might. So by flying Maria around the area, he was potentially inviting a Monday-morning court appearance for an emergency temporary injunction. It would look really odd if the Wildflower Coalition discovered Anderson's harvesting on Otran's land while flying around with him.

Dan knew he could wait until another day, after she found out about Anderson's harvesting another way. Or he could just go without her—without saying anything—but she would be furious. Tortured by indecision, he picked up the phone and called the Palmer Inn.

"Hello," the sleepy voice answered.

"This is the Republican Central Committee and we would like to know if for a mere three hundred dollars you would like to join the Voice of Congress Club."

"It's almost four in the morning," she said. Then in a more good-natured tone: "It must be awfully important. Either that or you're drunk."

"It's important. I want to take a plane over the Amada

compound on Sunday and look at that helicopter to see if it might be the one that emitted the signal.''

"You sure that's the reason you want to fly over the compound?"

"Uh-huh."

"Dan, you're not back on your idea of going in there?"

"It's just a consideration."

"Your boss and your client said no. It's stupid. You heard that guy on the phone. You could get killed."

"Maria?"

"Yes?"

"It means a lot to me that you're open-minded about this."

"Damn you."

Dan chuckled. "It's important to me to see that chopper." He said it warmly in a confident basso.

"I have meetings Sunday morning. Important meetings."

"I know. And you should attend them—"

"What's that mean?"

"It means I'd like to go alone."

"I liked you better as the Republican Central Committee. I'm going. What time does the plane take off?"

"I want to go at six A.M. I don't know when I'll be back."

"Call me when you get the exact departure time."

"What about the chemist and the bat guy? You mentioned that Patty McCafferty was working on it."

"She is. I'd like to go in person and talk to these people."

"How about the Corey Schneider gal?"

"I talked with the fund-raiser and got her to call Schneider."

"So what did she say: 'Where were you on the morning of June fifteenth?'"

"No, no. They got all cozy. Schneider offered a small donation. Small for Schneider at least. She likes to donate to the legal-defense fund for sit-in protesters that have been arrested. Anything in-your-face she likes.''

"So what happened?''

"Well, Penny gave her the inside scoop that we were supposed to get a big donation, but it never arrived. Penny said there was even a rumor that it was stolen by a woman. Then Penny said this: 'The only woman I know who would be gutsy enough to pull that off would be you.' There was a silence on the line, then Schneider said, 'Couldn't have been me because I was at the conference in Portland.' I checked and she was there. Several people saw her at the beginning and the end, and she was registered. So I'll see you at the plane, you just tell me when.''

Damn. Maybe they could somehow avoid flying over the area where Anderson was logging. With luck, they could fly low, straight to the compound.

Regrettably, Corey Schneider wasn't a whore. Oddly, Groiter had always been attracted to her.

Now as he sat looking at the wooded drive that led to her house, he thought carefully about his plan. It had amazed him that Corey's extended family had spoken with him so freely. But then it was a long time ago and she hadn't spoken to them in years.

The attorneys had become even more aggressive and were amassing quantities of information. Although he didn't admit it to Kenji, at this point no one really knew what they knew. Now they were going to fly over the compound taking pictures. Kenji had been furious about that. His failure to locate the device until just prior to landing the helicopter had been an incredible blunder, and Groiter knew it. Now was not the time to make a similar mistake.

He was driving a Mercedes with heavily tinted glass.

Taking his foot from the brake, he let the big car roll down the redwood-lined lane, until he came to a barely graveled and mostly overgrown side road. Turning off the motor, he coasted down it, listening to the barely audible sound of his tires crunching little stones and later the duff of the forest floor. He put on his full-face knit headpiece and donned a ski mask that left no hint of his hair or his skin revealed.

The small dead-end forest road, partially grown over with young alder sprouts, ended in a patch of wild blackberries. He decided that this was a good place to leave the car. His mother's favorite berry patch back in Germany looked much like this. While his mother picked for a pie, he and his brothers would eat their fill and play hide-and-seek amongst the thorns. Those were easier days.

When he stepped from the car the ground was soft with moisture. There was a chill in the air because the coastal fog was at least 20 road miles farther inland than usual this morning. The green of the forest had grown in an arch over the little road, and even if there had been sun it would have been obscured. Usually a stranger to the forest, Hans didn't like being surrounded by a thousand hiding places.

Just through the woods from Ghost Lane, as he now called it, he knew he would find the home of Corey Schneider. But this forest was somewhat problematic. He was near enough to the coast that the cut-over second-growth forests contained a fair number of dense brush patches. Using his compass to do a little figuring, he deduced that one such thicket lay directly in the line of travel.

Flipping the brass compass shut, he was pondering whether to avoid the brush by going left up a hill, or right down into a gulch, when he felt something at the back of his head. He knew it was a gun—even before he heard her words.

"Put your hands on your head. Berry pickers don't come out here in a Mercedes with new leather."

The thought that she had walked up on him so easily terrified him. She was good.

"Pleased to make your acquaintance."

"That won't last," she said dryly. "Now take off the head gear."

"Once I do that, you'll have to die. You know there's an endless supply of guys like me."

"I should worry that they'll send another dumb shit in a Mercedes, followed by another? What are you doing here?"

"I came to talk to you."

"With a mask and a gun?"

"Next time I'll bring flowers."

"You're the Kraut on the phone, aren't you?"

"What phone?"

"Imagine having your scrotum slit open, your eyes gouged out, and your tongue rolled around in garlic, onion, and flour, then fried in olive oil. Can you picture that?"

"What's your point?"

"I'm serving a blind man's tongue and balls with tartar sauce if I don't get some answers. And you're going to eat them one little piece at a time."

"Next question."

Suddenly his head felt like it had exploded. A few seconds disappeared on him, and he was on his knees with blood wetting his stocking cap. His temple throbbed and he felt nauseated.

A voice whispered in his ear. "I say when the next question comes. First you answer the last question or I'm gonna string you up and I'm going to take this knife—" Through blurred vision he could see a wicked-looking skinning knife with a long, curved blade turning slowly in her hand. "—and I'm going to cut you where the sun don't shine."

His head spun and he felt like he might lose consciousness. He didn't doubt that she would do everything she threatened, and more. Up until this moment his fright had been tempered. Being a cautious and thorough man, he had hired Garcia, a cocky young Spaniard, to watch his back. Garcia always rode a motorcycle unless the job required a car. Suddenly it occurred to him that if Garcia hadn't arrived by now, perhaps she had somehow found him first.

"Maybe we could make a deal," he said, stalling for time.

"I'd rather watch her cut your balls off," a voice interjected.

Hans could feel Corey Schneider whirl. By the time he got turned around, he saw Garcia with a submachine gun leveled at Corey's middle. Corey's gun was aimed in Garcia's direction, but his body was almost completely hidden behind a tree.

"Drop the gun," Hans said. "That Uzi will saw you in half and we won't be able to have our little talk."

Corey Schneider dropped the gun.

Hans shook his head, trying to get rid of the dizzy feeling. Slowly he stood. "It would be pointless to beat the shit out of you," he said. "But I'm going to do it anyway."

Corey never actually lost consciousness, but she became confused and sick. She couldn't recall how many times she'd thrown up. There was something scientific about the beating. It was calculated and brutal, but not deadly and not disfiguring. Most of the blows, other than a dozen open-handed slaps, were delivered to her torso and kidneys. At first she could tighten her muscles as a means of protection, but eventually she was a lifeless punching bag. She craved unconsciousness, but it wouldn't come.

There was an intermission to this beating when they marched her to the house. It resumed in her living room, where she noticed that she felt hot, as if she had a fever. Oddly, she recalled being grateful that there was no blood. When they stopped, she was lying facedown on the couch with one hand touching the floor. It was her father's plaid couch, and the crisscrossing of the red and greens seemed to add to her nausea. She closed her eyes. Letting her mind wander down her right arm to her hand, she didn't think anything was broken. She did the same for the left arm lying at her side.

Her right leg was bent at the knee but didn't seem unnaturally contorted. The left leg was almost straight. It was as though her body were a big room and her mind rolled around inside, checking the walls for cracks, looking for leaks in the roof.

"Would you care for a cup of coffee?" someone asked.

Opening her eyes, she tried to focus on the mahogany floor.

"Wait outside, I can take it from here."

"But—"

"I said get some fresh air."

"Shit." The Spaniard left. She heard the door close.

"Can you talk?"

"Yeah."

"I didn't want to hurt you. Really. I just needed to show you. You're going to do what I say?"

"That depends."

"Take off your clothes."

"No. No. No."

"You see, if you would have learned with the others in your life, they, too, would have left you alone. You just wouldn't learn. Now do you think you have learned?"

"Learned what?"

"Take off your clothes."

"No. I have learned."

"I couldn't hear you."

"I have learned."

"Good. Crawl over to that closet." She did as she was told. Hating herself for it.

"Get in."

"Can you hear me?" he asked an hour later.

"Yes."

"I want you to talk to me."

"About what?"

"I want you to tell me about where you grew up. About your father and your mother."

It was two hours before he let her out. For that entire time she talked of her early life. When he was finished asking her questions, he opened the door and took her to the bathroom. While he waited outside, he told her to take a shower. Before she showered, she peed painfully. Then she got dressed. It took almost forty-five minutes because she could barely move. As she was dressing, she slid open the bathroom window an inch. There were several places the Spaniard could be stationed, waiting if she tried to sneak out. Escaping could result in another beating, or worse. She was certain if she did as the man wanted, the worst had passed—at least for now.

They went back to the couch and he brought a tall glass of water. "Drink."

Then he drew her down. She lay with her head in his lap while he stroked her hair. It was disorienting. She felt like a small child.

"You're very good, you know. Nothing can touch you when you're allowed to be clever. When you're not opposing our cause. And when you oppose me, you oppose our cause. You'll lose for Mother Earth if you oppose me. Now we can work together. How do you feel about that?''

"OK."

"I take it, then, you agree that we're a team." His hand rubbed the back of her scalp; while arousing her hatred, it felt good.

"You beat the shit out of me."

"You wanna argue about this?"

"No."

"Good. Now you're not gonna have any of those nosy questions on the phone anymore, are you?"

"No."

"You're gonna hold up your end of the deal?"

"Fucking A, man."

"Don't give me lip."

"Yeah."

"Did you bury Denny in the woods out behind your house? After you shot him in the back of the head?"

"Yes."

"We're gonna dump Denny's body in the ocean with a concrete block tied to his ankles right after we work together on a few more projects. And these are all for the cause."

"What do you want?"

"I want you to tell me exactly what you did with Kim Lee. But first I want to know all about Denny."

Corey hesitated, feeling strangely attracted to this man while hating him. For reasons that came from a deep pit in a closed-over part of her mind, she wanted to please this German-sounding bastard.

"I killed him."

He stroked her forehead. "Good for you." He chuckled. It was sincere praise. Once again she felt the desire to please and hatred simultaneously. She went on to recite every detail.

"You are an amazing woman."

Then she told him about Kim Lee. Everything.

"You are so brilliant, the way you handle people. If you hadn't scared him to death, he would have told you everything. He would have held nothing back. It is a tribute to your powers of persuasion."

He put a hand on her shoulder, but it felt fatherly, not sexual.

"There was a transmitter in the briefcase you gave us. We talked about that."

The recollection of it and the shock of it helped bring her even further out of her fog.

"I don't know anything about a transmitter. It's like I said."

"You're sure?"

"I should have taken the money and dropped the briefcase. It was stupid."

"So either Maria Fischer and her group put it there or Dan Young and his group."

"Yes," she said.

"Working together, you and I, we will be far too clever to make a mistake like that again."

"Yes," she said, starting to believe it.

"You will get better soon. We were careful not to do any permanent damage." He stroked her head, then bent down and gave her a chaste kiss on the forehead. When he walked out, he shut the door quietly.

She lay there for perhaps two hours, dozing off and on, before she crawled on her hands and knees back to the shower. The thought of standing made her nauseous and dizzy. She managed over the course of about ten minutes to wriggle from her clothes and to once again crawl into the shower where she let the water beat down on her while she tried to survey the bruises that were running together on her torso, turning her a vibrant black and blue. Somewhere she recalled that hot water might make things worse, but she didn't care.

After that, the German called her frequently. Sometimes they would talk for the better part of an hour. There was something about his inner strength and deep voice that drew her. But it also made her restless. She dreamed deep, vivid, wild dreams, and often she was burning her father's body and crying.

14

Dan stood on the tarmac in the cool dawn, wishing he hadn't been so obvious in attempting to leave Maria behind. But there was nothing he could do now. Taking the best precautions he could, he had explained to Jason, the pilot, that he wanted to avoid the northeast corner of the Highlands Forest. It was the area nearest civilization and the location where Anderson was logging for Otran—right next to the main body of the Highlands in a small isthmus of old growth that protruded from the Highlands like a finger into the second-growth forest.

"Hey," he said with perhaps too much enthusiasm when Maria arrived.

"You seem awfully cheerful for this hour."

"Just anxious to take a look."

"You two can sit in back and talk over an intercom, if

you like, with headsets," Jason said. "If you want to talk to me, you can switch the intercom but you need to listen to make sure I'm not talking to air-traffic control."

Dan helped Maria into the Cessna 182. They shoved the passenger-side front seat all the way forward in the small plane to give Dan maximum legroom. The bench seat in back, which was to accommodate Dan and Maria, was fairly roomy in this plane. Maria sat next to Dan directly behind Jason. Because it was a high-wing aircraft, they would have excellent ground visibility.

As Jason went through the checklist strapped to his knee, Dan and Maria put on the headphones and figured out the intercom.

"I doubt we'll see much," Maria said. "We overfly the Highlands a lot."

"Those buildings seemed pretty large."

"The trees crowning above them were pretty big, and those buildings were just modular units that go on wheels, I think."

"I mainly want a picture of that helicopter."

"You don't fool me. You want to look and take pictures because you think you're going back in."

The plane took off and the ground fell away. It would only take minutes to reach the Highlands from the Palmer airport.

"Nothing is happening. The police are doing nothing," Dan said. "It's time to quit losing and make some progress."

"They all seem to buy Amada's story."

"Exactly, and it's bullshit. Some now-departed yew-tree scientist was interested in bats? We stole photos pertaining to the guy's *hobby?* And this is rich—the vaultlike file room with the microfiche is really a break room that previously was a storage area."

"Well, if we can find out what those equations mean, we may wipe the smirk off their faces."

"Will we ever meet these professors that Patty's lining up?"

"We will, but we have to do it carefully. You know we could be jeopardizing whoever talks to us." She pointed at the ground. "We're over the Highlands, the back end. Why'd we fly the long way around?"

Dan shrugged and tapped the pilot on the shoulder rather than switch the headset. Jason pulled off one side of his headphone.

"Can we go lower?" Dan shouted above the drone. Jason nodded and began to descend.

Below, they could see the long, winding access road, and a small, unimproved clearing next to a natural pond, complete with helicopter. Barely visible amongst the trees was a tiny portion of what looked like the main building.

"Unless you knew right where to look, and you have this angled view, you wouldn't see the building," Maria said.

"Doesn't that look like the helicopter we saw, except for the colors? I'm thinking it's the same bird."

"The one we saw was all white."

"I think they masked the numbers and the colored trim by spraying it with wash-off paint. Yeah. Accident-reconstruction people, car thieves, movie makers, they all have a water-soluble paint that can change the color of a car or truck temporarily."

"I guess it could be the one we saw," Maria said.

"It's the same." *I'll be damed. They gave half the money and have all of it back,* Dan thought. *What would Otran think of this?* From an altitude of 600 feet, Dan shot photos with a large-bore 300mm lens.

Clearly visible was a clearing with a large, round structure that looked like a swimming pool. A pipe ran from it to the side of the mountain. On the steep rock hillside there were boards, like a shack. Dan snapped pictures furiously and marked the spot on a handheld sat-nav global positioning system (GPS) device.

After a couple of passes Jason motioned to Dan. Dan switched the intercom to the pilot position.

"Somebody on the ground has a Unicom radio for the copter pad and they're telling us we're too low. Technically, you have to maintain one thousand feet over a populated area. I guess they consider their pad and their buildings a development."

"Nervous, aren't they?" Maria said. "Let's fly back over the lower part of the forest."

She tapped Jason.

"Let's go back that way. I'd like to look at the rest of the Highlands."

Jason looked at Dan, and Maria followed his gaze.

"What's going on?" Maria asked.

"Nothing. Jason, do you want to go back that way?"

"Tell me where to go, Dan," Jason said.

Dan groaned to himself at Jason's show of reluctance. The situation was deteriorating. "Go just where Maria wants," Dan said, hoping that somehow Jason would still be able to miss Otran's area or that the harvesting wouldn't be obvious.

"More that way," Maria said with uncanny accuracy.

"Your boyfriend is a state biologist, isn't he?" Dan had planned this topic for a completely different occasion, but hoped it would bring her mind and her eyes back inside the plane.

"Why?"

"I need to get into that compound and snoop around."

"What does that have to do with Ross?"

"He might be able to create a diversion. Make it so they can't have the dogs running around eating people."

"And when might that be?"

"When representatives of the Department of Fish and Game inspect timber-harvesting areas to determine effects on wildlife."

"What are you talking about?"

"We know that the wildlife guys let people like you tag along with them on private property when they are doing an inspection of timber-harvesting activity. They dress your kind up in green uniforms, or at least let you come with them in your civvies."

"Where did you get this idea?"

"Save your breath. I know it's a closely guarded secret. With the right story you could get the state to go looking around and you could even go with them if they were sure you wouldn't be recognized."

"OK. Just hypothetically, what if we could do that?"

"You would never have to admit anything to me. Just tell me when you're going and that's when I'll go through the fence. You know they won't have those guard dogs loose with state inspectors in there."

"It's too dangerous."

"The state can demand to look at the fence, the fallen trees."

"It's legal to cut trees if they are not sold for commercial purposes. You said so yourself."

"You know they'll let the state inspect. We've got to do something. They took the money. They shot at us. They broke into my house. They may have killed that senator's wife and made it look like rape."

"And they'll kill you too. This is not some B movie. This is real life, Dan. And real death. You have a little boy to think about. So just for once, don't listen to your testosterone. Let's do the research. Talk to the professors. Do all that we can do without getting killed in the process."

Her eyes went back to the window.

"Hey, over there," she said. "Fly over there."

Dan looked. Anderson was clearing a large log landing. They had felled an amazing number of trees for so early in the morning. There were cars back on the county road. Lots of them. Protesters.

"They're cutting right at the edge of the Highlands. God, they're cutting in the old growth!" She whipped around to Dan.

Dan opened his mouth but didn't speak.

"You knew," she said. "You knew. Well, answer me. You didn't want me to go. You didn't want to fly over here. You were hiding it."

"Now, let's just talk about this and—"

"Don't talk to me in that insipid tone of voice. You are treacherously deceitful."

"I can't disclose client confidences," Dan said.

He knew he shouldn't have said it the instant the words came out. Rage filled Maria's eyes and she looked away from him. Then she took off her headset and threw it on the seat, meaning that to communicate he would be reduced to talking in an unnaturally loud voice. Other than tapping Jason on the shoulder and asking him to circle the log landing that was being cleared by Anderson logging, no more words were spoken until they landed. Dan waited until they had thanked Jason and then walked her to her car before trying to redeem himself.

"I still think we should talk about this," Dan said.

She stopped and turned to him.

"So you can feed me more bullshit."

"It's obvious your people found it anyway."

"No thanks to you."

Dan knew that whatever he said next could affect his relationship with Maria for a long time to come.

"Answer me this," she continued. "Given what's happened in the last few days, the sort of trust that I thought maybe we were building, weren't you being deceitful this morning? Lying actually?"

Instantly he knew she was right. He knew it without analysis. But for some reason he felt compelled to analyze it. So he hesitated.

"Well?"

"You're probably right."

"You have insect-sized morals. You thought up every word you said this morning, hoping I wouldn't come, making it sound like it would interfere with my meetings. And if that wasn't enough, you schemed with the pilot behind my back."

"There are times when a lawyer has to—"

"That's it. I'm outta here."

While she angrily fumbled with her keys, he tried to think of something to keep her there. Nothing came.

"Damn it," he said under his breath as she pulled away.

When Dan called his cell-phone message center, there was a 6:00 A.M. message from Otran's vice president of natural resources.

"You know that THP we talked about that we were gonna start this weekend."

"We joked about bringing out a huge crew and dropping everything," Dan said.

"You and I were joking. Anderson went and tried it."

"We told him to do a normal operation."

"That's what we told him, but he didn't listen."

"What has he done?" Dan asked, not indicating that he already had a good idea of the corrupted timber harvest plan (THP).

"The asshole didn't follow instructions. Instead of doing as he's told, Anderson sends in a thirty-man falling crew on Friday and they go nuts. I guess they hatched this brilliant plot at the bar, and got out every faller they could find. Most of 'em never even worked for Anderson a day in their lives. They start dropping every tree in sight and tried to fall a major chunk of the clear-cut portion in three days. It's dangerous, and it's nuts. We found out first thing this morning when the media was called out by a bunch of hysterical enviros. We have our forester going out now to shut them down."

"We'll be in court first thing Monday morning and the judge will no doubt eat me for breakfast."

"I know," the vice president said. "I know."

Patty McCafferty sat in a lavender love seat in a small sitting area at one end of her large office. Maria seated herself in a matching love seat on the far side of a brass-and-glass coffee table.

"Dan Young is a class-A jerk," Maria began. "I'm so mad at him I could spit. He was hiding Anderson's logging. Not just hiding, trying to deceive me. And for no reason. Our people had already found the loggers."

"Which reminds me. We need a restraining order on that."

"Oh, I intend to get one first thing tomorrow morning. For this, I think we can get right to a judge."

"Did you know they were doing accelerated cutting?"

"What do you mean accelerated? I saw a lot of trees down."

"They brought in way more fallers than usual on Friday, Saturday, and this morning when you flew over. They're dropping all the trees first, then yarding them. They girdled trees they couldn't cut to make sure they would die. That way, no matter what the court decides, those trees would have to go."

It was like someone had hit her in the gut. She had been twice betrayed. Hiding Saturday- and Sunday-morning harvesting was one thing. Girdling trees with a plan to drop everything in sight before she could get a court order was another thing entirely. It bordered on criminal.

"I . . . I . . . don't know what to say."

"Can you take a case like this against Dan Young?" Patty asked.

"I certainly can. I'll gut him."

Patty nodded but didn't look entirely convinced. "What about working with him on the Highlands compound and the money?"

"I don't know what I'm going to do about that. Dan's on some kind of holy war. When they broke into his house . . . well, he's pissed. According to him, it's about the money they stole, the Highlands compound, bats, even the death of Catherine Swanson. But most of all, it's about his wife dying and what has happened to his life since then. I'm not sure he knows that."

"Well, I've sent those equations and the bat picture to the people at the university. Do you want to meet with them?"

"Definitely."

"Rumor has it that you are fond of Mr. Young."

Maria felt herself blush. "Right now I'd say that we are just survivors of a major trauma that in an odd way has drawn us together. That includes his housekeeper Pepacita and his little boy. We all got a little bit close. But it was nothing romantic. And it ended with this latest episode."

Patty's steely eyes locked with Maria's.

"Really," Maria said. "He's lost his wife. He's in no

condition to be romantic." Still, Patty said nothing. "Oh God, listen to me. Now I'm implying the only problem is his dead wife when I don't mean that at all."

"What do you mean?"

"I mean there is absolutely nothing between us. He's a liar. I could never trust him. And I can't imagine anything in the future."

"Your love life is your business. But you do have excitable clients—"

"You don't have to explain." Maria rose and came around the coffee table, sitting beside Patty. "You know I wouldn't keep it from you if I thought I was falling in love."

The older woman reached out and took Maria's hands. "I guess I value your work and your company so much that I selfishly didn't want you getting involved with this industry fellow."

"You haven't a thing to worry about. Now when can I get to those experts?"

"Ready when you are. So do you take Dan?"

"I don't know yet. I just don't know."

Walking down the hall to her office, Maria took out Dan's card and punched his home number into the phone. Only then did she realize how odd it was that her secretary had come in on Sunday.

It took a minute to talk to Nate and for those few moments she managed to stuff her anger. Then Dan came on.

"Just give me a straight answer, Dan, and I mean it. Did you know that Anderson was furiously chopping down trees with a huge crew, dropping everything and girdling the ones he couldn't cut—all over the weekend to avoid a court order?"

There was a long pause.

"Maria, believe me, I'd like to answer all of your questions on this, but attorney-client privilege—"

"Did you know?"

"I would never, ever condone girdling or this accelerated cutting you're talking about."

"I didn't ask if you condoned it, Dan." She felt on the verge of hurling the phone across the room. "I asked what you knew. And if you have to assert the privilege, then you knew."

"It's not what you think."

She hung up.

15

Night-vision goggles on, able to see in only the faintest glimmer of starlight, Corey moved through the darkness like a cat. After she completed a steep uphill hike, steam rose from her body into the chilly mountain air. In her pack she carried sugar, to mix with soil on-site, and a small arsenal— a relatively light incendiary bomb, a stun grenade, the .300 Weatherby, a can of military-strength pepper spray, hand-cuffs, and a razor-sharp stiletto.

It had all been easy to obtain except for the stun grenade and portions of the bomb, a homemade concoction of potas-sium permanganate, glycerin, and a high explosive. A timer controlled the mixing of the potassium permanganate and glycerin, which would ignite seconds after coming into con-tact, causing detonation of the explosive. The high explosive and the stun grenade had both been stolen from an armory in South Carolina by someone selling in the black market.

On a sunny spring day, the side of Tiger Mountain, gateway to the Highlands Forest, appeared as a multitextured, bushy, green patchwork. Brush patches, three to fifteen feet in height, intermingled with clumps of Douglas fir, redwood, Sitka spruce, and alder. In coastal fog the landscape took on a desolate, mysterious feel, the kind that could put a chill up the spine. But tonight the place was just dark, cold, and lonely.

Despite her load, Corey was able to move swiftly. Because she was far from her target, silence was not yet required. She had established a rhythm and kept to it, her breathing in sync with the raspy crunching sound of her boots on the soil and rock.

She thought of her body as that of a warrior's. There was an animal toughness in her square shoulders; her stomach was as flat as a granite wall; her biceps, her rock-hard thighs, and her calves were fighting trim. Not a body, she thought, a living sacrifice, in the service of Mother Earth.

Bile had risen in her throat as she watched Anderson loggers fell ancient giant trees in front of helpless-looking activists. The demonstrators were treated as a mere nuisance, petty criminals on the fringe of sanity. The quiet of her Sunday morning had been disturbed by the call. The only person in the regular movement who still spoke with her had rambled on, telling her of the biggest logging show they'd ever seen. It was on Otran land. No doubt Maria and her new buddy Dan Young were in on it. As Otran's attorney he must have known, and if he knew, she knew.

After thirty minutes she arrived at the base of the last steeply pitched bank, fifteen feet below the lip of the make-shift parking area, a one-hundred-foot square of tamped-down earth where the loggers were guarding their equipment in the night. She stopped to listen to their drunken laughter, her breathing calm and her heart rate steady despite the strenuous hike. Slowly she removed her pack and placed it six feet up the slope, then laid the Weatherby alongside it and began to climb the last short distance to her goal. But as soon as she had started, she froze. Something was close: a rustling in the nearby ferns; no doubt an animal, stalking its natural prey. Soon teeth would sink into hide, grabbing mouthfuls of fur and muscle; warm blood would spurt from freshly torn flesh. The images paraded through her mind in slow motion. The unseen men above her suddenly stopped talking as the rustling grew louder.

"Did you hear something?"

The morons would no doubt come and investigate. Nothing to worry about. These men were untrained and unmotivated.

"I'll check it out," a gritty voice said in a resigned tone.

She pressed her body to the ground, putting her head flat to the cool, dark soil that had cascaded down the hillside from the loggers' road-building. The damp earth sent a chill through her, but she remained motionless. If discovered, she knew, she would have to attack. No other choice, with all the terrorist paraphernalia she carried—even these jokers would figure it out.

Twenty feet to her right, a flashlight beam jumped erratically over the brush. "It's just some critter," said the man with the light, his head and torso coming into view past the lip of earth above her, silhouetted by the spotlight behind him.

Holding her breath, she reached for the rifle. Quietly she pulled it to herself, then raised it, the thumb of her right hand automatically releasing the safety as the forefinger began the squeeze. Two quick shots, to the chest—it would happen the instant he saw her. To her right the light moved across the hillside, coming closer and closer. When the logger's light crossed her body, she waited for the cry, but there was nothing. The beam continued on.

Exhaling slowly, she reengaged the safety. Her right leg began to twitch. Adrenaline.

Then she began the last tiresome crawl, an inch at a time. Drawing even with the pack, she moved it quietly two more feet up the slope. Then she repeated the process. Then again. It took twelve minutes to move the fifteen feet—the silence of the night utterly undisturbed. Not even a whisper of foliage against fabric.

Peeking over the lip, she saw the three men. The murderers were bundled up against the cold night air, so laden with insulated sportswear they couldn't have bent over to tie their shoes. They sat in a group next to the cold steel blade of an immense D9 Cat, warmed by camaraderie, booze, and a card game. Obviously, by their presence, they suspected that her kind would come snooping around, but they had probably concluded that three armed men would be sufficient to scare off any monkey-wrenching enviro without a fight. A smile played at the corners of her lips; the floodlight they'd installed on the Cat made them such an easy target.

She fingered the stun grenade. First she would take out the light and plunge them into darkness. After inserting her earplugs—the Weatherby was a loud and powerful weapon—she slid the rifle into place, exhaled slowly, and squeezed the trigger.

Flame roared out of the barrel; the concussion seemed like a cannon in the still night air. With the loggers engulfed in total darkness, Corey made her next move, rolling the stun grenade to their feet. In a couple of seconds, a blinding white light consumed the darkness. With her head down and eyes closed, Corey didn't see the overpowering brilliance of the grenade burst, but its shock wave made the rifle shot seem trivial. Then she sat up, removed her earplugs, and pulled on her night-vision goggles. The men, she saw, were walking around in small, confused circles. To them, she knew, the night appeared psychedelic, full of dots of light dancing madly in front of their eyes. They were effectively blind and nearly deaf.

Climbing over the lip, she walked calmly across the clearing toward the trio. Each held his face in his hands, screaming and moaning into the night. Already they were whining, she mused. She wondered how these men would react to real pain.

Moving to the largest man first, she put a hand on his shoulder. He jumped at the touch.

"Just relax and take it easy," she said reassuringly into his ear. "You'll be able to see in a minute. That's right, just lower your hands. Now, look at me." Mouth agape, the man turned to her, eyes wide but seeing nothing.

With a smile, taking her time now, Corey pointed and fired the military-grade pepper spray in the man's face. An ax might have taken off his legs at the knees, the way he dropped. The air whistled in his throat as he struggled to breathe, sounding like a death rattle. Reading his face, she was certain he knew, in the way a man knows about gravity, that he was about to die.

Next she turned to the other two men, who were moving their heads from side to side as if that might somehow shake off the blackness or restore their hearing. Such easy targets, Corey thought. The now-unguarded face of each turned crimson with the spray, and they, too, dropped to the fetal position on the ground.

The captain of her army stockade had once told Corey: "It's like sucking up hot lava."

Corey retrieved the sugar and sand, pouring both into the Cat's engine, along with soil from the landing. Then she moved to the other eight pieces of heavy equipment. It took twenty minutes to accomplish her business, including the time required to start all the equipment and attach the timed explosive device to the gas tank of the pickup.

The pickup truck was a nice touch. It'd look like a hulk from a war zone. They needed to know they were at war. Not some patty-cake war, with civil, orchestrated news releases gently chiding the timber barons for making a mess, but a real war, with broken bodies and twisted metal.

She approached the big one, who was now on his hands and knees, trying to stand. The captain, nicknamed Ivan the Terrible for good reason, had showed her how to subdue and calm "special" prisoners. This had been after telling her he realized she and he shared something the others lacked—something that people usually discovered only after years of being around "funny people" in cold little barred rooms smelling of vomit, excrement, and Lysol.

She told herself to concentrate on the kick. A little too hard with a steel-toed boot, and she would puncture a lung. Just about like a twenty-yard field goal, maybe a little softer. There was a thud at impact and the man gave a gut-wrenching groan that told her she'd probably snapped three ribs clean.

When she was through, the men sat groaning and barefoot, their breathing raspy and tortured. "It's a shame I can't kill you," she said, meaning what she said, feeling the power of the words flow through her. "But dead men can't talk. And I need you to tell the world how you suffered for your sins against Mother Earth."

Scanning the edge of the woods at the back of the clearing with her night-vision goggles, she located a small-diameter log that looked like it weighed somewhere around 150 pounds. Taking some tools from her pack, she walked over to the log, leaned over, and pounded three spikes into it, each through a heavy metal ring to which a pair of handcuffs was welded.

In two minutes all three men were sprawled around the log, handcuffed to it. She checked her watch. Twenty minutes since they had been sprayed—ten more and they would be more or less functional. Behind her, the machinery was starting to vibrate, engines beginning to cough as though infected by an angry virus.

"Pick up the log," she demanded.

The men, each in shock, stirred, tried to move, to obey. But not fast enough for Corey.

"You're not listening. You will each lose an ear." She said it without a thought, then stopped to consider the words, which dangled in the air like a spider on its thread. A chill of excitement ran through her and the blade shot from its handle with a quiet, cold click. People would talk about this; broken ribs would heal, but severed ears . . . These would be permanent offerings to Mother, more permanent than anything she'd done to them before.

On the ground before her, the men grasped desperately at the log.

"Too late. Stay where you are. The ear comes off first." The fat one. She grabbed his ear and made a clean, lightning-fast slice. The man's legs started shaking, and he stamped his heels on the ground involuntarily. The bleeding was profuse. She discarded his ear in the brush.

After watching this, the other two men became hysterical.

"Please don't," one of the men said. "Please don't." But before he could finish, his left ear was gone.

Then she turned to the third man and smiled at the look of resignation on his face. It was exhilarating—the knowledge that she could commit such violence, as much as the violence itself. The power was hers now. She would have to work fast, but she would get them all.

* * *

The men had learned to concentrate on this quiet, lethal voice, for behind it was a matter-of-fact malevolence like that of an eager butcher doing the spring lambs for sport. A creature that seemed capable of tearing muscle from sinew, bone from meat. Each man's vision was a mess. Through the flood of tears, points of light shimmered, wheeling and turning. Their remaining ears rang with the sounds of a thousand sirens. Struggling, the men lifted the log, the fractured ribs of each twisting in wounded flesh like battens in a wind-rent sail.

"Do not sit down until you get to the county road," she said when the men were standing. "If you sit down, you are liable to die of shock and exposure."

She went to the first man. "Don't sit down until the county road," she said. "Repeat it."

"Don't sit down until the county road."

"All of you together."

"Don't sit down until the county road," they chanted, barely able to make themselves audible.

"Move." They hobbled off into the night, blood pouring from the sides of their heads, their soft, bare, lily-white feet padding over the crushed rock of the roadway.

Corey Schneider turned and began moving down the hill. The exhilaration was ebbing, but it wasn't giving way to any uncertainty or remorse. This was her calling. She had been summoned by Mother Earth, who had led her to Uncle Sam to be trained. And who had then led her here, to this night, to repay with ruthless violence those who would destroy Mother Earth. Those who would dismiss her as a mere nuisance.

As she jogged down the hill, Corey pondered what she had done, wondering if it was enough. For what she had done had been nothing, really, compared to the magnitude of their crime.

Corey went straight to her refrigerator for the orange juice. Most of the vodka was in the living room with the two couples who came to party, but there was just enough remaining in a bottle on the counter for one mixed drink. The music was turned up so loud she could feel the vibration in her teeth. There would be time for only a few hours' sleep before she needed to rise and be about her business. For the morning she would need a much better alibi than these potheads could provide. As she guzzled the orange juice and vodka, she hunted for her speed. First thing in the morning, she'd need it.

Walking into the family room, she felt a sense of relief. This time they hadn't trashed the place.

"OK, boys and girls, everybody out. Your hostess needs her beauty rest." She shooed away the smoke with a hand in front of her lips. A person could get fried just standing in the room.

Once the music was off, it took only a couple of minutes to clean up their mess. They were so spaced that they probably truly believed she'd been home the whole time. She closed the door when the last in line walked out.

Unless Patty McCafferty had gotten even softer, there would be a court fight this morning. And industry would come out in force. It would be her chance.

The phone rang. It was 2:30 in the morning; must be a wrong number she thought—or him.

"Yeah," she said.

"You were brilliant; you showed them, but cutting off a few ears isn't gonna do it."

"It was good, though, wasn't it?" she said. "A good distraction for the main event, like you said."

"A brilliant distraction. And now it's time for the main event. Are you scared?"

"Fuck no."

A chuckle. "We have done good things. Now you and I will do some real good."

"Yeah, well, wait until tomorrow." Instantly she hated herself for saying it—for falling in with this German, shoulder to shoulder, as if she had given herself over to this man.

"Have you had any dreams, Corey?"

"None worth talking about."

"You can tell me."

"There is a man. He's faceless. He waits for me in the shadows outside my forest."

"Maybe the dreams will stop if you get this done."

"I don't know. I'm tired of the same dream over and over."

"Corey, using dope freaks for an alibi isn't the best. That little party—is that really the way to go?"

"You had someone here? At my house?"

"It's for your own good, Corey. You need extra eyes and ears." He hung up.

They had her place bugged; they watched her. She knew it. But she'd gone crazy tearing up the house and never found a thing. She shivered. Then told herself that maybe it wasn't so bad. The German knew things. Amazing things.

While she was collecting her thoughts, the phone rang again.

"Maria Fischer and Dan Young will both be at the courthouse at nine-thirty for the hearing. Traxler's courtroom."

"How do you know that?"

"We just know. And we know that Mother can count on you to get the job done."

* * *

Shohei arrived at her house early Monday morning after hearing about the loggers. His interest in Corey Schneider grew with each day. He would have loved a tap on her phone. Unfortunately, it was also impossible to tap Groiter or Kenji because Groiter swept the executive offices for bugs weekly and at random. Something was making Groiter cautious.

As Shohei contemplated the possibility that this Schneider woman might be linked to Groiter, he decided to ask Yoshinari if a bug of her phone might not be in order. It was highly illegal, and that might cause Yoshinari to balk. In fact, he knew it would.

A Mustang exited Corey Schneider's garage. Since he was in the bushes, a half mile away from his car, a hopeless feeling came over Shohei. Nevertheless, once she had passed, he sprinted up her driveway back to the road and back to his car. Driving flat out, he caught sight of her just as she entered Palmer.

He followed her to a video store, where she got out of her car and strutted like a peacock in her short skirt. This seemed highly out of character. He would wait.

Only hours after she left the earless loggers, Corey walked into Old Town Video wearing shades, short skirt, high heels, and a flashy blouse. It was a locally owned Palmer store that used to be a pool hall. A large rectangular room, it had high racks running its length. Along the back wall were small rooms, each with a video player and a TV that could be rented. The girl behind the counter, name of Macy, used to work for Jack Morgan, the pot farmer, and knew Corey. Macy was a faded blonde with a lot of miles on her, out-in-the-sun weathered skin, a pot slowed brain, and too long without vitamins. Corey thought she looked like she lived on Twinkies.

"Hey, long time no see."

"That's right." Corey took off her sunglasses to look at a young couple at the counter. "How are you folks today?"

"Oh, fine," they said, maybe a little self-conscious at the familiar attitude of this stranger.

"Do I know you? I could swear I know you. Corey Schneider is my name."

"Don't think so," the young woman said.

"Well, anyway, it's nice to see you."

A thirtyish man came out of the stacks, looked her up and down. No wedding band. He was tall and flat-stomached with good shoulders. He flashed a kind of sneer smile that reminded her of the heavy in a *Grease* sort of movie. Definitely the man thought he was cool. Heavy beard, lots of testosterone.

"Hi there." Corey gave it her best.

"Hi there to you," he said, looking intrigued. "You live around here?"

"Sort of. I live in the mountains."

"So how does a guy have a beer with a woman who lives in the mountains?"

"He calls her and talks to her until he convinces her he's not some kind of nutcase."

"And how does a guy get her number?"

"Like this." Corey took out a simple white card with her name and phone on it. Nothing else.

"Spartan card," the man said.

"I like things simple and neat," she said. "Call me." She turned to Macy as if to dismiss him for the moment.

He proceeded to check out the video and leave.

"He's a regular. And you obviously made a hit with him. I haven't seen you dressed like that before."

"Yeah." Corey smiled. "But you know I can't stay single forever."

"What brings you here?"

"Oh, I'm going to go to the library, but I forgot the damn thing doesn't open until eleven, so I thought I'd get a movie, kill time. Too far to go home."

Corey checked out *Malcolm X* and went to the viewing room in the far corner. Inside, she turned on the movie, stripped off her clothes, and took boots and overalls from a sizeable bag over her shoulder. Then she took out her cell phone, called Old Town Video, and slipped out the door of the viewing room. Macy stepped halfway behind a wall to answer the phone. Her habit was to lean against the wall, well back from the counter. Corey could walk all the way to the front door without being seen when Macy leaned against the wall.

"You got *Ancient of Days* there?" Corey said in her deepest, almost unintelligible drawl, already out the door.

"I've never heard of it."

"Well, could you look it up and see?"

"Well, I suppose."

Leaving the shiny Mustang right in front of the store, she walked around the block to a parked van.

"You know," she told Macy, "never mind. On second thought I don't have time to watch a movie."

16

"Look, you have your tail tied in a knot without knowing the facts." In the hallway outside the courtroom, it took Dan a second to notice Ross, who came forward to stand next to Maria.

"Save it for the judge. He may be sympathetic to your particular line of bullshit."

She wore a stylish business suit, deep blue with gold buttons, dark blue shoes, and an embroidered white blouse—a change from the usual. Her crossed arms and intense bearing said as much as her words.

"You don't seem all outraged about the ears your buddies lifted from the loggers." Ross grabbed her elbow.

"If you'd close your fist, you'd get a little more sizzle in that right," Dan said, smiling wanly.

"Don't tempt me."

"Come on." Ross urged Maria toward the courtroom.

"I see you're out serving the morally challenged as usual," she snapped as she backed away in response to Ross's tugs.

"I think if we could talk about this, you might—"

"Save your breath," she said, disappearing through the doors.

The people jamming the old-fashioned courtroom sat on polished-teak seats for the gallery. Matching the dark tones of the benches were a teak jury box and witness stand, and a pair of mahogany counsel tables, all sitting atop a worn marble floor. It was said that the teak was salvaged from sailing ships of the 1890s that used to stop for cargoes of milled redwood. Present in the historic room were members of the press, activists, and mill workers.

Maria stood behind the counsel table nearest the jury box. Dan sat behind the other, trying to make eye contact while she stared everywhere but at him. Soon the bailiff called the case and the judge took the bench. He was a salt-and-pepper gray-haired man who tended to dangle his glasses in his right hand.

"Are both counsels ready?"

"Your Honor, perhaps we could talk in chambers?" Dan said as he rose.

The look on the judge's face told everyone in the packed courthouse that he was favorably disposed to the suggestion. Translated into lawyerspeak, Dan was asking to go in the back room and make a deal. A quick settlement would be just what the doctor ordered. Like all state judges, Traxler was an elected official, and any decision he might make in this case would be extremely unpopular with many people.

Maria displayed no reaction to what was happening, even though she would likely prefer a much different order of events. Excoriating the industry for accelerated weekend cutting and girdling trees would best be done in open court. She could obtain a temporary court order halting the logging, grab headlines, declare victory, and then negotiate from a position of strength prior to the next hearing. None of that would be possible in a back-room deal.

"Your Honor, if I could be heard. I think the public deserves an open and fair hearing," Maria began before Dan or the judge could speak further. "I know Mr. Young wants to go in chambers, out of the hearing of all these good people, and try to cut a deal. Well, I'm happy to do that. But at the right time."

"What are you saying about settlement, Ms. Fischer? Exactly."

"The matters before this court are important to the public. As evidence of that, I would point out that there are hundreds of people both inside and outside this building. I appreciate the court's concern for achieving a settlement, and such a thing may be possible after the public's right of participation is taken care of, but right now I think settlement would be premature."

"Am I to understand that before you'll talk settlement, you want to address the court?"

"Your Honor, if Ms. Fischer makes a highly inflammatory argument and then we go off to discuss settlement, it may make it more difficult."

"Mr. Young, it will only look like your clients are losing if she makes a more compelling case." Then he eyed Maria. "I wouldn't let you grandstand if I didn't think your side had something to commend. But if I let you go on like Daniel Webster, I want some assurance that we're going to have some settlement talks before I rule."

"We are certainly willing to listen and the court can more effectively guide the settlement talks if it is apprised of all the facts."

"OK." Traxler sighed. "There will be order in this court-room." He banged his gavel, quieting the sizeable crowd. "No clapping or speaking will be allowed at any time. Ms. Fischer, this is your motion. You may proceed."

Corey had a medium-sized hand truck with a lashing strap that would wrap around the cargo and pull tight with a small hand crank. On it were two five-gallon drums, one atop the other. Her blue denim coveralls said JOHNSON HEATING AND ELECTRIC. Through careful investigation she had learned that they did much of the electrical work in the courthouse. She had duplicated a Johnson van down to the fine print lettering on the outside. As if she belonged, as if she owned the place, she drove right up to the back service entrance. Her hair was under a cap and she had bound her breasts so that she looked like a man.

Her black boot hit the grainy asphalt with a businesslike scrape and she moved with the determined nonchalance of a busy workman. Without rushing but with precision, she removed the dolly and placed the two five-gallon drums on it. They were taped together, one on top of the other, at the joint. Labels indicated thirty-gauge electrical wire. Behind the drums and against the dolly, she put a heavy three-foot crowbar.

Unlike federal courthouses, there was no metal detector or security other than a few laid-back deputies who didn't expect to see any action; there hadn't been an incident of courthouse violence for as long as anyone could remember. She wheeled her load into the service entrance and entered the elevator alone. A couple of sheriff's deputies were entering the building as the elevator door was closing, but she made no move to push the button that would have held the elevator and reopened the doors. No sense inviting trouble.

The elevator groaned to the second floor and the doors opened. A black lady with a cleaning cart stopped whistling when the doors parted and rolled her collection of janitorial materials in beside Maria.

"What you doing with all that wire?"

"Project on the roof. You know the first-floor rest room is awful. Why don't you start there?"

"It is?"

"Sure is."

"Well, I guess I'll ride it back down."

When Corey got off at the fifth floor, the woman went

back down. The chances were that everybody on the first floor would be able to get out before lethal exposure. No sense killing an innocent worker when it wasn't necessary. Corey knew there wasn't enough cyanide to get everybody; the vents she was using fed only three second-floor court-rooms and one hallway. She hoped to get Maria Fischer and Dan Young.

There would be none of her kind—real radical activists— in the courtroom. She had spread a rumor that in retaliation for the ears, the sheriff was out to arrest monkey-wrenchers who showed up at the hearing. Corey had told everyone that the sheriff had a list of names, so she was confident they wouldn't show up.

There were three clerks in the hall. When she wheeled the drums past them, she nodded at no one for fear they might ask her a question. When she got to the door leading to the stairs, she looked through the small rectangular window. Much to her shock, there were two workmen at the door to the crawl space. Immediately she turned, said, "Oh damn" as if she had forgotten something, and headed back down the hall to a storage room she had seen earlier. Trouble was, it was locked and she had no key. Fortunately, it was to the left and out of sight of the three clerks.

When she turned the corner, she noted with relief that no one was in this section of the hall. Maintenance people would be trouble. Leaning the dolly next to the storage-room door, she put one foot against the wall and leaned back as if she had all the time in the world. It was precisely what she did not have. She would wait fifteen minutes and try one more time. It was 9:30 A.M. exactly. The hearing would be starting now.

*   *   *

"Your Honor, I represent the Friends of the Wilderness, the Wildlife Society, the Wildflower Coalition, and other environmental organizations," Maria said. "Trees on this harvest plan at the Highlands are known to be over one thousand years old. In fact, it's possible some of the trees in the three hundred acres of old growth at White Horse Creek were growing when Christ walked the earth. These ancient trees are up to fifteen feet in diameter and over three hundred feet tall. We had no idea that this ill-conceived logging plan was under review. We made a mistake by not anticipating this. It's just that simple. Trees that are a national treasure—and can never be replaced—are going to be destroyed without serious thought, just because we made a mistake. Now, please note that we are not saying they can never be cut. We don't have to decide that now. What we are deciding here is whether this extraordinary decision, one that will affect priceless living things, should be made without a few moments of reflection. Can't our need to consume everything in sight be put on hold for even a few days, until the next hearing on this matter?

"Your Honor, it's not just the trees, although that would certainly be enough to give us pause. White Horse Creek runs right through the heart of this plan. For years it has been vital to local Coho salmon populations. The proposed plan will devastate it. Already half full of muck from logging, it will become even worse. For the salmon, for the trees, for our children and their children after them, we want those few moments of contemplation by this court to be informed moments. We want the court to have all the information reasonably available when the fate of these living things hangs in the balance.

"This forest has grown in silence since long before our country was founded. Give us just a few days to speak for it and to act on its behalf."

"Yes!" Hushed exclamations went up from the environmentalists around the room; while around them, the industry supporters were obvious in their angry silence.

Maria paused a moment. "Consider, Your Honor, another critical circumstance in this case. Anderson Logging, working together with their counsel, Dan Young"—she paused to enunciate his name—"deliberately attempted to steal our entitlement to those few moments of consideration by this court. We believe Anderson Logging and their counsel knew a suit would be filed, because they knew this old growth was part of the Highlands complex, lying as it does right against the border of the larger pieces. We know that over the weekend they sent in a greatly oversize crew and began cutting at a frenzied rate, laughing at members of our organization who suggested they wait until the court could consider the matter. Then they began killing trees by girdling, cutting the vital cambium layer because it was faster than harvesting the tree normally. A cynical way to make sure the forest died.

"Your Honor, they were holding in contempt our system of justice, which provides for the resolution of disputes through orderly processes. They were belittling those few moments of consideration that the law gives us to protect the public welfare. The court must not unwittingly become an accomplice to the attempt of a few greedy men to deprive society of a few moments of sober reflection concerning what we are about to do, which once done can never be repaired."

Maria sat down, and true pandemonium broke out. "Yes!" came the voices again from the gallery.

Traxler banged his gavel. "Order in the court! Order in the court!" But his words were drowned in the cheers. "This will not be tolerated!" the judge boomed. "One more sound and this court will be cleared!"

Standing, Maria Fischer turned and held up her hands like a teacher before a classroom full of children. Instantly there was silence, but the people continued with their passionate stares, barely able to restrain themselves. Around them, the mill workers and loggers were stone-faced, waiting for their champion.

Traxler was visibly moved. "Is this true? They were girdling trees they didn't have time to cut over the weekend so they could be sure of harvest later? Did they actually send in extra cutters over the weekend to beat a court order?"

Dan felt the stress in the tightened muscles of his chest and back. Even he had not realized how powerful a presentation could be made from these facts. He was staring at a tidal wave with no place to run.

Shohei waited behind the wheel of his Altima, puzzled. From what little he knew about Corey Schneider, she didn't seem like someone who would spend forty-five minutes shopping for a rental video. For a Monday-morning activity it didn't feel right. Yet the Mustang was still there, in front of the video shop.

Perhaps she had gone out the back door and this was a ploy to ditch any tails. Not wanting to attract attention, he walked across the street at a normal pace, hoping he wouldn't run into her on the way out. If she saw his face, the difficulties of his assignment would be significantly increased.

Inside, a few women browsed the stacks. None was Corey Schneider.

"Can I help you with something?"

"Is this everything?" He indicated the room.

"Well, yes." She smiled. "What were you expecting?"

"People come in here and stay for hours?"

"Oh, they're probably back there, watching movies in the private rooms."

"I see. Well, my friend came in here. She is blond."

"Corey?"

"Yes."

"She's right back there, waiting for the library to open."

"Ah." Shohei nodded. But it still didn't seem right. Walking back in the corner where the woman had pointed, he opened the door. A movie was running, but no one was inside.

"Did you find her?"

"Yes. Thank you." He stepped outside quickly. Like everyone else who listened to the radio, Shohei knew about today's duel at the courthouse. With all the demonstrators expected to attend, maybe she went there. But why so secretly? Unless . . .

Whipping his car around, he headed for the courthouse, the largest building in Palmer. He drove around the backside of the building, where he saw a dark van like the one Corey had recently parked in her garage. The lettering could easily have been added. Beside him sat his laptop. Quickly he scrolled through to Corey Schneider. The license plates on this van were not hers, so it was probably unrelated. But he had nothing else to go on.

Parking the car, he decided to inquire after the Johnson Electric man—or woman.

When Corey returned to the door to the roof, she put on an air of unconcern in case anyone was looking. Trying to control the tension, she peered through the window. *Shit.* They were there, coiling an electrical extension cord and putting away tools and a portable light. She looked up and down the hall, realizing that now a second turnaround would raise a question in the mind of anyone who had seen the first. But there didn't seem to be anyone. A woman came walking from the cafeteria with a cup of something, probably her midmorning coffee. Corey kept the bill of her hat low and went back down the hall toward storage, hoping the workmen would not also go there.

She was running out of time. They needed to be packed into the courtroom for the best chance at a kill. It had been thirty-four minutes since she entered the building and twenty-three minutes since the hearing started, assuming it started on time. As she stood against the wall, each minute carved its worry mark in her mind. Failure was not acceptable.

Two women walked by and both looked longer and harder than any of the others. Then one of them made some comment. A minute later, a deputy sheriff came by, a burly man with thin sandy hair and badly receding hairline. On his face was a large mole and he had a funny habit of running his tongue across his teeth. He was the officious type, manifestly concerned about everything.

"What are you waiting on?" From his tone Corey figured the women must have said something.

"My crew chief is coming to tell me. We're laying wire on the roof for something."

"Roof's down there."

"I know, but I was told to wait here by storage. I guess some of the wire is going in here until we need it."

"Hell, that's just a little janitorial supply room."

"I just follow orders. I ain't got a contractor's license."

"It just seems strange, them sending you here."

* * *

"Well, Your Honor," Dan explained, "I've asked the state officials to go into the harvest area today because I knew the court might want a full report."

"So you thought about this in advance."

"No, Your Honor. I was dealing with a situation."

"That's fine, but it's not what I asked. I want to know if these ancient redwoods were being cut at an unusually fast rate because Anderson and Otran Enterprises knew or suspected a court order was coming. I also want to know if unfelled trees were deliberately killed."

Dan was cornered. Obfuscation would anger the judge. Denial would be lying to the court, which was out of the question. He glanced at Maria Fischer and received an ugly glare in return.

"I believe Anderson, without the knowledge and against the wishes of Otran, cut on the weekend with more than the usual number of fallers. Anderson knew a court order was a possibility and wanted to keep his men working. But that's not against the law. And when Otran found out, they got them stopped by noon on Sunday. Only three trees were girdled, and the fallers who did it were thrown off the job."

"Mr. Young, tell us what time fallers normally stop dropping trees."

"It varies." The judge stiffened. "But often it's three or four P.M., sometimes earlier because the wind comes up in the afternoon."

Dan knew he had to turn things around if he was going to make a settlement. Right now, he was sure the judge was convinced justice lay with Maria Fischer.

"Your Honor, I'd like to offer the rest of the story. The pure unvarnished truth."

"I let Ms. Fischer have her say," Traxler said. "I'll listen to your clients' views as well."

"Your Honor, I want everybody here to get the big picture. She's coming into this court with mental images of clear-cuts and people naturally tend to think they are ugly and therefore bad. The implication is that clear-cutting is destruction and we should stop it. Well, I'm here to tell you that this kind of thinking is pure ignorance.

"We are saving the world by growing forests."

There was outright laughter in the courtroom. A prominent member of the local press was smiling and shaking his head.

"Hear me out." The courtroom quieted. "Humankind is making more carbon dioxide today than at any time in our history. We burn fossil fuels and spew the stuff out. Because we don't manage government forests and thin them, they burn up. We make more CO_2 by allowing our federal forests to burn. Hopefully, we all understand you can't breathe CO_2. In addition to choking babies, the stuff warms the planet and we get global warming. Growing trees helps solve in a major way each of those problems. When you see a clear-cut and all those little hand-planted trees, you know somebody is trying to *save* you. This isn't the Amazon, where they chop them down and make a plowed field. In the temperate northwest we're cutting trees for the sake of growing trees.

"People of the future are going to realize that growing forests is the best way to counteract the effects of burning fossil fuels like gasoline and diesel. They will learn that by managing them, we can better control wildfire. It's one of the best ways to convert the sun's energy into something we can use at the same time we are cleaning the atmosphere. We can make ethanol from trees. We already make 1.8 billion gallons of the stuff as a fuel additive, and we need more. It will run a fuel cell or an engine and it emits far less CO_2 than gasoline and is the best smog-control available.

So we clean the air, make fuel, and reduce CO_2 emissions all at the same time. I'm telling you if we had invented trees we couldn't have done it any better.

"Growing forests, people, is what we need. Not stagnant forests full of rotting old trees like Ms. Fischer advocates, but young vibrant forests that suck up the CO_2 and produce oxygen. These growing trees are the best scrubbers of our atmosphere. It's that simple, Your Honor. Old-growth forests were for the days when the only pollution to speak of came from plankton, forest fires, farting buffalo, and the few Native Americans who ate them. Clear-cuts *grow* trees because redwoods and most conifers won't grow in the shade. People are going to figure that out when the government gets off its ass and teaches them."

"Mr. Young," the judge called out.

"I apologize for using a term like 'ass' in the courtroom, Your Honor. In no way would I want to imply that somebody who doesn't agree with me is an ass. We never refer to ignorant people that way in a civilized society."

There was a lot of laughter and clapping from the mill workers.

"Mr. Young."

"So my first point, Your Honor, is that a little ugly for a little while does a lot of good. Our replanting programs create young forests that will save the planet for future generations. Smart management controls fire.

"Now I'd like to make my second point."

"I wish you would," the judge said.

"Our opponents always want us to selectively harvest; it looks good to them like a park. But it's usually bad. Private forests have been ruined by selective harvesting. When you cut the biggest and the best, it's like killing the first three finishers in a horse race and then using the fourth place finisher to stand at stud. You reduce the genetic viability of the forest through selective harvesting. Worse yet, the tree species that were there before a selective harvest won't grow back because the remaining trees provide too much shade. So in a word you ruin the forest. Today the average-sized tree on Otran lands is only eighteen inches because of uniform selective harvest practices. After one hundred years of modern clear-cutting techniques throughout the next century, the average-sized tree will be over thirty-two inches. The trees will be large once again, as they were before the Europeans arrived. So what looks ugly—namely a clear-cut—is really good. Forced selective harvesting will make sick, stunted forests. It's pure ignorance. These stunted forests do less for the CO_2.

"I have just one more point, Your Honor. In 1968, the government came into our community and said that they were going to save the old-growth redwoods. They took private property, reduced our timber base, closed our mills, and gave our workers government handouts. The government put tens of thousands of redwood acres in a park.

"But what happened then? Ten years passed, and concerned citizens noticed that not all the old-growth redwoods were in parks. I guess they wanted more places where the trees won't grow. By that I mean they wanted to produce an old rotting forest that does nothing. Inland away from the coast such forests burn in a horrible inferno because we put out the wildfires and also never cut because we have some weird idea about what's bad and what's good. On the coast such forests just stop vigorous growth and therefore do less for the air we breathe. These are the kind of concerned citizens who may do more harm than good.

"And in 1978 the government came in again and studied the matter, weighing all the options. And again, private property was taken, mills were closed, people were put out of work, and the welfare rolls were expanded.

"Now, it is true that when the Native Americans occupied the redwood coast, there were far more old-growth redwoods than there are today. But they didn't have cars; they didn't need fuel for cars and planes. They didn't have a problem with the greenhouse effect. And I admit we should have a few old-growth forests like we have museums. Keep them around. But the vast majority of the forests should not be old and stagnant. We need the rapid growth of a developing forest. And for God's sake, if we're going to manage a forest instead of leaving it untouched, then let's not make it sick. Let's not decide to intervene and destroy the forest by foolish selective harvesting methods. If we're going to cut, let's do it right so it grows back and grows back vigorously.

"And let's give a break to the people for a change. Let's follow the law. Let's not let ten minutes' worth of emotion overcome twenty years of planning. We don't need another vegetable dump. And that, Your Honor, about sums up my position."

Finished, Dan turned to his chair. Before he could even sit, the mill workers broke out in passionate cheers and whistles. On the bench Traxler banged his gavel; next to him, the marshal screamed "Quiet!"—but all to no avail. Emotions were too high now. A fight erupted near the back of the courtroom between a logger and an environmentalist. Screams and shouts filled the air as the audience tried to pull them apart. The bailiff, a fat man in his thirties, tried to make it to the melee, but ended up hopelessly locked in the crowd.

Fifteen feet away from him, Dan could see Maria Fischer climbing on the counsel table.

"Stop!" she shouted with more volume than Dan would have thought possible.

Perhaps it was the strange spectacle of a female lawyer standing on a table, but whatever it was, it quieted the crowd.

Stepping down, Maria addressed the court. "Perhaps, Your Honor, we could meet in chambers now. But I have got to say that Mr. Young is hallucinating about the science. He's just oversimplifying." More shouting erupted in the courtroom gallery.

Traxler banged the gavel. "Court is adjourned for thirty minutes or at the request of either party." Then he was gone, off the bench as fast as he could move without actually running.

At the judge's suggestion, the two lawyers entered the jury deliberation room alone. There, Maria sat at the head of the table, and Dan took a seat immediately to her left. It was only then that Dan noticed Ross taking a seat beside Maria.

"I believe this is an attorneys' settlement conference," Dan said. There was silence as Maria looked first at Dan, then at Ross. She sighed.

"You are really a prick," Ross said.

"Why torture yourself?" Dan said. "If you've got her, she'll come home. Following her around like a sick puppy isn't—"

"That's enough!" Maria shouted, and slammed her hand on the table. "You shut up," she said to Dan. "Ross, come here," she said, rising. "We'll talk outside. This man can't be civil, so don't give him the satisfaction of watching while the bailiff kicks you out." Ross followed Maria, who slammed the door on their way out.

In a minute she returned, livid.

"Did you send him home to Sacramento?" Dan said.

She sat down and opened her briefcase, removing a yellow pad.

"This may be your idea of a joke—"

"Will you just listen for a few minutes? Please."

"What?" she snapped.

"I didn't plot and plan against you. I wasn't sitting there on the weekend hoping they'd cut down your trees. I had no idea anybody was girdling trees or cutting with a huge crew. Of course I didn't want to spill the beans about what I thought was an ordinary logging job. I may in the past have made some unfortunate jokes about cutting on the weekend but, Maria, it isn't what you think."

"Yeah, you're not a deceitful sort of guy. Right. You sit in the dark like a spy, and let me go on and on in a restaurant thinking you're some kind of . . . soul mate. You oversimplified the carbon issue in your argument to the court. God, you think like Allen Funt."

"I have a job to do. If you don't like it, just walk down to engineering and they can fight with my boss," Corey said. "We have an ionizer to fix. That's all I know. Complete rewiring. If you have a problem, then why don't you and I go onto the roof and talk to my boss." She hoped he would take her up on it.

The deputy hesitated. "Your boss is on the roof?"

She nodded, then took off her hat and shook out her hair. "We could go look at the sights," she said with tones that were a touch friendlier and a lot more adventuresome.

Immediately the deputy's face was transformed. He was talking to a beautiful woman and not a snot-nosed boy out of high school.

"Let's go," he said. "Jeez, I thought you were a . . ."

"A what, Deputy?"

"Well, a boy. That's what they said."

Quickly she put on her hat and tucked her hair back up under it. "I find sometimes it helps to let people think that. I gotta take them this anyway," she said, picking up the crowbar.

He waited until she walked ahead. Unfortunately, he seemed very alert and still slightly suspicious. They opened the door and walked past the workmen who nodded and said nothing. The deputy pulled out a big ring of keys and unlocked the roof door. It meant she wouldn't have to knock out the small window again. She could use the crowbar for something else. They walked up the concrete stairs that rose through a cut in the roof.

She gripped the bar. Glancing back, she saw the deputy's hand go to his baton—probably just habit. Or maybe something was bothering him. His footfalls were heavy behind hers. He was close. Her second hand curled around the bar so that she held it like a bat. There were three stairs to go. When she touched the top stair, she whirled in one smooth motion. He was four stairs down. At chest height his head split like a watermelon as the bar slammed into his ear. A red film shot into the air and gray brain matter went flying.

The deputy's body crumpled. She grabbed it so he wouldn't roll down the stairs. The body convulsed in her hands. A stain spread across the front of his pants and a stench came with bowel sounds. He was dead. Using all her strength, she dragged the big man the rest of the way up the stairs and laid the body on the roof. Quickly she went to the southerly side of the building and found the large sunken chamber in the roof. She climbed ten feet down the metal ladder to the bottom of the rectangular, concave area. On the inboard wall of the chamber were large louvers. From her pocket she removed a red ribbon, tied it on a louver, and let it stream through the opening.

Quickly she climbed the ladder, ran across the roof, went down the stairs and through the door, noting with satisfaction that the workmen were gone. Right where she left it, she picked up the loaded furniture dolly and wheeled it down the hall around a corner, and into the small hall that bordered the southern side. Mechanic rooms, like the door to the roof, had small eight-inch windows. There were two off this hall.

She would try the first. Taking the bloody crowbar in both hands, she looked up and down the hall, then with one sharp blow knocked out the window. Opening the door, she wheeled the dolly inside and closed the door quietly. From the tool bag she removed a wooden square with black paper that she quickly taped over the window hole. Next she pulled out a small flashlight and found the light switch.

All around the dusty room were duct pipes, blowers, and electrical panels. She pulled a Colt .45 from her overalls, then took from her tool case a grease-filled sound suppressor and screwed it into the barrel. The first three or four shots would be almost silent. She returned the gun to its hiding spot.

She walked ahead toward the side of the building, winding through the various pieces of the heating, cooling, and duct system. When she neared the outer wall, she saw the light pouring through the louvers and the small ribbon.

Certain now that she had the right vent for the outside air intake to the south-facing courtrooms, she walked over and examined the equipment. Air from the outside poured into the equipment room and was drawn into a sheet-metal box a little smaller than a Volkswagen Beetle. The box sat about five feet from the louvered wall through which the ribbon fluttered. Its fans drew air from the outside and down into the courtrooms.

Directly in front of the box and its air intake louvers, she placed the two drums. But she inverted them, allowing the drum full of sulfuric acid to contact its specially designed plastic lid. It would take five minutes for the acid to penetrate the lid and hit the sodium cyanide. Heading back toward the door, she was shocked to see the board knocked off the window hole. Then a man dressed in uniformly dark clothing stepped out of the shadows. A small man but confident—

it registered in her brain. Reaching into her overalls, she fished for the gun.

He moved so swiftly he seemed more apparition than man. As the gun came up, his foot snatched it, hurling it against the wall. Open-mouthed, she raised the heavy crowbar, gripping it like a bat. She could beat any man with this advantage.

"What have you done?" The man had an Asian accent.

"You'll find out the hard way if you don't get your ass out of here."

She swung. Easily he stepped away. Never had she seen anyone this fast. No martial-arts instructor, no boxer. Nobody.

"Put it down or I will take it away."

It was as if he were speaking to a child. Furious, she aimed for his head. It missed, but she saw anger ignite in his eyes.

He lunged; she swung but it was a feint. In the split second that the bar flashed past him, he was delivering a blurring kick that nearly dislocated her shoulder and sent the bar flying.

"Be sensible," he said.

She jumped toward the door. He cut her off.

"Tell me what you have done. Then you may leave."

"Fuck you." She launched her best kick. It landed on his ribs, a glancing blow. New respect lit his eyes.

"It was good. But you are only a student. Now tell me."

This time she attacked with a feinted kick followed by a punch. The block was so hard it felt like it broke her arm; then she was flying upward, and her legs went out from under her. She hit the concrete with a horrible slap that knocked the wind out of her.

Before she had time even to blink, her hand was twisted at her side. White-hot pain shot up her arm.

"Tell me."

She breathed deep and fast, certain she could stand any pain. His other hand at her neck set it on fire.

"Oh," she moaned. "Fuck you. Fuck you." It was like a mantra and she repeated it over and over. She could take it. She could hate her way through it. Nothing would stop her. They would both die in minutes.

He bent her over, pushing her nose into the concrete. She was on her knees in seething constant pain. Then he released her just slightly.

"I can see you can take pain. I do not wish to blind you. But I can cause you another kind of pain. Do not make me."

"Die, fucker."

There was a click of a stiletto. At first she thought he would carve her face. Then, like a whisper, she felt her overalls part up the center of her buttocks. The slice was so clean, the knife so sharp, he did it without touching her body. She could feel the air on her panties. Then her panties were pulled down.

Something broke inside. "No, no, no, motherfucker, motherfucker." It was her father; it was everything she loathed, everything she couldn't stand.

"One more chance or I will put you in pain like you have never known."

But it wasn't the physical pain that she feared. It was something else, something she didn't understand. "Over by the wall," she gasped, hating herself. "Two drums. You're too late. It's gas."

He dragged her over by the wall until he saw the drums. "Go." He released her.

Hiking her panties, she ran for the door, grabbing her cap and Colt off the floor. By sheer force of will, she adopted a walk of brusque nonchalance as she left and closed the door. Maybe the little bastard wouldn't be in time.

Shohei paused and thought. There were no good options. He picked up the drums and moved them to the corner opposite the door, about fifty feet from the air intake. He had no idea what else it was near that might matter. Then he tried to force the vents closed, but the controls were electronic. He didn't have the slightest idea how the mechanism worked, nor how this gas bomb worked. Without further hesitation he was out the door, hearing a boiling sound as he headed down the hall.

Within five steps a maintenance man came running round the corner.

"Leave immediately," Shohei said.

"Who are you and what are you—"

Shohei could see it was hopeless and rendered the man unconscious. Flopping the man over him in a fireman's carry, he walked twenty feet to a fire alarm. An instant before he pulled the lever, it sounded anyway.

With a free hand he pulled out a cell phone and called 911.

"Nolo County Sheriff," the crisp voice answered.

"Turn off the air-conditioning and all vents in the courthouse. There is poison gas."

"Say again. The alarm is loud—"

"Poison gas in the courthouse. Turn off vents and air-conditioning."

"Got it. Turn off vents and—"

Shohei hung up.

"When will you stop with your bullshit and admit those trees are a national treasure—"

"Wait," Dan said. "I smell something—it smells like gas. Get out of here!" Dan screamed.

"What?" she said, not sure she smelled a thing. Grabbing

her, he shoved her toward the door and she started moving ahead of him. He seemed a crazy man.

"Go, go, go," he shouted, grabbing her hand, yanking her. Then shoving her.

"Just a minute," she said. He pulled her down the small side hallway leading from the judge's chambers.

"No 'just a minute'! We're out of here," he yelled, literally picking her up and running for twenty feet or so.

"All right," she said as they burst into the corridor and ran down to the stairway. Now something was stinging her eyes. He yanked a fire alarm.

"Everybody out," he shouted as they reached the stairwell.

The stairs were filled with running people. A man stumbled after them into the stairwell, looking violently ill and vomiting. They ran down the stairs and out the door, not stopping until they were across the street.

In minutes the entire courthouse had emptied onto the lawn. Detectives came through, telling everyone to stay. Yellow ribbons were strung around, separating those who had come from the courthouse from the gawkers.

"Where were you?" A young officer approached Dan and Maria with a clipboard and radios hanging off him.

"Judge Traxler's courtroom."

"How many in there?"

"Lots," Dan said.

"Everybody who was in Judge Traxler's courtroom, right over here."

"Actually, we were in the jury room just off the courtroom," Dan explained further. "Court had just adjourned. They may have been in the hall."

The questions seemed endless, it was warm, and after all the adrenaline rush, drowsiness set in. People were allowed to leave after giving complete statements. An hour and a half later, Dan and Maria had given their statements to the police and been excused to the coffee shop where they settled the case. After a time they got word that nobody died. Someone had called in and said to turn off the air conditioner, and the intake fans had already been on low. But thirty people were taken to the hospital. Ross wasn't among them; Maria called and found him at the Palmer Inn, oblivious to what had happened and grateful she was safe.

Dan wrote as Maria sipped her coffee and occasionally argued about a word or a phrase. The devil was always in the details. As she watched him concentrate on the page, she noticed the way his shoulders and arms filled the suit, the thick strength of his neck. Across his chest his blue dress shirt was nearly stretched tight. Although he'd gained a little since the photos she had seen, his face was still relatively lean and there was sharpness in his blue eyes. Periodically he glanced at her from under his heavy brows. She decided that they made him look wise and that in middle age a pair of gold reading glasses would only add to his charm. His thick blond hair was becoming uneven and had grown over his ears; he should have it cut. Then she considered that such a thought—considering her long-haired boyfriend, and all her many wavy-haired colleagues—must be some kind of mental regression. Perhaps it was a throwback to the days when she would tell her father he needed a haircut. She caught herself smiling, on the verge of laughter.

Then she noticed some of her friends from the café looking at her and felt suddenly very uncomfortable. Almost ashamed.

"What?" he said, searching her face.

"Utterly nothing. Just nothing."

Then the whole courtroom scene and his words overtook her again and she could feel her jaw set, angry with herself that she was acting like a schoolgirl.

As they finished penciling the settlement stipulation, Dan seemed to notice Maria's people gathering at a nearby table—and staring.

"This isn't real comfortable," she said.

"Why? We're settling a case."

"We already did that."

"You'd rather be with them."

"Dan, this isn't the twelfth grade. I'm heading to the john and then I'm going to go be with my friends and coworkers. I'll call you."

"You're still mad about what I said in court."

"You mean calling me an ass?"

"Well, it wasn't personal. It was a debate over something we both have deep convictions about."

"We can talk about it later." As she rose, he followed.

"I suppose you're looking for some kind of apology about my 'ass' joke. And the attorney-client–privilege stuff."

"Is that your idea or mine?"

Walking behind Maria, down the hallway to the rest room, he couldn't help but take in her appearance. Her suit, somehow both powerful and soft. The gentle, perfect sway of her hips.

"Great outfit," he whispered.

Maria halted abruptly and turned, causing Dan to come within inches of running her down. There they stood, her nose eight inches from his chest. Dan wondered if he detected a slight change in her demeanor.

He felt both tired and irreverent. "A beauty unlike any other." He smiled. "I am speaking, of course, of your oral argument."

"Dan, there can never be anything between us," she responded flatly.

He shrugged. "I also thought you looked terrific on the counsel table."

Her eyes betrayed nothing. "You are a hopeless throw-back to the Old West, when white people butchered Native Americans and destroyed everything in their path. Frankly, after that display in the courtroom, we shouldn't have anything to say to each other."

"Going to battle together doesn't count?"

"It does and it doesn't. I'll call you."

"Now that we've got a deal, I feel like maybe I could bend the rules and tell you what happened."

"So now ethics don't matter?"

"For five minutes, why don't you just quit being a hard-ass?"

She stood with her weight on her right foot and crossed her arms. "OK, spill your guts."

"This is just between you and me. Nobody else."

"Why should you trust me?"

"Because you may be a lot of things but you aren't untrustworthy."

"Don't tell me anything about the future. Only tell me about the past. I'm only curious about what you did."

Dan took a deep breath. "All right. I fought them tooth and nail on the extra cutters. So did Otran's chief of forestry. To shut us up, Anderson led us to believe they wouldn't do any accelerated cutting. I thought they were doing the usual thing. So did Otran's foresters all the way up to the vice president of natural resources. Normal work on the weekends, nothing else."

"You told them not to do anything out of the ordinary. No winks, nothing like that."

"No winks. I thought it was in their own best interests not to do that sort of thing. So did Otran's people."

"You know you'd be a real asshole to lie to me now."

"I'm not lying to you. I was absolutely trying to keep you away from the Anderson logging show on Sunday morning.

Everything you said about that is true. I suppose nothing will make this right between us?"

"More self-flagellation might be a start." She turned to leave. "I can tell you hate it," she said over her shoulder.

"Hey," he called out. "We have to discuss the chemists and the zoologist. We gotta keep going."

"Yes, we do." She turned to face him. "I was going to call you when I thought I could be civil. I have a zoologist who has spent his life studying bats. And he's rounded up a chemist. Perhaps I should go see them and give you a report."

"Look, Maria, as one human being to another, I'm sorry about these trees. I know how important they are to you."

She shook her head. "You couldn't possibly know. You probably believe that the tooth fairy is a Rockefeller."

"Peace." He held out his hand. Even as she shook her head as if she had reservations, she took his hand in hers. "So let's make an appointment for this zoologist."

"I have a feeling, Dan. We're into something dangerous. You have a little boy. Are you sure you want to pursue this?"

"I'm sure." He squeezed her hand. For a moment she squeezed back and then the touch was gone.

17

Other than security people everywhere, the next day people returned to the courthouse as if nothing had happened. Maria had not called Dan.

She first saw him standing in the courtroom doorway, watching her argue another case. Once again there were plenty of people in the gallery. A San Francisco attorney for Metco was opposing her, and she was in her element, showing the judge a six-foot blowup of a clear-cut. Although she knew Dan would label her argument as full of grand generalizations, simplistic and biased, she also knew she was effective. And on these ancient trees, she was certain she was right.

Maria began gathering her things on the counsel table. When she turned around, she noticed him; for a brief second, before she caught herself, she flashed him her trademark smile.

In the main hallway, the crowd was thinning. Maria watched as Dan greeted Nate and an attractive red-haired woman.

She slowed to say hello.

"Pepacita had to tend to a sick cousin for a few hours," Dan said. "She left Nate with Lynette at the office, and he wanted to come see his dad."

"Actually, *my* son is sick and I have to go home," Lynette said. "I'm afraid if I take Nate, he'll get sick too. And then the boss will get sick."

"Vicious cycle," Dan said, smiling. "There is the old expression that is too common for the likes of you, Lynette, but I'll say it anyway: 'I don't know what I would have done without you.' " He glanced at Maria. "She's my organizer, some days my sanity, and when Pepacita's gone and Katie's at work, she's my second backup child-care person."

"Don't forget nag. I'm his nag. When I get done with my husband, I start in on Dan."

"Maria Fischer, this is my assistant, Lynette Tisdale," Dan said. "And this"—he smiled, tousling the boy's hair— "as you may already know . . . is your admirer."

"Well, I haven't seen you for a while," she told Nate. "You're getting more handsome every day."

Nate grinned at her.

"Well, gotta go. See you later," Lynette said, nodding and moving off through the crowd.

"Hey, dude," Dan exclaimed to Nate.

"Hey, dude," the boy replied. "Are you done in court?"

"All done with the first one. I have one more quick one."

"Were you in court against Ms. Fischer again?"

"No, that was Monday."

"Who won?" He looked at them both.

Dan glanced at Maria. She did not try to hide her interest in his answer.

"We both won."

"Were you mad?" Nate asked Maria.

"Nate apparently has some questions for you," Dan said.

"I can tell." She sat on a bench, getting to Nate's eye level. "I was mad. People cut down trees that I loved and I didn't have a chance to talk about it first."

"I like trees," he said. "But my dad likes to cut 'em so the mill people have jobs. He says growing new ones cleans the air."

"I think your dad's been teaching you."

"My dad's a pretty good guy, you know."

"Yes, Nate, I know he is."

"Could I get that on tape?" Dan said.

"It's a matter of perspective that I think might be lost on the tape," Maria said with a smile.

"Hey, we gotta talk. Let's get the science guys on the phone."

"I know, I know. Yesterday was awful. I'm doing what I can."

"Come for dinner. We can talk things out."

At that moment, Judge Traxler stuck his head into the corridor. "Could I see you a minute?" he said to Dan.

Dan hesitated, then reached for Nate's hand before following the judge.

"If you won't be long, I'll stay with Nate," Maria volunteered.

"You would?"

"I would be happy to entertain the better half of the family," she said. "Besides, I'm sure Judge Traxler would like your undivided attention."

Nate signaled to his father that he wanted to whisper, and Dan leaned over.

Finally Dan stood straight. "If you were to come for dinner. Nate and I would help Pepacita cook for you," he said. "Nate figures that's an important sales feature that I omitted."

Maria was actually tempted for just a moment.

"Really, we need to talk about what I've figured out," Dan added. "Kim Lee disappears. Somebody tries to gas us. You know it was meant for you and me."

"That's what I'm afraid of."

"It would be a working dinner."

"That's really thin." She half-smiled. "We don't need to go to your house to work."

"Please," Nate said.

Maria caught herself looking around to see if anyone was listening. "Just this one more time."

"Maybe you could just take Nate on home then."

"Yes, maybe I could."

"I've watched my dad in court before." Nate's round eyes widened and a look of concentration came over his face as he formed his next question. "Are you an enviro?"

"I'm an environmental activist. Can you say that?"

"Sure—'environmental activist.' " His pronunciation was flawless. "Is that the same as an enviro?"

"I think so, yes. But tell me the correct name again."

"Environmental activist."

Like a sponge, she thought to herself.

"My mom died, you know."

"Yes. I was very sorry to hear that."

"You know, my friend Kenneth got a stepmom."

"He did, huh? What do you think about that?"

"I wish I could remember more about Mom. My dad tries to tell me, but he says it hurts too much."

Maria looked at Nate. Dan Young was a good parent, to have such a great kid—either that or awfully lucky.

Maria laughed. "Let's go," she said, walking to the exit. "You're a real charmer."

Nathaniel brightened at her tone. "What's a charmer?"

"A charmer is someone who pleases other people."

Nathaniel thought for a moment, then nodded. "Do you like my dad?"

Maria smiled at him. His simplicity was pure, unspoiled—simple light in a world of shadowed complexities. "In some ways, Nathaniel, I think I do like him. I don't know him very well, though, and we don't agree about things."

"I like you a lot, but I don't know you very well," Nate said. "I can tell you're good."

"Now, how can you tell that?"

"You hold my hand tight like you don't want anything awful to happen. You'd yell at me if I played in the street."

Maria laughed. "Well, that's all true. But you need to be careful about making up your mind about grown-ups too quickly."

Nathaniel gave her a conspiratorial look. "My dad likes you."

"And how do you know that?"

"Will I get in trouble?" he asked with mischief in his tone.

"I won't tell."

"He let me go with you." He paused as if there were more. He motioned her to lean down in the manner that his father had earlier, and she stopped to put her ear to his lips. "He looks at you funny."

"I see."

"Are you married?" Nate asked as Maria backed her Cherokee out of its parking space.

"No, I'm not, but I have a man friend."

"Is he nice?"

"Yes, I think he is."

"Are you sure?" His serious demeanor and penetrating gaze called for a serious response.

"These would normally be considered very private questions," she said. Looking at him, she saw the disappointment in his eyes. "But among friends, I guess the question is OK. I suppose I'm not sure."

"My dad's nice."

Maria smiled and shook her head. She had never met such a determined nine-year-old. "You and I can be good friends, but your father and I might just be what we call casual friends."

"What's 'casual'? I thought that was like pants." Nate thought for a moment. "So you and my dad don't do stuff together?"

"Right. But that doesn't mean you and I can't be friends."

"We turn here," Nathaniel said suddenly. "This is the way my dad goes."

* * *

Nate was fast asleep in his bedroom, Pepacita was cleaning up in the kitchen, and they were in the den. It was 8:30 P.M. Maria was drinking coffee, Dan his Bud Light.

"Look at this picture," Dan said.

"It's a pretty good blowup of the giant round thing we saw. Almost looks like a kid's swimming pool."

"And this."

"What's that? It looks like a collapsed shack."

"Or a boarded-over hole in the side of the mountain."

"Like a mine."

"But this is still in the area where the mountains have a heavy coastal sediment content. I don't think there are any tunnel mines anywhere near the northern California coast. I've looked for historical mines."

He held up a listing of old mines kept by the state department of mines and geology. "There are none. And look closely here." He gave her a magnifying glass.

"Some kind of a line running from the pool to these boards or whatever this is."

"Something is going on here that doesn't look like Taxol."

"OK."

"I've got to go in there. And we've got to see our chemist. Maybe some of this would make sense."

"Seeing the chemist seems fine, but going back in is nuts."

"We can talk about it. Let's just find out everything we can for now."

"No, I mean it, Dan. If you don't control yourself, I'm going to the sheriff and fink on you. He knows how to be a real jerk. I speak from experience."

His jaw dropped.

"This can become an obsession. You aren't a cop. This has gone far enough. Sometimes breaking a bad law is justified. But this is just dangerous shit. You've got a boy."

Dan sighed.

"If we are going to do this together, promise me you won't sneak around without telling me. We're using *our* contacts at the university," she added. Dan frowned. "Please promise me, no secrets on this."

"All right. You know I'm growing to like you."

She studied him, curious about his meaning.

"In a friendship sort of way."

"Thanks for the vote of confidence," Maria said.

Part of Kenji's face was going numb. The doctor said it was stress. He was also having nightmares. Dan Young standing in the fog watching him on a rickety footbridge, the bridge starting to unravel under his feet. He woke before the bridge disintegrated but not before his heart rate elevated to more than one hundred beats per minute.

The chemists were making some progress. They could now neutralize the effluent in small quantities, using a process suitable for mass-production efforts, but the cost was still too high. Ominously, a spring near the mine was coming up with trace amounts of the effluent—enough to kill wildlife that came to drink. That scared Kenji. If it ever got out that it was seeping into aquifers, he was finished. On the other hand, the only chemist who knew said if it traveled far enough—particularly far enough to get off Amada land—the earth would do the cleansing.

Even more worrisome, Dan Young was not giving up. Tired of palpating his numb upper cheek, Kenji rose from his desk and took the elevator to Groiter's office one floor below. It was late but he figured Groiter would be there. Groiter was dedicated if nothing else. It was locked. He knocked.

Groiter opened the door. "I've got a live feed to the recorder. When I'm listening, I keep the door closed."

"Can this be traced to us?"

"Not with all the relays. Not the way it's set up. If somebody tried to tamper with it, the network would self-destruct."

"Well, don't feed it in here. I don't give a shit how foolproof you think it is. Nothing is going right."

"They're intimidated. Or she is. She's stopped him from going back out to the compound."

"What about the pictures?"

"You've told us not to break into Young's house again. They won't learn anything critical."

"And Schneider?"

"Even if they figured her out, she doesn't know who we are."

"She saw a helicopter. We're not some petty criminals. She knows that."

"She has alibis for everything. Good ones. So I don't think they can squeeze her."

"You seem awfully sure of yourself for someone who hasn't succeeded at much in this mess. Why the fuck aren't those two lawyers dead?"

"Fluke. But they're contained. Maria Fischer is nervous for the boy."

"Make her more nervous."

"It could backfire."

"Don't use Schneider, just hire some thug who'd like to fuck her. I don't care how you do it. Just deliver a strong message. Got it? Don't you have someone just sitting on his ass up in Palmer?"

Groiter nodded.

"Call him. Now."

* * *

"I want to talk about something more personal," Maria said.

"Have at it."

"You're not doing well, are you?"

"What do you mean?"

"I think after your wife died you started drinking a lot."

Dan shrugged. "I hoist a few."

"A lot, they say."

"Who says?"

"Just people. It doesn't matter who says. Just tell me to mind my own business if you want to. Choice is yours."

"Go on."

"You figure you're tough. People die. People get over it. You'll handle it." When she spoke again, her voice was much softer, much more understanding. "Well, am I right?"

"I suppose."

"You're in control of your life? You don't notice any depression, lack of energy, or mood swings—nothing like that? The drinking and the isolation are by your choice?"

"I can deal with it."

"As good a father as you are, can you see this is affecting Nathaniel?" She locked eyes with him.

"Yeah."

"You can trust me and yourself on that."

Dan knew she was right.

"So," she said, staring at him. "How do your friends see you?"

Dan smiled. "Oh, they probably say I'm not quite my old self, drink more."

"What does Lynette think?"

"We're really close. She helps me."

She put a hand over his. "Am I intruding too much for someone from the enemy camp?"

"Of course," he said. "But we've gone this far, we might as well get all your theories out on the table. Lynette arranged a counselor, nagged me into going. I went a couple of times, but I'm not the counseling type."

"What we really need here is a temporary truce. This isn't the timber wars. This is just two colleagues talking. Tell me about how Nate has coped with his mother's death."

Dan sat forward. "The other day, right out of the blue, Nate asked if his mother used to fold his socks. After explaining how she did it, I followed him back to his room and peeked in at him. On the floor there was a box full of old clothes. He'd taken out a pair of socks that were all turned in and rolled up with the toes sticking out, the way she used to do it. And he was just sitting there gently rolling those socks around on the bed. I wanted to talk to him. About her."

For a moment she didn't say anything.

"How about a change of scenery? Let's go down to Mazzotti's and have a tiramisu."

Dan leaned back, dubious.

"You have a couple bites," Maria said. "I'll eat the rest and work it off at aerobics in the morning."

"What's wrong?" Maria asked, touching his forearm.

"Nothing." Dan reached to pour her more wine.

The Italian place was run by a short, pudgy fellow who made the best minestrone Dan had ever tasted. That, and Italian desserts.

"We'll call the science guys tomorrow, OK?"

"Great." He took a sip. "Do they know anything? I mean, why all the suspense? Why didn't they just tell you?"

"I've dealt only with their department secretaries. I get the feeling that they figure they're doing us a favor and we should come and appreciate their help in person. I might be able to set up a conference call, but I'd like to go down there."

"You're right. You can't smile over the phone."

"What does that mean?"

"Your warm-up-the-audience smile." He leaned back. "Best I've ever seen."

The waiter brought the tab with some coffee. For the first time she noticed that one of his blue eyes had a spot of hazel in the cornea. He'd probably shaved early in the morning and his beard, with its late-night shadow, was now rough and blond with a hint of red. She liked it.

"Now you're making me nervous. Are your friends doing more evil deeds that you haven't told me about?"

"It's like your boyfriend. We don't talk about him. We don't discuss my friends' upcoming evil deeds."

"You seem to have a thing about my boyfriend."

"One of us has to."

"I've got to excuse myself to the ladies' room."

After getting directions from a waiter, Maria moved down a shadowy hall. She forced herself to shrug off what seemed to be an irrational sense of alarm. She locked the bathroom door behind her.

On her way back to the dining area, her uneasiness turned to fear. Silhouetted by a light at the end of the hall, a large figure stepped out of the men's room in front of her. A shiver ran up her spine. He was a big man. Don't be silly, she told herself as she approached him. What can happen in a restaurant? She tried to make out his face, but couldn't see much in the silhouette he formed. As she turned to edge past him, she felt herself lifted and thrown head first against the wall—so hard it knocked the wind out of her and made her see stars. There she was held, engulfed in a sea of flesh, pressed flat, unable to move. A large hand clamped over her mouth, and she began getting dizzy.

"Don't move or I'll snap your neck right where you stand," he whispered. He smelled of stale sweat and whiskey. She tried to breath, but couldn't, and the voice continued. "Why don't you take your goddamn nosy attitude someplace else? Down to the Sierras, maybe." While he talked, she forced her right hand behind her, feeling for his crotch. "Bad things could happen around here if you and Young don't lay off. Real bad things, like to that kid of his. What's his name? Nate?" He slammed her against the wall again to make his point. "I promise I'll be back for a real dance. Unless you two lay off."

He ground his pelvis into her buttocks and consequently into her hand. She found his large testicles through his pants. Using her body weight, she squeezed, pulled, and twisted in one fluid motion. Every ounce of her energy went to her straining hands.

A scream burst into her ear and a meaty fist slammed the side of her head, then went to her throat. She yanked up again and then down. The hand disappeared. Choking sounds escaped her lips; then she felt herself dropping, crumpling to the floor. Only then did she release his testicles. His scream had turned to grunting. He staggered back.

"Oh fuck," he muttered, holding himself.

She tried to crawl up the wall, but her legs wouldn't work. Stumbling toward her, he took a swipe at her neck with one hand while he held himself with the other. He missed. She began sliding backward on the floor and screamed, but on the second try his hand took her neck and clamped her throat shut. No blood, no air. She felt the coldness that is death. Bending down to her, he put his face next to hers. When he began to speak—words that her mind never heard—she used her last bit of strength to ram her thumbs into his eyes, causing him to fall back.

From the floor she rammed her heel into his kneecap. Then she managed to get to her feet and half-ran, half-stumbled up the hall with him bellowing his pain as she reached the dining room, her head swirled and she fell head-long into Dan, who grabbed her.

Some crazy logger, she tried to tell herself. But she knew it was the Highlands and the lab and the bats and the damn equations, whatever it meant. This didn't happen because she was an environmentalist or because she had befriended Dan. It happened because Dan Young was after the Amada people. And they had to have been spying on them, trying to make it look like a coincidental meeting with a redneck.

"Are you all right?" Dan was saying.

"I think so."

"Can I help?" It was a young man.

"Someone attacked you?" Dan said.

"Bastard," she said.

"Hold her," Dan said.

"He's long gone and in a world of hurt," she said to Dan, who was moving rapidly toward the back hall.

She teetered as the waiter held her arm. Barely able to stand, she leaned against the wall to take inventory. Nothing felt broken, but she knew she'd have massive bruises. She hobbled back around a corner toward where they had been seated.

Dan ran into the back hallway, found the ladies' room, went to the back where the hallway ended in a T. To the left was a busy kitchen, to the right a storage area, and straight ahead the back door. Opening the door, he found an empty alley. Back inside he stepped into the kitchen. Only the kid washing dishes would have seen the hallway.

"Did you hear a scream and see a guy leave?"

"I seen a guy. Looked hurt bad. I couldn't tell where the scream came from. I thought it was in the alley."

"Can you remember anything about this guy?"

"Big, and wore a dark green shirtlike thing. He was doubled over."

"What color was the man's hair?"

"I don't know. I think he was wearing a stocking cap. He was in the shadows and didn't look my way."

Returning to the restaurant, Dan found the waiter and Maria exactly where he had left them.

He took her to his car, a 1990 Mercedes in virtually new condition. He and Tess had used it on special occasions.

"We've got to report this to the police," Dan said. "And I've got to go back to that compound."

"No. Absolutely not. They threatened Nate. You have *got* to stop fighting them. Let the police do it."

"I think you said that already."

"I'm afraid it's not sinking in. It was a warning, Dan. Somebody doesn't want us doing what we're doing. They may start with me, but it'll end with Nate."

Her words made him silent.

18

"If you won't go to the emergency room, then at least come and sleep on the couch in my house. If you feel worse during the night, we can take you in."

They were parked in the Mercedes outside the Palmer Inn after filing a report with the police and then another session with the sheriff, who'd been angry when Dan told him they had checked out Corey Schneider and her alibi without talking to him.

"My adrenaline is pumping," Maria said. "I don't think I can sleep."

"Then you'll come," Dan said, starting the engine.

"You're forgetting something. My suitcase is in my room."

"Forget it. I still have the same toothbrush you used last time. The pj's you wore are cleaned. You're all set. I'll drop you off back here in the morning on my way to work."

"I have a favor to ask."

"What?"

"Are you not sleepy, either?" she asked.

"Not really. Not after all that. But it's eleven o'clock, and I have to try to get to sleep at least by midnight."

"So we have an hour."

"Yeah? What are you thinking?"

"Show me Tess's grave."

"What? Are you nuts?"

"I want to see it. And I want you to take me there."

"It's dark. And . . ."

"Many cemeteries are lit at night. Isn't this one?"

"Well, I think so. Some."

"Then take me."

"Not tonight. Some other time."

"What, you think I'm going to be stopping regularly for this?"

"Why do you want to go there? You never even knew her."

"You did. You been there?"

"You know I haven't."

"Frankly, it's Nate I'm thinking about. If you can't go there yourself, you won't be taking him there."

"What is it with you and visiting graves?"

She didn't answer.

"You think I have some emotional hang-up, that I'm not grieving, or something."

She said nothing, just looked straight ahead.

"You're all beat-up. It makes no sense to go right now, in the middle of the night."

"Say no and stop with the arguing if you won't take me. You don't owe me an explanation."

"Damn, you're stubborn."

"I believe the cemetery is to the left up here. True?"

Dan pulled the wheel around and the tires squeaked as the car went left toward the cemetery. He didn't know what this would prove. He was reluctant, but many healthy people didn't go to graves. He took a deep breath. This was no big deal and it would make her happy.

There were soft low lights around the cemetery and along the paths, just enough so that visitors could find their way. A big sign said the gates would be locked at midnight and the lights turned off. He pulled in by the gate and stopped the car.

"You should go by yourself," she said.

It seemed that everybody but him thought he should go to the cemetery. Lynette, his mother, everybody who knew him, thought it, in one form or another. They thought he should make his peace with Tess's death. Or maybe it was that he should face it. Without saying anything, he got out of the car and began walking. He knew exactly where it was.

Sitting down on the grass next to the stone marker, he stared at the engraving: TESS YOUNG — BELOVED WIFE OF DAN YOUNG AND MOTHER OF NATHANIEL. What did he want to say to her? He closed his eyes and imagined her as he had seen her last: Nathaniel clinging to her leg, his cheek against her thigh; her eyes laughing at him as she explained that she wanted to steal him away to a desert island, where they would live off coconuts. It was almost as if she were right there in front of him.

And before he knew what was happening, Dan began talking, the words pouring like water through a burst dam. "I loved to listen to your heartbeat. I remember how it felt when you put your hand on my face, what your eyes did when they looked into mine." On and on, he recounted his memories.

If she were here, what would she say? She had a practical side to her. "Can you find something new, something different?" she'd ask.

In his mind he searched the face of his dead wife, for some sorrow, some torment, some anguish of soul, but found none. "How do I accept this loss?"

She was someplace far away, or no place. If she were here, what could she say?

"I don't want to hope," he said aloud. He smacked his palm with his fist and rocked. "I don't want to hope for another you. I'm angry, and I don't want to hope."

The car was parked near a streetlamp, and away from the deep shadows. Maria looked out at a large white Victorian structure that served as the funeral home. Down its sides ivy had been strung on trellises, and grown vigorously, forming luxuriant green carpets, making it seem more a place for the living than the dead. But for the frogs and the crickets, it was silent.

She reasoned that having just been attacked, she would not be assaulted again—for the moment. The logic was only slightly reassuring. Under ordinary circumstances Maria would have preferred not sitting alone on a dark street after just being assaulted. Additionally, there was her throbbing jaw and accompanying headache, not to mention the anguish from her bruised ribs. She would tell none of this to Dan Young.

It was midnight when she saw him coming down the path. He had been gone a long time. She unlocked the car, grateful for the company but nervous, not knowing what to expect.

He got in the car, looking completely composed.

"Well, I did it." He turned to her, looking so relaxed it seemed odd.

"There is something I always wanted to tell her. But never did."

"Do you want to tell me?"

"I don't know." He sat silent for a time. "After we'd been married maybe three years, there were still other women I would think about. Of course everybody thinks about other people. But I just ... you know ... would think about the possibilities."

"I understand."

"And I knew there was this certain closeness that Tess and I never had. So one night in bed, I held her close and I formed this mental image. It was like a mental game and I had to concentrate very hard. I imagined a big beautiful casket with a clear glass top. It sat over a hole in the ground. Tess and I were in the casket together. They closed it. Standing around was everyone we knew, especially the women I thought about. It was hard to focus on those women, to see their faces, to look into their eyes as we were being lowered. But I concentrated and in my imagination I made their faces clear. And the crowd waved and the other women threw flowers. And then they all slowly disappeared. You with me so far?"

"I'm with you."

"This hole in the ground was like the Alice-in-Wonderland

hole because it had no bottom. In my mind it came out in this Garden of Eden. And we were going there for the night. Just the two of us. So once I had watched everybody disappear, I began concentrating on Tess. My fingers were on her back, lightly, her body tight against mine. I'd say in my mind over and over, 'Just the two of us, just the two of us.' Every millimeter of my body was taken up with sensing her.

"Now when this was going on in my head I never said a word; I only held her and let my fingers run over her back. The first time I did it, she cried, happy tears, and asked me what I was doing. I said: 'Does it feel different?' She said, 'It's the most wonderful thing I've ever felt. What were you thinking about?'

"And I said, 'Just the two of us.' She said, 'That's all?' I told her I was concentrating on a particular mental image. 'What's the image?' she asked.

"And I waited a minute. Then I said, 'If I tell you, maybe it won't work.' I didn't want to get into explaining about the other women. And the looking in their eyes and watching them disappear. Or maybe I thought it would sound too crazy. I think I thought if we talked about it, then it might not work. Anyway, I promised that I would tell her sometime. And it was our anniversary coming up. We had agreed that I would tell her. I'd done this little meditation quite a bit by then and it was as close to magic as I'll ever come. I know it sounds dumb."

"No, no. God no. It doesn't sound dumb at all. But you didn't tell her?"

"I never had a chance. Our anniversary was the day she died. And on that day I knew I should go and pick up Nate. I knew it. It was my turn. And if I had . . ."

"And you've been thinking about that."

"I lie in bed at night and try to get back that picture of

me and her together in the glass-topped casket. Just me and her. But ever since the day she died, I can't. I can only think I should have gone to get Nate. And she would be alive.''

"I'm sure she knew even if she didn't understand. She knew that you were pushing the others out of your heart and leaving room only for her.''

"I can't get her back even in my head.'' His voice didn't crack until the last word. Then he wept the most profound sobs she had ever witnessed. "I can't get her back.''

Overwhelmed by his sorrow, she forgot who he was, who she was, the many expectations that imprisoned them both. She wrapped her arms around his head and held him.

Back at the house they each took a sofa in the family room. After Maria had changed into her now-official nightwear for these sleep-overs, she returned to find him trying to put sheets on the couch.

"A sleeping bag worked fine,'' she said.

"Well, that was when we had a tent,'' he joked, looking at the lumpy sheets.

"Here, I'll help you fold them back up and we can get the sleeping bags.''

As they were folding, she looked at him and smiled.

"My face must look horrible.''

"Just a little bruised. Probably doesn't look nearly as bad as it feels.''

"Forget calling the scientists. I want to go to L.A. tomorrow. We can take Nate. He can stay at my parents' with my mother while we're at the university. We should get out of here and take stock.''

"Your mother?'' He looked shocked.

"You have gotten the idea that my parents are dead. I

called her from here the other night. My mother and I are best friends.''

"What about the log cabin, and the dishwater that froze before it hit the ground, and the cross-country skiing, and all of that?''

"It's true. I lived in a cabin in the far north.''

"Where were your parents?''

"Where they've always been. I went to Alaska after college. I got out of high school two years early and got my undergraduate degree in three years.''

"Well, what are your parents like? What's your dad do?''

"You're trying to place my family on the old socioeconomic ladder, huh?''

"You a little touchy about it?''

"Actually, I am. What I tell you about myself stays strictly between you and me. Got it?'' She stepped toward him with the sheet and found her finger pointing at his nose.

"I got it,'' he said.

"My dad's a wealthy businessman. So now you know.''

Dan started chuckling. "Well, I'll be damned. And you had a falling-out?''

"It all started one day when we were watching a football game. We did that a lot, my daddy and me. I was just about to graduate from Stanford. He was taking an unusually long time pouring his drink. I remember he was wearing a golf shirt with a little polo emblem on it that I got him when I was shopping near school. Funny what you remember. Anyway, he turns around, looks at me, and says, 'I have the law school picked out.'

"I said, 'I hope it's Yale because I think I'll get accepted.'

" 'It's Boalt Hall. I don't want you all the way on the East Coast. If we're spending my money,' he said. Well, you know about my temper. And he had been a little overbearing in recent times and there was this edge between us.

It felt like a situation that could explode. I looked at him and said, 'Did you say, "spending my money"?' And there were a few more words about money and control and I got up and walked out and packed my backpack. Skipped the graduation ceremony. And flew to Alaska. On my way out the door, I heard my mother talking to my father. It was the only time in my life I have ever heard her use a four-letter word."

"What did she say?"

"She said, 'This time, dear, I think you really fucked up.' I had friends in Alaska, a married couple, in Fairbanks."

Fairbanks was twenty degrees below zero on the November night that Maria arrived. Fortunately, she had the presence of mind to shop in Anchorage and get outfitted with insulated boots, gloves, a parka, and heavy sweaters. Even with all the trappings, the cold still cut through her, made her bones ache, and pretty much pushed her indoors every moment she could get near heat. Standing only moments in the still night air, she took a cab to 2640 Lambert. It was a nice house, Sam Nehi was the manager of a wholesale petroleum outfit, the head of the local office, and Margi, his wife, was a homemaker. They welcomed Maria with open arms.

Quickly she found a cabin and a job tending huskies for a man named Cotter, whose hobby was racing dog sleds. Her cabin was near the dogs, their yelping, their smell, their food, and their droppings. It was 22'x14', all one room, no running water, a good woodstove, kerosene lanterns, an outhouse if you could stand it, a bucket if you couldn't. There was a sturdy pine table, four chairs, a small sofa, and a brass bed, with a mediocre mattress. Oddly, she found it satisfactory.

Within two weeks she had enrolled in a correspondence law school. In the mornings she tended the dogs, exercised them, groomed them, doctored them, and fed them. Afternoons and evenings she studied.

Cotter was a good man, ran his own feed store, and was greatly amused at the sprightly, well-educated young woman who came out of nowhere to tend and eventually race his dogs. She could mush the dogs as well as any woman around and was better than most of the men.

Cotter had two homes, one in town where he spent most nights, and one near Maria's cabin at Cotter Hollow. The reason for the town house was that it was not easy to get to Cotter Hollow and once you got there you found nothing but Cotter's compound. In winter, access was by snowmobile and cross-country ski. Unless she was hauling supplies, Maria preferred the skis. It was twenty minutes of hard work to get to the parking lot and the four-wheel-drive Cherokee she ultimately acquired out of her meager wages and some money that her mother required her to accept. Her father wasn't allowed to require anything.

On all the holidays that Maria could get away for, she went home to visit. Barely speaking to her father, she maintained a rigorous chilly formality that thawed by fractions of a degree with each visit. Her mother was dismayed but stayed out of it.

Just after Maria passed the California bar exam, days before she was due to leave Alaska for the offices of Patty McCafferty, something happened. During the almost three years that Maria lived at Cotter Hollow, she had come to know the Prestons. They lived in a beautiful and grand log house situated adjacent to the trailhead to Cotter Hollow, where Maria parked her car in one of Cotter's three garages. Maria, who had a natural affinity for kids, got to know Amy Preston on short winter visits over hot chocolate.

Amy's father was a trapper who never ran a line or stretched a pelt. Her mother called herself Sarah Preston (although her native name was different and mostly unpronounceable) and was a successful weaver who made custom blankets that were really art.

Maria arrived several times a week at the Preston home on her skis. In front of Cotter's nearby garage, she would remove her skis, load them onto her Jeep Cherokee and—with a heater efficient enough to raise the temperature slightly above freezing on a cold day—drive to Fairbanks with something less than a certain conviction that she would make it.

Passing the Preston house day after day on her way to town, Maria became familiar with the place: when the lights came on in the morning and went off in the evening, that Thursday was garbage day, that Mr. Preston heated the engine blocks on the cars at about 6:00 on those mornings when he wasn't alcoholically incapacitated, that Mr. Preston usually shoveled snow on Saturdays when the inebriation exception didn't apply—and in that event he waited until Sunday.

Eventually she got to know Mrs. Preston and her beautiful blankets, and the story of Mr. Preston before he became a morose drunk. One late evening, as she passed by the Prestons', she noticed the house dark except for a shimmering strange light in the windows. And she thought she heard a cry. Shuffling closer on her skis, she became certain of the sound and rushed to the front steps.

There by the side of the steps, frozen solid in a dirty T-shirt, bottle still clenched in an icy hand, was Mr. Preston—stone dead. She threw off her skis and dashed to the heavy oak front door. It was locked. Through the window she saw that the dancing light was a roaring fire. Maria *took a flying leap through the living-room window; protected by her thick parka, she landed on the inside floor unscathed.*

"Is anyone here?" she screamed.

Amy appeared at the top of the stairs, shaking and screaming long screams, her hair wild and mussed, holding out her arms as if she wanted to be picked up. The stairway was an inferno. Unlocking the front door, Maria ran back outside, only to be chased by flames looking for oxygen. Hoping to contain the fire, she slammed the door. A ladder, a tree, she couldn't think. There was no way up. Over the front porch was a slanted roof, above that roof a window. There was no way to make it to the roof. "God help me," she muttered, desperate, the little girl's face filling her mind.

Then she saw her semifaded red Cherokee. Running through the knee-deep snow on the walkway, she made it to the Jeep, jumped in, and drove for the front porch. Pushing the wheels up the steps, she drove until the front end of the vehicle was a foot from the front door. By climbing onto the top of the Jeep cab, she was able to pull herself atop the porch roof and dive through a window into the master bedroom.

Flames were everywhere. Her parka caught fire and she yanked it off while staying flat on the floor. Crawling forward, she found the door, the hallway, the top of the stairs. Amy lay unconscious, the smoke thick and dirty. Maria hadn't bothered to breathe and was running out of air. Grabbing the little girl, she got out of the house by leaping from the second story into a snow bank. But not before a falling timber had caught her midriff and burned in a permanent six-inch scar across her belly.

"I showed you mine," Dan said as she completed her story. They had bedded down on the two family-room couches that nearly converged in an L shape. His head was a couple feet from hers.

"What do you mean?"

"I spilled my guts; you should show me your scar so I can tell you it isn't a big deal."

"I'm not showing you my scar."

"You want to."

"Go to sleep, Dan."

They were in the bowels of a USC science lab in the section devoted to zoology. The large, somewhat haphazard work space lay under a maze of old pipes wrapped in something that looked like plaster-cast material. Evidently, the bat people weren't graced with the best digs. Dr. Michael Sanford welcomed them into his office and brought out the photos.

"We'll start with the bat. There are about one hundred species of bats that we know of. Nearly one quarter of all mammal species worldwide are bats." His eyes glistened with enthusiasm. "Bats belong to the order *Chiroptera*. But they defy generalization because their dietary habits and habitats vary so widely. Now this fellow here looks like a hoary bat. Notice I said 'looks like.' He isn't quite. Coloring around the neck is a little different. I had to do quite a bit of comparing to figure that out. Almost classifies as a subspecies. It's always exciting to find something new." He sighed and took off his glasses. "I don't suppose you know where I could get a carcass?"

"No," Dan said. "If you knew they were in a particular area, would you know how to find them?"

"Oh yes. They live in trees, come out at night, and feed on insects. Any relative would be very interesting, especially if its behavior differed."

"Do they ever come out during the day?"

"Never. Unless you kick them out of the tree, but then they'll go immediately to another and roost again."

"Anything odd about this one other than this neck color?"

"Not that I can see. But there could be all kinds of things if we actually had a carcass."

"What about the math? And these chemical equations?"

"You know, these pages are electro-chemical equations on one side and quantum neural mechanics on the other. The chemistry and applied math seem completely unrelated. I showed this around to some chemistry professors and applied math men. The fellow who did this math in the photo is expert in artificial intelligence. The math guys got a kick out of it, wrote a sort of informal memo for me. Here it is," he said, handing it to Dan with a wink. "You can read it later, when you're having trouble falling asleep."

Dan folded it up and put it in his pocket.

"Enjoy," the professor said. "I hope it helps. It's written for a layman. Sort of. The gist of it is that this guy was doodling in quantum mathematics. The man who wrote this equation has a theory that quantum mathematics is the best model for describing intelligence or artificial intelligence if you were trying to replicate what a mammal does. The same math we use for describing the universe. In layman's terms we could say it's a richly descriptive language for that purpose. Whoever did this was interested in quantum neural dynamics, otherwise known as quantum consciousness. You want me to explain that?"

"Yes, please."

"Using Hilbert math or quantum math, we can better describe thoughts because a thought may be more than the sum of its parts. A thought is the sum total of a pattern of neural firing. In traditional math a thought could never be more than the sum of its parts. Not so with quantum neural mechanics. In that realm the sum of the parts could be much more than the whole. Hence, a thought. Or thoughts about a thought. Or, for a nonhuman mammal, an image associated with a feeling. You're furrowing your brow. Read the paper. It'll help. We can simplify for our discussion. Judging from what we see here, we can assume this fellow was very interested in solving some riddle about brains.''

"How could bats relate to all this?"

"Any evidence of bats behaving strangely?"

Maria and Dan looked at one another. "You say that bats never fly in the daytime. We observed one do just that."

"So the person who wrote this equation may have been a specialist in mammalian neural networks. In the context of your situation, perhaps he was pondering bat behavior. He may have been a zoologist who knew a lot about neural networks and this was just some of his chicken scratch. Thinking on paper, so to speak. Contemplating odd bat behavior would be consistent with his training."

"If he was a zoologist with a picture of this bat, he would have been interested in the new species aspect as well."

"Anybody in that line of work would."

"If this is a bat that's merely *like* a hoary bat, is it possible that it flies around in the daylight?"

"It would be the only known bat species that does that and it would be terribly fascinating."

"So if the scientific community knew of a forest habitat where they could find a colony of these bats, what would happen?"

"Army of zoologists, that's what. You don't know of such a forest, do you?"

"No. We saw one bat flying in the daylight."

"Where?"

"You don't want to go there," Maria said.

"Try me."

"No way. Now what about the chemistry?"

"I'll call my colleague. He's standing by in his office."

While they waited, the professor told them all about bats, more than they expected to hear, and tried to wheedle information about the location of their bat sighting. They remained firm. About fifteen minutes later the chemistry professor showed up. He reminded Dan of Jack Nicholson without hair.

"Well, Frank, tell them about the chemistry," Dr. Sanford said after making introductions all around.

"That's fairly easy except you only got a small part of the equation. This is a portion of an equation that I believe describes a process for the conversion of wood fiber into something like an alcohol or a methanol. Unfortunately, you didn't get the interesting part. Nothing in the middle or the end. I'd love to see it. My gut tells me they are on to something new."

"Could it be valuable?"

"Turning wood into liquid gold? Yeah, it could be valuable. How valuable is Saudi Arabia if its wells never run dry? A new process to convert wood to fuel that's cheaper and maybe more efficient and you have something analogous to Saudi Arabia with no end in the oil supply. You can always grow a new tree."

"Does whoever wrote this have such a process?"

"It looks interesting, but I need the rest."

"So all we can discern is that they are turning wood into a fuel, like a petroleum substitute."

"I think you have it."

They were on their way to La Jolla and Maria's parents. Maria's mother had met them at the airport upon their arrival and had taken Nate home while they proceeded to the university. Now Dan couldn't resist asking, "Is there something you haven't told me about all this? You've been nervous all day."

"Like what?"

"Like why a hard-driving businessman would be home in the early afternoon to see a daughter with whom he has only a formal, chilly—I believe that is the word—relationship. Like why you're nervous about it."

"Do I look nervous?" she asked. "You know it's really irritating when you smirk like that. And I said that it was a slowly thawing, chilly relationship."

"What's the matter?" he asked.

"Well, maybe this whole business of taking Nate to the zoo looks a little like something it's not."

"We've gone over that ad nauseam."

"So we have."

"But my parents may not believe we're all business. That we're just doing this to get away from this mess and for Nate."

"So?"

"So my father may want to meet you."

"This is the father whom you barely speak to. Why would you care?"

"It's complicated. We're in the end stage of the fight. The maneuvering stage. So just try to get through it the best you can. I'm debating on going inside by myself to pick up Nate."

"I'm that much of an embarrassment?"

"No. Don't you get it? You represent Jeb Otran. You're fucking perfect. He'll fawn all over you. He'll want to smoke cigars, drink bourbon, and do whatever it is you business guys do when you're sniffing around each other's butts."

"Can't really say as I'm familiar with this butt-sniffing ritual."

"You know what I mean."

"I think you mean you're terrified I'll get along famously with your father, something you can't do, and you'll be mad as hell."

"You could help me out here, you know. Just a quick introduction and explain how anxious you are to get Nate to the zoo."

"Why don't you just tell him I have pink hearts on my boxer shorts? Maybe I've turned gay or something."

"You're going to torture me, aren't you?"

"Maybe not. Say, not to change the subject, but how is your boyfriend, Ross?"

"I think he's fine. We haven't seen each other a lot recently."

"Does he know you're turning lukewarm?"

"Beg pardon?"

"Oh, come on, I thought we were the no-bullshit team."

Maria looked away. "I think he thinks we're just taking a little breather."

"From sleeping together?"

Maria smiled and shook her head as if shocked by the question. "Candor is one thing. Rude is another."

"Well, you can tell me to shut up."

"Good. Shut up."

"Look, it's no big deal, maybe Ross would like to go to the zoo with us."

"Dan?"

"Yes."

"Stop it. We're absolutely clear on what we're about."

"Absolutely clear. So me having a drink with your dad, a little talk, shouldn't hurt anything?"

"That's it. You wait in the car. I'll get Nate."

"Awfully rude, don't you think? Not to say even hello?"

"Please don't do this to me."

"We could make a deal. I won't say anything about us to your dad if you'll tell me about Ross."

"There is no 'us.' "

"Right, and I'll make that perfectly crystal clear if you tell me about Ross."

"It depends on what you want to know."

"He's a biologist, isn't he? Works for the state? What level is he?"

"If you're suggesting my father doesn't like him for his occupation, you're wrong. Even my father isn't quite that crass."

"Why doesn't he like him?"

"Because Ross is a very calm sort of even-tempered guy who doesn't go off the deep end about things. Are you happy?"

"When I've seen him, he sure hasn't been calm."

"I mean about life, not about you."

"You mean he's unambitious."

"You can really be a jerk, you know."

"You've got chutzpah. Your dad probably just wants an even match in a husband."

"You and my dad, with your power trips." She shook her head. "He's gonna love you. So just don't let him get the wrong idea. Please."

19

Kenji sat beneath a crystal chandelier at the Bankers Club, a private luncheon establishment known for its good food and fast service. Often he stayed in San Francisco and worked in the city offices instead of driving to the operations headquarters for Amada in Palmer.

"I'm worried about exactly what Schneider got out of Kim Lee," he said to Groiter.

"You have my report. Nothing but a mention of bats and Catherine Swanson."

"What about Catherine Swanson?"

"He was incoherent. Said Catherine Swanson was in his briefcase or something. We looked and there was nothing of Catherine Swanson."

"Do you believe her?"

"In a word, yes. She might hide a few things. On the whole we have an understanding."

"Because you beat her senseless?"

"No, it's much deeper than that."

"What do you mean?"

"I think I know what makes her tick."

"That bitch could have tortured Kim Lee. Pumped him for information. Got him to spill his guts."

"Relax. It didn't happen."

"Those lawyers are making you look like an idiot. Schneider is supposed to kill them at the courthouse, and then she claims some guy stopped her. Who?"

"She thinks he was Japanese."

Kenji gripped the table sides. "Japanese? Why didn't you tell me this immediately?"

"I wanted to be certain, but all we have is her word. She thinks he was Japanese."

"You don't think he's from my wife's family?"

"Let's not jump to conclusions."

"Somebody broke into the compound and killed the dogs. Could—"

The waiter came across the room with a brown envelope in his hand.

"A lady asked me to give you this," he said, handing it to Groiter.

The envelope was made of thick paper and sealed with masking tape. Kenji could see that it came from Groiter's assistant. From in front of his place setting, Groiter took the sharp knife and deftly cut through the tape and the top flap as well. Parting the envelope, he looked inside. He pulled out a white sheet of paper and handed it to Kenji.

"It's a summary from the wiretap and the surveillance," he said. It explained in some detail how two of Groiter's men had followed Young and Fischer to the University of Southern California campus to meet with a zoologist whose specialty was bats.

"So they're still at it. Your warning meant nothing."

"It's kept them out of the compound. They don't think anybody could possibly know about the visit to the university."

"It could unravel everything."

"Next time we'll get it right. If she takes out Dan Young, that will do it," Groiter said.

"I don't want to hear about it. I just want them to go away. Got it?"

"Got it. Consider it over."

With a cup of coffee in her hand, Corey walked to the phone without so much as a limp. It amazed her that she had recovered from the beatings so quickly. The German and Asian were both technicians.

"After a little rest you will be ready to do something big."

"What should I do?"

"Dan Young is corrupting what little good was coming from Maria Fischer."

"Which one should I kill first?"

"We'll talk later. How are you feeling?"

"Like shit," she lied. She actually wanted this man's sympathy.

"I am sorry. You will feel better, I promise. As always, let us be your eyes and ears."

Literally within sixty seconds a knock came on her front door. She jacked a round in her Colt and looked out the fish-eye viewer. Nobody. What she saw made her suck in her breath. Set back on the porch, in the light of a small lantern, was a sign. It said only: DAN YOUNG.

Not surprisingly, by morning the sign was gone.

The Fischers' home was a spacious, modern affair, an angular collection of glass and white stucco. It shared a scenic hillside with a number of other homes of similar size and distinction, none closer than one hundred yards away. A sweeping circular drive passed through a portico at both ends, and guests entered the house through massive oak double doors.

Dan chuckled when they drove up. And laughed when he saw her stiffen.

"OK, you've had your laugh."

"I'll take it easy," he said.

Mrs. Fischer, who wore a long, flowing, deep blue housecoat, greeted him warmly with a double handshake before kissing her daughter.

"Nathaniel is playing Nintendo," Mrs. Fischer said. Trim, with no gray streaks in her blond hair and the same high cheekbones and big eyes as Maria, Laura Fischer appeared to be in her late forties, at least a decade younger than she must be. "Welcome. We're just delighted you could come."

"Well, I actually promised Nate a trip to the zoo," Dan said as if on cue.

"Maria, my beautiful daughter." Amiel Fischer came out of a large hallway to the left. A balding man, about 5' 10", with a strong baritone voice. "And you've brought your friend." He extended his hand to Dan.

"Colleague," Maria corrected.

"Colleague and coadventurer, I understand from your mother. Surely, you two don't have to rush off. At the least I'd like to show Dan my den, my scotch, and my humidor. It's not often I meet a friend of my daughter's."

Fischer gestured powerfully with his hands even as he spoke in smooth, unhurried tones. Intelligence lit his eyes, and a thin, black mustache, as dapper as the crisp white handkerchief in the pocket of his herringbone blazer, accented his dark, handsome face. He seemed an avalanche of energy, and suddenly Dan understood the intensity of Maria's conflict with her father. He was an intriguing man, and Dan found himself curious. It was as Maria had feared.

"I promised to take Nate to the zoo. We don't really have time."

Amiel looked at Maria. "Not even for a single drink? Just a few minutes for your old man?"

Maria hesitated. "Dan, I think we could take a few minutes, what do you think?"

"Sure," Dan said.

"But, Daddy, I *know* Dan wants to get going, so please don't capture him." Maria's emphasis on the word "know" sounded as if she were jumping on the single syllable with both feet.

"Well, we'll hurry with that one drink, then."

Mr. Fischer led Dan on a brief tour. The foyer was large,

two stories tall, with massive vertical beams along the side-walls and matching beams above. Custom milled, with dark oak moldings, the windows and doors matched the crown molding throughout the house. A hardwood staircase with Persian runner and stained balustrade climbed to the balcony overlooking the foyer. Past the foyer was a spacious living room, bordered by a formal dining room. Immediately to the right were double swinging doors, beyond which lay the kitchen and the adjoining family room. To the left and down the hall, there was a library with cherry or mahogany ceiling, deep-hued paneling and bookcases. At one end was a massive fireplace. Through the back corner of the library was a den hidden behind what was probably a bedroom accessed through the main downstairs hallway.

In the den were two soft leather chairs in dark brown and a fabric couch in earth tones. There were two beautiful oils, one of Laura Fischer and one of Maria in her late teens. On his desk and the shelves behind were photographs of his wife and daughter. Most were of Maria. Dan winced at some indefinable thought about Amiel Fischer and his daughter. For a moment he couldn't put his finger on it. Then he knew: Amiel felt he had lost Maria and so he had surrounded himself with her pictures. The parallel with Dan's own life was unmistakable.

Amiel pushed a button on a disc player and soft jazz came on.

"What do you drink?"

"Mostly beer, but Dewar's and water is good."

"I have that." He opened a massive liquor cabinet with one of the best stocks Dan had ever seen. The Dewar's was way in the back in the economy class. Up front were twenty-five-year-old Glenlivet, Crown Royal, and the like. Amiel poured him a heavy tumbler, more than he could possibly drink and stay rock-hard sober.

"I hear you're a big football fan."

"Yeah, that's true. Niners."

"Well, of course I'm a Rams man myself. USC coach and I get together all the time. In the off season we watch tapes when he's getting ready for the next season."

Dan nodded appropriately.

"Not to change the subject but I listen to my wife. She says my daughter is at least a little bit fond of you."

Dan sighed, and sipped his drink. At least Amiel was getting right to the point.

"One thing I'll say for you, Mr. Fischer."

"Please call me Amiel." -

"You don't waste a lot of time with small talk."

"That comes later. I know you're no weak sister. Maybe you drink a bit much lately, but you've got guts. Why should I waste time on trivialities?"

"We each have our issues—Maria and I—so we both get jumpy when you use words like 'fond.' "

"So you do this pretend thing?"

"Well, I'm not sure it's all pretend, but more or less. Yeah. We gotta be saying it's one thing while maybe we're doing something else."

"I love my daughter more than life itself. At the moment I'm afraid it's not mutual."

"Actually, I think it is."

"You do?"

"I think she desperately wants to find a way back."

"Do you love her?"

"I don't know. Maybe on occasion it's starting to feel something like that, but that has to stay between you and me."

"I confess I've done some checking. Probably not right. I found out you're a good man. I run across Jeb Otran from time to time. I called him."

Dan shook his head and smiled.

"If you end up together, I would really like to get to know you. When it's appropriate."

"I understand," Dan said.

"What do you think of her boyfriend, Ross?"

"I don't know him very well."

"Come on."

"She's falling out of love with him, but she'd never tell you or me that."

"She was never in love with him. He was the opposite of me. That's all he had going for him."

"And you think deep down she wants somebody like you?"

"Not just like me. A New Age man who's you know— sensitive. Respects women as they call it. I mean I respect women, but you know, I don't try to get in touch with my feminine side. I stay firmly attached to my balls."

Dan laughed. "Yeah, I can see where you and your daughter must get down and dirty when you fight."

"We've both got strong wills. Now how you gonna knock her boyfriend off? You going to wait till he falls off a cliff or push a little?"

"Amiel, I don't know if we should be having this conversation. You know she's gonna pump me for everything we talked about."

"That's what I like about you. You got character. I'm just overanxious. I only have one daughter."

"Amiel, when there's something to talk about, we'll talk. And if you have any hope that your grandchildren won't be fathered by a state biologist, you should let it rest and give it time. Maria and I are a long way from anywhere. I'm not getting in the middle of whatever you and your daughter have going."

"Smart man. But promise me something."

"What?"

"Promise me you'll tell me when you fall in love with her."

Dan thought for a moment. "Fair enough."

"And one more thing. What's said on the trail stays on the trail."

"And I gather that goes for the den too?"

"The den too." Amiel chuckled. "Hey, before you go, I wanna show you something. Play of the century."

Grabbing a remote, he hit the play button and there were the 49ers and the Rams.

Dan knew this had to be a setup. Amiel must want to know if he really understood his football. This he relished.

There was a knock on the door. Amiel punched off the player.

"We need full concentration for this."

Maria opened the door, looking slightly impatient.

"Well, boys?"

"Just one play, dear, just one play." Again he pushed the button. Niners had the ball on their own thirty-yard line. The snap, handoff, and a run up the middle that made a forty-yard gain, but for one lucky tackle, it would have been a touchdown.

"What did you see?" Amiel asked.

"Interesting the way the Niners countered to the short side of the field from the left hash. They took advantage of the defense's fear of Jackson's speed to the strong side."

"Get some eyes, Young," Maria interjected before Amiel could speak. "The Rams were in a Split-six D with the tackles pinching hard. The pulling right guard has no leverage, running into the tackle that way. Notwithstanding the forty-yard gain, the Niners would have been better served to have faked the play up the middle, and play-actioned on the tight-end delay." She paused. "That would have been six points."

Wanting to get even, Dan thought for a second. "You embarrass all your boyfriends in front of your daddy?"

"Now you're jerking my chain. Let's go."

They tore Nathaniel away from Nintendo and chocolate chip cookies, then said good-bye to Amiel and Laura Fischer. Everybody looked a little overanxious except Amiel, who appeared unfazed.

Once in the car, Maria turned her attention to Nate.

"So you are a real Nintendo player."

"She doesn't seem old enough to be your mother. She's good at Nintendo."

"Yes, my mother is good at lots of things."

"Your father's nice too."

"Yes, in his old-world way, I guess he can be charming." She looked at Dan as she said it.

"He was a real card. And he loves you. That I can guarantee."

"And what did you find to discuss?"

"Not much. Amiel headed into forbidden territory pretty fast, and we ended up talking about the fact that we shouldn't be talking about what we were about to be talking about. It was obvious he thinks about you all the time."

"And what exactly did you two discuss?"

"Well, we never really got there. It was more a discussion about what we weren't going to discuss?"

"Which was?"

"Well, how can I discuss that?"

"She's getting mad, Dad," Nate said.

"Thank you, Nate," Maria said. "That was well said."

"Yeah. Well, Amiel was—" Dan began talking with one hand, but no words were coming.

"He was talking about my boyfriend. He was asking you

if you and I were romantic. And all I want to know is what you said.''

''I said we shouldn't discuss it. That you and I were a long way from anywhere. And I said you had issues.''

''You probably made it sound like we're on the threshold of the promised land but for my 'issues.' You were supposed to say that we're in Egypt and living with Pharaoh, with no travel plans, no travel arrangements, and no travel agent, for God's sake. And what was that crack about you being my boyfriend?''

''You were supposed to act like an enviro.''

''Oh and what's that like?''

''Barefoot, stupid, hair under your arms. And nothing about football.''

Nate laughed.

Back in Palmer, Dan dropped Nate at home with Pepacita before taking Maria to her car. They talked easily, Dan driving a circuitous route. When they pulled up behind the Cherokee, they both went silent. After nervous smiles, Dan helped Maria put her luggage in her car, then came around to close her door. She was about to get in and then hesitated. For just an instant in time he knew that kissing her would be the most natural thing in the world. They were looking right at each other—not talking. With a slight smile she held out her hand. Then before he could react, she dropped it and hugged him. It was somewhere in between a brother hug and a boyfriend hug. She kissed him on the cheek.

''Call me,'' she said. ''Soon. Like when you get home.''

Dan got on his cell phone on the drive to his house. He called Otran's home. It felt a little unusual. Normally, he was relaxed around Otran, but this time he felt tight. Just the way he felt before they opened the gate on his last bull ride.

"I've got another issue I need to discuss," he began after the customary pleasantries. "Maria Fischer and I have been checking each other out for a while now. Maybe I'm doing most of the checking. We still disagree on everything having to do with trees." He paused, nervously tapping the wheel of his car. "It's conceivable that all this chemistry could, you know, make a battery or something. I thought you ought to know in case you felt it would constitute a conflict of interest."

"A what?"

"A conflict of interest. That's when—"

"I know what a conflict of interest is," Jeb interrupted. "So does Maria Fischer have to call up Patty McCafferty and tell her the same thing?"

"Probably not. She's still in the denial phase."

"You're sure?"

"What about love is sure?"

Otran chuckled. "You sound as nervous as a long-tailed cat in a room full of rocking chairs. But I don't care about the details of your as-yet-hypothetical love life. The real issues are: Are you emotionally attached to her, and if so, would it affect your judgment? Would it affect your ability to help me on the Highlands?"

"What do you need me to do?"

"I'm buying out Metco's half of the old growth. And I'm going to need convincing timber-harvest plans and someone to litigate them if I'm ever going to persuade the government to buy it."

"This is a shock," Dan said.

"It was to me too," Otran said, "but the price was right. So will you help me?"

Dan was silent, wondering how to respond.

"It's that bad, huh?" Otran laughed.

"I'm not sure. Maria's ideas don't change the way I think. Tell me this. You don't actually expect to harvest the lower Highlands, right?"

"We're figuring the government will buy it. Save us all a big fight. Make a little money for our side."

"But if the government doesn't act right away?"

"We'd have to go ahead and start cutting if it came to it. How can you make the government move if you just sit there and let the trees rot for free?"

"Could we tell Maria it's a bluff? That we won't actually cut?"

"If you tell her that, we're liable to lose that shrill intensity of hers. We absolutely have to make the world believe we'll cut. Besides, if they don't buy it, we have to manage it for long-term timber production. And to do that, we have to cut it."

Dan sighed.

"I just hope we don't have to deal with it," Jeb said. "Cutting the Highlands *or* the romance. Hell, I don't care about a stolen kiss, but if she's going to be a fixture ... We'll just have to talk. I mean, knowing her is great. It's always good to know your adversary. But for God's sake, how would it be to get in bed at night with the enviro who's been nipping at your heels all day?"

"Maybe violins and flowers have taken over my brain," Dan said.

"At least you're thinking with your brain," Otran said.

The minute Dan got home he called Maria's room at the Palmer Inn.

"Long time no see," he said. "Listen, let's get a drink in the pub."

"Now?"

"I know we've been together for two days, but I need to talk."

"I'll have *one* beer," she said.

Dan chuckled. "It's impossible to ignore the emphasis. You don't approve of my having two beers."

"I guess that's none of my business. But as long you ask, when do you have just two?"

"Touché."

It was only a couple of miles from his house to the Palmer Inn, and before Dan could decide how to bring up the most difficult topic of the evening, he had rolled into the lot.

"You look nice," he told Maria. She wore a khaki pants suit and yellow print blouse.

"What's the matter?" she asked.

"What do you mean? I just said you looked nice."

"You have the knitted-brow look, last displayed when Judge Traxler asked you point-blank if there had been accelerated harvesting. So what's up?"

They were through the main lobby and at the head of the stairs to the pub.

"In a couple days a story will break about a sale of the lower Highlands."

They were walking down a narrow staircase and a noisy drunk was coming up from below. She moved to Dan's side of the stairs to let the man pass. For an instant she leaned up against Dan. Her hair smelled of orchids, and the warmth of her body felt good. He knew he wanted more of her, and what he was about to say would give him less.

"What? Tell me."

"Come on," he said, pushing her by the elbow, just the way he used to nudge Tess. It was a little test and she let him. "Let's sit down and I'll tell you."

They sat in a booth. Instead of sitting opposite her, he slid in beside her, putting her on the inside next to the wall.

"Is there something wrong with the other side of the table?"

"Just that it's the other side of the table."

"Somebody is sure to see us."

"Crowd's light. And so what?"

"So it's my career, not to mention yours. Imagine what Amada could do with this."

"For one night let's just forget it."

"For one beer we'll forget it. Now tell me about the lower Highlands."

"Otran's going to buy it."

A look of utter amazement crossed her face.

"How long have you known this?"

"I just found out." Her eyes searched his. "I decided to tell you right away."

"But it's not the telling me that's got you bothered. Is it?"

"No. It's not."

"Jeb Otran is tough. What does he want with it?"

"He's going to manage it for timber unless the government buys it. Between you and me, I hope the government buys it and gives us all some relief. So does Otran. But that's purely personal. I just don't want to fight about it."

"Are you going to help write harvest plans and defend them in court?"

"It's my job."

"Well, it's my job to save those trees. So let me out."

"Not until you listen to me."

She fixed her eyes straight ahead and sat stiff as a statue.

"Come on," he urged her.

She didn't move. A single tear coursed down her cheek until she brushed it aside.

"This has got nothing to do with you and me. Or at least it doesn't have to."

"Just for the record, my boyfriend and I decided to call it quits. But I guess that's a moot point now, isn't it?"

"This isn't personal."

"Do you believe in this?" she asked. "Laying waste to this forest?"

"I believe we can have a fair debate and let someone else decide. One park more or less won't decide the future of mankind. Nobody's going to turn it into a wasteland."

"That's a cop-out. This time I mean it. Let me out." She turned to him, her eyes bright-fired with determination.

He slid out. "You're taking this all wrong."

She muttered some obscenity as she left. He could guess what she said.

20

One beer led to another. Then a couple of boilermakers. The whiskey burn felt good. Filling the hole inside with liquid comfort seemed an acceptable idea until the pub started to move. Certain that Maria wasn't looking at this thing correctly, Dan decided to pay her a visit.

When he rose to walk, he realized that sitting down had made the earth flat. Standing, he didn't feel right, either. He knew he'd had too much alcohol. He needed to make a trip to Maria's room to sober up.

The stairs weren't too bad because there was a stout railing on both sides and no traffic. When he reached the lobby, he knew he had to concentrate. For a moment he sat in an overstuffed chair and considered his predicament. No way would the clerk give him Maria's room number. Although he knew it earlier in the day when he came to pick her up, he was now having a tough time. It was 328 or 338 or perhaps 318. Probably he could remember if he saw the door and its placement in the hallway.

Making his way to the elevator, he entered with some young guy. Something about his jacket seemed familiar, but he didn't look him in the face until he was standing at the back wall.

"You're drunk, asshole," the man said.

Then he knew who it was.

"Well, if it isn't the *ex*-boyfriend."

"She's too good for you. Why don't you go find some tight-ass Republican?"

" 'Cause I found a tight-ass Democrat."

"You prick." Ross shoved him against the wall. Anger flashed through Dan, and he shoved back, throwing Ross against the wall. Ross reacted instantly, slugging him in the gut. It hurt and it made him angrier still. Putting his hand in Ross's face, he shoved him back.

"She ain't interested, and you can't face it."

It was the wrong thing to say. Ross began swinging wildly and hit Dan in the face. But even drunk, Dan outmatched him. Although the punches were lethargic, one of them connected on the point of Ross's nose. He crumpled, and that was the end of the fight. Both men had blood down the front of their shirts.

When the door opened at the third floor, Ross remained leaning on the wall of the elevator. When it closed, Dan was in the hall and Ross was on his way back down.

Maria's eyes took in Dan, his bloodied shirt. He had found her door on the first try.

"What happened?"

"Did you know your biologist was going to be here?"

"You got in a fight."

"I didn't start it."

"Did you hurt him? Where did he go?" she asked.

"Back down in the elevator."

She pulled Dan inside and closed the door gently.

"I can't begin to tell you how little I think of you."

"You're still mad?"

"I'm calling Pepacita to come for you."

"She's not home. Nate's at Lynette's."

"You're disgusting." She pushed him toward the bathroom. He began to fall, and she caught him.

"I hate you," she said.

Corey stood in the light drizzle outside the Palmer Inn. With its white stucco sides crisscrossed by dark brown moldings and steep pitched roof, it was a combination of Tudor and Bavarian design and one of the most ornate and imposing structures in Palmer. She liked the feeling of the rain, liked the coastal sleet and fog of Palmer; she would never complain about the lack of sun.

Never far from her consciousness these days stood a shadow. The German loomed over everything she did, every decision she made. He was even in her dreams. In her fantasies she pleased him one minute, then vanquished him in the next. But the thought of pleasing him was like an anesthetic. It quieted her fear of the Japanese man who had bested her in the equipment room.

She knew that Maria Fischer stayed at the Palmer every time she was in town. Upon arriving, Maria would go from parking area to the open breezeway and on to the back door of the inn. She could be shot in the breezeway proper; or maybe a little sooner, as she crossed the parking lot, just after exiting her car. The more Corey thought about it, the better she liked the idea of lying in wait here at the inn; she could count on Maria approaching and leaving her car repeatedly; she would wait for just the right opportunity to strike. Problem was, she was here to kill Dan Young.

The German had just advised that Dan Young had spent the night with Maria Fischer and his car was in the area. Because she had worked so hard on Kim Lee's bomb, that was the method of choice. The only difficulty was that it was rigged on a timer, meant for a situation where she could see him coming. She had fixed that. First she had to find the car, then worry about the detonation.

Starting on foot, she walked away from the back of the inn, the rain pelting her face now, trickling under her windbreaker, down her neck to the skin of her chest in chilly little ant trails. Traveling in a 180-degree arc behind the inn at a distance of a block, she carefully searched for the silver-gray Mercedes or the blue Chevy pickup that he normally drove. Evidently, the man was a little nervous about being tagged for an all-nighter with Maria Fischer. Otherwise, he could have put it in the parking lot.

She had gone only a block when she found it. A twelve-year-old Mercedes with sheepskin on the seats. How many of those could there be? Fortunately, it was a bit outdated; otherwise, she would have had alarm problems.

The bomb would go under the driver beneath the car. The wires would go one to the solenoid and one to ground. Determined to be careful, she had tested the detonation device on an actual solenoid for that make, model, and year Mercedes.

To do the job, she pulled up behind the Mercedes, but she had not considered that it was a Saturday morning. There were kids playing baseball in the street right in front of the car. It would be dangerous enough without the kids; with them, impossible. She would wait. Whether this morning or later, sometime this weekend she needed to blow Dan Young away.

Dan's headache loomed like a mountain. The pain started between his eyes and radiated to his temples. Trying to open his eyes, he rolled over, winking open one eye and expecting to see his grandmother's mahogany highboy. Instead, he saw a long room with a second double bed. Searching through his memory, he recalled the drinks in the bar. He moaned audibly, then found the inevitable red-letter digital clock on the nightstand: 9:00 A.M.

Looking around with both eyes now open, he saw the sign beside him on the bed, two words scrawled in red lipstick: GET OUT!!!

Of all the times not to have been wearing underwear. For some reason there hadn't been any clean, so he had just pulled on his pants. It wasn't embarrassment at nudity that galled him, it was simply being caught without underwear—there was something second-class about not wearing shorts.

Perhaps because of his embarrassment the two words scrawled in lipstick took on extra force. "Fine, just give me my clothes," he muttered.

They were nowhere to be found. Casting aside the blanket, he remembered the research he was going to do on local mines, the further work on Corey Schneider, the memo from the professor he had to study, and all the other things that would come to mind when he returned to his den and bulletin board with a cup of coffee.

In the closet he found his clothes, hand-washed and half-dried. Given that he came in the middle of the night, that must have taken some doing. He pulled on his pants and T-shirt, socks, and shoes. He would go home to his den, regroup, and try to find her.

Dan walked across the street. There was nobody about but a lone dog pawing at a garbage can. Palmer seemed particularly desolate this morning. Other than the Mercedes, there was only a single car parked on the street, a van. He looked at his wrist. He'd left his watch in the hotel room. That was what was wrong.

He wondered if Maria had propped him up under the shower. Vaguely he remembered her robe getting wet. Fundamentally, he was humiliated but really didn't want to go there in his mind. Normally, he controlled his drinking to the extent that he never became falling-down drunk. Last night he was nearly that, and it unnerved him. On the way back to the room, he decided he had taken his last drink. The decision made him feel better. In three minutes he was back at the car. He put his cell phone in the carriage, looked in the rearview mirror, and saw Maria's Cherokee pull up behind him.

In the hope of salvaging the situation, he climbed out of the Mercedes and walked back. Out of the corner of his eye, he noticed the van pull away.

"Hi," he said. He knew that despite himself he had a grim frown on his face. "I've had my last drink. I mean, I decided that would be best."

"I believe you," she said without hesitation. "But if you want anything to do with me, don't ever, ever forget you said that."

"Nothing like a clear understanding," he said.

"Someone else in your office could work on the Highlands. You don't have to do it personally. That's a choice."

"Plunging right in, are we? This is my area. I don't want to give it away."

"There isn't anything else you want more?"

"Well, like what?"

"I still can't accept our little rapprochement if you're fighting to cut the Highlands."

"What if I said I would like to be friends. Kind of a personal thing."

"I'd say prove it."

"Well, shit."

She started the Cherokee, threw it in gear, and backed up. Evidently, his expression had spoken as loudly as his words.

21

Dan slouched into his chair and stirred the papers on his desk. He couldn't stop thinking about Maria. While he drank his coffee and waited for some brilliant plan for reconciliation to reveal itself, he thought about the Highlands and all his projects for the day.

He felt tired in his mind. When Tess was alive, it used to be that late on Saturday morning after his trip to the office he would get recharged by an intense physical workout. Get the blood flowing, the arteries expanded, and turn his body into a physical machine that glowed warm and healthy. Now he was starting to feel weak in every respect. His exercise routine was turning into a few halfhearted push-ups and a little jog. The alcohol had done that. He knew he could work smarter, do more, think clearer, if he went back to his old habits. Before he started in on the afternoon's sleuthing, he would work out. Like the old days.

A little less angry after an hour of trying to parse through the mysteries of the Highlands, he tried chasing down Maria. First he called the local Environmental Center, where the woman's voice turned cold when he identified himself over the telephone. They hadn't seen Maria Fischer all day. He tried Maria's room at the Palmer Inn three times about ten minutes apart and got no answer. Just when he was about to go out the door, he called one more time.

"Hello," she said crisply, surprising him.

"I'd like to talk. We have things to talk about."

"So talk." Her voice sounded worse than distant, harsher than cold.

"Maybe we could meet for a cup of coffee."

"Oh yeah, and then dinner, then coffee at your house. Lose the line, lose the gimmicks. What do you want?"

"I want the friendship back."

"Good luck." There was a click and she was gone. What a hard edge that woman had on her. At least she didn't deny that there was a "friendship" of sorts. He decided to view that as a start.

It took twelve minutes to drive home from his office, one minute longer than usual. Pepacita looked positively shocked when he began rummaging through the boxes in his closet for his gym shorts and jockstrap. After more than two years, some of the elastic stretch was gone. The shorts would fit but barely. Disgusting. He had thickened a little around the middle.

"Wanna go?" he asked Nate, who had been standing by watching with a somewhat doubtful eye.

"I think this is gonna be like Mrs. Ogletree singing 'The Star-Spangled Banner,' Dad."

"And what is that like?"

"She wheezes and we all wish she'd stop."

"Well, thank you, son. Didn't know I was that bad off."

"Well, you aren't fat like Mrs. Mullins."

"Another vote of confidence."

"You used to be really buff."

He stood straight and pulled his stomach tight. "I'm not that bad. You could shoot baskets while I work out."

"There's a bunch of tall guys that'll just grab the ball."

"Life is full of tall guys."

"I don't have to play with 'em."

Finally he had his old white socks, shoes, and sweat clothes free of the boxes. Realizing he hadn't called his mother for a week, he picked up the phone and found her in the house reading. By the time he finished a somewhat halting explanation of Maria Fischer, twenty minutes had passed. On his way to the gym, he spent another fifteen minutes on the cell phone talking with his sister, Katie, trying to avoid her somewhat pointed questions about Maria. He refused to allow any hint of desperation in his tone.

Feeling slightly exhilarated at the prospect of a workout, he pulled into the parking lot of the health club with building confidence. Then he saw the clientele going and coming. Out of eight people in the lot, one had a beer belly and most didn't look all that athletic. Still, there was that one hard-body guy. By the time he got the car lined up for the narrow parking space, everybody was in the building or gone—save one couple. They were leaving and looked beat, especially her, but the way she leaned on her guy had a warmth to it and he remembered what he missed.

Corey watched Dan pull into the health-club parking lot. Frustration at not being able to get to the Mercedes and blow his ass to hell had turned to fury. On her seat under a newspaper was her silenced Colt. As she watched Dan

Young walking out of the back of the lot, she gripped the gun and fingered the trigger. Shoot the bastard. For a second her knee shook, her mind perched on a razor blade of indecision.

People had faded away into the club. There was only a couple in the lot. If they drove off, she could just blow him away. She could actually do it and be done in thirty seconds. She released the brake, rolling forward. Then she stopped abruptly. Am I losing it? We didn't plan this. She and the German had discussed a bomb at length. He had given her the concept.

She snapped around, expecting to see the Japanese bastard. God, he had unnerved her. Something had happened to her. No shrimp shit of a man like that could make a plaything out of her. Those placid eyes. She strained to remember every tiny detail, to understand why her kick hadn't broken ribs. The next time her gun would be ready. The little shit couldn't move faster than a bullet.

She put her head on the wheel and took a deep breath. There were no Orientals. He hadn't followed her. To reassure herself, she carefully looked over the cars, behind her, to both sides. She needed to get a grip and follow the plan. Glancing in the backseat, she saw the box with the bomb. It was simple. You wired it to the solenoid and it blew up when you started the car. She knew exactly what she had to do. Slowly she rolled forward right past the Nazi Dan Young.

"I'm going to blow you straight to hell," she said aloud.

Dan still had plenty of meat on him, but after 2 ½ years it had begun to undergo a slight metamorphosis. He was living with the beginnings of transformation from muscle man to slack man, and the consequent globules of adipose tissue that formed on the abdomen wall. And the loss of his wind. After over two years of marginal exercise, the first thing to go was cardiovascular stamina. Now he knew that a two-mile jog would have him puffing as if it were a five-mile run of three years ago. When Tess was alive, he did five back-to-back seven-minute miles.

In the entrance the place had a trendy juice bar complete with a hard-body female blonde to inspire effort and pour drinks. Beyond that were overstuffed couches in front of large-windowed racquetball courts. You didn't play in these unless you were good, or you just didn't give a damn.

He'd need to get a towel, he reasoned, and probably look for a locker, although he wasn't clear on how that worked. They'd moved into this newer facility and absolutely everything had changed since the last time he worked out.

The blonde was serving some vegetable-juice blend to three guys, obviously regular patrons, with *Baywatch* bodies.

"Excuse me. I'd like to work out," he said to the blonde.

"Well, you've come to the right place."

"Good."

"You look in pretty good shape," she said, giving him a genuine smile. "Here's your towel; here's your lock." As she was talking, Maria Fischer came around the corner, apparently headed for the carrot juice. She wore a simple but elegant black, gray, and white suit, complete with leggings and really good court shoes.

With her were two male lawyers from the Sierra Club legal-defense fund who weren't nearly as sweaty as she was.

"Well, what a pleasant surprise," she said. "Look who's here to work out."

He felt exactly like a butterfly about to be stuck to a collector's board with long, sharp pins.

"Yeah, well, I thought I'd start again. Light workout."

"Uh-huh," Maria said. Her two friends hung back, only seeming to let their attentions wander elsewhere.

"I guess I better go get changed."

"Good," she said in a tone that sounded like anything but good.

It took him about ten minutes. Maria was still by the juice bar. Her two friends had disappeared.

Corey parked two cars over from the Mercedes. After turning off the key, she sat and stared in her lap. Fear bowed to rage. But now the fear was sometimes so strong that she hadn't enough rage. The German and the Japanese, they swirled in her mind. How much better it was when she had been alone, feeling next to nothing. Back then, more than anything, she wanted to kill Dan Young. Now maybe she wanted to kill the Japanese even more—it happened the second he had beaten her and called her a student. In that moment she had felt her life's redemption might lie in killing the small man. It was a moment of clarity.

Shit, what am I thinking about? If the Japanese came, she would kill him. If the German wasn't pleased, he could fuck himself. Snapping her head around, she was certain for a second that the Japanese was behind the car.

Nothing.

Then she glanced to the side again. And there he was. Smiling at her, the shit. Slowly she reached over and pressed the electric window button. He waved. Her eyes bored into his and he pretended not to know her. She raised the gun, drew a bead. She saw his mouth open, feigning astonishment. The asshole thought he was God, that he couldn't die.

Wait! He had a hearing aid. There was no hearing aid on

the Japanese. And this one was slight not strong-shouldered. Oh God. She dropped the gun.

"Just kidding," she called out, forcing a smile. She was sweating like a pig. Shaking.

"Not funny," the man said.

For just a second she wondered if she was losing her mind. No, it was a likeness. Just two men who looked amazingly similar. Stick to the plan. Stick to the plan. Flicking on the safety, she worked on herself, telling herself to calm down. Had it been the Japanese, she would have shot him through the head. It was comforting. Calming. He would be dead, lying on the pavement with the back of his head blown off. She would have done it. She could have done it. She had the power.

Amazingly, no one else had seen. If she went to work on the Mercedes, it would be OK. She opened the door, went to the trunk, and got her tools. For show, she raised her hood. No, it would call attention. She lowered it and closed it firmly. Shit, she was wasting time. Forcing herself to focus, she went to the backseat and got out the box and went to the Mercedes. In seconds she was under it, reaching up to the solenoid. It took a couple of minutes to get the right wrench, to get it on and to loosen the small nut.

Quickly she fastened the wires. From the toolbox she took a putty knife and scraped the car's underbody, then taped the heavy pipe to the bottom of the car.

After a quick check of her handiwork, Corey grabbed her tool bag and jumped in her car, almost peeling rubber as she left. More than anything she wanted to watch Dan Young explode. If she stayed, maybe she would actually see him disintegrate. But she dare not stick around. Somebody might notice her, and this time she hadn't bothered with an airtight alibi. She would drive her motorcycle like hell to Crescent City.

Already a woman looking like her would be there, the German had said, charging things, checking into a room. If anybody ever checked, they would conclude that it wasn't humanly possible to get there that fast. It wasn't great, but it would have to do.

Dan went up some stairs that were an architect's dream, complete with painted steel railroad rail, wall murals, and roughened tiles color-coordinated to be part of the murals. Even in a small town like Palmer, there must be money in this, he thought. The stairs led to a large mezzanine looking over the entire racquetball complex. The exercise bikes were located here.

Much to his surprise, Maria followed.

"This club was probably completed after you quit working out, huh?"

"Yeah. Matter of fact."

"What level you gonna ride on?" she said, slipping on one next to his.

"What about you?"

"Twelve."

Without comment he put his on level twelve. She was giving him a hard time. Given his lack of conditioning, he should have been on level six at the very maximum. He knew the machines well and at his peak had ridden on level twelve. There were only twelve levels.

"I thought I'd ride on level twelve, but since you're just getting into shape again, maybe you should try three or four," she said.

"An old farmer once said, 'Any woman can make a racehorse feel like a donkey. But it's a hell of a trick to make a donkey feel like a racehorse.' I'll do twelve."

"Jeez, you've got heart. I'll give you that."

"Yeah. That's my role here."

"Oh, and what's mine?"

"Let me keep it."

Sweat formed on his chin with frightening speed. Burning legs and burning lungs took over his mind. He glanced sideward, hoping for a letup but refusing to give up.

"If you're getting tired, don't keep going on my account," she said.

His breaths were deep and he began to think about whether he had capacity left. Sweat dripped onto the bike and he tried to wipe himself with a towel while he kept the pedals turning. After several minutes he dropped the towel, which meant the sweat was an uncontrolled river. Soon his breathing was tortured and then even desperate-sounding. Trying to remember the way it was, making his body like it used to be by sheer force of will, helped a little.

He looked at her again. Almost coming clear of the seat with every revolution, her body weight was barely enough to turn the pedals. There was a slight quiver in her legs. She probably rode on level eight except when she was trying to kill somebody. Now her breaths were moderately labored. He could sense that she hadn't quite counted on this level of stamina.

Blanking out everything, he focused his mind on turning the pedals, nothing else, especially not the pain that he tried to crowd behind a great wall of pride. As he began to ponder what words to use before lowering the level to three, he felt a hand on his arm.

"I'm going to level six."

Gulping for air, he couldn't talk, so he just nodded.

Immediately he steadied himself to punch in six, and as he did so, he felt instant relief. But it was short-lived. Even six was way too hard after level twelve. He knew she could keep it up for an hour if she had to. Nausea was starting to build. Everything hurt now.

"Why don't you put it on level four?" she said. "This is childish."

More determined than ever, he just gasped and rode.

"All right," she said, "you're gonna pop. I'm going to level four."

When he climbed off the bike after twenty-six minutes on level four, he doubled over and couldn't move. She tugged on his arm.

"Weights," she said.

Knowing that for a couple of reps he might do big weight, he adopted an air of studied nonchalance and, after a brief warm-up, loaded the bar to 300 pounds. Everybody around the place was watching when he slid under the weight.

"OK, you've made your point. You're still a tough guy. This is ridiculous. Take off a hundred pounds."

"Pound sand," he said.

"You wanna be friends or not?" There was a sharpness in her voice. "I baited you into this. Now get out from under there."

Angry at being told what to do, he thought for a minute. He was pretty sure he could do it if she spotted for him. Then he reviewed his priorities.

"Take off fifty pounds," he said.

"Seventy-five, and it's a deal," she said.

They took off the weight.

"Maybe we could call it a draw," he said.

She nodded.

What followed was a steady barrage of "push, push, push, and harder." His muscle turned to jelly and every part of him shook with the effort. But he knew he was still impressive.

When they were done, and it was time to shower, she stood by him, as if pondering something.

"So what does our smart-ass farmer have to say now?"

" 'If you've acted like a donkey and you still feel like a racehorse, don't forget to thank her.' "

She smiled.

"Before I go home to my Sherlock gallery, let's go have a bite and talk," he said. She hesitated. Unconsciously, he held his breath.

"OK," she said.

After he showered, he went to the front lobby and sat on the leather couch, waiting. He was looking out through the glass doors and saw what looked like a familiar face and red head of hair. It was Lynette. Although he knew she worked out, he couldn't quite picture her in this place.

"Hey, you," he said as she came through the door.

"Well, look who's here. I thought that was the Mercedes, but honestly I couldn't believe you would be here. And if you were, I thought you'd be in your truck. The Mercedes was supposed to go to the shop. You had a Saturday appointment at one o'clock."

"Oh God." He slapped his forehead in disbelief.

"You could still take it. They're used to you."

"Maria is in the dressing room and we're gonna get a bite and I'm going to invite her over and she's kinda—" He waggled his hand like an airplane on a bumpy ride.

"Let me run it over. It's five minutes and I'll get one of the guys to give me a ride back here."

"Could you?"

"Why not? I'll just be doing it next week if I don't do it now, and it's a lot farther from the office."

Dan was looking out the window and waiting for Maria when he watched his good friend die.

* * *

Maria bent over to tie her shoes and was telling herself not to be giddy. Dan still hadn't promised to cease on the Highlands. Not one step had been taken toward a resolution and she could feel herself, despite her stubborn will, ready to keep talking to him—as opposed to shutting him off and letting him suffer. It was a fact that Dan suffered quietly but couldn't hide it. In the battle of the sexes, it was an endearing weakness.

Then the building shook and a concussive shock wave frightened her to the core. There had been a massive explosion. For a second every woman in the dressing room was dead silent. Then there was pandemonium. Instantly she thought: "Bomb." Then she thought "Dan." She ran from the dressing room, knocking into another woman. Along with a small herd of others, she came around the corner to the juice bar.

"Oh God," she moaned when she saw him. It was after she threw her arms around him that she realized Dan was staring out the window with tears running down his face. He didn't speak. Out in the parking lot the Mercedes was blown in two. The explosion hadn't occurred until the car was pulling out of the lot onto the street in front of the club. There was an ache in Maria's heart as she watched Dan's face.

"Who?" she said.

But he didn't speak. His face shook. "Lynette," he finally gasped, then moved toward the door.

"No," she said, holding him back. "Don't go out there. Come over here." She pulled him toward a couch facing away from the window. "I'll bring the police here."

"I should—"

"No, no. Trust me on this. I'll go."

An officer came inside and took a long statement from both of them. They referred the officer to the sheriff for all the background on the Highlands when he was asked if there was a reason someone might want to kill Dan. It might be the man who had been seen at the courthouse, they explained. They understood that police sketches were being made. And finally both Dan and Maria repeated their prior suspicions of one Corey Schneider.

The officer offered Dan police protection and Dan, as she knew he would, adamantly refused.

After the officer left, Maria saw a most amazing transformation in Dan. It was as if he had gathered up the parts of his mind and put it back together, but missing a piece. It wasn't quite right, she could tell. Still he seemed calm, focused, and almost unaffected by what had just happened.

"I need to protect Nate. Could you take him to your parents'? Katie's place may not be safe. And my mother's ranch is somewhat isolated, but it would be easy for them to find him and then to take him. They wouldn't think of your mother."

"What are you going to do?"

"I'm going into the Highlands, but I'll need your help."

She thought for a few moments. This was crazy. But so was the grotesque pile of rubble and flesh in the parking lot.

"Only if you promise me not to do this on your own and you swear you will wait until I get back from delivering Nate."

"I'll wait," he said.

"You won't do anything."

He nodded in reply.

22

Maria sped down to La Jolla with Nate and returned the same day. Her mother took Nate to visit a Florida cousin, also a Fischer, who had a sprawling place, almost a mansion, with kids about Nate's age. Even Dan didn't want to know exactly where they were.

The moment Maria returned, she knew Dan had become a man obsessed. Motioning, he took her outside to the far corner of the backyard.

"They know too much. They knew to look in your purse. They knew to be at the restaurant. They knew we would be in court. They've got the house or the office bugged or both."

"That's pretty hard—"

But at the house he began ripping up everything, looking under furniture and pulling up the carpets. It took only twenty minutes to find the spike mike. Two hours later a detective and the phone company found the illegal tap. At least now the flow of information would stop.

The sign on Luna's was the worse for wear. In yellow neon, with part of the elements burned out, it looked like Lua's with a big gap after the *u*. Inside you could smell the burned oil hanging in the air, watch the waitresses with near-popping buttons, and listen to truck drivers hack their morning phlegm while washing down bacon and eggs with black coffee. It was 4:00 A.M.

"No one has ever figured out where to spit," Dan said as Maria curled her lip in disgust. "So I think they all swallow it."

"You just love grossing me out, don't you?"

"Not me."

"They teach you that at . . . where did you say you went to law school? Cal Northern in Chico?"

He nodded.

"You talk like a cowboy except when you forget yourself."

"What do you mean?"

"Oh, I don't know, that you put on this country-boy effect."

"Most of the girls think it's cute."

"The girls probably do. What about the women?"

"Sometimes I get the feeling that this 'save the world' stuff is like a telephone pole up your ass."

Maria laughed. "Oh, let's get down and dirty."

"You asked. Besides, I'm serious about what I believe," Dan said. "I think the best solution to saving the planet is to harvest and replant temperate forests at a rate that is perpetually sustainable."

"I'm sorry about Lynette, but fighting with me won't bring her back."

Dan paused. "I know; I'm sorry; it's a distraction."

"Perhaps a distraction other than pounding on me, please. And stop being scared to death to be sincere. Why don't you encourage me by being yourself?"

"What do you mean?"

"You graduated from Harvard."

"You've been spying on me."

"Daddy's been spying on you." They rose to leave and he helped her on with her jacket.

"Now you look really embarrassed," she said.

She put her hand on his shoulder and looked in his eyes. "I have my good side. You just need to get there." They walked outside the café. The sun was just over the horizon, the sky tinged with red, the moon still full. It was cold, and the coastal wind whipped through the parking lot. "Wait," she said as they were walking to their cars.

"Yeah?" he said, turning toward her. "What's the matter?"

"These people are big-time dangerous. I don't think you should go."

"We've got it—"

"All planned. I know. It's all set up, but who cares? It doesn't matter. Listen to me. You have Nate. You're all he's got. He doesn't have a mother. You should think of him and put him first. We don't need to do this. I can go in with the state inspectors and just see what I can see."

"Oh, and they're going to show you all their secrets."

"Dan, I know how you feel, but who says you'll learn anything by sneaking around outside?"

"I can try."

"You swore you wouldn't go in the buildings. Look at me, you bastard. Tell me."

"I won't go in the buildings."

"Or any old mines."

"I'm not promising about that. I want to figure out what they're doing with that pipe, and the tank, and the old shack or mine, or whatever it is. And if I knew that, I might figure out why they feel the need to kill people." He grabbed her shoulders. "They almost caused a holocaust at the courthouse. They murdered Lynette. What'll they do next? You make the diversion and don't worry about me. I'll be fine."

"All right. Forget it. Do your damned macho thing. I'll see you when you get out."

"All right," he said as he turned back to his truck, obviously wanting to leave before she tried again to talk him out of it.

"Please be careful," she said in a tired voice.

Kenji seemed amazingly calm as he sat across the desk from Groiter. Kenji had come to Groiter's office, meaning that he would want him to do something he might not want to do.

"I think you have to get more directly involved. This isn't working out."

"There was no way to predict that his secretary would get in that car."

"It didn't work. Nothing else matters," Kenji said.

"Next time I'll supervise."

"And now we haven't even got the taps. We don't have a clue what's going on."

"I'll take Maria Fischer. With Corey. We'll bleed everything she knows; then we'll deep-six her. It's that simple."

"That simple, huh?"

"It'll take some planning."

"Why do you need Schneider?"

"Because there has to be a villain, and it can't be me or you."

Groiter's confidence was boosted by his photo of two corpses—a dead Catherine Swanson and the photographer—he had retrieved from Corey. If everything went to hell and Kenji began to get dangerous, he would use it.

"OK. But this time make it work. Find out everything she knows and then bury her where nobody will ever find her."

When Kenji left, Groiter went to a phone booth at the nearest strip mall. He found Corey at home. Now that he called her regularly he had learned her patterns.

"You were brilliant," he reiterated as if he hadn't said it five times before. "It's incredible that he stuck his secretary in that car."

"I don't understand it," she said. "I just don't understand. Why would he do that?"

"Papers said she was doing him a favor, taking it to the mechanic. It was a last-minute deal."

"Shit."

"Maybe he knew it was dangerous. Maybe he was acting like the king who has a taster eat his food to see if it's poisoned."

"He's still walking around," she said. "Whatever the reason. I used up a perfectly good bomb on a dumb bitch."

"So next time we'll do it together. And wouldn't you rather do them both? One right after the other?"

"I would."

"And what if we got her to talk. Admit they were taking money."

"Could we make a video and show it to the movement?"

"Sure. Why not? But we need a place to take her." There was a pause.

"I know a perfect place."

"I'll call you soon to hear your ideas."

Groiter felt that at last he was making progress. She was starting to rely on him.

Dan watched the fence, listening intently for dogs or people. Only after seeing the fence for the second time, observing the meticulously coiled razor wire, did he contemplate his enemies' determination to protect their secrets.

It was 7:00 A.M. The forest was drippy with moisture, cool and dark. Angled shafts of early-morning sun barely penetrated the upper layers of the forest. The ground was in deep shadow. The clarity and pureness of a spring day made emerald green of the grasses and trees.

Nothing moved. The owls were perched, and the daytime predators were not making themselves known. A dusky-footed wood rat had scurried by, no doubt looking for the nearest windfall.

For 2 ½ hours Dan attempted to retrace the route he and Maria took the day of the car chase. Finally he recognized the large barrier logs and the hemlock they'd used to bridge the windfalls. Now he crouched just outside the double chain-link fence. Not a dog in sight. The diversion seemed to have worked.

Because of its warm-when-wet properties, he wore wool head to toe. That was at Maria's insistence. She even found him wool pants. Wool was not only warm, she said, but unlike fabrics like Gore-Tex it was also quiet when moving through the forest. No matter how hard she had tried to make her assistance seem trivial, it was endearing.

She had gone in with the biologists as a public representative. Whatever that was. The whole concept of self-appointed public do-gooders marching around on private land irritated Dan. After all, the government was supposed to represent the public, and the bureaucrats were bad enough without volunteer bureaucrats. Yet here he was using the very system he hated in order to snoop and trespass. The world was a complicated place.

He wondered if there were electronic sensors or infrared beams that would enable them to detect him when he passed through the fenced area. The thought was hard on the nerves. He had been acting like a fearless commando around Maria. Now, by himself, without an audience, how brave was he? It was that precise thought that brought a curse to his lips and brought out the wire cutters.

Quickly he snipped the heavy chain-link fencing. Pushing

himself so he wouldn't mentally freeze and crawl back under his bush, he cut quickly, and in seconds he had chopped up a three-foot section and bent it inward. Sweating profusely, he tossed the cutters through the hole in the first fence and crawled through after them. He used the same technique on the second fence and was soon on the far side.

No alarms had sounded. Moving slowly through the woods with a light pack on his back, he stayed in the thick undergrowth and used a compass along with the handheld GPS, moving toward the area of the tank. He had no idea where the lab was located or what other amenities might be found on the property. Every time he stepped, he made a sound unless he deliberately disciplined himself. After more than a few crackles and snaps, he decided to take off his boots and socks and put them in his pack. This enabled nearly silent movement. His tender feet could feel any twig about to snap and the leaves were moist enough that they were a mere whisper against his skin.

He found himself wishing he had brought a handgun. Fear did that. In the more rational confines of his office, he had come up with several good reasons not to bring a weapon of any kind. After many minutes he came to a lightly graveled road. In most places the gravel had sunk into the soft ground, leaving a surface that was partially dirt. It appeared that heavy vehicles used the road frequently. He wondered if the workers came and went at night so as not to attract attention.

Shrinking into the forest, he began to parallel the road, and in a few minutes he came to what resembled the letter *Y*. The ground was becoming rapidly steeper. The trees remained giant with few breaks in the overhead canopy, the road largely winding around their trunks. Where a tree had been removed, a telltale patch of blue sky shone through.

There was nothing to distinguish the fork of the Y bearing right from the one bearing to the left except that the left-hand fork rose at a steeper gradient. If he were correct about his position relative to the main buildings, the road to the right probably led to the gate. The one to the left had an unknown purpose and was therefore the more intriguing. He decided to keep to the left and look for the tank and the boards on the side of the mountain.

He walked what he guessed was a hundred yards before he came to a small clearing. At the edge of the clearing, but back under the tree canopy and nearly out of sight from the air, he found the man-made reservoir, some forty feet in diameter. It looked to be about five feet deep. Like an aboveground backyard pool, it appeared to have a liner, but its sides were made of concrete. Leading in two directions from the reservoir was a four-inch-diameter plastic hose. One hose went in the direction Dan had come; the other went nowhere and was coiled near the edge of the clearing.

Vehicles obviously frequented the area; this reservoir must be a center of activity. Looking to the far side of the clearing, he saw a portable toilet. In front of the plastic structure, a heavy man sat in a chair not far from what looked like a boarded-up mine shaft. The man was reading a book with a bloodred cover. Although still in the bushes and virtually invisible, Dan nearly stepped into the clearing. The thought was unnerving. Stooping down, he removed a pair of field glasses from his pack.

Dan saw that the man was armed with a prominently displayed semiautomatic pistol. With the binoculars he saw what looked to be an underground tunnel entry that was not seriously boarded up; someone had merely leaned the lumber against the rock face and over the opening. Somehow, he guessed, the reservoir and the mine were connected. In fact, the coiled-up line could have led from the reservoir to the mine. He had to look in that mine shaft. Removing his camera from the pack, he took several photos at slow-shutter speed from a tiny collapsible tripod.

As he studied the guard, it became apparent that he was not watching the area. In the movies someone would knock him out, but the whole notion of attacking a potentially innocent man and giving him a concussion was out of the question. He would just have to hope the guy didn't look around.

If they were operating in secret, it made sense that they would close everything down for an inspection. He wondered if Maria's group would observe this area or if they would be led around it.

Within about forty feet of the mine entrance, there was heavy forest. Moving as quickly as he could, he walked around the perimeter of the clearing, careful to remain far enough back in the trees to stay hidden.

When he arrived at the forest edge nearest the mine entrance, he quickly put on his socks and boots. It made him feel less vulnerable. The guard turned a page and didn't pause to look up. A heavy black holster with cuffs and pepper spray on his belt completed the police-officer look that private-security people often affect. The man could, Dan realized, be an off-duty cop.

It would only take one glance for the guard to see a man running in the open to the mine. Even peripheral vision might do it. Maybe he shouldn't try. To psych himself for the sprint, he made himself think of all the reasons the man wouldn't risk shooting him on sight.

He forced himself to breathe deeply and slowly, took a last look around, and ran on his toes, as quietly as he was able, all the way to the mine entrance. In seconds he moved three boards to the side, then slipped in. In a few more seconds he had the boards back in place.

Not a sound came from the guard. Dan waited a moment

for his heart to slow. Light shone through the wooden slats, creating a halo near the entrance. Behind him it was black and cool. Reaching into his pack, he pulled out a penlight and played it around the confined space. On the rock wall were pegs; on the pegs hung eight yellow suits smeared with gray, dustlike particles of soil.

Those outfits, he was certain, served as a barrier against some kind of toxin. Next to the suits there were bottles of compressed air. Of course, if it were an old sulphur mine, it could be that the earth had acted as a retort and created acid. He had read about that. But if that were true, why would these people want to go down inside?

Dan knew nothing about mines, nor did he understand the use of toxic suits. For that reason his next thought pushed bile up his throat. He had to explore inside to learn what concerned the people who owned it. He had to see what lay at the end of the plastic pipe.

Fear is just a state of mind, he told himself as he began to put on one of the larger-looking suits, leaving seven suits on the wall and one empty peg. Even a casual glance would reveal that an intruder was down the shaft.

On the suit's headpiece was a light that could be turned on by twisting the portion that housed the lens and the bulb. A mask fitted with the air supply sealed off his face. He checked the regulator and verified that the tank was nearly full. It was similar to the scuba regulators he had used when diving off Hawaii. With everything on, including gloves, no portion of his body was exposed. He removed the mask and let it hang around his neck, thinking that he would wait until the air turned bad. As he walked, he remembered stories about miners and canaries. The need for such a bird would imply that bad air might not be easily sensed. Doubt filled him as he stopped to put on the mask and turn on the regulator.

As he continued deep into the mine, there was an unsettling sense of aloneness. Beyond the beam of his light, darkness housed the lurking unknown. Other than the sounds of his footsteps and his deep breaths, there was silence. Without the breeze there was an uncommon stillness.

Down the center of the mine ran an old set of rails, miniature by train standards but sufficient to handle a half ton of ore in a tiny car that could be pushed by men or pulled by cable. In many places the rails were loosened from the dilapidated ties. The mine could be a century or more old, he realized.

The rock sidewalls and ceiling of the shaft were blue-gray in color and the floor relatively smooth but overlaid with fine gray-white dust, except along the walls, where shards of rock had been pushed to make walking easier. There were old rotten timbers overlaid with new. In many places only the original timbers remained in place. It looked like a reasonably serious but temporary patch job.

After hundreds of yards he came to a Y and followed the plastic pipe down the left fork. Going a little farther, he came to a vertical shaft. The horizontal shaft ended about twenty yards beyond the downturn. Above the vertical shaft were beams, one of which held a large rusted metal pulley. Next to it, affixed to a new timber, was a smaller and shiny stainless-steel pulley that held a ¼-inch cable that ran onto a power drum. Affixed to the cable were stirrups that would enable a person to ride the cable down the shaft.

Over the edge he could see only darkness at the end of the headlamp's reach. Cracking open his air mask, he noticed a noxious odor, like gasoline. It wasn't suffocating, but it was clearly noticeable, and it was coming up the shaft.

Dan walked over to the power winch and examined it. Two buttons on a handheld box controlled the winch motor. It had to be operated from where he stood, which meant that for one man to go down on the cable, another had to run the controls.

Hunting around the machinery, he found a toolbox with a screwdriver. By jamming the screwdriver in alongside the power button, he discovered it would stay in the on position. This way he could at least ride the cable down. To come up, he planned to climb, although he wondered what he would do if it were hundreds of feet down. He studied the drum. The way it looked, there couldn't be over a couple of hundred feet of cable. That was reassuring. Looking down the shaft once again, he studied the walls and noted with satisfaction that they were irregular. At least near the top there were outcroppings large enough to stand on, which meant he could rest and climb. No way could a man climb a ¼-inch cable without footholds.

Still, it was a serious risk. He knew that if he never came out Maria would find a way to get the police into the compound and maybe with luck she would guess where to look. But it was a slim chance that she could find him if something went wrong. He hesitated. He had his son to think about. His mother would give it a valiant try, but she was getting along in years. It would be hard for her to raise a nine-year-old boy to manhood all by herself. Dan's father was dead and his brother was single and running the ranch. Katie would try but how would she deal with Nate and a panic attack at the same time?

Nate was a good reason not to go down. He found himself sweating and breathing deeply.

Then he heard voices.

23

He ran toward the voices as quietly as he could, hoping to determine something about whoever it was before they became aware of him. Maybe nobody had thought to count suits or maybe they would think he was just another Amada worker.

Voice sounds carried extremely well in the otherwise quiet rock chambers. Either that or they were very close.

"Get your damn gun up, dildo," he heard.

"Why, he wouldn't know what to do with it."

"Shut up and do your jobs—all of you," a serious voice cut in. "I don't want any shots fired until I say so."

Dan reversed course and ran until he came back to the vertical shaft. Now staying up could be just as dangerous as going down. Jamming the screwdriver alongside the down button, he hopped in a stirrup and began the descent. He told himself, all the way down, that large mines normally had more than one entrance.

As he descended, he studied the rock walls, trying to reassure himself that they could be climbed. Soon his head-lamp wouldn't reach the stainless-steel pulley and estimating vertical distance became difficult. It might be too far to climb even with rests and outcroppings. He couldn't hear the voices anymore. Not knowing whether he was armed, they were probably coming slowly, looking in every crevice and dead-end side tunnel.

When next he looked down, he saw a pool. He looked

around for something to stand on and was relieved to see a lateral tunnel just above the pool. Jumping off into it, he pulled the cable after him and began coiling it at his feet. What if the cable wasn't anchored to the drum? He knew the answer; the end would drop uselessly at his feet.

He watched the cable, knowing that at any moment he would have his answer.

Just as he was near panic, the cable began retrieving. It had been anchored to the drum and now was being reeled in even though the drum continued to turn in a clockwise direction. There were seven dust-coated stirrups on the ground, and the first of the seven was going back up. Damn! Frantically he looked around for something to hold the cable and stop the drum. The sixth stirrup was rising.

He saw some timber and wrapped the cable, then waited anxiously to see if the winch would move the timber and start a cave-in. When the cable snapped taut, it stopped.

The moment of relief was broken when he noticed the cable line relaxing. A few seconds later, the winch started and the cable snapped taut again. Once more, it loosened and pulled. Over and over, somebody loosened and pulled. The timber gave an eerie creak. The next time, it moved an inch and groaned terribly.

"Stop, you dumb shit." He heard the words from above clearly. The winch stopped. "Hey, you down there. Come on up. You're trespassing."

He remained silent.

As the last stirrup lifted off the ground, he had to make a choice. In a split second he decided not to go. If he arrived at the top and found armed men, the men who had thrown the stun grenade, the men who had hurt Maria and killed Lynette, they might just give him a shove and end his investigation forever.

After the stirrup had risen well into the vertical shaft, it stopped. A large light shone down and hit the pool. He could only imagine the muzzles of the guns aimed down the shaft. Rescuers would have kept the cable rising.

"Where are you?" the voice asked.

"Enjoy your stay, dumb shit," another voice said, and the cable motor turned on once again. It didn't come down.

They turned off the light and above there was only blackness. He was trapped.

It took a moment before he fully realized his predicament. He had about one liter of water, some trail mix, and that was all. Loosening his mask, he verified that the fumes were coming from the pool. Even a small whiff choked him. When he ran out of air, he would die—unless he could get far enough away from the pool that the fumes didn't overcome him. There was no telling what kind of deadly material the pool contained.

"There's no way out of there, mister. You better come up." It was a different, more reasonable-sounding voice. "You're going to run out of air, my friend. You've got to come up." Quickly looking around for a weapon, or a place to hide, or something that might help deliver him from the madness of his predicament, he found nothing. There was only a pool of noxious liquid.

He turned and began to jog. Here the ground was rougher. Rock that had fallen from above lay where it hit the ground. There was a track at this level, so he knew it was likely that this tunnel went a long way. It twisted and turned, depriving him of any sense of direction. He stopped long enough to pull out his compass but didn't know what good it would do since the tunnel offered no options.

Determined to control the jitters, he began regular deep breathing and maintained a brisk walk. The passage was narrowing and in places he had to stoop. Soon outcroppings and debris slides to either side narrowed the passage further.

He came to a partial cave-in where timbers had fallen. He squeezed his way between the rough timbers and over a pile of rock that went almost to the ceiling.

Air from the tank might run out at any time, and he had no idea whether he could breathe in these shafts. Instantly he cracked the mask and was greeted by the same pungent smell—but not as strong. Coughing hard, he replaced the mask. To continue on might well be suicide. He had no guarantee that the air would improve. It probably wouldn't. If he went back, he had no idea what they would do to him.

He looked at the gauge and discovered it was half empty. Undoubtedly, stress was causing him to gobble the air supply. He began to control his breathing. Walking around the next bend, he came to an old chamber filled with debris and partially collapsed timbers. Leading off this chamber were three passages. This was obviously some kind of a hub near a concentration of whatever ore they had been mining. There were four options. One of them was a vertical shaft going up. It might lead to the level above, perhaps to the right fork of the shaft through which he had entered.

"You're daydreaming," he said to himself, staring upward into the blackness, trying to figure if he could even climb it. In studying the vertical tunnel, he turned around 180 degrees. Then he sucked in his breath.

In his direction came the faint glimmer of a light. How could they be so near? Quickly he ran into the largest-looking shaft and went perhaps a hundred yards before he came to another debris slide and an unfinished vertical shaft. There were massive timbers partially caved in and large boulders, perhaps from a blast before the mine was abandoned. He couldn't keep running. There was an old, rusted crowbar about six feet long lying in the dirt. It was his first bit of luck.

Sighing at the improbability of what he was about to

attempt, he climbed up the debris and began the vertical ascent of a narrow chimney. It looked like the start of an abandoned vertical shaft. Wedging himself in an alcove above the main shaft, he waited. The bar was heavy and he laid it on an outcropping. In the process he glanced up and what he saw stopped his breath.

A hand.

Pulling himself up to the next ledge, he found a headless body dressed in a filthy, blood-soaked blue blazer.

Forcing his mind back to the men who were after him, he lowered himself down and listened. His heart beat like a drum. Trying desperately to quiet his breathing, he attempted meditation, but he was unskilled and the fear crowded his mind. He was in a terrible spot. If two of them came down this passage, he might get the first and catch a bullet from the second.

He didn't know if he had the stomach to ambush some faceless, nameless guy whose intent was unknown. Until someone shot at you, there was no way to know for sure that they were out to kill you. There was no black and white here, no obvious villain. Then again, the guard had a gun, and those guys in the mine had guns and were talking about using them. Above him someone had hidden a corpse.

In that moment he knew that everything in his existence boiled down to one thing—his son needed a father. He never should have risked Nate's future by coming here. Maria was right.

Then he saw a light. He held his breath instinctively.

Think, think. Breathe. Get control of yourself.

His breaths began coming again, shallow but regular.

Still the light bounced around the walls. It was taking forever.

"Nothing yet," he heard the words, low in tone, like a

whisper. The guy had to have a radio. Sweat broke out on his forehead, stinging his eyes, as if he'd run for miles.

He gripped the iron bar and saw that his hand wasn't quite steady.

The light was bright now, completely lighting the walls.

The first thing he saw was a silencer on a semiautomatic weapon. This was no goody-two-shoes rescue group.

He aimed one end of the iron bar at the side of the man's head. It struck his hard hat with an ugly whack. Then Dan dropped his 240 pounds right on top of the man even as the man collapsed. They hit the ground in a tangle. Dan had one hand on the gun, the other on the man's throat, overpowering him. Glancing around, he saw no more lights. They were apparently alone for the moment. The man struggled feebly, barely conscious.

Dan choked down on the man and could feel the man's body shaking in some kind of nervous spasm. Perhaps by instinct Dan rolled the half-conscious man so that both of them were sitting with his adversary's back in the direction of the large chamber. The man's arms windmilled and there was a loud smack, like a fist hitting mud, and the man's body jerked violently. Instantly Dan knew they had shot their own by accident. Yanking the man's gun from his hand, he snapped off both his light and the man's, then retreated into the mine. After three steps he realized the man would be carrying more clips of ammunition.

Knowing he was taking a terrible risk, he stepped back to the body, grabbed the man's radio, his air tank, and two clips from leather pouches on his belt. The man groaned and Dan could feel the body armor. In all probability he wouldn't die unless the bad air killed him. Again he retreated around the corner. Everything was quiet for several minutes. Then he heard the man gasping.

"Help," he said. "Help."

Dan cracked his mask. The air was bad but didn't seem sufficiently bad to cause suffocation. He held down the broadcast button on the radio.

"Come and get your man. You cretins shot him."

"Yeah? Well, you can prove that in court. Right now you need to give up that gun."

"Help me," the man screamed.

"I have no gun. You're the ones with the guns and that fellow didn't look like Roger the ranger out trying to help a lost soul."

"Come out and we'll talk. We can work this out."

"Body armor and automatic weapons with silencers? That doesn't seem to me like a real talking-type group."

"Go get the dumb son of a bitch," he heard the boss say.

"What if he shoots?"

"He's an officer of the court. He won't shoot you in cold blood." A hint of sarcasm in the tone.

They know who I am.

"I'm dying," the man groaned.

"Don't shoot. Red Cross coming through here." He saw a light coming up the passage.

"I'm dying," the man said again.

Dan was staring around the corner with his gun pointed at the ground and his light off. The rescuer approached the downed man and put his own mask over the man's face. He could hear the deep sucking breaths.

"Put your gun down when you carry him out."

"What?"

"You heard me. Put down that gun when you carry him out of here."

"You bastard. You never said—"

"You try walking out of here with that gun and I'll shoot you in the back."

"Keep the gun," the boss said. Dan squeezed off three shots right next to the rescuer.

"Shit, you idiot," the man screamed in panic. "You're gonna kill somebody. Bullets ricochet in here."

"Throw the gun or wave bye-bye to your fat ass."

He threw the gun.

"Smart man."

"I hope you got life insurance," the leader said. "That kid of yours will need it."

"You shouldn't be telling me you're going to kill me. Makes me harder to catch."

"Well, fuck you."

Dan took the second gun and began feeling his way back down the tunnel toward his pursuers. He wanted out of this hole, and he figured an outright attack this soon would surprise them. Feeling with his hand enabled him to distinguish large boulders and the wall. It was hard not to stumble. When he came around a bend with a straight view to the main chamber, he saw four headlamps. Now was his chance. He could nail at least one or two of them as if they were pigeons to ground-sluice. He wanted to see Nate again, and killing these men was the surest way to do it.

His body was shaking, hands slick with sweat. He wanted to kill them. He wanted to walk out over their dead bodies. Somehow his finger would not pull the trigger.

Then it was too late. They turned off their lights.

He ran perhaps twenty paces, kicked a rock, and then deliberately hit the ground. At the sound there was a spray of gunfire lighting the darkness. Bullets popped everywhere. Instantly he was slithering fast, without thinking, oblivious to the pain of the hard rock on his knees, elbows, and belly. The shooting stopped. Ammunition would be a problem he knew. They weren't expecting a war.

He could feel the fear like a hot flame in his body fueling

his adrenaline. He could see nothing. There was a debris pile, he knew. Reaching for it, he had a premonition. Or maybe he was thinking like the enemy. The leader would have crawled right in front of the debris pile—right where Dan would come through—and would wait. He moved to the side, flat against the wall. Clearly, the questions were: Who would first turn on a light? Or would somebody start shooting at noises?

In the mine, noises were hard to place; echoes confused the ear. Perhaps if he made a noise, he could seduce a light. Scraping the barrel of the gun lightly along the rock might do it. He reached as far from his body as he could, then yanked the gun back. A spray of bullets smacked the wall and fire erupted from a barrel not ten feet away. If the shooter hadn't hesitated at the sound, Dan would have lost his arm. He fired into the blackness at the spot he had seen the fire.

The weapon Dan had taken was a fully automatic handheld machine gun. If you pulled the trigger, it shot until the clip emptied. That was all he needed to know until he ran out of ammunition. Then he needed to know how to replace a clip and how to get the first bullet from the new clip into the chamber. He began fumbling around in the dark with the clip when he realized that the second gun was hanging from his shoulder.

There was an awful groaning coming from the far side of the debris pile.

"You've got a man down. Maybe you better help him."

There was silence.

"Please help me," the man wailed. It wasn't the leader. He rambled and begged, and said he wanted to see his family. Then he began wailing.

"Mother, God, I want my mother." The leader had put another man at the debris pile. The screaming turned Dan's stomach. This was nearly the worst moment of his life, second only to holding his wife's dead body.

He was tired. Tired not just in his body, but in his mind and in his spirit. How did men get to such a sorry state that they were killing each other in a hole in the ground? And for what? Out there in the dark the leader waited in silence for him to turn on his light or reveal his presence—then he would shoot. Somewhere there was a fourth man.

Some things were just as bad as being shot. Suffocating in a hole was probably one of them. Either way he would leave his son an orphan. Even as he thought it, sucking air became harder. Now he was running out. As quickly and as quietly as he could, he fumbled and changed tanks.

Without warning Dan jumped up and slid over the debris pile, then began walking in the pitch black, his gun pointed straight ahead. The man screaming tended to drown out everything else. His hand reached out for the rock wall and soon he felt the cold of the earth. He followed the wall.

Staying low, he walked the perimeter of the large chamber, recalling that there was one passage before he reached the main passage that led back to the pool. All of a sudden the staccato spitting of a silenced automatic weapon had bullets smacking the wall just ahead of him. They knew what he was doing, and they were getting desperate. He hit the ground and kept crawling.

This time he hadn't seen the muzzle flash. Perhaps the shooter was smart enough to stand beside a boulder to hide the flame. He came to the first tunnel off the main chamber. Putting out his hand, he crawled until he felt the far wall and then resumed a duckwalk along the wall. Based on the sound of the shots, he was sure they had come from the center of the chamber.

Smack, smack, smack. More shots were fired, but this time he saw the muzzle blast. Trying to fix the spot in his mind, he fired back into the blackness. He could not have hit the shooter except by dumb luck.

He knew they would try to cut him off. Probably they would move to the wall. Any moment he should arrive at the main shaft leading back to the pool. He stopped. These men were determined. They would not let him walk out of here and the most likely spot to stop him was the mouth of the main shaft.

Think.

If they waited, he could wait. They all had about the same amount of air and he had a little more. The closer they got to the pool, the worse the air. Soon everybody would have to move away from the pool or get out of the mine.

Seconds ticked by. Every muscle in his back and neck felt stiff. His tongue was dry like toughened leather. He needed cover. He duckwalked forward, feeling for some debris. Something in front of him felt like a boulder. In an instant the exit tunnel was lit by a bright light. It was ahead of him. Without hesitating, he emptied the clip at the light and blew it away. Breathing hard and trying to see where nothing could be seen, he forced himself to wait and to think.

They had attempted to surprise him. Had he been upright he would be dead. Anger filled him. He took a full clip from his pocket; he felt for the clip release. A small button by the trigger guard didn't do it. Probably the safety. Near the top of the clip, he found a lever. It worked. Sliding the new clip into place, he pulled back the small bolt on the ejector. It had an action vaguely similar to his Browning semiautomatic twelve-gauge shotgun.

Sitting on the hard stone, he took off his boots. They scraped the rock in the dark and made soundless travel impossible. He tied the laces together and hung the boots around his neck. Duckwalking, he moved back toward the center of the cave in the direction of the light. It was the last thing they would expect and that's why he liked it. Leveling his gun in front of him, he kept his finger on the trigger. One way or another, this would end. When he had gone about thirty feet in complete silence, he tossed a stone. It hit, and before it rolled, the darkness exploded in machine-gun fire only a few feet from his chest. He shot back and knew he had a hit.

"Who is that?" he cried into the mike, trying to sound like one of them.

"All right, let's call a truce," came a frightened voice over the radio.

Maybe he had hit the leader; he sensed the survivors were spooked out of their minds.

"You out there, lawyer man?" a shaky voice said.

He remained silent.

A terrified, whispering voice came back over the radio. "Are we shooting at each other?"

"Turn on your light," one man said to the other.

"Fuck you," came the reply.

"Boss, you there?"

There were two of them talking. He was certain that he had shot two and knocked one silly with the crowbar. But they had body armor, so maybe they weren't dead or even dying. He turned off his radio and concentrated on hearing the next sound.

"We can't just sit here; we'll run out of air."

"What the fuck do you suggest?"

"I'll come to you."

"How will I know it's you?"

"Some things you gotta take on faith."

One voice was straight ahead. Dan was sure that he stood between the speaker and the exit. Quickly he turned and duckwalked back to the entrance of the main shaft, put his boots back on, and hurried down the corridor. After making the first turn, he switched on his headlamp and began running. Then he stopped, turned off his light, and fired a single shot.

"I got the bastard," he spoke into his radio.

"Who was that?" He heard an obviously bewildered voice.

"Maybe it's Meat. That you, Meat?"

There was silence.

"If that's Meat, then who operated the winch? And why ain't he talkin' to us?"

"I don't know, but it sounded to me like one of our guys got the snoop. Maybe Meat's radio went dead. I'm getting out of here. Screw this. Without air we'll turn puke yellow and shake to death."

"I'm coming too."

Dan found a boulder and waited. So at least they were convinced their leader was dead or unconscious. Soon he saw headlamps bouncing off the wall. The men were moving erratically, no doubt peering around corners and trying to stay behind cover. Retreating, he found a straight stretch with no place to hide, backed up until he came to a large rock outcropping at a bend. There he waited.

He knew that their hands shook like his, their throats were tight—it was in their voices—barely holding it together until they could rip off those masks and breathe in the goodness of open air. He waited for them, breathing shallowly, not moving a muscle. It was obvious from the light on the rocks that they were getting close. When he guessed they were twenty feet away, he peered around the corner, saw them as vague shadows behind their six-inch lights. He aimed. In the eerie light, with unsteady knees and the quiver in his hands, he hoped the bullets would go over them.

"Freeze," he shouted.

Instantly they turned off their lights. He squeezed off a single shot. Bullets poured back through the tunnel, hitting the rock wall twenty feet beyond him. They were utterly panicked, just emptying their guns at where they had seen the muzzle blast. When he heard the click of a man pulling a clip, he flipped on his light, catching them both like deer in the headlights.

"Drop your guns or I will blow you away."

They did as he said. "You're using up a lot of air. You got no place to go. Either we all go up or we all die. Come on forward. Do exactly as I say, or I'll kill you so I can get out of here alive."

Dan collected both guns, slinging one over his shoulder. Before they made their way back to the heavy stink of the pond, he took their lights and threw away their shoes. They teetered when they walked.

"What the hell is in here?"

"We don't know."

He tossed one gun in the pool and kept the other, replacing the clip. Now he had two guns and almost two full clips of ammunition. Quickly he removed a sample screw-topped capsule from his pack, took a sample from the pond, and put it in his pocket. One of the radios crackled to life.

"Where's McCall?"

"Answer," Dan whispered.

"Dead."

"Who's left?"

"Me and Willy."

"And one more," Dan whispered again with his gun prodding at the man's back.

"And Wilson."

"Jeez. How'd he take down Jansen and McCall?"

"It wasn't hard once he got a gun. You can't see anything

down here. You got these damn suits on. Get us up; we're running low on air.''

The cable started to rise and Dan stepped in the loop. In turn, each of the two men followed suit and they all rose toward the faint glimmer of light above.

There was a slight shimmy in the cable that Dan didn't recall. Probably they had damaged the assembly when jerking on the timber. Something wasn't as tight on his mask and he could smell petroleum vapor or something similar. As he rose, he strained to see what waited at the top, but it was useless. There could be an army with guns ready and there was nothing he could do except die fast in a hail of lead.

He wondered if the men below him knew he wouldn't bother killing them just because somebody was trying to kill him. No purpose in it.

When he got within twenty feet of the top, he could see the winch operator. Although he had an automatic in his hand, he didn't look very spooked. This guy hadn't heard the muted pops, the screaming men, nor felt the terror of hundreds of rounds smacking rock in the dark. Just sat up here thanking God it wasn't him.

As Dan reached the top, he realized that there was nobody topside to do the thinking. The operator was no candidate for higher education. Meat was perhaps a suitable moniker. Dan stepped off the cable, reached out, and took Meat's gun as if he were taking it from a child. Tossing it down the hole, he saluted the man who still hadn't been able to discern his face behind the mask.

"Hey," Meat said. "What're you doing?"

"Hey," Dan said. "You have a real good day, Meat. Afraid I gotta take your shoes, though."

"Who are you?" Meat said as the other two stepped off.

"I'm Superman. Hurry with the shoes."

"You bastard," Meat said as the other two stood by.

Dan stepped back twenty feet or so. "You gentlemen will want to stay right here, because if I should see you again when I go around that corner, I'll turn you into bratwurst. You got that?"

Dan watched Meat, cursing and swearing, untie his shoes. Interestingly, the man sat on the ground, almost as if he were a child having a tantrum.

"How does a guy get a name like Meat?"

"It's on account of his last name," Ed said.

"And what might that be?" Dan asked.

"It's Ball."

"That would explain it," Dan muttered to himself as he began running, desperately hoping that no one stood between him and the mine entrance.

24

The search warrant had turned up nothing.

Dan had taken to clicking his ballpoint pen with tedious regularity. The rumors were mind-boggling—namely, that when the police arrived there were no bodies and no blood to be found in the mine, even the footprints had been swept away. Given the number of men down there, it must have been a massive undertaking to remove all evidence of their passage.

Sheriff McNiel walked in looking weary. "I'll be blunt, Dan. They say you must be hallucinating. There was a guard sitting right in front of that mine shaft."

"Yeah, reading a paperback novel. He never saw me go in, and he wasn't there when I came out."

"All we found was a massive cave-in that looks fresh, about two hundred feet in."

"A cave-in?"

"Yeah. Tons of rock. You'd have to dig a whole new tunnel just to get in there. And I'm telling you the county can't afford that. My deputies said it looked like somebody might have swept the place. There were no Hazmat suit hangers at the entrance and of course no Hazmat suits. We found no pool of anything, no fumes, no vertical shaft, and no winch."

"If it's plugged at two hundred feet, you won't find anything. And let me guess, to dig it out would cost millions?"

"More money than the county has."

"Well, if that isn't just mouse turds in the cornmeal."

"Stop talking like a hick," Maria said under her breath.

"They had all the time in the world to dynamite the mine," Dan said. "It's twenty or thirty miles from anything. Nobody would hear it."

"We don't have evidence to prosecute," McNiel said with finality. "Who would we prosecute?"

"I understand," Dan said. "What do they say about the big reservoir out there and the plastic pipe?"

"They're growing pacific yew in hedges and they use that to mix pesticides."

"That's bullshit."

"Well, what do we do, arrest them for lying?"

"I've seen the hedges," Maria said. "I'll bet they've already run agricultural chemicals through the pond, so if we looked for residue, we'd find bug killer. But shouldn't we at least look?"

"I'll never get another search warrant. What is it we suspect they do with that reservoir that's illegal?"

"Do they have permits to spray pesticides?" Maria asked.

"They do," the sheriff said.

"There's got to be something," said Dan. "Maybe the DA has—"

"Oh, believe me, we're talking to him. He wants evidence. Even if we took your testimony, Dan, we don't know who was shooting at you. Some guy named Meat Ball is all we have and you threatened him, not the other way around. We'll be watching them. If they sneeze, we'll be on it, but as it stands now we can't charge anyone."

Dan sat stunned, not quite believing it. Without saying a word he got up and walked to the door.

The woman's hands flowed over his back. She was an artist. Slowly she stripped the tension from his shoulders and loosened his lower back. Whatever his secretary paid her, it wasn't enough. Kenji was in the wintertime conference room that was something of a sunroom, a library, and a good place for a drink. It contained a collapsible massage table that he was beginning to use with regularity.

Nothing, not even the best massage, brought his stress level to normal, but it was an improvement over a back full of violin-string muscles. His enemies were everywhere, poking into everything. Blowing up the mine was only a temporary measure and would set back research immensely because now they had no volume of effluent on which to run their tests. And a ghost was stirring in the grave, thanks to Dan Young.

Hans Groiter entered the sunroom and dismissed the masseuse.

"He was in the mine," Kenji said. "Do you suppose he found the body?"

Groiter didn't bother telling him that if he did, it was headless.

"I hid it well."

"They're going to look into it. I guarantee you that."

"Let them investigate. There's a mountain of rock in the way. And we took everything out, including the photographer's body."

"You took the body out without my authorization?"

"Yeah. But you don't want to be involved in the details. You're better off not knowing."

"Who else knows?"

"Only those who absolutely need to know. You're safe. Relax."

"Don't tell me to relax. I told you to stop them. Since that time you've accomplished nothing. They have come onto Amada land, forced us to derail a major project, and set us months behind. They're going to cost us hundreds of millions and you tell me to relax."

"It takes time. We will get Maria Fischer. That will divert him, and we'll know everything they know."

Groiter's threat about the photographer's body was only implied, but it was just beneath the surface of his words. Of course Hans wanted Kenji to believe that if something should happen to him, the people who "needed to know" about the photographer's body might pay a visit to the sheriff. When the time was right, he would deal with Groiter. Probably send him off to the South Seas with a nice pension that would disappear if the photographer didn't stay buried. Right now the unnerving uncertainty was good for both of them.

"Suppose he did get a sample of the effluent. How long do we have before they've analyzed it?"

"Three or four days. But what's it going to tell them?" Groiter said.

"It's going to tell them that we're doing something with

wood distillates and that it has nothing to do with yew trees.''

"It'll tell them that somebody spilled a wood alcohol by-product in the mine.''

"Even that tells them too much. But you can't explain that effluent without understanding the catalyst. So that tells them a lot. Way too much," Kenji said. "Those two fucking lawyers did something the police could never have done without a warrant. Up until now they had no way or reason to get one.''

"Once we snatch Fischer, everyone will be distracted.''

"I need time," Kenji said. "Sixty days to get this lab wrapped up and moved. We can't hang onto it any longer. We've lost all the effluent and it will be tough to continue working on bulk conversion. Until I get out of the country, I want those two lawyers dead or distracted.''

Corey was not averse to all of the wishes of the German. This morning she had to take care of a major detail in what had become their plan to take down Maria Fischer.

In her kitchen after her second cup of green tea, she went to the drawer and removed a razor-sharp fillet knife from the knife rack, then picked up a day pack that she had already loaded. On the way through the garage, she picked up a torch and the TV/VCR player. She climbed into the front seat and turned the key, sending the van rumbling to life.

It took about sixty minutes to drive from her house to the grower's place deep in the mountains at the end of an isolated back road. Jack Morgan was a pot farmer who grew most of his crop on property Corey had acquired with a tiny portion of her father's money. For $10,000 every six months, paid in small-denomination bills, Jack had the use of 160 forested acres with good access to water. Located miles away from any residence, the property was almost surrounded by Forest Service land.

Jack Morgan lived in a two-story yellow farmhouse with gables and a steep-pitched roof. When Corey arrived at the front door, the bearded, balding grower greeted her but didn't invite her in. A short, rail-thin man, Jack Morgan glanced around nervously, obviously not wanting anyone to see him with Corey Schneider.

"Hang loose," said Corey. "You got a tick up your dick? You think there's guys hidin' in the bushes?"

"Let's go out back." Jack led Corey around the back of the house and into a large barn. There he seemed to relax. Reeking of hay and livestock, the place felt like a real farm. Jack stopped just inside the door, near a stack of gray fifty-five-gallon drums marked DIESEL. They looked military. "I've got workers coming and going—I don't want them spreading rumors I talk to you. There should be no connection between you, me, and that property."

"Fine by me."

"So why did you come?"

"Well, it's like this. You owe me thirty thousand including interest and haven't paid me back. Furthermore, you have ten thousand in rent coming due."

"Two of my places got raided. It's only a couple of months till the crop comes in. I borrowed the money for planting. You know that."

"You're late, Jack."

"I don't have it. Spent it on lawyers after the raid. They got the pot and my lawyers got what money I had."

"Fortunately for you, I have a way you can work your way out of this. Somebody will pay you the forty grand you need to pay me."

Jack eyed her suspiciously. "I can pay you the forty grand after the harvest. I thought you understood that."

"I need the money now. I have a plan I'm working on, and you're going to help me. One Maria Fischer has gone over to the other side, and you are going to help me detain her and ask her a few questions."

"I don't know, Corey. I gotta keep a kinda low profile out here, you know? I don't know that I wanna get involved."

"Way I see it, Jack, you don't have much choice. Cops could find out about this place in a hurry, for sure."

"But I'm on your land too."

"They don't have to find out about that. And even if, for whatever reason, you are dumb enough to tell them about my place over by the South Fork, I never go there. So I rent you some property. I'm not responsible for anything illegal you have going on, am I?"

"They could take your land."

"Oh sure, after they take your farm and put you and your family behind bars."

"You'd do that?"

"Damn right, Jack."

Jack looked torn.

"I saw Otran's mouthpiece go into Maria Fischer's room at the Palmer Inn. I know the right-thinking people in this movement might care if their all-star, troublemakin' bitch is in heat for the Otran guy."

Jack grinned despite himself. "Hard to imagine two lawyers who don't want to screw each other, though."

"And the rest of us too," Corey added. "Anyway, here's how I have it figured. Why don't we get her out here, and use a little persuasion to get her to tell her story on tape? I know she's been taking big money from the timber industry."

"No lie?"

"Believe me, I know it."

"The law will try to do something, but there won't be a lot of heat. If we're careful, they won't catch us."

"Are you nuts, man? We'll go to jail, and they'll throw away the key," Jack retorted.

"They won't know who did it."

"Leave me out of this one. This is way over my head."

"I need your help," Corey said.

"I don't know, Corey. This just isn't for me."

"You can skip two ten-thousand payments when we pull this off. That's not insignificant. On top of that, you get five extra acres of good ground, with water, for the same money you pay now."

Jack frowned and shook his head. "No, I just don't think so."

Slowly he looked into Corey's eyes. She knew that what he saw there scared the hell out of him, causing him to back away tentatively. With her right hand Corey drew her army .45 from the back of her pants and moved with him, step for step, the gun inches from Jack's chest. With her left she pulled a Taser stun gun. "I know you pretty well, Jack. I figured that would be your reaction."

"Take it easy, Corey. You and I both know you aren't going to shoot me."

Corey made it a point to smile her crazy smile.

There was a snapping sound and Jack grabbed his chest as he fell backward.

Effortlessly Corey rolled him over and put plastic tie-wraps on his wrists, pinning his hands behind his back. From her pocket she removed a black hood, then sat on the floor holding Jack's head in her lap. In a moment he became coherent.

"What are you gonna do?"

She put the hood over his face.

"Don't hurt me."

"We can do this the easy way or the hard way."

"I'll do whatever you say."

"You don't sound convincing, Jack." She shoved a can of pepper spray under the hood and released a two-second squirt.

Jack convulsed and gasped with a convincing death rattle. She removed the hood.

"Now don't fight me, Jack. We're just going to have a little talk."

Corey scanned the barn. She grabbed a line hanging from the rafters, probably for hanging deer or a slaughtered cow. Quickly she fashioned a noose, then put it over Jack's head and pulled until he was lifted up on his knees. The noose was tight, but not choking him completely. Next she located two concrete blocks and had Jack stand with one foot on each. Adjusting the rope so that Jack would hang himself if he moved from the blocks, Corey stood back.

"We need to have a discussion. It's tough for a woman to convince a man that she's the big dog. I could fix that by making you not a man, Jack."

"I'll do anything you want," said Jack.

"Oh no, Jack, it's not going to be that easy. You'll tell me whatever I want to hear, then welsh later—maybe shoot me in the back. No, I want real sincerity."

"I said I would help."

"Great. But first, you have to watch my show." With that, Corey walked out of the barn. When she returned from the van, she held a small TV with a built-in VCR. Hanging about the barn were light sockets on the ends of insulated electrical cord. Cobwebs made a ghostly skein around each wire. One of them had a plug-in, in place of a light. Inserting the plug to the television, she turned it on and pressed play. It was a narrated video, complete with background music, featuring Jack's pot gardens, showing their locations and Jack at work with his wife, his son, and the hired help.

"If something happens to me, this tape goes to the cops—and, Jack, you and your wife will go down for at least five years. There's a note with the tape explaining exactly why it was made—you threatened to kill me if I didn't let you grow on my property. If I die under strange circumstances, the cops will get the tape."

"OK, so let me down."

"We haven't made a bargain yet. You can skip two payments on the land, and I'll give you an additional five acres for twenty thousand per year, two ten-thousand payments. Pretty good, huh, Jack?"

"Sounds fine to me."

"You're still not sincere, Jack. I can read your mind. You're still thinking maybe there's some way out of this."

"No, Corey, I swear; I'm willing to do it."

"Good. We'll celebrate over dinner."

Again, Corey turned and walked out of the barn. This time she returned carrying a frying pan, a small torch, and a day pack. Suddenly Jack began to sweat.

Corey lit the burner and poured oil in the frying pan. "You haven't asked me what's for dinner."

Jack's jaw began to quiver. He swallowed hard. Corey began unlacing his boots. She pulled them off one at a time, then his white socks.

"I'm gonna fry your feet." With that, she spooned up a drop of hot oil and dropped it on his foot. He spasmed, kicked the blocks out, and began choking. Wildly he struggled, then tried to find his footing. She let him hang until he started passing out; then she lifted him and got his feet back on the blocks.

"Oh God, Corey, don't—I promise I'll help," he choked out.

Corey took out her alcohol and put it on the burn.

"And again," she said, this time scooping up a whole teaspoon of oil, "don't jump around so much or you'll hang yourself."

"No!" Jack shrieked, causing Corey to kick the blocks from under his feet to quiet him. She never had a chance to use the oil. Jack began to choke, turning blue as the rope cut at his neck. Corey waited twenty seconds, then replaced the blocks.

When Jack had more or less recovered, Corey spoke. "The problem is, Jack, you won't really believe I'd do it unless I actually fry one of these feet." She paused. "You notice I'm being real sanitary about this. I've got the right antibiotics. Your old lady can nurse you. She'll keep it from getting infected."

"Corey, I swear to God I'll help you with Maria Fischer—please."

She waited a suitable time. "I think you believe me."

She untied Jack and packed up her things. "Jack, you and I have a perfect understanding—right?"

Jack lay on the floor, rubbing his badly bruised neck with one hand and gripping his burned foot with the other.

"Absolutely."

"Just remember. I'm a crazy bitch. Don't let your ego get in the way or you may go off to prison with burned feet and no balls. Lot of ramifications there, Jack. Lot of ramifications. And, Jack?"

"Yes?"

"You know absolutely that I would do it. You know I'm like that, don't you?"

"Not a doubt in my mind."

"Good then. We've made progress. Tomorrow you'll meet the German. I know you'll love him. We're going to build an interrogation room right here in your barn. We'll dismantle it when we're through with it. And I need you to take the van and have a few specialty items installed.''

Groiter had a feeling and he couldn't shake it. Satoru was always pressing, always wanting to know. It felt like the walls of his world were moving ever closer and that each wall had its own set of prying eyes.

Groiter bought an airline ticket for the east coast under his own name. Took aside his most trusted guy, Barnes, and had him fake an ID. It was a California driver's license with Hans Groiter's license number and address but Barnes's face. It took some work but the man actually looked a lot like Groiter. Groiter boarded the airline while Barnes boarded the Amada corporate jet and was quite illegally not listed on the jet's log. When Groiter arrived in New York he immediately returned on the private jet. Barnes remained in New York regularly using the Groiter ID. Upon his return to San Francisco, Groiter immediately went to a small rural airport just outside of Santa Rosa. There he entered Mama's Café, a bustling little place where people waited in line to eat. It was a nondescript concrete-block building painted yellow and brown. It had a bad case of the uglies. Inside was better, with green plants everywhere, even in the rafters.

Something about walking through all the plants felt good. He liked his plan.

He entered the men's room in the very back of the place and opened the window. There was no screen. Not a hundred feet away, parked on the grass, was the helicopter he had ordered. Quickly, hoping he wouldn't be seen, he crawled out the window and jumped down in a small enclosure that stored the garbage cans and housed the air conditioner. It was an easy vault over the low wall and a quick walk to the helicopter. Hans could fly passably, and it was a sunny calm day.

Without filing a flight plan and with the transponder off, he flew below 1,000 feet for 200 miles to a strip in Fortuna, California, where he picked up the Spaniard, pulled fuel in cans from a hangar, and then flew to Jack Morgan's. Nobody but the Spaniard could put him anywhere near Palmer. Legitimate receipts would show that he checked into the Waldorf-Astoria in New York.

25

Maria and Dan were in the public library reviewing a Sunday-magazine newspaper insert article about the death of Catherine Swanson.

"I'm sure the body in the mine was the photographer, so we know he didn't kill her."

"It was a body without a head," Maria said.

"Clothing matches. He was skinny like the photographer."

"OK, I'll concede that. I think you should leave town for a while."

"No way."

After a short argument and a longer discussion, Dan changed the subject, explaining that he had to meet some clients the next day even though it was a Saturday.

"It's a bit of a problem," Dan said.

"Why's that?"

"Pepacita's going to visit her family. And worse yet, Nate

was supposed to stay with his friend John Barge. Debbie Barge is great, but I'm reluctantly coming to the conclusion that her live-in boyfriend is into drugs. Now that Lynette's gone . . ."

"Are you working up to something?"

"Well, I'm in a bind."

"You know I'll do it," Maria said between bites of her tuna sandwich. "I just want you to ask, instead of sliding all around it."

"He's liable to have an attitude. The boyfriend was taking them for a ride in his drag boat."

"I can deal with it."

On the first floor of the castle, there was a large ceremonial room. History was prominently featured with swords and body armor from various eras, even equestrian armor, and all manner of ancient fighting implements. The floor of the long rectangular room was gleaming mahogany from a nearly extinct species. The walls were redwood and the ceiling Japanese white cedar. Functions for up to 200 could be held in this room.

Off of the ceremonial room lay a relatively small study. This room looked much more Western and prominently featured several large computer screens. Yoshinari sat in front of one such screen that displayed a detailed map of northern California. Shohei had just called by satellite phone. Groiter had disappeared at a Santa Rosa airport. Shortly after he entered a public eating establishment, a helicopter took off and Groiter could not thereafter be found.

Shohei could wait in San Francisco and collaborate with Satoru, or he could go to Palmer and wait. Yoshinari studied the map. There was nothing of great interest in San Francisco. Maria Fischer was from Sacramento. Dan Young was from Palmer. Kenji's laboratory was near Palmer and Corey Schneider was there as well.

"Go to Palmer. You have a radio that will monitor the police?"

"Yes."

"Use it. The pressure on Kenji is great. Groiter may do whatever he's working so hard to conceal at any moment. Let me know the minute you hear anything out of the ordinary."

"Ossu."

Yoshinari flirted with the idea of sending more men but thought better of it. More men meant greater risk of exposure. And Shohei was incredibly talented.

He dialed his daughter.

"Micha."

"Father," she said softly. "How wonderful to hear your voice."

"How are you, my daughter? Beautiful flower in my garden."

"I would love to see you and Mother."

"Maybe we will take that shiny plastic bubble of a thing and aim it at America."

"Father, it's a Gulfstream GV. Kenji envies you."

"Nothing but wires and metal. No beauty. But if it will take us to you, maybe there is something to be said for it."

"Something is on your mind."

"How did you know?"

"Mother comes on the line first when you are not worried."

Yoshinari smiled. His daughter was indeed observant. "How is Kenji?"

"He paces in the night. His teeth grind in his sleep."

"So what do you think is worrying him?"

"He keeps me far from his worries."

"Yes."

"And if I ask, he gets angry. So I don't ask."

"I see."

"How is my granddaughter?"

"She is well. You should come and see her. Already she paints like Mother. She has your love of the garden."

"I will come soon."

"Rest easily, Father. You will figure it out. You always do."

He hung up. For better or worse he had just told his daughter that he was very worried. Now she would be doubly alert. Turning off the screen, he rose to retire to his garden. And wait.

Corey looked out the window of the study. Through a break in the overcast, a shaft of sunlight beamed through the shadows. Looking down at her glass-topped desk, she saw that both the sun and the clouds were reflected there in an interplay of gray and gold.

Sitting back in the oak chair, the straightness of it feeling good against her back, she focused her anger and reviewed the plan. Maria was supposedly in Palmer this afternoon and was to remain through the weekend. But that information had come from a fund-raiser who had talked to Maria's assistant; it was two days old. After thinking it over for a minute, Corey picked up the phone.

"Maria Fischer's legal assistant, please."

"This is John."

"John, this is Terry Hatcher. I'm an attorney and I'd like to consult with Maria Fischer. Will she be in this afternoon?"

"No, but she'll call for messages. Would you like her voice mail?"

"I'd like to talk with her in person. Where could I reach her tomorrow?"

"I can take your name and number and get back to you."

"Certainly. But you know, I was told she was going to be in Palmer tomorrow and I was hoping I might catch her there."

"I believe she will be in Palmer. If I could just take your number, I'll tell Maria you called."

"I'll be out. I'll have to call back."

The harlot and the pimp, she had taken to calling them. The phrase felt good and bolstered her determination. At the German's insistence the three of them were to have one more meeting before the big event. If Jack was nervous about her, he was incoherently frightened by the German. Now she was convinced Jack would put his heart into this thing to save himself. Wisely, he had sent his entire family to Mexico. These days he looked like a man who had seen his darkest moments, and when September brought this year's crop, she imagined he might move out of Nolo County altogether.

Startled by the ringing phone, she answered, certain that it would be the German.

"Corey?" It was her aunt. She would know the voice anywhere. A shock. They hadn't spoken in two years, and then it was about a dying cousin. She hadn't cared then, and she didn't care now.

"What?"

"I know you don't like us bothering you, but we thought you should know."

"Know what?"

"A few weeks ago a man came here. A private investigator. He wanted to know all about you. He was very nice. He said it was about an inheritance and they were trying to locate you."

"And you had to talk to him." She knew her aunt would

talk with anyone if they made her feel important. Corey
hated her all over again. "What did you tell him?"

"Well, everything in general, about . . . you know."

"About Max, his drinking, his suicide, the rest?"

"More or less."

"Yes or no?"

"Yes."

"You told him about me. About my real father."

"Well, it seemed pertinent to the inheritance."

"Shit." Corey slammed down the phone, cracking the
handset. There was no use talking. It had been some hench-
man of the German. Immediately she understood how he
knew to lock her in the closet. To pump her. She wasn't
stupid! She *wasn't* stupid!

She flung her coffee cup against the wall. It left a dent
in the Sheetrock where it shattered. Goddamn manipulating
bastard. He had made an ass out of her. He wasn't anything
to her. Not a goddamn thing. And he had worked his way
into her. Coddled her. Told her how wonderful she was.
Humiliation burned in her, then turned to rage. She promised
at that moment to reverse everything or die, and then spent
a good hour figuring what she would do.

Corey planned to go along with the German until an
opportunity to do otherwise presented itself. She detested
the Spaniard who followed the German everywhere, but one
thing, the only thing, she now appreciated about the German
was his penchant for meticulous planning.

Corey checked out the equipment in the van, as she knew
the German would. She had to admire Jack's handiwork.
Gutting the interior of the van had been easy, but Jack had
gone to some effort to arrange for the installation of the
round table bolted to the floor—one of those Formica and
plywood creations found in cheap cocktail lounges. Behind

the table, likewise bolted to the floor, a gray vinyl bench seat faced the rear doors.

Resting the Colt AR-15 on the pile of sandbags she had arranged on the table, Corey assumed a firing position. The rifle's green-camouflaged plastic stock felt smooth and businesslike against her cheek. The rightness of the way it felt in the firing brace, close to her, an extension of her, came from the thousands of times she had fieldstripped, assembled, and fired rifles like this. Like a ritual, a mantra. Ivan the Terrible had taught her well. When you pick it up, it must *become* you: you think through it, breathe through it, live through it.

She pressed the foot pedal and watched with satisfaction as the rear window lowered—all the way down in just four seconds. None of it was terribly fancy or high-tech, but it was all sturdy and would serve its purpose well. If anyone followed the van, they would get a surprise.

She drove to Jack Morgan's place, forty-five mind-numbing minutes of twisty driving to the sounds of the local country-western station. The house was dark, and only a sliver of light shone from the barn. She headed straight there and parked by a white Ford Taurus with absolutely nothing memorable about it save a small antenna protruding from the back window.

In the barn she found the familiar fifty-five-gallon drums and the tractors; at the far end near the hayloft was the German in his black hood. No way was this man ever going to let any of them identify him. The Spaniard waited off to the side, running his eyes over her body as obviously as he could. She approached the German and stopped about ten feet short. She felt unnerved and knew that was precisely what he intended. Jack sat in a folding chair about ten feet away, jiggling his knee like a nervous kid.

"Are you ready?" the German asked.

"I am."

"Fischer will come out of the Palmer Inn on Saturday morning, as usual. We have reason to believe she's going on an outing. Follow her. If you get a good opportunity, take her. If not, bide your time. I don't want any screwups. Make sure no one is watching when you grab her. The rifle is a last resort. If we haven't got her by Saturday evening, we've devised a ruse to get her out of the hotel very early Sunday morning. But that's the end of the time window, so we want to try to take her before that. Jack, you do what Corey tells you."

They then proceeded to go over the details of the plan. Over the weekend Jack had completed the remodeling of the barn, finished the Sheetrock, and installed a solid wood door and a two-way mirror, all to the German's specifications. From inside the interrogation room, it was impossible to discern that you were in a barn. Maria would see only white walls, fully carpeted floors, fluorescent bulbs, and the large mirror. As the German and Jack had planned, the room could be dismantled in minutes, leaving no trace of its presence save a few nail holes in the rafters.

Corey knew she would get only one chance to double-cross the German, and if she failed, she could end up dead— or worse. She had to get all the evidence he had on her, and then she had to kill him.

"Hi," Maria said as Nate climbed into her old Jeep Cherokee.

"Hi." He sat there, arms crossed and a grim look on his face.

"Nate, I think I understand how you feel. I'll bet that drag boat sounded pretty good. If you don't want to go somewhere today, I'll understand. We can stay home and you can play around the house.''

He shrugged. ''Maybe we should go someplace.''

''Did you bring your boots?''

''Uh-huh.'' He pointed to his pack, which he'd tossed in the backseat.

''Your father didn't fill you in on what we're doing, did he? It was supposed to be a secret.'' Nate just grunted, a ''no'' from the sound of it. ''Well, we were going fishing, but you can stay home. Really, it's OK.''

''I wanna go,'' he said, making it sound like a groan.

''I suppose you don't like trout fishing,'' she said casually as they entered the National Forest. ''So would you like to leave the fishing poles in the car or take them with us?''

''I don't care,'' Nate said, looking straight ahead.

Something has got to change, she thought. She went to the back of the car to get her pack. ''We were going to scout places to fish. That was my big surprise. But I guess we don't have to do that.''

Nate's eyes flickered at her for just a second. ''We could take the pole,'' he said.

''Who would use it?''

''Well. Um. I would.''

The boy squelched his enthusiasm masterfully, she thought to herself. Poor kid.

Soon they started up a steep incline through the forest, mostly second growth that had filled in since the early 1900s, the redwood trees some four and even five feet thick at the base. They climbed quickly, Nate with his head down and a determined look on his face. After a time the path came to a rushing stream, then followed it up the hillside. Eventually they came to a fork in the trail. To the left the trail continued alongside the stream, toward a waterfall, from the roaring sound in the distance. To the right the trail moved off into the trees, up the mountain.

"This way," Maria said, pointing left.

Finally they came to the end of the trail: a small gorge with a roaring cascade at one end, which sent a cool mist floating through the rays of sunlight pouring down from overhead. Spanning the gorge was a thick log, which from the look of the damp green stuff covering it would be quite slippery to walk across.

"Pretty nice place, huh?" Maria whispered, looking at the crystal-clear water from the falls as it poured over some boulders in the gorge below. A shiver of pleasure ran through her; there was nothing like this, the feeling of being closed in by lush green—the trees, the moss, the lichen.

"It's like a magic forest." Nate pointed his finger. "That'd be a good place to fish."

Looking downstream, Maria saw a still pool off to the side of some rushing waters, covered over by a couple of old, fallen logs. Perfect place for trout to hide. "Yes, it would," she said. "But to get down there, we'll have to cross the log."

Together they looked at it. An old Doug fir, it was over one hundred feet long, the topside worn smooth and slightly flat, and pockmarked by burrowing bugs and the spiny, sharp cork boots that loggers wear. Four feet through at the big end, nearest Nate and Maria, the log spanned a chasm fifty feet across and perhaps forty feet deep at the center.

"Well?" Maria asked, smiling.

Nathaniel looked at her, wide-eyed. "I don't know," he said, bewildered. "How?"

"Well, you could walk or crawl."

Nate peeked down at the rocks in the stream far below. "Are you going too?" he finally asked.

"Of course," she said. Maria recalled the feeling she'd

had the first time she had to cross a sheer drop like this one, which could kill with one slip. A sensation of a cool draft, even if there is no wind, the feeling of lightness that is an adjunct to dread.

"If you go, I'll go," Nate said. "I think."

Maria smiled. A tough guy—sort of—just like his dad. "I have a safety harness in my pack. You can put it on, and it would catch you if you fell. I will be right with you. You can do it, Nate. I'll show you how and I won't let you fall."

"OK."

Maria quickly removed two harnesses. Then she donned some Gore-Tex climbing gear and helped Nate into some rubber pants.

"You do this a lot?" Nate watched as her fingers adjusted the harnesses.

"Yup." She snapped a tether from her harness to Nate's.

"Sit," she said after leading him to the log. Following her instructions, he climbed up on the natural bridge, straddling it.

"Look at that tree on the other side," Maria said. "Stare at it. Don't look down."

She sat immediately behind him, Nate almost in her lap. Then, picking him up, she scooted him forward. "Look at the tree," she said, encouraging him to repeat the movement on his own.

Within minutes they were across. When they stood, Nate turned to her, respect in his eyes.

"We did it," he said, a tinge of excitement in his voice.

"Yes, we did. And it took two of us. So you would be making me feel safe if you promised not to do that by yourself. OK?"

Nathaniel nodded.

Then they fished. Assembling a small collapsible rod, she taught him how to use a fly with a barbless hook and a bobber. Small trout took the fly repeatedly. After reeling them in, Nate and Maria released them. After they'd reeled in a half-dozen small trout, Maria led Nate to a pool near the base of the falls. The shore was crowded with huckleberry and thimbleberry, so they had to crowd past the many spiny stems and damp, leafy branches to get to the creek's edge. There she pointed to a log that angled across the pool's edge, above a back eddy that made the foam move upstream past an old alder log.

As they neared the log, Maria hunkered down, indicating to Nate that he should do the same. Together they crept the last few feet to the log and the deep pool beyond it. Even with the roar of the falls, the place had a tranquillity that they didn't want to disrupt with shouting, so they gestured as if sharing secrets.

Standing behind Nate, Maria placed her hands over his, then gently cast the fly near the falls, letting the fly drift down the stream's center and into the eddy, where it moved back up past their log like a tiny float in a parade. It was a special caddis fly, with gray wings and a tiny silver strand around its furry body. Jutting out from the body were little whiskers that stood the fly on the water, each whisker making its own tiny dimple in the glassy surface. Without warning, a swirl appeared where the fly had been, and the reel began to sing as the line peeled out across the creek. Nate shrieked.

"Keep the tip up," Maria said calmly in his ear, reaching to tighten the brake on the reel. Then the line went slack. "Reel quickly," Maria urged.

As Nate took up the slack, the fish once again swam for the far side of the creek, bending the slight rod in a half circle and eliciting another cry from Nate. Then the eighteen-inch-long silver-sided monster exploded from the water, shook its head, and dropped the fly as easily as a child spits out a pea.

"Oh man!" Nate shouted, his face lit with excitement.

When Nathan's enthusiasm had about peaked for one day, they packed up their stuff and due to the ease of descending made much better time. They wound down the trail in the quiet forest, hearing only an occasional scampering, the blowing of a startled deer, and the mad whir of a blue grouse.

"I'm going to the outhouse," Nate said.

The park service maintained a pit toilet at the other end of the lot. She nodded as Nate trotted off, then turned to load her stuff into her Cherokee. She pulled an apple from her pack and leaned on the tailgate, watching a red-tailed hawk. A nondescript blue van pulled into the lot and parked one space over. Nate was taking a while. Walking to the driver's-side door, she opened it and reached down to pick up her tennis shoes, thinking she would remove her boots.

The sliding sound of a van door made her realize with a start that someone had been taking their time in getting out of the van. She was unlacing her boots when she felt a hand on her shoulder. Then suddenly she was assaulted by searing pain in her eyes and nostrils. Her lungs felt as though they were being filled with a thousand angry hornets. As she felt her knees buckle, strong arms grabbed her. Burning mush filled her chest; terror gripped her mind. Something horribly confining, even suffocating, was over her face, and she was suddenly, vaguely aware that she was lying down.

"Where's the kid?" she heard.

"Forget him. Let's get the hell out of here."

Soon she calmed enough to realize that the cloth bag over her head was tied at her throat, that her hands and feet were tightly trussed, and that she was on the floor of a large moving vehicle. Then she thought of Nate, the engaging smile under his cowlick.

At least he had been spared.

26

Dan paced his office. He had raged at the sheriff, urging him to use the information they did have to the maximum. Then, calming himself, he sat and called Amiel Fischer.

"Hi, this is Dan Young."

"Dan, how are you?"

"Maria has been kidnapped."

Amiel Fischer took the news as calmly as Dan could imagine any father doing. He asked for all the details and listened without commenting while Dan told him what he knew.

"She took Nate fishing in the National Forest just outside Palmer. When they got back to the parking lot, Nate went to the toilet. Bless him, he hid but saw the whole thing and got the license number of the van that was used to take her. They had stolen plates, of course. He said two skinny men dressed in black sprayed her in the face. Nate was very fast, and found somebody five minutes later with a cell phone. They had to drive ten minutes to get a signal, but then the plates and a description of the vehicle went straight to the Highway Patrol. A patrolman recalled a blue van going away from the coast in the area where Maria was abducted. About ten minutes had gone by before he did a U-turn and tried to find them. That gives us a general region, if it's the same van. The officer never noted the plates."

"Her mother and I will be right up there," Amiel said. "We'll take the company plane."

"You should know that Maria tried to fight. She tore a red bandanna off one of her assailants. It fell on the ground, and Nate had the presence of mind to pick it up and take it with him. The lab is analyzing it right now."

In the minutes that followed that most difficult of phone calls, Dan made himself the center of a whirlwind of urgent activity. Within minutes of telling Patty McCafferty, the Wildflower Coalition machine went into motion to send an army of enviros into the woods.

Next he called Jeb Otran.

"Maria Fischer's been kidnapped. My little boy saw it."

"He what?"

"Long story. She offered to baby-sit and took him trout fishing. I had to meet with clients and my housekeeper was gone."

"What can I do?"

"Helicopter. We know the area. She was taken in a blue van. Your pilot needs to call the sheriff's office."

"You got it. But I'm sure it'll be an hour before it gets to Palmer."

"Tell them to call me the minute they have an ETA for Palmer. I want to ride with them and look for the van."

"I'll tell 'em."

"How about a bunch of foresters and some pickups?"

"Sure."

"I'm grateful. I know she isn't one of your favorite people."

"Come on. I'll do anything I can to help." Jeb disconnected.

A recent photo of Maria was distributed to all those who volunteered. An APB was put out on the van Nate had seen in the forest-service parking lot.

Sitting down, he took out a yellow pad and wrote down everything he knew. Amada owned the compound in the

Highlands Forest. Amada was run by a Japanese man named Kenji Yamada. People locally knew very little about him. The mill manager was known to everyone but didn't call the shots except about the operation of the sawmill and the flakeboard plant. No one knew the scientific type that had held Dan and Maria at the compound. Evidently he went straight in and out to San Francisco for his social life. Not hard for someone with a corporate helicopter.

This secret Amada operation was distilling wood to make gasoline and methanol. They had a pool of something bad, they had a body in the cave, and they were desperate. Someone had snatched Maria; someone was a violent monkey-wrencher; someone had kidnapped and murdered Kim Lee; finally someone had stolen the money. In some bizarre way, most of this had to be related.

Dan called in Gail, his new secretary, a longtimer at the firm.

"I'm so sorry," Gail said. "Everybody knows you're fond of her."

"Thanks, I appreciate it. This is sheer desperation, but could you call every garage in town and ask them if they've done any work recently on a late-model blue van, California license number 312 EWH?"

Gail took the license number and left.

"Sheriff's office is on the line."

Dan picked up.

"We're scouring the countryside for the van but haven't found anything. We know the plates came from a junked-out Dodge in Los Angeles and the serial numbers on the body would indicate that it was sold at auction in L.A. We're trying to find out who bought it."

"We're calling local garages on the off chance they worked on it after the stolen plates were put on it."

"That's thinking. Tell us if you turn anything up. Keep a list of who you call."

"Will do."

Gail rang him on the intercom line. "Bingo. Second place. The guy said yes, then got flustered and hung up. Said somebody called Morgan had the work done. Apparently, they installed an electric motor to raise and lower the back window. Put tinted-glass windows in all the way around the van."

"That's the van," Dan said. "Where's the place?"

"Sak's garage at the corner of Fifth and D."

"I know it. Old masonry building. Looks defunct."

Dan called the sheriff with what they had.

"We'll send an officer," the sheriff said. "We know these people. Edwin Gilbert owns it. He's always in the gray zone. We think among other things he's a fence and he supplies a lot of pot growers with their equipment. Funny they made this dumb a mistake, telling you on the phone."

"Maybe they didn't. Somebody called Little Gilbert did."

"That's Big Gilbert's brother. He's not real swift."

"How about you let me talk to Little Gilbert first and then send an officer."

There was a pause. "What are you going to do?"

"Give him a ration. A story, see what I can find out."

"You sure you want to do it this way?"

"Yup."

"We'll give you ten minutes with this guy, then we're taking him downtown."

"Fair enough."

"By the way, the red bandanna had cannabis resin in it. Probably worn by a pot smoker. Maybe a grower."

Dan drove straight to the bank, all the time keeping an eye on his watch for the time of the chopper's arrival. At the bank he removed $5,000 in cash. He got twenty-four

$100 bills and the rest $1 bills. He made twenty-four piles in his briefcase, each stack topped by a $100 bill. Then, sprinting from the bank and leaving an openmouthed teller, he jumped in the car and went to Sak's.

"Here we go," Dan whispered to himself, jumping out of his car. Trotting down to the big shop building, he spotted a guy with MANAGER stitched over the pocket of his blue work coat. "You must be Gilbert."

"That's me, unless you're lookin' for Big Gilbert." The man shouted over the whine of two departing diesel tractors that the mechanics were revving.

"No, I'm lookin' for you. I'm Jake," Dan said in a voice that said that name should mean a great deal to Little Gilbert.

"Well, so?" Little Gilbert said.

"Can we go inside?" Dan said.

They walked through the lube area behind the rows of workstations to a small office with a gray desk on a concrete floor. It was a cluttered mess, the desktop covered with junk-food wrappers, old receipts, an adding machine, and an old girlie calendar. Dan closed the door.

"Didn't Big Gilbert tell you?" Dan said, the surprise evident on his face.

"Tell me what?"

"Tell you that I'd be coming with the twenty grand. You're supposed to tell me how to find that blue van, the one you did the windows on."

"Did somebody call earlier?" Little Gilbert asked, stress and suspicion becoming apparent in his voice.

Dan exploded with a shout, grabbed the smaller man by the collar, and slammed him against the wall, letting all his anger and frustration escape. Literally, he wanted to hurt the man. "You hicks can't get anything right. This is what I'm talkin' about, you dumb greaseball."

He let the man sag to the floor. Setting the briefcase on

the desk, he opened it a crack, then slammed it shut before Little Gilbert got more than a tiny peek at the money inside.

"He said I'd know where to find the pot grower who brought in the van?" Little Gilbert moaned.

"Absolutely. The one who always wears the red bandanna. Can't think of his name." Dan clicked his fingers like he was trying to think. "And if you can't find him, the whole deal's off, and Big Gilbert can do without his twenty thousand. My guess is that when I leave here with Big Gilbert's money, he's gonna kick what's left of your ass good."

"God," Little Gilbert groaned. "He never told me, I swear it. Let me make some calls."

"There's no time." Dan slammed the man back up against the wall. He put a knee into his testicles, then dropped him to the floor. Dan feigned hysterical violence, kicking the man in the ribs but making sure not to connect too hard. Finally he stopped.

"Please, one call," the man choked out, rolling on the floor.

"One call, but then I really kick the shit out of you." Dan watched over Little Gilbert's shoulder as he called Big Gilbert's housekeeper and heard that she didn't know Big Gilbert's whereabouts.

Dan shook his head sadly. "I'm gonna beat you to death."

Little Gilbert looked like he was going to cry. "I'll try his mobile." He punched the buttons so fast he misdialed twice.

"This cowboy with the twenty grand is here, and I need to know how to find Jack Morgan. Whaddya mean what guy? He's beating the shit out of me." Little Gilbert listened, then looked up at Dan.

"I won't say a thing," he said into the receiver.

"It's Jack Morgan. Now get the hell out of my shop. Big Gilbert's gonna tear me limb from limb."

"I doubt it, this time," Dan said, picking up his case. On his way out the door, Dan met a sheriff's deputy. "He's all yours," Dan said, dialing the sheriff. "We're looking for a pot grower. Jack Morgan."

27

"You like your face, bitch?" Corey whispered. "I've got a razor here that will do some funky things to it."

Maria tensed behind her blindfold but said nothing.

Corey took out her stiletto and popped the blade. Teasing the blade down Maria's cheek, barely touching it, she chuckled quietly. "What have you got to say?"

"Your video won't look like much if I have a Halloween face," Maria said in a strong voice.

Corey exploded with a backhanded slap, snapping Maria's head back and raising an ugly welt on her cheek.

Then, calm again, as though the outburst had been merely an affectation, Corey grabbed the heavy hood and put it over Maria's head.

"You're right. We gotta do it slow, and we can't make a mess. We'll just take some of that spray you liked so well earlier and drip it on the mask. Right over your nose and mouth. No permanent damage except mental. It'll feel like you drowned about once every sixty seconds. Only you never die. You just want to. Here goes the first drop."

The noxious fumes exploded in the tiny room, causing Corey to step back.

Maria began gagging.

Corey grabbed the hood off. She put her lips an inch from Maria's ear. "This ain't a war. They don't give medals for refusing to talk. All we want is a little information about cooperation between you and the mouthpiece. And McCafferty and her buddies in industry."

Corey waited, pacing back and forth while Maria continued choking. Finally Maria spoke. "Nothing happens until you loosen the pressure on the handcuffs. They're cutting off my circulation."

Corey thought for a moment. Given enough time, she was certain she could get Maria talking without loosening the handcuffs—but she had no time. Speeding the dialogue and making the woman look better on videotape was all important. And any chance of escape was nil—the door to the makeshift room was locked, her feet were tied, her waist was taped to the chair, and Jack was standing guard just outside. And if that wasn't enough, the German was watching in the next room.

She loosened the cuffs slightly.

Dropping the foot prop on the recliner chair, Hans sat bolt upright. He didn't like what he was seeing through the two-way mirror. He wasn't sure that Corey was experienced enough to be loosening those cuffs. Then again he sensed she was hurrying and that was good.

Hans went to the door and spoke softly. "Goddamn it, Jack, if you want two eyes tomorrow morning, you make sure that if Maria Fischer comes through that door she's a dead Maria Fischer." Then he carefully locked the door. Initially he had felt good about the setup. That was until he found out they didn't kill the kid. If that kid saw something, anything, there could be trouble and soon. He liked Corey's style, but he needed results.

Corey needed a little coaching.

* * *

Dan drove to the airport to meet Otran's helicopter and the two officers assigned to it. Like most things involving aviation, it was a little slower than anticipated. As he was turning into the road for the airport, his cell phone rang. It was Gail.

"The title guys and foresters found no property in the name of Jack Morgan. They have six people calling every outlying post office, as well as all the major branches. They say if someone by that name gets mail in this county, they'll figure it out."

The news hit Dan hard. If Morgan was a renter or squatter, it could take days to find him.

"I'm sorry," Gail said.

Dan got a call-waiting beep.

"This is Dan Young."

"This is Murray, the title man. The Geary Creek Post Office holds mail for a Jack Morgan and family. They're a bit reclusive—actually, the whole bunch up there is a bit that way."

"I know the general area. People grow pot up there," Dan said.

"You said it, I didn't. Anyway, the house is only four miles up Geary Creek Road from the post office. You turn right a quarter mile past the sign that says 'Geary Creek Dump.' The road to the dump is on the left, and the road to Morgan's is on the right. The gravel road to Morgan's is a half mile long. There are two other houses on it, and you bear right consistently to get to Morgan's. The Morgans have a two-story yellow house with a big red barn out back. There's some pasture off to the north. I swore to the postal guy that we wouldn't ever divulge how we got the info."

"Great work. Conference me into the sheriff."

* * *

Corey turned when she heard Jack's voice.

"Boss wants to see you."

Corey nodded, frustrated at the setup. She was never going to get near the German, who stayed behind the two-way mirror. He was in complete control and she knew it. That had to change.

"He wants you out here now," Jack repeated.

Corey nodded and went back to Maria, still speaking in a perfectly controlled whisper. "The blindfold stays on. You touch it and the negotiations are over. Watch her," she told Jack.

On her exit from the interrogation room, Corey was confronted by the German. For some reason the Spaniard had stepped out of the barn.

"We do not have time for any more preliminaries. Cut her face now. Get her talking."

"What about the video? I thought we agreed we were making a video to show the grassroots people."

"Just find out what she knows, and make it fast. We need to close this place down. You should have killed the boy."

It was about what Corey had expected. Typical German efficiency. Make sure all the witnesses are dead, including Corey.

Corey fingered her stiletto, trying to make the move look natural, staying calm. She still didn't see the Spaniard. The German's eyes were nervous.

"How will we prove it to the grass—"

With incredible speed the German grabbed her knife and put her in a stranglehold. In the instant she felt the stranglehold on her throat, her years of training took over. Rather than grabbing the strangling hand, she kicked straight for his kneecap. But she was being lifted, and the balance

344   *David Dun*

required for a well-executed kick was gone. Although the boot struck its target, it did not have the force necessary to maim.

The German raised her still higher in the air, moving her toward the wall. It took her two seconds longer than normal to kick again, this time the groin. For a split second his grip on her knife hand weakened. It was enough. She had practiced the move so often she could execute it with her dying breath—which right now was still seconds away. She lacked full power in the upward stroke, but the blade nevertheless split the man's forearm like an overripe tomato.

The German bellowed, and Corey slipped from his fingers, hitting the ground and raising her knife. But she was unprepared for the pistol that came up in his left hand, now aimed straight at her chest.

"Drop the knife, Corey."

For the first time since her father died, Corey Schneider had allowed herself to get into a situation where a man's treachery might defeat her. She dropped the knife.

The moment she let it go, the German spoke to Jack without turning to him. He seemed not to notice his own wounded arm, which he tended by transferring the gun to his right and using his left hand to clamp a handkerchief over the gaping laceration. "I want this woman hanging from the rafter. Tie a noose and put it on her."

When he turned to look at Jack, his jaw dropped. Jack trained a double-barreled twelve-gauge shotgun on the German's center mass, ten feet separating the scattergun's barrel from his heart.

"I'm getting out of here. We were just going to video the mouthpiece, that was it," Jack said. "Drop the gun or I blow you in two."

The German's eyes met Jack's. His pistol—a fine German Heckler & Koch, Corey now noted with satisfaction—was pointed at the floor, his other hand still clamped on the wound.

"I swear to God I'll kill you," Jack said, now shaking so bad Corey wasn't positive he could hit the German square.

"You shoot me and I shoot Corey," the German countered.

"I don't give a shit what you do. I'll blow you to kingdom come."

Finally the German let the pistol slip and clatter to the floor. Corey stepped to Jack.

"Let me have it, Jack. As soon as we take care of the Spaniard, you can get out of here." Jack nodded dumbly and let Corey take the shotgun. Backing up, Corey reached into a feed room and pulled out a six-foot pole with a fine wire loop on the end. Recognition flickered in the German's eyes.

"You know what this is, don't you, Kraut?"

Corey fit the piano-wire loop over Groiter's head as she stood behind him with the shotgun. Running up the hollowed-out center of the heavy dowel, the wire could be pulled tight with a handle from Corey's end. It could cut through the arteries in seconds. With a little less pressure, slow strangulation was possible. Yanking off his hood, she paused for a second at the sight of his freckled face—somehow older than she had imagined—then pulled the wire tight enough to turn him blue while Jack taped his hands. All the time she watched for the Spaniard.

"Hold this," she whispered to Jack, giving him the end of the wire loop. "If he does anything, you choke him to death. Understand?"

"He's choking to death now," Jack whispered.

"No, he's not. He just looks it."

Outside, Corey saw a light on in the house. So the Spaniard was in there. Quickly she made her way to the back door and noticed it was ajar. From inside she heard moans and a woman crying. Looking a little farther, she saw the Spaniard hunched over the kitchen table on top of a young woman. He held a knife to her throat. So intent was he on raping the girl that Corey was beside him before he noticed.

As soon as her captor left the room, Maria went to work on the handcuffs. As a child, she had learned to slide out of play cuffs by stretching her thumb and using her double-jointed socket. Like Houdini, she needed only the slightest loosening. When she folded her thumb into the palm of her hand and pulled, pain from the chafing skin made her grunt. She tried to force her hand through, not caring about the ripping skin.

From outside, there were sounds of a struggle and threats. They were fighting each other. Hope invigorated her.

Slick with blood, her right hand popped free of the cuff, then her left. She ripped off the blindfold and began working on the tape at her waist, using her fingernails to pull up an edge. Free of the tape, she grabbed the plastic tie-wraps at her feet, ignoring the free-flowing blood from her hands that dripped onto the carpet. As she worked, it became apparent she was in a windowless room with a large mirror on one wall. She pulled frantically on the plastic tie-wraps that held her ankles together and fastened them to the chair. Finally she was able to stretch the plastic until she got enough slack to twist it. On the floor she found a screwdriver and moved the chair enough to grab it, then used it to further twist the plastic. She broke the plastic tie-wrap on her right leg. The left went faster.

When she moved to the door, she could only make out hazy figures across the barn. The chemical would not leave her eyes no matter how many tears she shed. She forced herself to wait, watching as best she could, knowing that they would probably see her the minute she went out the door. Through the blur it looked like a man had something pointed at the back of another man's head, probably a gun. Then someone else came with a gun pointed at a second man. A woman's voice. She sounded in a rage and she was tying up one of the others. In minutes he started yelling in a foreign language. Then the yelling turned to incredible, agonized screams. If ever they would be distracted, it was now.

Crouched down, she ran out the door and down the wall of the barn. At any moment, she expected to be discovered by the lunatics behind her. And then she saw it. A broken board in the side of the barn next to several bales of hay. Approaching it, she discovered a hole that looked like it might be big enough to crawl through. She lowered her head and scrunched her shoulders, barely squeezing into the opening. God, it hurt, first pinching her shoulders, then her hips. At last, she popped free. Ahead, she saw the forest.

Freedom.

She began to run, the eerie screams driving her first up a small path, and then off the trail, through a patch of ferns, trying to put as much distance between herself and the barn as possible.

When Corey was through with the Spaniard, he was moaning in shock. The girl, a young woman really, was still crying, and Jack looked haggard. The German showed no emotion.

"She's your daughter?" she asked Jack.

Jack only nodded.

"I thought you said they all went to Mexico."

"I lied. She wouldn't go. I wanted to protect her. Now this."

"What's your name?" she asked the girl, gently touching her head.

"Janet."

"I did you a good turn. Can you do me one?"

"As long as I don't have to kill anybody," she said, staring at Corey's bloody arms.

"You don't. I still need my videotape."

"That's all you're going to do?" Jack asked.

"Absolutely. We better check the bitch."

Corey was shocked when she opened the interrogation-room door and found the empty chair.

She walked back across the barn to Jack and Janet. "Jack, did you let her go?"

"Not me."

The German had to take some satisfaction in this turn of events, but he did not smile.

Corey tried to think. They were surrounded by forest. She couldn't be far. But now they couldn't stay here.

"Jack, you and Janet deposit the German in my basement. I've got handcuffs, a place to cuff him. Take him while I chase down the bitch." Then she proceeded to explain in detail what she wanted and how to get into the basement room.

"Why don't you just shoot me now?" the German asked as Corey pushed his head down to stuff him in the back of the van.

"You won't be that lucky."

Before he could say more, she sprayed him full in the face with pepper spray. He lay on his side, emitting muffled groans. She slid his hood over his face, then reached in his pocket, found a wallet and a card.

"What a dumb shit, a wallet with ID. I'll be damned. I thought you looked familiar. You're Hans Groiter, the security guy for the Amada corporation. Shit. Unbelievable.

"Tie his feet tight, Jack, and don't forget to stack some straw bales in front of the cabinet that leads to the room. It's in the cellar, right where I told you. Don't ever take the wire off his neck. Control him with it. And you know whose side you're on?"

"I'm a dead man if we don't deal with this dude," Jack replied.

"I'm real happy you figured that out."

"I want him dead, but I don't want to do it."

"That's my job. And remember those videotapes of your farm and family."

Jack nodded.

"Now let's you and me go back in the barn and make sure all the physical evidence here will incriminate him. This card will come in handy."

A minute later, Corey walked out of the barn, the Colt AR-15 strapped across her back. After popping the Spaniard in the head with the German's fancy Heckler & Koch, she left the bloody hulk sitting in the corner and began her search for Maria Fischer's trail.

It took Corey only minutes to find the hole in the barn and the small trail leading away from it. Reaching the fern patch, she saw the disturbed foliage and began following what she hoped was Fischer's escape route. Halfway through the ferns, she heard the helicopter. In minutes the area would be crawling with police. The adrenaline surged through her body and she let herself become the hunter—every scent, every folded leaf, every impression in the ground, held a meaning.

She had to silence Maria Fischer.

* * *

Listening to the tap and hum of the big twin turbine-jet helicopter, Dan watched the mountains roll underneath. Sitting next to him was a young officer they called Shane. Curly blond hair framed intense blue eyes that seemed to take in everything. The guy was slender but strong and fit. When they couldn't get Kier Wintripp, a Tilok Indian from the next county who was evidently on his honeymoon in Hawaii, they got Shane.

Next to Shane sat Sergeant Frank Spinoza, a dark-haired man with a reputation for grim determination that often irritated the sheriff but usually resulted in a conviction. Squad cars were to arrive in thirty minutes, but Shane and Frank were authorized to go in if it looked manageable. The highway-patrol copter would go in first. Dan was to remain in Otran's chopper with the pilot until the all clear was given and under no circumstances was the aircraft to enter a live fire zone. The rules were irritating but unavoidable.

Upon arriving, they circled with the highway-patrol chopper. No vehicles were visible at the farm. Staying back about 300 yards, they watched the California Highway Patrol (CHP) copter land.

"We're down and taking no fire," the CHP radioed.

Frank nodded at Otran's pilot.

"We're coming in," the pilot said.

In seconds they were on the ground.

"House or barn first?" Shane asked Frank.

"Let's knock at the house first."

Dan watched them head out, impatient to look around but constrained by his promise to stay. On the front porch they drew their revolvers while the CHP headed toward the back door. No one came to the door. Dan watched them try to open it. Locked. In a couple of minutes the CHP opened the front door. Obviously, they had walked in the back.

"No one home, but two cars in the carport," Frank said over the police radio as they exited the house.

"Ground to Helo," Shane said.

"Helo here," the pilot said.

"Any signs of life?"

"Not yet."

"Stick around. We're going in the barn."

After what seemed like minutes, the radio crackled.

"Come on in," Shane said.

Dan jumped from the copter, his heart in his throat. At the door he slowed.

"Careful," Frank said. "There's no Maria Fischer so far, but it's a murder scene. Don't touch anything. Don't step in anything. You shouldn't even be in here." Frank walked ahead, nodding at the body in the corner.

Dan involuntarily began to retch.

"Somebody castrated him."

"They did more than that. Cut off everything down there. Not to mention his eyes."

"Anyone home?" Frank shouted again. He received no reply.

"Look at that," Frank whispered, nodding at the hangman's noose and the two concrete blocks, bathed in bright light.

"Somebody built themselves a special little room," Shane said, entering what looked like a giant plywood box. It was crude on the outside, but Dan marveled at the finish work within—Sheetrock, carpet, the large two-way mirror. And a single chair. Cuffs on the ground. Blood. A lingering odor—pepper spray.

"They had her in here, I'll bet," Shane said.

Dan went back out and to the other side of the mirror.

The camcorder, mounted and ready to record, sat beside the huge recliner. A single bottle of German beer sat by the chair with no more than two or three swigs gone.

"We'll print it all," said Frank.

Shane nodded, analyzing the scene.

"Maybe they were interrupted," Dan said.

"Why would anybody want to go to this much trouble to interrogate Maria Fischer?" Frank asked.

"I would guess because somebody wanted to know what she knew about a lot of things."

"Like what?"

"Turning trees into gasoline, toxic ponds, stuff like that. And maybe somebody wanted to know if Patty McCafferty was selling favors to the timber industry."

"Can they really turn trees into oil?"

"Price is the issue. It can be done, though. In twenty years it'll be commonplace."

"How do you know about all this?"

"Seems Ms. Fischer and I are a nosy pair." Dan looked at the empty interrogation chair, the bloody cuffs. He bit his lip and offered a wordless prayer that she had escaped.

There must be something, some kind of clue, he thought, walking out of the room and along the perimeter of the barn. Minutes later Dan came to the broken board. He studied the hole. Then he noticed a handprint just outside, in the mud, and seconds later he made out the plaid fibers of a Pendleton shirt on the board's rough edge. Maria liked those shirts. A big fan of wool. She had even bought him one.

"Frank, Shane, come here," Dan called. "She went through here."

Two minutes later, Dan was back in the helicopter, flying under the high overcast, studying the terrain. Frank Spinoza had joined him, the pilot, and the sheriff's deputy while Shane followed the trail on the ground.

Situated on a bench near a ridge top, the house was surrounded by thick, mixed conifer forests, with the exception of two small emerald-green meadow areas nearby. At low altitude the forest looked like a textured, rolling mosaic of pointy dark greens—the conifers—and bubblelike, lighter greens—the hardwoods—with occasional flecks of gray and earth-tone reds in areas of thinner growth, where tree trunks were visible. The trail leading from the barn was exceedingly hard to make out, but it was apparent to Dan that if Maria had stayed on the flat bench paralleling the ridge top, she would have remained in the thick forest.

About a mile and a quarter from the house, the bench narrowed and met the headwaters of the Marmon River. Dan willed his eyesight to improve, desperate to see Maria safe, but the forest floor was for the most part obscured from the air; they could fly over a small army and not know it. Occasionally, though, he did catch a glimpse of Shane, moving quickly, jumping over logs, and zigzagging through the trees along the bench like a determined tailback hurtling toward the goal line.

Frank pointed. ''More than likely, if she stayed on the bench, she hit that creek and went down it. It's human nature to run downhill when you're in trouble—and water always leads to civilization. Let's concentrate there.''

28

Maria moved quickly despite the pain in her hands and the watering of her eyes, able through years of conditioning to maintain a steady jog except in the most obstructed areas. By her reckoning, she was now more than a mile from the barn. Moving through some dense brush, she suddenly imagined that she could hear a low-flying helicopter. She stopped, looked up, but could see nothing through the dense canopy of leaves. Could be the police, she thought—or it could be the bad guys. She plunged on through the forest, head down, moving like an animal, making herself small by shrugging her shoulders inward, squeezing along narrow pathways in the underbrush.

After traveling for about forty-five minutes, she began following a small stream downhill, but the stream's course was choked with fallen trees. Growing up through the criss-crossed logs were huckleberry, salmonberry, thimbleberry, young alders, and a host of other greenery, all of it forming an almost impassable wall. It was tough-going: a bruising, scraping, and soon bloody experience. She was forced to move up the sidehill, higher up the ravine above the creek bottom.

She had been running for maybe twenty minutes when she came to the first marijuana patch. Black plastic pipe traversed the hillside, sometimes partly buried and some-times above ground, feeding the young marijuana plants in their large clay pots. The pots had been placed next to large trees, effectively concealed from prying eyes in police helicopters.

Knowing she was in danger from growers determined to keep their gardens a secret, Maria moved quickly down-stream, where the country opened up. The trees and under-growth thinned, allowing her to move easily—not hunched over all the time—but also making her more vulnerable to detection. Natural meadows formed great green ribbons down the hillside. Interspersed with the meadows were patches of forest comprised of leafy hardwoods and arrow-shaped conifers. Maria moved along the meadow edges now, trying to stay hidden without delving into the denser forest. Deep blue-gray gullies were water-carved, appearing like giant tears flowing down the flanks of the mountain, often choked with brush, sometimes vertical sided and not easily crossable. She suspected she was on Bureau of Land Management (BLM) property, designated a wilderness area despite the pot-growing squatters.

About thirty more minutes downstream, she turned and looked up at the terrain she'd just descended. What she saw sent a wave of fear through her. Far up on the sidehill, near the ridgeline above the creek, a lone figure moved quickly down the mountain. While the figure was not directly on her trail, he or she was moving in the same general direction and was no more than half a mile behind. Maria's heart began to pound. If she could see the pursuer, then the pursuer might well have seen her. She considered her options. She could try to hide by losing herself in the brush, or she could run. Hiding might mean an overnight stay under a clump of trees, in nothing but a wool shirt. Capture by the kidnappers would be unlikely, even if they had radios and several hunters, but the chilly night could be brutal. Running in the dark was not a much more enticing option. What if she hurt herself on the trail? Run or hide?

Until dark, at least, she had to keep moving.

Turning downstream toward civilization would be the likely choice for Maria, but Corey knew that lower on the slopes she would find pot gardens, probably guarded by unpredictable men with tangled hair and beards, men living in hovels, who could or would do nothing else for a living, who lived outside the law. Such men didn't mind long stretches without much company under hard, primitive conditions. Each year they suffered the elements, thieves among their own kind, government raids, the threat of imprisonment, and the risk of great bodily harm or death at the hands of whoever happened to oppose them—and there were many who had reason to oppose them.

She considered how she might turn that situation to her advantage.

The second marijuana plantation was much larger than the first. Plants were everywhere, by almost every big tree. Some trees had several pots. And the plants were big. Already some were four feet high. Maria realized she was looking at millions of dollars in marijuana. What wouldn't they do to protect it? She had to get away from this place, across the creek and to the far side of the canyon, where there was no southern exposure—without the sun there would be no gardens. But as she tried to find a place to descend the precipitous mountainside to get to the creek, she was suddenly shaken by the coarse, boisterous blaring of an air horn. Adrenaline shot into her system as she looked around. Then at her feet she saw a trip wire. Damn. She was in the open near a steep embankment. She could hear someone coming. Galvanized into action, she went feetfirst down an almost vertical bank.

Within seconds she heard voices.

"Well, la-di-da." She whipped around and saw a sandy-haired man with a sly grin coming at her, a knife in his right hand and a military-style rifle in his left. The gun was pointed at her midriff.

"Take it easy now or I'm gonna put a bullet in you."

He wore a stained, heavy wool, half-unbuttoned shirt that revealed soiled long underwear beneath. There were small shells hanging around his neck, five earrings going up his ear, and a little patch of hair on his chin, with several days' growth on the rest of his face. Three feet away from her, he stopped. The muzzle of the rifle was in her belly.

He spoke into a radio.

"I think it was just another deer."

"I'm telling you I saw a woman coming down that hill."

"I'll keep looking."

He grinned at her again.

"I don't want to bother the rest of them just yet. Best I'd get is sloppy seconds."

Her insides turned sick. "You want sex?"

"Aren't you a mind reader?"

"Show me your hard-on," she said.

He laughed. "You gotta be shittin' me."

"I like to fuck as well as the next girl, but I wanna see what I got to work with."

He looked around for a moment.

"You first."

"Oh, come on, inspire me." She stepped close, sliding past the gun barrel, walking right up to the knife.

"You try anything and I'll twist this knife right in your gut."

He stank of stale sweat and had breath like rotten bananas. She had to concentrate in order not to retch. Forcing a smile, she ran her fingers over the front of his jeans, deliberately hurrying before he became erect.

She reached for the top button with her right hand. With her left she touched the stubble on his face. Apparently wanting to feel her breasts and use both hands, he turned the knife flat against her. It was a mistake. She put everything she had into her knee to the testicles and two thumbs into the eyes.

He fell to the ground, thrashing. Sharp thumbnails had gone deep; he was clawing at his eyes. She jumped away and ran. Only after getting twenty feet down the hill did she think about the gun. She cursed herself. Spinning around, she plowed back up through the brush only to see a second armed man coming toward the first.

Leaping back downhill, she barely maintained her balance as she ran full out.

"I'll shoot!" somebody said to her side as shots rang out. She disappeared over a six-foot drop-off. Even with all the noise of cascading rock, she could hear them coming after her.

"She's right down here," one of them shouted.

As she bounded down the hill, she saw a tiny clearing and a ramshackle cabin about the size of a two-car garage, made of unpainted plywood. It had a big black stovepipe running up the side. Darting around the structure, she looked wildly for a place to hide. Knowing that she was running to a creek bottom in unfamiliar territory, she realized they would no doubt get close enough to shoot when she tried going up the opposite hill.

Slamming through the door, her hands shaking, she looked for a gun. Junk was piled everywhere. There were boxes and sacks of supplies stacked two or three deep all along the wall with three bunk beds and a table in the middle. Against one wall by the door, there was an old wood cookstove. No gun. A knife on the table. She grabbed it and crawled behind some sacks of fertilizer. These people lived like animals. Desperately she clamped her sides, trying to calm her breathing, trying to make a plan.

"Hell, it's hard to find her in this brush," came a voice from outside.

"We'll find her. You run downstream on the trail and then come back up the draw."

"Wait. What if she went in the cabin?"

"Shit. You take off, I'll look."

She tried to make her hands stop shaking, to get control.

It seemed her whole convulsing body would give her away. The door creaked on its hinges.

"Come out, come out, wherever you are."

He started at the far end, looking behind some boxes. Scrunching down as tight as she could, she tried to make herself invisible.

She had no illusions. Getting caught would be a death sentence—after they were finished raping her. It made her desperate. Believing she had nothing to lose, she decided to lunge with the knife. He was five feet away and almost to the stacks of fertilizer. Trying to look around the six-foot stacks without exposing himself, he moved with slow deliberation. Any second he would see her.

His hand draped over a sack about three feet in front of her and above her. Frightened out of her mind, she lunged, skewering the hand with the knife, running it through and pinning it to the sack.

The man let out an earsplitting scream and dropped his gun to clutch at his hand. She dashed out of the cabin and with a backward glance saw him remove the knife.

"I'll fuckin' kill you!" He started shooting wildly.

"What the hell?" a second voice said.

There were at least four men, but now two were wounded. She crashed through the brush, hitting small saplings with bruising frequency. Charging down through brush so dense she couldn't see three feet, she had no idea where she would end up. She broke into a small clearing. There was a wiry short man with a grim, determined expression ten feet away pointing a gun at her middle.

"Party time," he said. "Wanna wrestle?"

Instead of shooting, he bolted after her, grabbing her around the middle. He stank like the first.

She turned, slapping the palms of her hands over his ears.

"Shit," he said, dropping his gun and trying to hold her arms.

Grabbing his ear with her teeth, she ripped the flesh and came away with a hunk the size of a quarter.

While he was feeling for his ear, she managed to kick his unprotected groin and connected. When he doubled, she kicked him in the face, hitting his eye with the toe of her boot. She picked up his gun. Deep, ragged breaths poured out as she tried to will herself to shoot him, then cursed at herself because she couldn't. He was hurt, but he could still hunt her. It was a weakness.

"What the hell?" a voice said as she ran.

Two men hurt but not incapacitated. Maybe a third was out for good, blinded with two swollen eyes. With only one uninjured man, the odds were getting better. She wondered how many shots the pistol had left in it. In Alaska she had learned about guns. Although she never had to use one, she had carried them in case a grizzly turned her way.

She knew her life depended on flight. Given her inexperience, she would not win a shoot-out against three men. She had to flee down the creek. Turning at an angle to the stream, she went down and away from the men, running the whole way. Then something grabbed her foot, she was flung through the air, and a horn blast went off. Another trip wire. On the steep bank the gun went flying. Straight down the hill, she turned, running a hundred yards through heavy brush.

Sliding and jumping downhill, she traveled maybe twenty yards, then crashed through more brush and over the edge of a rock outcropping, continuing down an almost-vertical rock face. Aware that she was starting to free-fall, she reached out and clasped a tree root. A searing pain went through her shoulder, but she managed to hold on. With her other hand she pawed desperately at the rock, finally finding another handhold. She looked down. Hanging over a large expanse of watery brown muck bordered by an almost impenetrable wall of marsh grasses, she was trapped.

She heard the crunching sounds of a man in the woods.

"I saw her running down the mountain over here." A deep voice.

"All right, all right, but I don't know what a lone woman, without a pack, without even a coat, is doing out here. How Spike let her crunch his balls and gouge his eyes, I'll never know. She's the type who'd turn us in tomorrow."

"Maybe with a little encouragement she'd warm our beds tonight."

"We have three million dollars in plants to worry about. She's already half-killed Spike. Dutch is half blind. Let's just shoot the bitch and be done with it."

The voices were getting closer. Silence was crucial.

"I say we chain her in the shack first."

"We'll figure that out when you find her. Dutch, use the eye you got left to search down in the bottom. English, you circle around up the hill. I'm gonna hang around in this area."

"My hand hurts."

"I don't give a shit."

From where she hung, Maria watched the shadow of the man moving to the creek bottom until he appeared below her, downstream about fifty feet. Dutch. He was tall and skeletal, skin like tanned leather, an uneven pirate-looking beard. She held her breath. She was plastered as close as possible to the rock, but she would be visible if he looked up. She studied him as he debated stepping in the mud, tentatively placed his boot on the watery surface, and began sinking rapidly. Quickly he yanked his boot clear of the muck. Shaking his head, he eyed the putrid swamp.

"No one could have walked through this mud without leaving huge tracks," he shouted up to the leader. Turning, he began walking back uphill, climbing the rock slope using all fours, obviously in pain. Then having turned well above her, he could be heard crashing through the brush. She heaved a quiet sigh of relief. Obviously, they didn't realize how far down the hill she had gotten.

From above, Maria heard more crunching sounds of footfalls on the brushy slope. There were at least three men. Knowing that she could not hang on indefinitely, and that she would be discovered if she crawled up the outcropping, she began to consider a drop to the mud. By dropping under the lip of the rock, she could remain well-hidden.

She was in a small steep-sided mountain valley, where for a few hundred yards the creek ran nearly flat, and where the land acted as a natural settling pond before it spilled the water on down the mountain in riffles and cascades. On one side of the creek, the side from which she hung, there were some large gray rock formations near the water's edge; the other side had fewer sheer drops and was more soil-covered, the trees growing in places to the water's edge but not so densely that on a climb out, her invisibility would be guaranteed. The Douglas fir and the scattered oak were rich green in the sunlight of the day, but now in the lengthening shadows some were turning black, making the place seem deadly solemn.

The leader called out from a distance well above the rock. "I see another one coming. This one's got a gun."

Realizing her pursuers were distracted, she decided to drop. Letting the root slide through her hand, and using her fingers and toes to cling to the rock, she accomplished a controlled but painful slide. She moved down three feet, paused for a split second, and then pushed herself off—plummeting ten feet to the mud, her chin barely missing a stone projection as she fell.

Instantly she sank to her thighs in soft, velvety ooze. She

had never heard of quicksand anywhere in California, but that hardly put her at ease. If it was quicksand, she knew thrashing would be stupid. But she had read about swimming in quicksand. The horror was that you got only one swimming lesson—and if you failed, you died.

She looked down again. Her belt was closer to the muck. Maybe she had just leaned over and wasn't really sinking. No—she had been still. Straining to pick up her right foot, she tried to move forward, but she received only shooting pains through her ankle for the effort and a loud sucking sound. The noise was frightening. And now the mud was touching her belt.

Above her she heard the growers on the hillside, waiting for whoever had been following her. With luck they would kill or run off her pursuers, but would that really help her? For the first time she felt cold, and wondered how long she could stand in the mud before her lowered body temperature would become life-threatening.

She looked down, barely saw her belt. How long until the mud reached her neck? Maybe she should just try crawling forward and gamble that they wouldn't hear her movements. What irony if she should die in this mud hole after escaping both the growers and her kidnappers. Tears came to her eyes. Don't be a wimp, she scolded herself.

She listened intently and soon realized that the leader was sitting just above her. Occasionally he would call out to the others who were searching the hillside. Any movement on her part created water and mud noise sufficient that she would be heard. Only a real struggle would free her.

Maria shivered uncontrollably as the sun began to slip below the ridge in the western distance. She was having a harder and harder time remaining conscious. She had ceased being in pain from the cold and the bruising; now she was numb, and she knew that was bad. Struggling and pulling

herself out might soon be her only option. Dan's face kept
flashing through her mind. He was coming, she kept telling
herself, fighting the cold with the only weapon left to her:
hope.

Then she heard the helicopter in the distance. This time
it seemed to be coming nearer. It grew progressively louder,
finally flying directly toward her. The big buzzing bird came
into view from behind the rock face, flying overhead.

But as it turned, glinting and reddened in the failing sun,
heading back up the mountainside, her hope turned to bitter
despair.

Janet Morgan pointed to where they had stowed the German behind them in the van. "Would he hurt us if we just
let him go?"

"Damn straight he would," Jack said. "He said Corey
should have killed that little boy."

"She's crazy," Janet said. "The way she just went all
nuts and cut that guy, and gouged out his eyes. She was
using her fingers."

"I don't think she'd kill a kid. And that guy was . . ."
Jack paused. There was a thumping from the back.

"Hey, asshole," Janet shouted as she drove. "Child killer.
If you don't shut up, I'm gonna spray your ugly face again."

But still the pounding went on. After several more minutes, Janet slammed on the brakes. Grabbing the pepper
spray, she walked around to the side door of the van.

"Wait," Jack said, getting out the shotgun. "You gotta
be careful." With the gun trained on the entry, he let her
open the door and shove the can under the hood. Muffled
gagging sounds erupted when she released the spray—then
the foot stopped. But the van immediately filled with a foul
odor.

"Well, now you know why he was banging his foot," Jack said.

"The German's revenge," she said as she rolled down the windows.

A couple of minutes later, Jack heard Janet gasp.

"Take it easy," Jack said. It was a state patrol car turning onto the highway ahead of her. Janet slowed.

"Keep going normally."

A couple of hundred yards up the road, the patrol car turned into what Jack remembered as Corey's place. His face went white.

"That is the place," Jack said. "Just keep on driving."

"Damn!" Janet muttered, speeding past the driveway. He studied the mirror on his side. Just as they entered a bend, he saw the highway-patrol vehicle exit Corey's driveway and head in the opposite direction.

Jack exhaled sharply. "He was just turning around."

The first patch had been small, with no obvious alarms or booby traps. It was unguarded; Corey passed on.

The second was much larger, and she almost missed the first trip wire. After stepping over it, she heard the voices.

"I'm tellin' you, I saw a second one, dressed for the hike and carrying a gun."

"Make the same pattern you did before, and keep your eyes open this time," an authoritative voice responded.

Corey put the nylon stocking over her face and moved toward the voice. As she approached, she could see the two subordinates moving off through the brush no more than twenty yards from her. One of them held a bloody hand under his arm, the other had a swollen bloody face. Walking when they walked, stopping when they did, she slowly crept upslope and around behind her target. Now she was downstream from the leader, assuming that his attention was directed at the mountainside. She waited, knowing that if she moved closer he might hear her. Carefully she stepped out from behind a redwood stump the size of a small car, stealing a quick look to ensure that he was still facing in the opposite direction.

Tossing a stone in the bushes was a tired trick, but it worked. He immediately started for the spot where the stone had landed. Moving behind some bruʳh, Corey raised her rifle. Soon she heard the crackle of his footsteps; seconds later, he walked straight into her sights. He wore a bandanna tied around his head. Tangled red hair hung from under it. Built low, broad-shouldered and squat with long arms, he looked slightly apelike, with a bit of a belly and a flat-looking face like her wooden masks.

"Hold it," she said. "Drop the gun."

The man hesitated, considering his situation. Finally he dropped the gun, cursing.

"The woman you're hunting is a lady lawyer. You give her to me, and I'll walk her out of here and cancel her ticket."

"Go screw yourself."

Corey shook her head. "Turn around and spread-eagle against that tree."

The man just stared at her. She unholstered her army Colt .45, strapped on the rifle, removed her stiletto, and approached him with her pistol aimed at his chest. A quiet click, and the blade on the stiletto appeared, glinting in the late-afternoon sunlight.

"Do it, asshole."

The man looked at her, gauging her, weighing his chances.

Totally at ease and as cold as an arctic night, she sighed. "I'm gonna kill you."

"All right." He turned and spread his legs against the tree.

"Farther," she said, kicking his legs apart. Frisking him thoroughly, she found a knife and a pistol on his calf. The razor-sharp stiletto cut into the skin of his torso as she began shallow but bloody carving. He groaned and tried to move away. She put the gun hard in the hollow at the base of his skull. "You're a sixteenth of an inch from having your head blown off."

"Don't shoot," he croaked.

"Don't move," she said, continuing to cut him. "Call your boys and tell them you found me. Make it convincing or the knife goes right into your kidney."

"Get on over here, boys!"

"Now turn and face me; stay on the trail. Keep your mouth shut or you're a dead man," she said, stepping behind the stump to hide.

Soon the men came to the clearing. "Hey, Greg, whatcha doin'? You're bleeding. Did you see her?" Both men walked toward their boss, curious as to his silence.

"You're not pissed, are you?" one man said in a worried voice.

When the two men were within twenty feet of their boss, Corey stepped out from behind the stump. "Drop the guns or he takes a bullet right in his fat ass."

Startled, the two men dropped their guns.

"Get over by him."

They moved to their boss's side.

"What a sorry bunch of losers. You look like you walked into a meat grinder."

"Fuck you," the leader said. Slowly she approached him. Faster than a rattlesnake, she stabbed his thigh, then removed her knife.

"Oh shit," he groaned, holding pressure on the bleeding puncture wound.

"Did she get one of your guns?" Corey demanded.

"She got an AK-47 from me, but she dropped it. We found it in the brush."

"You got knives or guns hidden on you?"

"No," said the one with the bloody hand.

"Likewise," said the swollen face.

"You're going to strip," Corey said. "If you lied, I'm gonna slit your bellies. Now take 'em off."

"Uh, ma'am," said bad hand, eyeing the boss's bloody shirt and pants.

"What do you want?" she replied.

"I forgot about a knife on my leg and a gun in the small of my back."

"Me too," the other said.

"Get 'em out and throw them on the ground. I don't think you assholes take me seriously." Then without warning, she stabbed their boss in the same leg, eliciting a louder scream. "Don't fuck with me," she said, twisting the knife.

"Please, Holy Jesus." He was gasping in pain.

The two men hurriedly began taking off their clothes.

"Forget the strip show. I haven't got time." She frisked them both.

"How many more trip wires you got?" Corey asked.

"Four on the slope and five on the ridge," one of them answered, quickly pointing out various landmarks.

"OK. Two of you will pick points on the hill fifty yards away from one another. Boss man here will stand in the creek bottom down there at the narrowest spot. We can only cover the bottom portion of the hillside, but that's where she ran from you morons. The odds are she's hunkered down. If she went past this area, she probably would have hit one of the wires. If she stays put, she'll eventually die

from exposure. Move in slow circles around your point.
Don't get more than twenty-five yards from your spot. If I
hear you moving in the brush, or catch you leaving your
station, boss man here gets it in the other leg. So don't let
me hear you. When she moves, we'll hear her. Now get
moving."

Just then, the helicopter buzzed low overhead. Seconds
later, it circled away.

"When she is dead, you can get back to your plants. Not
a second sooner."

29

As the likelihood of rescue dimmed, it became easier to give
in to the seduction of the cold. But Maria was stubborn. She
had forests to save. She had Dan to contend with. Nate to
apologize to. She looked down at herself. Clearly, she had
stopped sinking. No quicksand, just deep mud. She decided
to move.

Using her arms like stiff oars, she pulled herself ahead.
She seemed stuck. She threw herself forward, then rocked
back, loosening the mud. Throwing herself again as hard as
she could, she began to come loose. At first, she could barely
move but soon she discovered that she could crawl on her
belly. Downstream twenty yards, the mud was knee-deep in
thigh-deep water and she could walk. Within a hundred
paces the ground became firmer. Then she rounded a bend
and saw a man, standing. Although she could climb the
canyon wall on either side, she would be exposed, and it

would be very slow and noisy. Despair flooded her. She stopped, hiding in the rocks. Soon the gray light of evening would give way to bone-deep cold and the pitch dark of night in a wilderness canyon. Then she turned, and not fifty yards back and fifty feet up, she saw someone with a rifle.

Dan and Frank were getting frustrated. They could see little in the trees, and the pilot was running out of fuel. Only twenty minutes' worth remained. They were way beyond safe reserves. They would have to return to the airport, and then it would be dark.

"Let's run down the river drainage one more time before we land," Dan said.

"We gotta go," the pilot said.

"I still think she followed the creek," Dan replied. "Fly down it on the way back. Get down low and let me out."

"It's getting dark," Frank said.

"I know, but she's out there. I can feel it."

"Can't let you do it. After we try the creek again, we're outta here," Frank added.

The pilot banked the copter and aimed at the drainage. Looking back up the mountain, they could see foresters' trucks and sheriffs' vehicles pouring onto Jack Morgan's property. Dan prayed.

Frustrated that they were finding nothing, Corey went to the leader's position down in the creek. "Did you search the entire creek bottom?"

"Dutch looked down here," he replied.

"How exactly did he do that?"

"He went down next to the rock face and tried looking around the corner. There were no tracks. No sign of her."

Corey was not convinced. Making her way back up and over to the bluff, she looked for the best spot to approach the precipice. After traversing a steep rock shelf fifty yards long, she located a portion of the slope that appeared to have good handholds. She began the climb down, clinging to the rock surface as she approached the edge of the sheer drop. Lodging her fingers and toes in cracks as she went, she barely managed to avoid a precipitous slide. Reaching the drop-off, she could tell there was a considerable overhang. And no easy way to look down over the lip and maintain a good handhold. She dug her fingers into the only two available cracks and peered over the edge, half-expecting to slide out of control and over the cliff.

"Morons," she said as she saw the obvious trail in the mud along the rock wall.

Dan looked so hard his eyes hurt, but they saw nothing save Shane, who walked head down as if following a track.

"Put me down," Dan said, sounding more determined than he'd ever been.

"All right," Frank said, shaking his head.

Within seconds the copter was diving for the creek at a point where the brush patch and meadows began. Going down into the bowels of the ravine, they flew heart-stoppingly close to the steep hillsides, just 200 feet off the water. Slowing the copter to forty miles per hour, the pilot soon located a small clearing.

The landing point was a brushy spot just ahead of Shane, right by the creek. In seconds they had plummeted to six feet off the ground, and the pilot, in an obvious hurry, signaled a jump.

Dan hit the ground and they were gone. It was eerily

quiet. Then he saw someone running toward him with a gun.

As Corey ran downstream, the wilderness calm was broken by a cop's ringing shout.

"Everybody freeze, put your hands up." The copter had come down ahead of her. Must have dropped a cop.

Knowing she might have just one last chance to kill Maria Fischer before they closed in, she sprinted the one hundred yards to the point where the rock wall became a steep incline and the muddy bench ended. She was still one hundred yards above the leader. At the creek's edge, she turned and looked back upstream. There were no tracks in the brown sand. She climbed back up on the rock bluff and moved upstream, perhaps another fifty yards. Not even thinking about protecting herself from a fall, she slid headfirst to the cliff's edge, barely managing to stop. The copter was now a quarter mile away and moving rapidly up the hill and away.

"Yes!" she shouted in a hoarse whisper after her first glance over the edge. There she was—seventy yards downstream, standing next to the rock wall. She swung the AR-15 around; the safety came off with a flick of her thumb. Maria was moving around a rocky outcropping. Shifting position, Corey steadied the rifle.

Dan had been traveling downstream fast and was below the man with the gun. Judging from Shane's far-off shout and the gunman's clothing, it couldn't be Shane. From his vantage point he was able to discern that the shooter was looking at the creek bottom somewhere below him. Refusing to think about the risks, he scrambled down the slope and peered over the edge, desperate at the thought of Maria pinned down in the rocks.

Seeing that the shooter was drawing down on her, Maria dived behind a rock no larger than a living-room chair. There was so little cover. She had to think. She couldn't even hear the chopper anymore. Risking a look, she saw the gunman moving toward her once again. She had to run before he got any closer. Sprinting down the rock wall of the creek as fast as the water and muck would allow, she found a small crevice and slid in. A shot smacked the rocks inches behind her, sending the grit flying. If she hadn't been moving, she'd be dead.

Dan flinched at the gunshot and kept running at the barely visible black-clad figure.

The radio rasped to life.

"Helo. 10-49 to my 10-20. 10-49 to my 10-20. I'm down the creek in the brush fields."

"This is Helo. We copy. We had to leave."

Having measured the distance to the muddy creek bottom at twenty feet, Dan figured he could jump and not kill himself. Before he hit the mud, he saw Maria, and when he splashed into the shallow water, he estimated the shooter at fifty yards. Too far away for him to hit even if he'd been armed. Maria, however, was close enough to reach in time. He hoped.

Shane's voice crackled over Dan's radio as he ran. "I hear shots from the gorge in the area straight ahead of me."

As he neared Maria, Dan took a quick glance back, saw the gunman on the cliff's edge, aiming at her. He dived in front of Maria, waiting for the shot.

* * *

Corey cursed. Only Maria's hip was visible under the cowboy-looking cop on top of her. She wanted a clean kill, not a martyr with a wounded leg and a dead cop. Then the cop shifted and she saw the middle of Maria's back. A heart shot.

"Oh yeah," Corey said breathily, bearing down on the trigger.

Her rifle bucked skyward. Her hands stung with the impact. But there had been no shot.

The little Japanese stood next to her, awaiting her reaction. She swung the barrel, but with blinding speed, his hand caught it. His other hand took her shoulder and severe pain shot down her left arm.

With her right she reached for her hand gun. A hard kick to the inside of her upper right arm brought a scream to her lips and immobilized the arm.

"Go," he said. "Or I will kill you."

Spooked out of her mind, she let him take the rifle as if she were a child. She scrambled up the cliff and never looked back.

The shooter, unaccountably, had disappeared. Shane was combing the area and finding nothing.

"You're an idiot," Maria said with a bone-tired smile.

"I know."

Crying, she kissed him full on the lips.

"Let's get out of here," he said.

Kenji Yamada was more than worried. Groiter wasn't answering his cell phone. Groiter had called him when they brought in Maria Fischer, just to reassure him. They should have finished with her by now. Something had to have gone wrong. But Groiter was experienced, and he had the Spaniard, who was equally deadly.

Kenji was certain that Groiter had proof concerning Catherine Swanson. He also had the photographer's remains. If something happened to Groiter, Kenji could be the victim of leaked evidence to the police. He had two men in San Francisco he could trust. There were two more at the forest compound that he would need to trust. He would dispatch all four men to learn what happened at Jack Morgan's.

At the emergency room there was no wait because the sheriff was personally involved. There was an awkward moment when Maria was ushered into the treatment room.

"Dan, you and Dad stay in the waiting room while Mom comes with me," Maria said. "I'm really all right and I'm sure I'll be right back out."

Dan wondered why he hadn't remained in the waiting room in the first place. He was with Maria, but he had no status. Any minute Ross could show up—he was supposedly just a friend now, but he didn't seem quite content with his new status.

"Dan, go in and sit with Maria for a while," Laura Fischer said. "She'd like that."

Amiel winked at him.

"Sure," Dan said. "I'd love to." They buzzed him into the treatment area.

"Maria Fischer, please," he said to the nurse. She pointed the way, and when he entered the room, he was greeted by a bruised face and a big smile. She was lying on a gurney in a curtained-off area with a hospital gown, a blanket, bandaged wrists, and an IV.

"Quite a shiner," he said.

"Yes. It hurts but nothing is broken, I'm sure. How's Nate?"

"Great. Worried about you. Wants to see you."

"I'm sure we can arrange that."

"I want to know who's behind all this, once and for all," he said.

"We will. There was a woman. The same woman, I think. She's nuts, and I think she's associated with the environmental movement."

"How could someone like that be connected with Amada?"

"That's what we've got to figure out. And we will. But I need a little time out from that subject."

"Oh?" He wondered what could possibly be more important or interesting.

"Before I left with Nate, I really and finally broke up with Ross. I thought you should know. I don't want you to feel like you need to say anything. It's a little embarrassing telling you this way."

"Maybe it was just comfortable, having that . . . I don't know what."

"I know exactly what you mean. And we still have that something in a way. But you're the industry and I'm the environment, so don't go getting all weird on me."

Once again they found themselves seated in the well-designed conference-room chairs as a guest of Sheriff Robert McNiel. This time they waited no time at all. He entered the room still talking to someone through the doorway. For some reason he had shaved his droopy mustache. Dan's was back, somewhere between stubble and full growth.

"Somebody does not get along with you," he said to Maria.

"The timber industry?"

"You think this was somebody from the industry?"

"Actually, I'm not sure, but maybe it was some really wacko fringe element of the environmental movement. I mean really wacko. Or maybe it was industry, I don't know."

"It wasn't any industry I know," Dan said.

"Well, we've got forensics people all over up there. They've got a lot of hair samples, fingerprints, all that stuff. But none of it has been run yet. Oddly, we did find a business card of one Hans Groiter. Have to be as dumb as a post to leave that around."

"Isn't he with Amada?"

"Yup. Sure is. And he doesn't seem to be around. Plumb disappeared."

"So are we making progress?" Maria asked.

"Maybe. But you know something as obvious as a business card looks like a plant. You've got to at least consider a frame-up."

"Uh-huh. But those are the same guys who shot at me in the mine."

"Oh, I know, I know. We're all over it. Now where will you be?" he asked, nodding at Maria.

"For the time being at the Palmer Inn with my parents. After that, back to Sacramento."

"Well, as long as you're here, I'm putting two plain-clothes deputies on your tail. And I might recommend that unless the police in Sacramento are going to do that, you might want to stay here until we get this figured out or at least until we get some time under our belt."

"I will take that under advisement."

"And no playing cop, OK?"

"Absolutely," Dan said.

* * *

By midnight Corey was home and in her basement with Janet. The entire basement area was open except for a load-bearing wall down the middle with a passage at either end, and a single room. Everywhere it was gray concrete. They went to the room and removed a large padlock. It was a furnace room converted by the prior owner to a small work-shop and had a number of heavy pipes in the overhead. Here the concrete walls were covered with tool racks and a built-in worktable and a freestanding bench.

Groiter was sitting on a bench, looking like a caged beast. Chain had been looped through his handcuffs and then looped around two of the heaviest pipes with a bicycle lock. His feet were spread-eagled, each fitted with a handcuff that was chained to the built-in worktable. As a final touch, Janet had stuffed his mouth full of handkerchiefs and fastened a gag.

Corey walked up to Groiter, took out his gag, and put a bottle of water beside him. Then she put her lips to his ear. "It would be pointless to beat the shit out of you, but I'm going to anyway."

Corey placed a rubber strap around the bare torso of Hans Groiter, taping other wires to his chest, and putting finger clips on his fingers. Janet's eyes followed Corey's every move.

"You will of course recognize the leads for a simple lie detector," she said to Groiter. "While I have a fairly cheap model, it seems to work quite well. I perfected the technique, as you know, on Kim Lee."

It was 7:30 A.M. and they were waiting for the coffee to brew in Corey's spacious kitchen.

"We're going to have a cup of coffee, then we'll be down to begin the morning's work."

Corey and Janet adjourned to the kitchen.

"Do you think you'll actually have to do anything?"

"Groiter's a professional. He knows what I can do. Some people need some pain before they talk while others are more pragmatic. But last night I got even with the bastard."

"Why did you bother?"

"It's personal."

Corey picked up her cup and returned to the basement. With Janet's assistance she took a carpet that rolled into a twelve-foot length and carried the giant sausage of fabric over in front of Groiter.

"You see that roll of carpet," she said. "Imagine being rolled in it. Tied tight and then lashed to a pole. We put you over an open-pit barbecue and heat the carpet to one hundred fifty degrees and constantly pour water over it, onto the coals. Slow-cook you in the steam. When we do this, your head is a good three feet down inside the end of the roll, but we pump air to you to make sure you stay alive. We do that until you answer all our questions."

She watched the needles, then tore off a strip of paper from the machine and wrote "Carpet Trick" on the bottom.

"OK, Hans, that was very good. Now for the next option. We take these fire ants . . . ."

When she was through, she came and sat a foot away from Hans. "I'm pleased to say there's one thing that sends you off the chart, Hans. So tell me, when did you become terrified of tight places, like a rolled-up carpet?"

"Little kid."

"Tell me about it."

"We gonna make a deal?"

"You need that reassurance, don't you?"

Hans was silent.

"You tell me everything I want to know and I won't roll you up in the carpet and cook you."

"How do I know?"

"Because you didn't let that Spaniard tie me down and fuck me like he wanted to. Now, who called me on the phone?"

"I did."

"That's a good start. I know you'll keep in mind that I'm going to pentathol you when we're through. You know what will happen if you don't pass with flying colors?" She paused. "I don't hear you."

"I know what will happen."

"All right. So what's with the bats? And what are your boys doing around the mine?"

Kenji was in a panic. According to his men who had listened to the police bands and scouted Morgan's farm, Groiter had disappeared off the face of the earth. Cops were still crawling all over Morgan's, and Corey Schneider wasn't answering her phone. He would need to flee to Japan or get personally involved. There were too many loose ends and too much potential evidence against him to leave the country. Extradition back from Japan would be a distinct possibility. Instead, he would go to Palmer and work with the two San Francisco men. The men would meet him at the Palmer airport and together they would find Groiter and Corey Schneider.

Ninety minutes later, Kenji was in the company Hawker Sidley 700 business jet, staring down at the Golden Gate Bridge. As he sat with his feet up on the opposite seat and contemplated his predicament, his finger traced the swirls in the maple fold-out table, and he kept seeing Groiter's face in the pattern.

* * *

Maria had a date with Nate, who was traumatized by what he had seen when she was taken. She'd convinced Dan it would be better if she and Nate went alone. Although Dan was initially reluctant, he realized that with the police following her around Palmer, nothing was likely to happen.

When she pulled up to the curb for Nate, he bounded up to the car, looking eager. Inside, he sat with his hands squeezed tightly together in his lap and glanced sideways at her, not making eye contact.

"I'm so proud of you. You saved my life. How about a hug." He squeezed tight enough that her bruised ribs hurt. She said nothing, enjoying the intensity of the moment. "One of these days we'll have to go get some more fish. But maybe we'll wait until they catch the bad guys first."

Glancing in the rearview mirror, she saw the two plain-clothes officers in their white Crown Victoria.

"Those are the cops, huh?"

"That's right. We're going to have a little company, but they won't bother us."

The light fog coursed over the kelp-strewn water's edge, pushing past the beach and inland some quarter of a mile. There, the sun shone to the earth unhindered, turning the coastal mountains an Oz-like golden green. Maria and Nate hiked over the rocky beach, their nostrils flared with the smells of salt and seaweed; their leg muscles burned as they walked barefoot on the cool, damp sand. Ahead of them the beach stretched in a crescent to a finger of land pushed prominently out to sea, its tip spewing out several rocky little islands. Behind them were the massive jetties: two gray-white arms reaching out into the ocean, forming a safe passage to Palmer Bay.

Maria and Nate had said little since leaving the car, communicating instead through gently squeezed fingers and lazily swinging arms.

"Hey," Nate said finally, breaking the silence. "What's that?"

Together they spied a form on the beach.

"I'm not sure," Maria responded. "But it looks like a sea lion."

"Wow. It's big. What's it doing? Is it hurt? Will it run away when we get close?"

Maria laughed. "I don't know. Let's find out."

Soon they were close enough to look the creature in the eye. Just then it rose up, gave a roaring bark, and fell lamely back to the sand. The tide was going down, and the sea lion lay on its side, its body moving in little tremors, struggling to rouse itself and head back out to sea. But it was so sick or so exhausted that it could not. The animal had no outward wounds, but Maria suspected it was struggling with age and the infirmities of an old body. She put a hand on Nate's shoulder.

"I'm afraid this poor old guy is getting ready to die."

"Like Mom," Nate said softly.

"Yes," Maria said, squeezing his shoulder.

"But she was just gone all of a sudden."

"I know."

"I don't want that to happen anymore," Nate said, his voice breaking.

Then she held him and he cried for what seemed like a half hour. On the way back to the car, Maria could see a change in his eyes. She wasn't sure what or how, but something had been resolved.

30

They were to meet in the lobby of the Palmer Inn. Sitting in front of a mammoth stone fireplace in a brown overstuffed couch, she browsed through a *New York Times* that she had managed to find at the front desk. They had reserved a private booth at the back of the restaurant. It was 4:00 P.M. She wasn't hungry, her insides were in turmoil, and her feelings bounced from anger to desperation to hope, while her mind fought to see a rational path out of her quandary. They really needed a very private place—a place she could yell and pace. When she agreed to meet him here, she hadn't thought of that.

She felt a hand on her shoulder.

She turned around, and there was Dan, smiling and relaxed.

"You aren't getting yourself all worked up, are you?"

"Yes. I am getting myself all worked up."

"Well, let's go in the coffee shop and have a talk, then maybe we'll go for a drive."

"OK," she said.

They were greeted by a friendly waiter who had no one to wait on. Apparently gauging Maria, he handed them their menus immediately after seating them and said he would return in a while. No chitchat.

The decor was blush pink and black, a little worn, but not nearly as tough as the conversation she contemplated.

"I'm grateful to be alive."

"Yeah. It must feel good coming so close on the heels of almost dying."

"It does. We've been saying . . ." She paused and started again. "We've been talking about the Highlands and our—" She hesitated, trying to think of how to say it.

"Maybe I could help out here. I mean, you might not have to carry all the water yourself."

"Why don't you just grab a bucket and have at it?"

"Well, I'd like to change venues if I'm going to help you out. I'm sure the waiter will forgive us. I'll leave a generous tip."

"OK," she said, uncertain but willing.

"You have to promise to hold this discussion in abeyance until we reach our destination."

Dan rose, pulled out his wallet, and offered his arm. As they walked, the waiter rose from his perch with a quizzical frown. Dan smiled and slipped him a five.

"I'm sorry, I just realized there was some important business that I need to attend to," Dan said.

"Where are we going?"

"My house. Pepacita's just leaving and Nate's with Katie."

"I see." They were quiet during the walk to the car.

"I'm really curious now. Do you have food, or what? You look so devilish. I'm almost worried."

"There's no crew at my house chopping down all the trees if that's what you're concerned about."

"The suspense is killing me. Can't you just give me a hint? Just a little one."

"We'll be there in just a minute."

"Have you talked to my dad?"

"Now, now, you promised."

"No," she groaned. "That's not the same subject."

"Oh, come on. You'll have to do better than that. Everything to do with your family is the same subject."

In minutes they turned into the driveway.

"We're here. I promise we'll deal with everything inside."

They went in through the front door this time. Just as they went in, Pepacita slid past them, smiling mysteriously and kissing Maria on the cheek as she went. Everything looked normal, neat and thoroughly groomed, just as she remembered it. Then they proceeded through the dining area and soon nothing looked the same. Down the hall to the kitchen and family-room area, she could see flowing white diaphanous fabric. Through the doorway there was a soft glow.

She tried to form a question but found herself speechless.

The family room had been converted to a tent with fabric over the bookcases and across the ceiling. There were soft candlelike lights and two candelabras with live, burning candles—Pepacita must have just lit them. The furniture had been cleared, and there was one very large recliner couch that looked like a holdover from the Roman Empire. On it lay a single red rose. Beside it stood a silver champagne bucket packed with ice and a large bottle. A lacquered cart held strawberries and a marvelous array of sushi. There were four flower arrangements—each head-high with lilies, orchids, and irises in an Asian motif.

Dan put his hand on her shoulder and guided her toward the recliner.

Reaching down, he picked up a filmy peignoir and a partly translucent gown. Beside them were men's silk pajamas.

"You'll need a costume," he said.

"You are completely crazy."

"I can't help you with that bucket of water if you don't put on your costume. You can use the back bedroom."

"I thought I could deal with anything. But I'm not so sure about this."

"Relax. It's only a gown. The lights are soft. You'll be safe as safe can be." She looked at him. "I promise."

"OK," she said.

On the bed in Dan's room, she found this note:

> *Eyes can speak things only the soul can hear;*
> *Minds can intertwine with greater bliss than touch;*
> *A look can stir the heart, never slipping a button;*
> *A face has magic enough for heart, soul, and loins.*
> *I don't need to see the rest until you're ready.*

Feeling her old confidence and deciding the gown wasn't bad at all, she walked back to the living room to find him waiting.

"Right this way," he said, inviting her to slide under a heavy silken sheet. As she did so, she turned on her side, facing him. In a second his face was a foot from hers; he also perched on his elbow.

"Now I would like to take up where we left off."

"This is nice," she said.

"I'm thrilled you like it. It was planned just for you."

"Did Nate see this?"

Dan nodded. "Most of it. He thought it was pretty cool."

"It is crazy but in a very charming way."

"So I think it's my turn now."

"Yes."

"I think we were about to say that Dan Young has fallen utterly in love with Maria, and this presents some interesting dilemmas. In order for you to decide how you might approach that thorny subject, you need to have a talk with him. And we were about to have that talk."

"Yes."

"May I take your hand?"

She held it out. He lay back and took it in both of his and began caressing her palm. Instantly her hand seemed intimately connected to her whole body. Lying supine on the angled couch, he continued with her hand while he slid up close. Putting her head down, she watched him until he kissed her eyelids. She was going to say something, but decided to wait, enjoying the feel of his lips on her face.

His thoughts were dancing in his eyes and he seemed terribly alive, his look making her body warm.

"I love you. I'll do whatever it takes," he said.

"Oh God, I was so hoping you would say that. But how can I ask more from you than I would give?"

He looked at her as if he were waiting.

When she said nothing, he said, "Trust me."

Something inside her exploded. Crawling on top of him, she began kissing him. He pulled her tight and kissed her back, his tongue exploring hers. She felt bound and pent up. While she pulled at the peignoir, he slipped it over her shoulders. Reaching beneath her, he stopped kissing her only long enough to slip the gown over her head. They collided so hard she heard their teeth click. With her gently tugging his arm, he rolled on top of her as she began popping buttons on the pajamas.

"Slow down, lover," he said when she had stripped off the pajamas. "Remember I haven't done this in a while."

"You look fine to me," she said, holding him and stroking him.

He kissed her nipples while she held the back of his head. Her breasts were large and firm, the nipples dark rose. Then he pulled her on top and began using his hands on her back, caressing in long deep strokes. He could feel her relax and move to his touch. All the time he planted kisses on her face and neck.

"Oh God," she said as he went to work on her shoulders. "This is so good."

Gradually he moved his hands once again to her lower back; then as he felt her telling him, he moved to her bottom and the tops of her thighs, making his touch feather light. Gradually he could feel her hips start to move, grinding on him, trying to find the place. She reached for him to put him inside her.

"My tongue is an instrument of peace," he said with a grin.

"Noooo," she said as he rolled her over. "I haven't—"

"Trust me," he said, licking her as she laughed nervously. For a while she was quiet and slightly tense. He went everywhere but the core of her sensitivity. Then gradually he began to flick his tongue.

"Oh my God," she cried out as he began the little circles. On her thighs his hands listened for the subtle tremors that guided his tongue.

She grabbed his hair and he knew to keep on and on. Then she pulled him down tight. From deep inside, the groans began as he moved his tongue in rhythm with her hips.

"Trust me, trust me." The words echoed in her body without his ever speaking them again. It was a fierce dance and he could feel her falling into abandon, giving herself away. Tossing her head, she moaned as if in delirium, and chills went up his spine as he felt her going with him. Her glistening belly moved like rippling grass with the tremors through her body. She breathed as if she had sprinted a mile, her whole body finally falling rag-doll limp.

"Now you've done it," she said between breaths, and held his head gently.

"Only once," he whispered, moving on top of her, feeling her open like a flower.

Slipping inside her, he could feel her exquisite sensitivity and knew to keep his movements slow and gentle.

"I love you," he whispered in her ear. Her hands gripped his shoulder blades, her nails digging into him. He made his tongue gentle on hers. Then she let her head sink into the pillow, held his face, and looked in his eyes; he knew she saw his hope, his desperation. Gradually he felt her body start to quicken; then he saw her eyelids flutter. Kissing her deep and hard, he knew her wanting even as he lifted his weight so she could move beneath him. Gradually he found her rhythm, then understood it and rolled her on top of him, putting his tongue to her nipple in an echo of her thighs. Perspiration dripped from her as she rode him, her whispers turning to moans in the candlelight until at last his mind lost itself in desire and he gave himself to climax.

Later, she lay draped over him facedown on his chest, enjoying a piece of sushi.

"Don't move," she said when he reached for the tray. She popped a California roll into his mouth. "You're trapped," she said. "You can't go anywhere. You're mine and I've got you."

"I like being got."

"Good."

"This is the deal," he said.

"Oh. Tarzan." She laughed in mock, breathless wonder.

"I will have nothing to do with the Highlands. After that, you do any kind of environmental law you desire but never against timber owned by Otran. Never. Not even a smidgen."

"Yes?"

"And I will do no timber law except Otran."

"Will Otran go for this?"

"He already has."

"I'll need to talk to Patty."

"We already have."

"We? Who we?"

"Your father."

"Ah, I don't—"

He kissed her heavily on the mouth. "Don't start." He kissed her again. "Trust me."

"You absolutely will have utterly nothing to do with the Highlands."

"Utterly nothing."

"I do love you," she said.

"I suppose you won."

"You won me," she whispered.

31

Certain that Maria would be recuperating somewhere—probably at her parents'—Corey placed a call to Jessica Lyon. Jessica, a successful fund-raiser, was one of the few members of the McCafferty inner circle who would give her information.

"Haven't heard from you in a while," Jessica said in her usual fund-raising voice.

"So what's going on these days?"

"Well, I'm sure you heard Maria Fischer was kidnapped and escaped."

"No," Corey said. "What happened?"

"Well, nobody really knows. Some crazies snatched her and took her to a barn in the woods."

"Was she hurt?"

"I don't think so. She's in Palmer. Somebody said she called the office this morning."

For the next ten minutes, Corey forced herself to listen while Jessica chattered on about the kidnapping and upcoming environmental issues. Finally Corey closed by dangling a possible donation of $2,500, explaining that she was in Alaska and could do it only after she returned.

The German remained downstairs. Corey was surprised that he had broken so easily. She kept probing for more, but there wasn't any more. With no resistance Hans Groiter told her everything. When she gave him sodium pentathol, he became harder to understand but told her nothing new. She'd had enough experience to know when men were telling the truth. What troubled her was the fact that Groiter knew nothing of the little Jap shit who seemed to haunt her.

Seemingly nothing remained but to get rid of Dan, Maria, and then Groiter. Somehow she needed to convince the authorities that Groiter was the culprit and that he had fled. For that, she had sworn off a grave in the dirt. Bodies had a way of coming to light. She had a different plan for Hans. Even though it was a pain in the ass, she would keep him around for the few days it would take to create all the right fingerprints and other physical evidence.

Janet was turning into a fine soldier. Surprisingly, Corey was attracted to her in more ways than one. They slept in the same bed and both enjoyed the consolation of another warm body—a female body. That was the one thing that Janet had taught Corey instead of the other way around. Perhaps men were completely expendable, after all. And once she got some self-confidence, Janet had guts. So Corey took the risk of including her in her plans.

They needed a couple of extra-large travel cases on wheels and were going to town to buy them.

"Are you ready to go?" Corey asked Janet, who had just come up from the basement after feeding Groiter. True to her word, she gave Groiter real food because he talked.

"I'm ready. I fed the beast, emptied his bucket. He wants clothes, though."

"He's got his blanket. That's enough."

They walked into the garage, jumped in the Land Rover, and headed out the driveway.

"I want to get Kenji Yamada before this is over. That asshole is the one behind all this. Polluting, raping the land. He's gotta die if there's any justice."

"I suppose you're right," Janet said.

They were turning right onto the county road when Corey had an impulse. Reaching under the seat, she pulled out her Colt. From the glove compartment she took out a clean Smith & Wesson 9 mm and handed it to Janet. Backing up into the driveway, she turned away from town to check the small side road where she had found Groiter and the Spaniard the day they came calling. Poking the Land Rover's nose down the grown-over track, she saw the broken foliage. She slammed on the brakes.

"This could be from before—that I told you about. Or we might have some visitors. Probably berry pickers. Keep the gun hidden."

Corey stuck the .45 down the front of her pants and pulled out her blouse. Janet did the same. Walking quietly down the road, they heard a chattering squirrel and a jay in the distance. They came to a bend and Corey crept up to a tree. When she looked around, she saw a parked four-wheel-drive.

"I don't see any berry pickers." They approached the vehicle cautiously with the guns drawn. Nobody. It was a Toyota Land Cruiser. New and loaded.

"Come on," Corey said. They passed an obvious trail to

the house. Running to the end of the road, Corey turned off on a small trail clear enough that men could run single file. "Most don't go this way," Corey said over her shoulder. They made a large loop used by the berry pickers. To either side there were redwoods and dense huckleberry, mixed with salal ground cover. Eventually the smaller trail intersected the larger. As they neared the main trail, Corey slowed and then crept forward. They listened. Soon they heard the swish of brush. There were whispered words. Janet and Corey crouched low in the brush.

"Speak of the devil," Corey whispered, recognizing Kenji Yamada in the lead. "Dumb shits, all tight together in a row."

All three men wore bush clothing that looked like it came out of a Macy's catalog. Corey motioned Janet to kneel. The trio would pass within twenty feet. She held out her hand to Janet and mouthed the word: "Gun." Janet placed the Smith & Wesson in Corey's hand, and she popped the safety.

When the men were opposite Corey, she rose with utter calm, aiming point-blank. Mouths dropped open, open hands went up. Corey shot. Both pistols cracked simultaneously. Crimson mushrooms sprung onto the torsos of the two men following Yamada. They dropped with barely a quiver.

"Get your hands on your head or you're as dead as they are," Corey said to Kenji, who still stood openmouthed. When Corey turned to look at Janet, her partner was down on one knee, shaking. "Get used to it," she said to Janet. "These guys play for keeps."

Yoshinari watched the fish in his aquarium. It stood twelve feet high, two feet thick, and ten feet long with a capacity of 2,000 gallons of salt water. There was tranquillity in the looking, and he blocked out all that was going on in America, knowing that after a time of rest his mind would create clarity of vision. A rainsquall came and went; his grandchildren ate their lunch and retired for a nap. His wife, saying nothing, and making no sound save the slight rustle of her kimono, set tea in front of him. His eyes remained opaque, and he saw nothing but the fish.

When at last the rain began to fall a second time, he rose and walked to the edge of the porch overlooking the garden. It was time to decide.

There was a deep irony in the fact that the Schneider woman, a creature whose destiny had been tampered with by Groiter, now had him in her control. From all that they could tell, he had told her everything. So adept was Shohei that he had managed to get copies of all the woman's tapes— Groiter's entire confession. It was a fascinating tale indeed. Should he rescue Groiter? She would almost surely kill him. What should he do about the lawyers? About Kenji?

Maria spent most of her time in Dan's house, notwithstanding her insistence that she be free to go wherever and whenever she wished. Then, quite conveniently, Dan's home office became her office, with her laptop on-line instead of his floor-model computer. Dan's fax line became her fax line, his phone her phone. He emptied the filing cabinets so she could have files shipped from Sacramento. She had everything she needed right there. Dan and her mother made that point with regularity.

Pepacita needed help in the garden; Nate needed help with his homework. Since Dan's finances and Maria's business finances were going to overlap to some extent, she was the logical choice to take over the bookkeeping. Dan had no aptitude.

For some reason a cell phone wouldn't do. It had to be Dan's phone (now hers) in Dan's house (soon to be officially shared by her).

Being in love helped. There were worse prisons, she decided. And it did seem she could work many hours each day, planning her campaign to save the Highlands. So she gave in to the conspiracy and for the most part resolved to stay home.

On her fifth night at Dan's, she tried to imagine what marriage might be like. As nearly as she could recall, she was sitting with the shades open, taking in the last of the evening light. She had just finished running her fingers across a newly developed picture of Dan standing by her father, and was turning her attention to attacking a timber harvest plan when she was profoundly startled. A man's shadow fell across the desk. She stifled a scream. He had appeared literally out of nowhere, standing beside her, wearing a hat and sunglasses.

"Don't be afraid," he said.

"Well, I am," she said, aware now of her heart pounding.

His face was definitely Asian. He looked strong and had a flat, narrow waist under broad shoulders.

"We want to clear up all the mysteries. We have proof of what happened to you and what is happening in Amada's forest. Everything."

"Who sent you?" She tried to discern his features, but he seemed to gather the room's shadow around him like a cloak.

"My principal will make himself known to you in forty-eight hours."

"What about the police?"

"We will talk first."

"Why are you telling us?"

"One of your sacred ones once said: 'Seek and you shall find, knock and it shall be opened unto you.' "

"What's that mean?"

"It means you will be rewarded for your diligent efforts. But there is a condition."

"What is that?"

"You must come alone without your police. There will be no meeting if you bring them—you will not get your answers. There will be time enough for the police." Then the man bowed. "If you will excuse me."

She noticed that the door onto the patio was slightly ajar. How had he done that? Quickly he stepped out into the night and was gone. He could have killed her easily.

She looked at her watch. It was 9:20 P.M., and Dan was attending an office function with out-of-town clients. He had promised to leave early, and she expected him at any time. At 9:33 she heard the family-room door open. Forcing herself to wait, she counted to ten to ensure that Nate could get there first. Nervous with anticipation, she wondered how long these newlywed-type feelings would last. Then she walked faster than she intended into the family room to find him hugging Nate. Instantly Dan's eyes went to hers.

"Hey, Dad, we caught five fish this morning," Nate said.

"That's great," Dan said.

She put her hand on Nate's back and the other behind Dan's neck, kissing him firmly on the lips.

"Did you catch them in the same place?"

"Yeah. By the water tower. Hey, can I go over to Tim's and spend the night tomorrow?"

Dan tilted his head at Maria. She appreciated the consultation and nodded.

"Well, Maria and I are going to discuss it a little later, but I think it's gonna be fine."

"What's to discuss?"

"It's the principle of the thing, son. You know what that is?"

Nate smiled up at Maria. "She'd never say no if you said yes."

"I won't always be a pushover, buddy boy," she said, running her fingers through Nate's hair.

"I'm gonna go watch *The Simpsons* on video," Nate said.

"I had a really unusual visitor," Maria said when Nate had disappeared.

"What do you mean?"

She told him the story.

"Those cops outside are incompetent," he said. "I'm gonna go give them a ration—"

"No," she said, hugging him around the waist. "I think there's another set of players here and they mean us no harm. In fact, I think one of them stopped the shooter from killing you and me both. Maybe even this guy."

"We'll see. The police think the head of security over at Amada is implicated in all this. They have physical evidence at the barn that he was present. Amada's masters are Japanese. Nobody knows much about Kenji Yamada. And now you're telling me some Asian guy breaks into our house."

"There wasn't much breaking. He means us no harm. Trust me."

Corey's scheme worried her only because it was so ambitious and elaborate. It was all but impossible, which is what made it so delicious. She would show them all, especially the little Japanese bastard. Carefully she had studied the Hutchin Office Building, found old plans in the public library from the days when it was Mr. Carson's bank, and even crawled underneath it.

She had four bombs that she intended to plant in the crawl

space directly under Dan Young's chair. Dialing a cell phone and then punching in a code that would normally activate a voice-mail playback system would leave a lethal message. She had stolen the technology from an engineering contractor who blasted roads through mountain rock. The rest she had adapted from an electronically minded prankster.

Activation could occur from anyplace there was a digital-cell-phone signal by simply dialing the detonator and punching in a code. Specifically, it would work from the little knoll where she intended to terminate Maria Fischer by firing a single shot through a window. Convinced that the bombing and shooting could be combined, she intended to send them on their way together. Dan Young's house had constant police surveillance, but they didn't check beyond a hundred yards. Her shooting spot was 150 yards distant.

Tonight she would take care of Groiter and Kenji. A few minutes earlier, she and Janet had deposited them both chained in the bilge of a small fishing trawler. She didn't kill them first because she needed them to walk under the cloak of darkness. Once on the boat she hadn't killed them because she wanted to watch them contemplate their own deaths. For the time being, she had sedated them beyond such contemplation, worried that chains and gags might not be good enough. Last she had seen, they looked nearly dead.

Now parked in the van with yet another set of stolen plates, she waited for 11:00 P.M. before she and Janet began hauling the bombs and placing them under the building. All in all, including the setup of the detonator, she expected to spend about one hour at this location. She didn't want to stay much after midnight because the janitorial service arrived around 1:00 A.M. Working earlier increased the risk that some night-owl attorney might stop by the office.

After the bombs were set, she would go to the boat and Janet would take the Chevy home. Deathly seasick on anything but a lake, Janet wasn't into watching Groiter and Yamada slide screaming into the sea.

The street was quiet, streetlights glowed in the night fog, and she hadn't seen a car for minutes. A stone's throw from the waterfront, she could hear the quiet chug of a diesel— some bone-weary captain and his even more exhausted crew were docking the boat. In the distance the whistler buoy and the gong buoys made a ghost party in the mist. Much louder, the foghorn bellowed its melancholy at the jetties.

Wearing all-black clothing, she slipped from the van with a nervous shiver and nodded at Janet, who was parked in the Chevrolet behind her. Quickly Corey opened the van's rear door.

She and Janet would each carry one bomb at a time. She pulled out a pair of heavy-duty Atlantis travel cases on wheels, flipped open the tops, and signaled Janet to help with the placement of the first heavy round pipe, weighing in at eighty pounds. It was crammed with TNT, nails, and a twelve-ounce detonator.

Zipping up the first suitcase, they immediately repeated the process with the second and then hurried across the road. Once they reached the edge of the sidewalk, they grabbed the handle on the travel case and carried it over the decorative bark, setting it down in front of a hinged door. Two days earlier she and Janet had cut the lock with heavy bolt cutters. It had not been replaced. She zipped open the case and winced at the sound. In the utter silence it unnerved her. She looked around, saw no one, told herself to relax, and with Janet's help removed the pipe.

Janet held the door while Corey slid the pipe under the building. When they had repeated the process three more times, it was 11:15 P.M.

Once under the building with all four of her creations, she and Janet had to wrestle them to the intended location.

With a maximum of three feet under the building and in some areas only two, they had to struggle to get to the spot she had previously marked. Although the building was old, it had obviously been replumbed in recent times. The pipes were shiny copper and covered with modern insulating material. Little pieces of string affixed to these pipes led her to the chosen spot. At 11:30, after returning to the trapdoor for the third bomb, Corey decided to take a quick peek outside. Quietly she opened the door. And froze.

Two men stood on the sidewalk. She tried to hear, but they spoke in low tones. She made herself go to work anyway.

Returning to the bombs, she and Janet placed them in a perfect square about six feet apart. Although she might not have them located directly under Dan's chair, she was pretty certain she was under his office. Using copious amounts of duct tape, they managed to fasten the pipes in place. From each pipe a telephone cable protruded. Each cable was quickly plugged into a cable connector, then the cables fed into a central terminal that sat on the ground. Satisfied with her work, Corey activated the computer in the junction box and they each headed for the trapdoor with a travel case.

Gradually Corey opened the door. Five feet in front of them, a man watched the street. Something was wrong. The building was being watched. Probably a meeting with important people. And in the middle of the night. While she was pondering these things, she saw a car drive up. Instantly she recognized Dan Young's truck. Out stepped Maria Fischer and Dan Young.

"I'll be damned," she whispered to Janet. Maybe it would be easier than she thought to kill them both at once.

It was to be a midnight meeting in the conference room at Dan's office. Although bizarre, the desire of the Japanese for privacy without accidental intrusion by other attorneys seemed reasonable. There was a bone-chilling moment when Dan and Maria were told in a phone call that there would be five bodyguards surrounding the building. It was all very mysterious.

Dan and Maria arrived at 11:55. They entered through the front door, turned on some lights, and walked to the conference room.

At that moment there was a knock.

Dan left the conference room with Maria following. Three men waited at the door. The leader had a dignified bearing and Dan knew that he was in the presence of a powerful man. Wearing a long camel-hair coat against the cool of Palmer, the older man stepped over the threshold, followed by the other two. The second in line also wore a suit, whereas the younger man wore a black knit turtleneck. His eyes seemed everywhere and nowhere.

"I am Yoshinari Asaka, the chairman of the board of Kuru, the parent corporation of Amada. This is my lawyer, Kashi Nagura, and this gentleman, Shohei, looks after us."

"I am pleased to meet you," Dan said, shaking Yoshinari's hand and noticing the firm grip. "This is my fiancée, Maria."

Maria stepped forward and shook Yoshinari's hand, then followed Dan, shaking hands with the other two.

"This is new?" Yoshinari inquired, looking pointedly at Maria's diamond engagement ring.

"Yes, very," Dan said.

"Hard times winnow the heart, do they not?"

"Yes," Maria said, "they certainly do."

"May I take your coat?" Dan offered, appreciating the perfectly appointed blue pin-striped suit with hand-painted tie underneath. The lawyer looked anxious to get started. They walked to the conference room, where they all sat down. Yoshinari nodded to his lawyer. The younger man nodded his respect and began.

"We have recently discovered substantial irregularities in Amada. According to our sources, Kenji Yamada had discovered a means of manufacturing fuels from wood fiber. As an example, using the known technology it would cost thirty-four dollars per barrel to make crude oil. Using the method discovered by Kenji's scientist, it could be done for twelve dollars per barrel. Now, you probably wouldn't make crude oil, you'd make methanols and other fuels, but to make the point I'm using crude as an example.

"The implications if it worked are profound. With all the havoc in the Middle East you can imagine the value of this discovery. The only problem was that Kenji's new process used a special catalyst that created a dangerous effluent— dangerous enough to change the brain chemistry of the hoary bat subspecies that lived in the caves. They were storing the toxic by-product in a large plastic tank in the mine when it ruptured and made the pool that you saw. They left it there with the idea that they would develop a means of converting it to something useful or neutralize it. Then you came along."

"Why were they shooting the bats?"

"They had two major problems. First they had stumbled onto a new deep forest subspecies that would retreat to caves as well as tree hollows and the like. Any such subspecies would be a fascinating find for biologists who would start coming around. We think that compounding the problem, insects from the contaminated creek were affecting the bats' brains, particularly the area of the brain known as the cingulate gyrus in humans and the area that corresponds to the prefrontal cortex. There is increased activity in the former and decreased activity in the latter, according to records we found at the compound. In a human it could result in suicidal behavior. In bats it causes them to fly around in daylight. And this would bring enormous scrutiny on the compound and might lead to discovery of the contaminated water—not to mention the cave.

"At first they thought it was just exposure to fumes from the cave. But after they thought they got all the bats from the cave, they were still having the problem. Unfortunately, they probably killed the man who was working on the issue when he discovered the contaminated water and the insects. Made it look like a heart attack.

"Of course they had the more serious problem. The effluent is lethal to humans, and it had made its way into the creek. They had a theory that if you went downstream far enough it would become sufficiently diluted so as not to kill anybody—at least immediately. Try telling that to your press and government officials."

"Who stole the money from us?" Dan asked.

"Amada Chief of Security Hans Groiter, working through a woman by the name of Corey Schneider. And that's what this is for." The old man nodded and they placed the briefcase on the table in front of Maria. It was the one Dan had given her. Dan popped open the latches, and it was full of bills that looked exactly as he had packed it.

"We found it in the vault at the Highlands lab. But one hundred thousand had been taken by the thief, Corey Schneider. We've replaced the money she stole."

"Who was her accomplice?"

"A dead man. Our people will be turning his body over to authorities after we are on the plane."

"Why did Amada do it?"

"They had discovered a large natural-gas deposit under the lower Highlands. Their methanol-manufacturing process could be greatly enhanced by the natural gas. But a railroad company owned the mineral rights and wouldn't sell. Added to that, they had a mine full of toxic effluent. The last thing they wanted was a government purchase of the Highlands.''

''And they contributed the money knowing they would try to screw it up?''

''They saw the sale going ahead like a juggernaut. At first they tried to stop it with the donation idea, but they couldn't. That's why they changed direction so dramatically. One day they are fighting all of you on giving the environmentalists the money; the next day they're leading the effort. Once they knew that Metco and the others were pushing, and that the donations would happen with them or without them, they decided to play along but sabotage the effort from within. If they stole the money, they expected the crime to become public knowledge. It would come out that industry was collaborating with the activists, hence both congress and the public would be suspicious. But you managed to keep it all quiet.''

''What did Kenji know about all this?'' Dan asked.

The lawyer paused and looked at Yoshinari.

''I'm afraid my son-in-law knew all about it. Even ordered it.''

''Do you know about the photographer who was murdered out on Amada land a couple of months ago?''

Yoshinari bowed his head, a gesture of respect. ''You have been excellent detectives.''

''Was it his body I saw in the mine?''

''We believe so.''

''Did Kenji do it?''

''According to Groiter,'' the lawyer said.

''Why are you telling us all this?''

Again the lawyer ceded to Yoshinari.

''We are telling you because you risked your lives to make it right. And because we don't wish to deal directly with your authorities. Shohei will provide the evidence. We leave for Japan in an hour."

"So what happens to Kenji Yamada?"

"He is missing. He will come to Japan if we can find him. There he can fight extradition. He, frankly, is not my concern," the old man said. "His wife, who is my daughter, and her child are both coming with us tonight."

At that moment the sound of a radio interrupted them. Shohei removed a handset.

"Yes." He listened. "Out, now!" Shohei literally shoved Yoshinari to his feet and rushed him through the conference-room door.

They all followed, half-running, down the hallway. After throwing open the front door, even the old gentleman took the steps two at a time. From the front walk they heard the squealing of tires; a dark car pulled away into the night. As Dan grabbed Maria's hand, a wave of heat washed over his back and a thunderous explosion knocked him to the ground. Even as he hit the ground, he was twisting, reaching for Maria.

"I'm OK," he heard her say through the ringing in his ears.

"Thank God." They both looked around. The old man and the bodyguard were getting up. Simultaneously they turned to see the lawyer fifty feet behind writhing on the ground, a large metal shard protruding from his back and exiting his gut. He grunted horribly. Yoshinari ran to him, taking his head in his lap.

Maria had already dialed 911 on her cell phone and was giving the ambulance crew the address.

"Schneider," Dan said.

Shohei nodded. "I should have killed her. I will bring her to your police."

"No," Dan said. "Let us do it for you."

Yoshinari nodded almost imperceptibly at Shohei, who whirled and left.

"Wait," Dan called after him, running.

"The ambulance will get here any minute," Maria said.

They heard a wailing siren, but the Japanese lawyer had gone silent.

Dan reached the black Lincoln sedan just as it was about to pull away from the curb. It had a combination lock below the handle on the passenger side that wouldn't open. He jumped across the hood, pounded on the windshield, and heard the electronic door lock click open. Clambering off the hood, he jumped in.

"I'm coming with you," Dan said, pointing at the pair of taillights in the distance.

"I was afraid of that," said Shohei.

32

Maria dialed the sheriff's office directly on the run to Dan's truck, angry that Dan had left without her but understanding that he was trying to keep her out of harm's way.

"There has been an explosion at the Hutchin law firm, probably a bomb. It might have been detonated by one Corey Schneider. There is one man critically wounded. An ambulance has been called."

"We're already responding," said the dispatcher. "What is your name, please?"

She started the truck and followed Shohei's Lincoln. "Maria Fischer. And Dan Young and another man are trying to find the person responsible."

"Where are you?"

"Right behind them."

"Please remain at the scene, ma'am."

Maria disconnected. Then she saw the van. It was coming in the opposite direction, moving slowly, and it looked exactly like the one parked at the barn, the one they had abducted her in. Whipping the truck around in a U-turn, she planned to pull up behind it when it jerked forward, accelerating rapidly. Maria followed. It turned right, then left, then over a bridge that intersected a long peninsula. On the inland side of the peninsula lay Palmer Bay with its boat harbors and yacht basins. Seaward was the vast Pacific.

Quickly she got back on the phone.

"This is Maria Fischer again. May I speak with Sheriff McNiel, please?"

"He's not in."

"I know he's not in. It's the middle of the night. Look, I'm following a van that may have been involved."

"Ma'am, I asked you to stay at the scene."

"Well, I'm not at the scene; I'm pulling into the Grayson Island Marina behind the van."

"We'll send a squad car, but don't follow a suspect's vehicle."

"Give me the sheriff."

"OK, OK, I'll try. But please get away from that vehicle."

Maria watched as the van pulled into a large parking lot. She stayed back on the road leading to the lot, trying to see in the heavy shadows. Large lights illuminated the area, but budget-conscious bureaucrats had designed the lighting for minimal coverage. It was especially dark near the rest room and laundry facilities where the van had parked.

She coasted forward a little farther, straining to see. Someone had gotten out of the van and walked toward the docks behind the rest room.

Mist hung in the air, haloing the lights in the fog. Her fear made the eerie night chilling. Slowly she rolled the truck forward. If Corey Schneider was departing in a boat, she needed to identify it. At the edge of the parking lot, she climbed out, her shoes clicking on the asphalt, certain that any moment she would see a boat leaving the marina.

Where were the police?

She continued around the washroom facility, keeping clear of the shadows to the back and sides of the structure. Facing the marina stood a well-lit bulletin board that served as the local trading post. It was covered with little cards advertising boats and all their various parts and gadgets. Along the steeply inclining ramps that led to the various docks ran a wide asphalt sidewalk used by roller bladers and strolling lovers. She had no clue which of the numerous piers Corey, or whoever it was, had chosen. Most boats were dark. Some had a single light at the pilot's station. A few had cabin lights luminescent against the window coverings. She counted twelve separate gangways accessing twelve separate floating piers, each pier with slips running down either side. There were perhaps eighty boats per pier. Only a few berths were empty.

Her eyes scanned the marina for some sign of movement. In her right hand she clutched her cell phone, ready to push the call button to the sheriff's department. Approaching the second washroom, she began a systematic search of the floats.

A shadow startled her. She turned.

Her next thought was that her head hurt terribly. Strangely, her cheek now rested on a wooden deck, and the sound of a motor throbbed through the planks. Her hands and feet were bound. With a shudder she realized she would be thrown into the black deep. She imagined it would be a slow drowning.

* * *

It took only minutes before they found themselves behind a familiar black Chevy, following precisely the same route as before, only this time the driver was seemingly oblivious to the tail. And this time Dan had a cell phone.

"We should call the police," Dan said.

Shohei didn't take his eyes away from the road. "I can get a lot of information before the police arrive. I won't have to break a single bone or do anything permanent."

"What will you do?"

"You don't want to know, and I don't want to tell you."

"I've got to call the police." Dan dialed the phone. "This is Dan Young, attorney. A bomb just went off at my law firm. We're following a suspect."

"We know. Get the license number. Don't follow."

"They'll be stolen plates. They were last time. Besides we haven't gotten close enough to observe them."

"What's your location?"

"Old Mountain Road, just past the fork to Browns Point."

"You're in the mountains."

"That's affirmative."

"We'll have a squad car catch up with you. Don't approach the vehicle. We have a report from Maria Fischer, who advises that she is also following a suspicious van."

"Van?"

"That's affirmative."

"Where is she?"

"Last we heard she was at the marina. She is not answering her cell phone. We have a patrol car there now."

"Understand," Dan said. "We'll wait for a squad car." Dan turned to the bodyguard. "We gotta run that car off the road now. If that's not Cory Schneider, that means Maria followed her to the marina, and that means this is the wrong car.''

''I thought you were against taking the law into your own hands.''

The big sedan surged forward, quickly hitting eighty miles per hour. It took only a few seconds to pull alongside the Chevy. It tried to accelerate but Shohei adroitly pulled ahead. Once in front, Shohei slowed, checking the Chevy's movements so that it couldn't pass. When they were down to forty and the Chevy driver was laying on the horn, the Chevy swerved, turning off onto a logging road. Instantly the big sedan did a sliding reversal and was laying rubber. Again they quickly caught the Chevy. The car twisted and turned rounding corners.

''I can't pass,'' Shohei said.

''Something will happen.''

The Chevy took a corner too fast and careened into a tree. They jumped out, and Shohei tackled the young woman in the bushes. Dan could hear choking sounds and ran to them.

''Stop.''

The bodyguard ignored him. ''Tell me about the van and I will let you breathe. Where was it going?'' He released and she spit in his face. Again he choked her. ''You killed a man tonight. You don't have to die.''

Dan watched in sick fascination.

''I don't want to die.'' The woman choked out her answer when Shohei let her breathe.

''Tell me.''

There was silence, horrible choking, then a gurgled scream. ''Corey was in the van. She was going out to sea in a trawler. That's all I know.''

Dan called the dispatcher. ''Did they find Maria?''

''Haven't heard. I'll check.''

''Let's go,'' said Dan. ''Take her with us.''

Dan sat beside her in the backseat while Shohei drove at full speed.

"They haven't found Maria Fischer. They're still looking," the dispatcher said.

"Look for a boat. The suspect she was following was leaving on a trawler," Dan said.

"I'll pass it along."

"Call the coast guard. Look for any trawler exiting the jetties in the last hour," Dan continued. "What were they doing with the trawler?" he asked the woman next to him.

"I got no idea."

"Right. What did it look like?"

"A big fishing boat, that's all I know. It was dark."

They pulled up into the parking lot. Two empty police cruisers had their lights flashing. At the far end they found an officer on foot.

"We're looking for Maria Fischer," Dan said.

"So are we. She's disappeared."

"What about the coast guard? I told the police dispatcher to look for a fishing trawler."

"There are dozens of boats out this early. Cruisers, shrimpers, crabbers, long liners, draggers, and trawlers. They need a description."

"This woman was at the scene of the crime. She knows about the boat."

"Ma'am, you have the right to remain silent, anything you say can and will be used against you. You have the right to an attorney."

"I want to exercise my right to remain silent. That man choked me."

"It was to apprehend her, I expect?" the officer said.

"That bastard got me on the ground and choked me unless I talked."

Dan left them for the piers.

''Where you going?'' the cop called.

''Look for Maria,'' Dan said, with Shohei just behind.

They trotted down the gangway. A friend of Dan's, who also happened to be his doctor, owned a fast sportfishing boat that was docked in the harbor. By virtue of a few salmon fishing trips, Dan had learned where his friend hid the key.

Dan started the boat. A quick study, Shohei had the lines free in seconds. And then they were boiling up the bay to the jetties and the ocean bar.

The night was thick with fog and salt. Dan didn't know what he was searching for, but he had to try. He turned on the GPS navigator and the radar along with a bright searchlight on the bow.

On an electronic display Dan found their boat shown superimposed on a chart, its location heading and speed over the ocean bottom plainly visible. He accelerated to eighteen knots but suspected he didn't have the visibility for that speed. Frustrated, he slowed to sixteen knots and watched the radar. Crossing over the sandbar at the entrance to the bay, he saw three targets moving away from the jetties.

He took a bearing on the closest target, which appeared at the six-nautical-mile ring, also traveling out to sea at about ten knots. He could chase them down in less than forty minutes if he maintained his current speed. The fog could get no thicker, though, or he would have to slow even more.

33

Maria could taste her own death. She imagined the water closing over her nostrils and contemplated the agony of sucking the ocean down her throat. Whatever waited in the depths spawned its own peculiar terror. Death wanted to fill her mind, to crowd out reason and love and hope. The contemplation of her gruesome dying threatened to erode even her will to survive.

Groiter and Kenji looked groggy, drifting in and out of consciousness on the back of the fishing boat, each with his feet buried in quick-dry concrete and hands shackled at the wrists. Maria worked feverishly at the line on her own wrists, which, unlike the men's, were tied behind her. She had made little progress, and Corey checked her bindings regularly. Maria knew that at any moment Corey could kill her and reduce her workload by one. The only impetus for keeping her alive, Maria suspected, was Corey's desire to exert her power and watch her drown in some macabre grand finale.

Everything was wet from the mist, the ocean oily calm. Large deck lights poured over the black-painted aft deck, and stout halogens bolted to the spars shone over the deckhouse, illuminating the sea and making the bow wake sudsy white against the dark velvet of the Pacific.

"I'm cold," Groiter said.

"I wouldn't worry about the cold—you'll be dead soon," Corey said.

Kenji just stared at the dreary darkness and the ghostly mist.

"You want to go over the side dead or alive?" Corey asked. "Your choice. Bitch here goes over hog-tied and alive so I can watch her struggle. But you guys are going down like bricks."

The line around Maria's wrists had cut off the blood flow. A shark glided through the wake as if it knew that the ocean was about to be fertilized. On the black gunwales the moisture was shiny slick, making it seem as if they traveled on the devil's own vessel. The muffled horn at the harbor's mouth sounded regularly in the distance; occasionally a startled seabird leaped out of the water before the prow and glided through the air.

"I want to go over dead," Groiter said at last. "Get me square between the eyes, from up close."

Corey laughed. "You know I almost forgot something. I have something to show Kenji, but first I gotta go tweak the autopilot a few degrees to miss the outer buoy." When Corey returned, she held a photograph. "Mr. Kim Lee had rather cleverly hid this under the leather of his Gucci briefcase." She held it in the light in front of Kenji; it was obvious he didn't like what he saw. "I took the liberty of sending it to the cops."

"Wanna see, bitch? You might be interested in this."

Corey held it in front of Maria's nose like an excited child with a secret. Effortlessly Corey used a strong arm to turn Maria's body so that the halogens hit the picture square. It was a woman's nude and headless corpse and stuffed between her legs was a man's decapitated head, his mouth open as if in a scream. Maria's stomach turned.

"See, on those thighs, that TS tattooed on either side of that rose stem? That's because those thighs are dedicated to one Tom Swanson. And that's because those are the thighs of one Catherine Swanson. And that head came off the photographer who supposedly killed her. But if he killed her and fled the scene, how can it be that his head is between her thighs? Groiter here took the picture just in case he ever had boss trouble.''

Corey got in Kenji's face.

''Now, how did the lady lose her head? It seems that she had been blowing Kenji, and Groiter wasn't positive he could get every molecule of cum out of her mouth. All kinds of nasty new DNA tests, you know.''

''I want a knife,'' Kenji said.

''Oh, this isn't what I think it is? That hara-kiri thing?'' Corey laughed. ''We get to watch while you spill your guts on the deck? Is that it?''

''I want a knife.''

''This I gotta see,'' Corey said. ''Too bad Janet isn't here. You wanna slit your guts too, like your boss?''

Groiter didn't dignify her with a response.

Corey stepped into the boat's galley behind the wheelhouse and returned with a long, thin-bladed knife for filleting fish.

''This do?''

Kenji nodded.

''Let's see what you got, Jap. Impress us with your *cojones*.''

She set the knife at his feet and stepped back quickly with the gun leveled at him. Kenji stooped and retrieved the knife. ''I need my hands,'' he said, holding them out. Warily she unlocked the shackles.

Slowly he unbuttoned his shirt, each button made to seem special. Then he removed the garment and deliberately laid it over the rail. Staring into the distance as if he were alone, with both hands wrapped around the handle, he poised the knife in front of the left side of his belly. He waited.

Maria felt her throat constrict. ''Please don't.''

His eyes betrayed nothing—it was as if she hadn't spoken. In an instant he raised the knife and with all his strength drove it to its hilt, then pulled it across his belly, making a wound that gaped like a grotesque smile. There was a slight sound—like slop in a bucket. Intestines started to spill as he dropped the knife. Blood poured out, but not a sound escaped his lips. Kenji began to fall when Corey jumped, throwing her shoulder into the bloody mess as if she were desperate to get him over. He toppled with a splash, the force of the water on his shoulders dragging the concrete over the side. In a second or two he was gone, leaving only a crimson ribbon.

"Jesus Christ. He had balls after all." Corey carefully cleaned the knife on his abandoned shirt, then tied a lead weight to the garment and dropped it over. The knife she put behind her in the waistband of her pants.

"Shoot me in the head point-blank," Groiter said.

This final, last-ditch effort at escape was pathetically obvious. Maria was certain that Groiter wasn't fooling Corey. Groiter would try to grab the gun. But Corey appeared willing to play the game. For Corey it would be one last torture, a chance to snuff the tiny spark of hope that still remained.

She pointed the gun at his forehead. "Come on, asshole. Give it your best shot." One step at a time, Corey got closer, baiting him until the barrel was just two feet from his nose.

Quite predictably, he grabbed for the gun. Maria actually saw Corey's finger pull. Nothing. Horror crossed Corey's face in the split second she realized there would be no bullet.

Jerking on the gun with the brute strength of utter desperation, Groiter sent Corey hurtling toward the rear corner of the fishing platform. Instinctively, she saved herself from going overboard, grabbing the only thing in sight—an upright piece of pipe bolted to the deck, known as a downrigger. Swinging around the heavy metal, she jumped back into the boat and hit Groiter's hands with a well-aimed kick. The gun stayed in his grip, but the blow from her foot knocked him off balance. For a moment he windmilled his arms to stay upright. Finally, he squatted, flicked off the safety, and fired—but it was too late. Corey had darted around the deckhouse.

The rapid turn of events gave Maria cause for slightly more hope. Neither of her enemies was clearly in charge. She struggled with her bonds, knowing that if she could get to the wheel she might also have currency for negotiation. If she could turn the boat around in the face of a standoff, she might not even be required to negotiate. Groiter for the moment ignored her, concentrating instead on Corey.

Quickly Maria looked around and spied a sharp gaff hanging by its handle on the back of the deckhouse. The curved point was six inches off the deck. It would serve to jam into the knots that bound her wrists. With great effort she began to inch her body to the instrument.

Corey clenched the anchor chain and ground her jaw in rage. Hunkering down behind the large anchor windlass near the bow, she tried to seize upon the obvious solution. There wasn't one. They were passing through the coastal shipping area to San Francisco without a radar reflector in the fog.

The pair of Perkins 4-108 diesels droned quiet and smooth. The front hatch was battened down. Food and fresh water were below but inaccessible to all of them. Groiter had his concrete boots on, and if she moved, he would kill her. That left only the hog-tied Fischer bitch.

Perhaps she could get him when he dozed off. But most likely that would take a while. Throwing things might work, but he had seven shots remaining and could shoot when she rose to throw. If she were able to physically outlast him, she could take the gun when he fell unconscious.

As if reading her mind, Groiter spoke. "Hey, I'll shoot holes in the bottom if I have to."

"Let's talk, Groiter." Corey closed her eyes and tried to relax. She sighed and took deep breaths. Fear of something she could only barely define seized her. Maybe she was wrong.

It was nearing sunrise; they were miles out at sea now. Maria watched Groiter squatting in obvious pain, fighting to stay conscious.

For Maria there was only one means of deliverance. She had to free herself or she would die. Although the gaff was potentially helpful, she couldn't get the critical knots over the point. Attempting to loosen her wrists in order to complete the maneuver entailed pulling taut the loop around her throat. Now she felt the circulation being restricted in nauseating light-headedness with every effort. She didn't know how many times she had tried to lift the knots over the point of the gaff and failed.

By now she was desperate and prepared to risk strangling herself. Mustering her energy, she lifted both her wrists and her head, trying to get the knots positioned over the gaff. The rope bit into her neck and she wanted to gag, but she persisted. At last she got the point wedged into the knot. But now there was constant tension on her neck. Feverishly she worked at the knots, pulling the outer knot down over the point. She fought the urge to gag and panic.

Corey called out to Groiter from her place of safety. "If you drop the gun, I'll get you out of the concrete. I swear."

"You come out in the open and drive the boat back to the dock. As long as we're headed in the right direction, I won't shoot."

Corey's silence must mean that she was considering the proposition. Maria was certain she had slightly loosened the rope at her wrist and struggled harder. She figured Groiter could last two more days without water, maximum. Corey had been in the shade and had had fluids more recently than he. If she stepped out where he could shoot, he would have control. For Corey it was safer to stay put. That was Maria's only ace in the hole.

The ropes that bound her had stretched sufficiently so that she no longer felt strangulation was imminent.

Groiter's gaze fell upon her. He could surely see enough to figure what she was doing with her hands. As sure as she could feel the hardness of the deck under her shoulder, she could feel his desire to kill her. But she was his only potential salvation, and even if she weren't, it would waste a precious bullet. His hand played with the gun. A feeling of the chill air came over her and it began to look as though he might kill her anyway. It would mean punishing somebody rather than nobody.

"If I get free, I'm going to take the boat back to the harbor," Maria said.

Looking morose, Groiter said nothing. Maria could see him looking around, desperate, but obviously thinking something. There were large lead weights at the stern. Three were within reach. He picked one up. Maria cringed. Then she got it. By lobbing them over the pilothouse, using a sort of two-handed shot-putter's technique, he might seriously wound Corey.

On the third deep breath, he heaved the heavy lead ball.

Wham! Corey jumped at the loud thud—the sound of something gouging the planking on the cabin top. Instantly she knew what Groiter was doing. And knew she had to do something. A direct hit would maim, perhaps even kill her. But she could think of no way to protect herself except to move between the huge anchor-chain roller and the cabin. There she would be under the lip of the cabin roof—but vulnerable to a gunshot through the pilothouse wall.

Wham! The second toss smashed into the deck a foot from her hand, missing her shoulder by inches.

Move under the cabin roof, she urged herself. Groiter would not know she had moved or where to shoot.

And then she saw it in her peripheral vision—one small green light and numerous white lights burning through the fog-laden morning and into her mind, filling her with a tooth-rattling panic—the shadow of a supertanker bearing down on them.

34

Maria was ready for a vigorous pull. After a deep breath in anticipation of great pain, she shrank her hand by folding her thumb and yanked. Her arm shook; then her hand popped free. In seconds she had the second hand loose and crawled quickly for the deckhouse, with one eye on a nodding Groiter. As she opened the cabin door, Groiter jerked up, pointing the gun. Quickly she pulled herself inside, rolled, and once out of sight went to work on her feet.

"Hey, Maria Fischer," he called out.

"What do you want?"

"You and me, we can make a deal."

"Groiter, look, a ship," Corey said.

"I see it." His voice had the tones of a man resigned to his fate.

Maria jumped up. Her breath seized at the awesome sight of the multistory supertanker. Leaping from the galley into the pilothouse, she grabbed the wheel and spun it. Autopilot! She fumbled madly with a black box overhead.

"Off," she screamed, flipping the switch. Grabbing the wheel, she threw the spokes. This time she felt resistance as the rudder dug in. A wall of black steel. A huge bow wave. She was turning, but so was the tanker.

"Oh God, oh God!" Then she saw a small boat racing. "Dan," she said.

Having checked all three outbound boats—and finding nothing—Dan was beyond desperate. Then for three minutes he had watched the scene on the radar. A mere speck, perhaps a boat with no radar reflector, a tiny target, going headlong into a supertanker's path. The freighter appeared as a moving island on the screen. The smaller something was almost invisible. Turning up the gain on the radar did little good, the second vessel barely visible, explaining why he hadn't seen it as he crossed the bar. Either the skipper was asleep at the boat's helm or the boat was out of control. The tanker hadn't picked up the tiny wisp of a target, either.

He picked up the VHF and broadcast on Channel 16.

"Mayday, Mayday, southbound supertanker off Palmer, you are about to run over a trawler. Mayday, Mayday, southbound supertanker, you are about to run over a trawler."

Ignoring the fog and repeating the warning continuously, he pushed the boat to twenty-eight knots. It was dangerous. One seaborne log and he was all done. It didn't matter. In his gut he knew that this time he was right.

He strained his eyes. The fog was burning thinner.

"There," he said, pointing. Shohei grunted. They could see the boat before the tanker.

"Mayday, Mayday, southbound supertanker, you are about to run over a trawler."

"Damn, the big guy is moving to dodge *me*," Dan said in disbelief.

Dan threw his own wheel over, but the tanker continued turning into the trawler.

A horn blasted across the water like a shock wave. Behind the tanker the water boiled.

"Reverse. He's hitting reverse," Dan said.

Slamming the throttle forward, Dan headed for the trawler. In seconds it would be kindling.

Thunk! A bullet hit the pilothouse wall, missing Corey's nose by inches. A second bullet passed over her head. Least of her problems. In seconds it would be too late. Not hesitating, she dived off the bow and swam as hard and as fast as she could.

Maria shrank from the black wall that grew above the trawler.

Then bullets and wood flew as Groiter tried to shoot Corey.

Maria ran out of the wheelhouse. "Dan," she screamed, seeing his shock of blond hair.

Then a shot chunked the bulkhead next to her, sending splinters everywhere. *He's trying to kill me. To kill anything.* She leaped, hit the water, and swam.

There were a few seconds when Groiter hoped they might somehow pass in front of the tanker, but the giant bow backed by 100,000 tons of steel and petroleum hit the small fishing trawler amidships. The stern, which held Groiter, scraped along the tanker's vertical steel starboard wall for fifty yards or more, until cast aside by the ship's wake. As the lit stern of the tanker passed, Groiter, in water up to his waist, gripped the gun and began shooting wildly at the sea, hoping that against all odds he might hit Corey.

Desperately he tried to claw his way around the boat as it listed and turned, but the concrete was too heavy and he found no handholds. His fingernails made ugly noises as they scrabbled over the deck planking.

"Please," he said to no one in particular as he made his final attempt to stop his slide into the cold, dark water.

"You missed," he heard Corey call in the distance as he sank beneath the waves.

Corey looked to the east, where the sun would be shining on the beach, and began to swim.

Her hands stretched out flat with each stroke against the smooth, glassy sea; her breath pushed into the cold water; the bracing smell of salt was in her nostrils; the silky sensation of the water's passage lapped under her arms. She swam without thought of time save the rhythmic passing of her breaths, ignoring the folly of her will to live.

Then the sea became hard and brittle. Her hand cracked on something solid. She grabbed the metal. It was the stern of a small boat, and there was a man standing over her. He wore a deep blue down coat over a blue cotton dress shirt, deeply wrinkled, open at the neck.

Dan Young.

Reaching behind her, she drew the fillet knife from her waistband. He held out a hand. She grabbed. As he came low to swing her up, she thrust the blade straight for his heart, feeling every inch of the knife slice through flesh. She shrieked her satisfaction.

Then from above, hands closed on Corey's neck. She was shaken like a sapling. She heard screams of white-hot, crazy anger. Her own, she realized, as the deadly earnest grip tightened. Relaxing her body, she went totally limp. Her mind became a shrinking tunnel, and just before it closed to utter blackness, the hands departed.

Water closed over her head. Summoning all her rage, she stroked toward a breath. The first inhaling of sweet ocean air came in a stupor, leaving only the haziest memory. She floated away. There was the churning water of a wake and the fleeing vessel. The cold, cold water.

Maria clambered onto the boat nearly hysterical. Shohei held his hand tight to Dan's chest above his heart. Maria put her hands under his head, beside herself with fear for him.

"Drive, drive," Shohei was saying.

Forcing herself to put Dan's head on the deck, she jumped up and engaged the throttle. The GPS made the entry to the bay obvious on the electronic chart.

Ground speed was thirty-five knots. The boat flew. Sometimes she could see ahead and sometimes she just stared at the screen. If they hit something not visible on the radar, they would all die. If they slowed, Dan would lose whatever slim margin he had. With her whole being she wanted to hold him, but instinctively she knew Shohei was strong, that he understood bodies and that he could best stop the life from seeping out of Dan.

Glancing back, she saw Shohei blowing air into Dan. They broke into the sun and neared a coast guard vessel.

She picked up the radio. "Coast guard, we've got a wounded man. He's dying," she cried out, choking, nearly hysterical.

"This is the United States Coast Guard. We have a helicopter and a lifeboat coming your way."

Dan could feel the joy when he saw Maria bending over him. With a tired grin he looked into her eyes. Then, in a twinkling, he felt a terrible sting in his shoulder. His face burned. Where did Maria go?

A white light, a wave of foreboding.

"Dear God, dear God!"

He heard Maria's voice through the white light. Something utterly serious, he knew. Then the light grew warm. People gathering around, and in his ear, Maria's voice. "Don't die, Dan Young, don't die." He could see so many things. Tess and her calm smile. Maria in court, standing on the counsel table. Nathaniel.

"Daddy, Daddy" cried Nathaniel's voice.

He was in a glass-topped casket. Tess lay beside him now. People with red roses were standing all around. There was a man wearing vestments and holding a small black book. Those standing around began tossing the roses as they were lowered to the place where they would stay for a night.

* * *

Maria waited in a large anteroom of the St. Joseph's Episcopal Church. It wasn't a place in which she felt familiar. She had mostly forgotten her childhood experience of its customs and rituals. The woodwork was dark mahogany, very fine, the design Tudor. Two large windows allowed sunlight through head-high half-curtains. In the corner were large bouquets that had not yet been put out. For a moment the world had left her alone. Looking through the window, she saw a hearse drive up. Dan's brother got out. Tears flooded her eyes. Soon it would be time. She had to pull herself together. Any minute her mother would come.

As if the thought summoned the person, there was a knock.

"Come in," Maria said.

"We need to get you ready," Laura Fischer said.

"I know."

Mrs. Fischer removed the wedding dress from its stand and Maria slipped off her robe.

"I'd love to know what you were thinking." Her mother began helping her into the dress. It was a Vera Wang and very expensive. It embarrassed Maria. There would be people dressed in army boots at her wedding as well as people in designer originals.

"Do you see the hearse out front? The one covered with 'Just Married'?" Maria asked.

"Hearse?" Laura Fischer walked to the window and peered out.

"I've heard of practical jokes on your wedding day, but this is more interesting than most."

"It's a very special message." Maria pointed to several pages on a window seat. "That's the homily the priest is giving during the ceremony. It explains the hearse. Dan sent Nate with the homily. Nate confidentially advised me that his father was worried I might look out the window and not understand.''

''Nate was in here?''

''He's the *son* of the groom. That doesn't count.''

Laura finished the last button while Maria went to the vanity to inspect her makeup.

''I'm not really a makeup person. But my cowboy grew up looking at teenyboppers in Maupin with makeup. Tess wore makeup. Do you think I'm giving away too much of my own identity?''

''Oh yes. Shaving under your arms and a little blush will no doubt twist your soul, dear.''

''Ever since Dan Young started looking at me in the courthouse, I started changing what I wore, my hair, then lipstick. Jeez, why couldn't I just stay myself?''

''This would certainly explain it,'' Laura said, reading the homily. ''It's really one of the most touching things I've ever read. You're going off in a hearse because he's dying to every love but yours. There won't be a dry eye in the place. It's so un-macho of Dan.''

''There's more to macho Dan than meets the eye.''

''Apparently,'' Laura said. ''Let's do the veil.''

''We're ahead of schedule.''

There was a knock.

''That'll be the bridesmaids ready to go.''

''I don't understand how I can wear a veil. The symbolism is so outmoded.''

''The hearse is for you, honey; the wedding is for the rest of us. Wear the veil. I think your father has invited everyone he ever met, and then some.''

''He's gloating. But he doesn't really know what I've reeled in here. He hasn't completely won.''

Laura sighed a deep sigh.

"Mom, I love you. And you know what I'm going to whisper in Dad's ear when he gives me away?"

"What, dear?"

"I'm going to try to fix us. I'm going to tell him I want to sit in his den and watch football again."

"Oh dear. He'll cry in front of his friends."

Dan was in the pastor's conference room, which was also a kind of theological library. He stared in the mirror; everything seemed in order. Turning to Nate, he stooped down to help him with the cummerbund on his tuxedo.

"Dad?" Nate said.

"Mm-hmm."

"I still miss Mom."

"I do too. Always will."

"Maria says she can't be my new mom because Mom is still my mom."

"That's right."

"But she says she's going to be like my godmother. She's there to remind me what Mom would want, and to stand in at parties and games and stuff and remind me that Mom's proud of me. And she says she loves me like a mom. Is that right?"

"That's right."

"Do you think Mom knows?"

"She knew we loved her, Nate."

Dan was fluffing the large salmon fly in his hat.

"Does Maria know we love her?"

"I believe she does. Wouldn't hurt to tell her, though."

"You're not gonna wear your hat, are you, Dad?"

Dan looked down and smiled mysteriously.

"Dad, I don't think they allow cowboy hats with tuxedos."

"It's livin' at the edge, son."

Dan watched Nate screw up his face in disdainful puzzlement.

"I'm just kidding, Nate. There are times when a man can leave his hat behind."